THE
LAST
HOLIDAY

BOOKS BY AMY SHEPPARD

The Beach Party

AMY SHEPPARD

THE
LAST
HOLIDAY

bookouture

Published by Bookouture in 2023

An imprint of Storyfire Ltd.
Carmelite House
50 Victoria Embankment
London EC4Y 0DZ

www.bookouture.com

ISBN: 978-1-83790-586-7
eBook ISBN: 978-1-83790-585-0

PROLOGUE

We'd been friends since we were kids. We knew every scar, every secret, every story.

It's the little things that stay with you. The hurried rip of zips being opened. Limbs bouncing against tent fabric. The screams echoing across the campsite as flashlights scoured the ground.

In the hours and days that followed, a hole opened up. A hole where an expectation of goodness had once been. The knowledge that awful things can happen to the people you love.

The police investigation began immediately. Before her body had been removed. Before the sun had fully risen over the little tent village. They needed to know everything. Every scar, every secret, every story.

That's what happens when someone you love is murdered.

CHAPTER ONE

CHARLOTTE

Four days before

My phone flashed on the bedside table beside me. The alarm I'd carefully set the night before telling me it was 6 a.m. It wasn't needed, I'd been awake for three hours. Woken by the sound of Tristen getting home and quietly letting himself into the spare room. Woken by my subconscious anxiously creating lists and acting out possible scenarios.

In two hours, we'd be leaving for a camping trip to Cornwall. A camping trip with our old college friends. Me and Tristen had known Annie, Jack and Stella for twenty-five years. We were sixteen when we met. That's how long me and Tristen had been together. A lot had happened to us all in that time: kids, marriage... divorce. But me and Tristen had managed to stay together. Through endless military postings, through the arrival of Theo. Me and Tristen were hanging on by our fingertips, but we were still together.

I turned over in bed. Stroking the crisp whiteness of the sheets in the empty space next to me. I played possible versions of today over in my head. Jack and his wife, Kelly, had organised the camping trip. Kelly was Jack's second wife. They'd been together for five years, married for two. I'd not seen a lot of Jack in that time. It was still a shock every time we met up, that his first wife, Lisa, wasn't there. They had been married for eleven years and had two boys together. Over the time of their marriage, I'd become closer to Lisa than I was to Jack. A little while after the divorce, me and Lisa stopped calling each other. We stopped meeting up for coffee and the occasional night out. Eventually, even the Christmas cards stopped. It's hard to stay friends with the ex-wife of one of your oldest friends—even if you do prefer them to their new wife.

I pulled myself up and sat on the edge of the bed. My feet automatically scuffed the soft beige carpet in search of my slippers. I slid my toes into the ends of the plain moccasins and tried to summon the strength to stand. My thin cotton pyjamas stretched tightly over my thighs. I prodded the doughy flesh with frustration.

Stella and Annie would look incredible, they always did. Stella with her perfect, make-up-free skin. Her figure would be toned from rock climbing or surfing or whatever outdoor sport she was into now. Annie would be immaculate. Her hair would be smoothed into a perfect red glossy bob. She was short in stature and tiny in frame. Annie had spent thirty years denying herself food. Sugar carbs, fats... There were few things more important to her than staying slim. She'd be dressed head to toe in black. The only colour would be a slash of crimson across her full lips. It was like her uniform. An expensive, designer uniform.

I wondered what version of herself Annie would be this trip. She had always been one of the most generous people I knew. Someone who would fight your corner. Annie was wild, but she was someone you wanted on your side. Even at the best of times, she could be self-centred and forceful. This weekend might not be the best of times. I bit my lip with shame. Why was I thinking like this? After everything Annie had done for me over the years.

I walked to the dressing table mirror, studying my tired face in the small shard of light that escaped through a gap in the curtains. My mousy brown waves had turned to frizz overnight in the clammy August heat. Even in the darkness I could see how pale I was. How deep the lines around my eyes were. I tilted my head. Running my finger gently down the scar on my jaw. It wasn't as visible these days. But I was always aware of it. To me, it was as deep as if it had happened yesterday.

We were all forty-two. Me, Tristen, Annie, Stella and Jack. I was the only one who looked every single year of it.

The bottom of the bedroom door brushed against the carpet as it slowly slid open. Theo padded into the room. His tattered giraffe pressed against his sleepy face. He moved towards me. I bent down to receive his small pyjama-clad body into a hug. 'Good morning,' I whispered into his warm bed-creased ear.

'Good morning.' He replied much louder than I'd spoke.

'Shhh,' I told him in a low voice. 'Dad's still asleep.' I smiled as he pressed the threadbare giraffe to his face to hide his giggles. 'Are you excited about going camping?' I asked as I pushed his blonde waves from his eyes. Theo nodded as he snuggled his head into my shoulder. He'd recently turned four and was still full of the same sweetness he had when he was a toddler. I felt a familiar tightening of my throat when I thought about him starting school next September.

No child had ever been longed for more than Theo had. We had tried for thirteen years to get pregnant. Endless tests and hospital appointments and two failed IVF attempts had left their scars. On my mind and body. They had never been able to find a reason that I wasn't getting pregnant. 'Just keep trying,' they told us. 'It might happen when you least expect it,' said our consultant when she knew we'd come to the end of our treatment options. And then came Theo, our tiny little miracle. I had resigned myself to the fact that he would be our only one. That a sibling for Theo was very unlikely.

I never stopped feeling grateful for him. Not even for a moment.

Me and Theo crept downstairs to get breakfast. The narrow 1970s stairs groaned under our feet. We'd lived in the small three-bedroom terrace for four years. We'd moved in just after Theo was born. It had been Tristen's mum's home for the last few years of her life. When she died, the house had been left to us. I assumed we'd sell it. Use the money to buy somewhere we really wanted. Somewhere we'd chosen. Tristen had wanted to keep it. He had been in the army for over twenty years. We'd spent our lives in military housing, moving from base to base. He wanted a permanent home. One that we wouldn't have to leave every time he was deployed. It hadn't worked out that way. He was still deployed and moved to bases around the country, although I no longer moved with him. For most of the year, me and Theo were here by ourselves.

I gently pushed the kitchen door closed. The longer Tristen slept, the greater chance there would be for him to wake up in a good mood. 'What do you want for breakfast?' I asked Theo as he climbed onto one of the dining chairs.

'Cheerios!' he shouted, throwing his small fists into the air.

'Cheerios?' I smiled, raising my eyebrows.

'Please,' he added.

'Good boy,' I told him and placed the box of cereal and a bowl down in front of him. Most of the camping stuff had already been packed in the car. Tristen's old green army tent had been rolled into the boot last night. I'd suggested months ago that we buy something new for the trip. 'Why waste money?' he'd said. Tristen would have it set up in under twenty minutes. Him and Stella were the outdoorsy members of the group. Between them, the camp would be run like a military operation. And like a military operation, they would want to spend their week running and hiking and swimming.

There was still a pile of bags heaped against the back door and the list of things still to find was long. I pulled two large tubs out of the freezer. Frozen containers filled with Bolognese that I'd made a week ago. I gnawed on my bottom lip as I turned the plastic boxes over in my hands. Trying to gauge whether there was enough food to feed ten people. 'It's fine... it's fine,' I muttered, anxiously smoothing down the fabric of my top over my hips.

'Why are you talking to yourself?' Theo asked with a grin as he haphazardly sloshed milk over his cereal from an impossible height.

'Because mummy is crazy.' I said the last word in a low, silly voice and we both laughed. Theo was excited about the trip, I could tell. It made me feel terrible that I had put up so much resistance. I'd thought about ways to get out of it. Every day since the holiday had been suggested. I'd prayed for bad weather, overbooked campsites—even illness. Tristen wouldn't even discuss it. He loved camping. A week in a tent, spending time with his friends... it was his idea of a perfect holiday. He hadn't expressed a desire to do *anything* for such a long time, I didn't feel like I had any choice. Even if I had, it was Rose's eighteenth birthday. Rose was Annie's wonderful daughter. We'd all doted on her since she was a baby. I would never miss her milestone birthday.

'Daddy!' Theo shouted as Tristen walked into the kitchen. I jumped. I hadn't expected him up for a while. He wore grey jogging bottoms and his top half was bare. His body was still as taut and muscular as it had been twenty years ago. My stomach twisted with a familiar longing. Tristen had been away for a week on a training course. It had finished late. He'd driven through the night to get back to Surrey from an army barracks in Yorkshire. He must be exhausted.

'Theo!' Tristen embraced him in an all-consuming hug. Their matching dark hair meshed into one as Theo disappeared into his chest. Tristen moved around the small breakfast bar and planted a kiss on my forehead. 'How's the packing going?' he asked.

'OK,' I replied. I placed my hands playfully on his waist and my fingers crept around his back as I inched closer to him. I felt him flinch. It was only a tiny movement, but enough to make me drop my hands to my side. 'There's still lots to do,' I told him, flustered by the rejection. I heard Tristen exhale with frustration. It was something he did so often, I'm not sure he even knows he's doing it any more. 'It's going to be great,' I added, fixing my face in a bright smile.

I mustn't fuss. I need to relax this week. I need to be the happy, bubbly Charlotte he fell in love with. This week felt like it might be our last chance.

CHAPTER TWO

ANNIE

Four days before

'Mum, slow down,' Rose warned. I'd been dipping in and out of traffic on the motorway for nearly an hour. I was deep in thought and hadn't realised my foot had dropped on the accelerator.

'Sorry,' I told her absently, reducing the speed of my BMW convertible and drifting over to the middle lane. I watched Rose out of the corner of my eye. She hadn't been herself for a while now. It wasn't a surprise really. She'd worked so hard over the last few months. Rose was seventeen, eighteen in just a few days. She'd just finished her A levels. She barely went out and had hardly any friends. Her life was her studies. Now college was over, I wasn't sure how she would fill her time over the next few weeks.

I pulled the visor down as I squinted against the bright August sun. I'd turned the fans up high to try and get some air moving around the cramped car. It still felt tight and stuffy. The motorway was crowded. Lines of slow-moving vehicles creeping towards the coast for the holidays. I stretched my neck from side to side. Trying to work out some of the irritation.

'Have you heard from your dad?' I asked, fixing my eyes firmly on the road.

'Muuum,' she groaned. 'If you want to talk to dad, just call him.'

'I don't...' I protested, but I saw she was smiling. Even Rose, with her desire for solitude and her penchant for reading a book in social situations, knew my feelings for her dad. 'OK, OK.' I raised one of my hands in mock surrender, before returning it to the steering wheel. 'I just haven't heard from him for a while, that's all.'

'You know what he's like when he's on tour... It's all late nights and liquor,' she told me. I nodded. Rose kindly left out '... and women.' The groupies who would undoubtably follow the band back to their hotel room every night. Every night and every city across the globe. There was no reason he shouldn't enjoy the perks of being in a rock band. It's not like we were together. We'd never been together—not properly.

Taylor, Rose's dad, was the guitarist in indie-rock band Fearless Embers. They'd been together for twenty years, but it was only in the last five or six years that they'd become really famous. I met Taylor when they were just starting out. When we were in our early twenties. I was working in London, at the PR firm that had just started representing them. He had turned my world upside down in a way that no other man ever had. That I thought no man ever could. Just over a year after meeting him, I fell pregnant with Rose. I knew he'd never settle down. He'd been honest about that right from the start.

Everyone was surprised that I'd decided to keep the baby—to keep Rose. Even Charlotte, who knew me better than anyone. All they saw was wild Annie. The ambitious, tequila-swigging party girl. I suppose I thought that if me and Taylor had a baby together, then one day it might happen for us. One day we might be a family. I had no idea how painful it would be, watching his life from the sidelines. None of the group knew how I felt about him, not really. I'd always given the impression that the single-mum life had been my choice. That it was *me* who wasn't the settling-down type. It wasn't difficult to believe. Taylor was a good dad when he was around. Rose adored him.

After a while, the motorway turned into A roads. Concrete bridges and central reservations melted into the Cornish countryside. High green hedgerows, dotted with pink and purple wildflowers. Openings to dry, dusty farm tracks. Marked with the deep ridges of tractor tyres. Every corner was flanked by sloping green fields of cows. Sheep as still as statues. It had been a long time since I'd done this drive. Years in fact. There was a time, after college, that we all used to traipse back here every few weeks. Finding safety at home in our little group. A shelter from the realities of grown-up living.

'Did you never think about moving back to Cornwall?' asked Rose as she took in the scenery. It wasn't something she'd ever asked before.

'God no!' I replied quickly.

'But I thought you loved growing up there? You all talk about Cornwall like it was the centre of your world.' Rose was right. We had all romanticized growing up in Cornwall over the years. Told stories from our college days. Parties in the woods and drinking on the beach until the sun came up.

'I did. We all did,' I told her. 'Cornwall will always be special to us… but it has a way of keeping you close. Holding you back from other things. If I hadn't left after college, I'm not sure I ever would. Cornwall is like quicksand,' I told her. 'Beautiful, but still quicksand. It wasn't something I wanted for you. You liked growing up in London, didn't you?' I asked her.

'Of course,' she replied. But I knew it wasn't true. I knew she was only trying to make me feel better about my choices. London didn't have the same effect on Rose as it had on me.

The city energised and inspired me. It excited me in a way that no other place ever could. For Rose it was different. Rose had thrived in spite of it. London had been a sensory barrage. The traffic, the people, the lights. I would lie awake at night in our West London flat, listening to the sounds of buses and people. The drone of constant activity around the city. I was comforted in the knowledge that London never slept. Rose would fall asleep every night with headphones on. Her pursuit of quiet throughout her childhood was one of the many things that made me and Rose so different.

Rose's dislike of London was one of the reasons I'd bought an old farmhouse five years ago. Our second home, in Wiltshire. The plan was that we would drive up every Friday and spend the weekend there together, just the two of us. In the rural tranquil of the big Victorian house. 'West Mill', read the name by the gated entrance. Rose had instantly fallen in love with it.

When I bought the house, it had been in a serious state of disrepair. Bare wooden floors, peeling wallpaper and a rustic oak kitchen. There was no heating system. In the winter the only source of warmth were the open fires in each of the rooms and an Aga. For nearly three years I did nothing to the place. I couldn't afford to. We rattled around the five-bedroom property every weekend. Rose had never been happier.

A couple of years ago, I'd called in the builders. They worked on making every inch of the house perfect. If Rose had her way, it would have been left exactly as it was. The bare floorboards were covered with expensive tiles. The windows were hung with designer drapes. Eventually a swimming pool was added to the large, manicured gardens. Me and Rose were no longer alone there every weekend.

The completion of the house six months later coincided with me opening my own PR firm. It was a stretch financially, but I needed a place to entertain. Clients and journalists were invited every week to enjoy the secluded paradise. What had started as an occasional weekend retreat for people, became a country party house. I employed a part-time chef and a cleaner to manage the influx of guests every month. Quiet gatherings became alcohol-fuelled all-nighters, packed with minor celebrities and their agents. Very soon Rose stopped coming with me, preferring the new solitude of the London flat.

We'd stayed at the farmhouse together for the last two nights, just the two of us. It was the first time Rose had been there for over a year. She'd looked around it with disappointment. Like it was a stranger to her. Guilt prickled my body as I thought about how much she'd loved that house. But without the networking I'd done, I would never have got my PR business off the ground. Now it looked as if it had all been for nothing. I wondered if that might have been the last time me and Rose would ever go to the house together.

'It will be fun staying in the bell tent,' I said, trying to sound more positive than I felt. She'd rested her head against the window. Her dark curls cascaded around her face. Her pale skin. The dimple on the right side of her cheek, visible only when she smiled—that was all me. The dark hair was just like mine had been when I was a kid. I'd worn it in a sleek bob and had dyed it a deep crimson for many years. Her long willowy frame was all she'd got from Taylor.

When Rose was a baby, people were always surprised that she was mine. I never used to understand it, as we looked so similar. Maybe it was my vivid red hair. In reality, I think it was because I was so awkward with her. It took me a long time to get to grips with being a mum.

'What?' I asked when Rose didn't reply.

'I just don't know why we couldn't just bring a normal tent like everyone else. You know? *Proper* camping,' she sighed.

'Proper camping?' I tried to keep the irritation out of my voice. 'Not sure how much proper camping gear we'd be able to get in the back of this.' I nodded my head towards the tiny boot at the rear. It was only just big enough to hold our two bags. 'The bell tent will be great! The campsite is putting it up for us. We'll have real beds and even a fridge!' I thought about the bottles of Champagne that were warming in the back. Chilled fizz might be the only thing that will get me through this week. 'Anyway... me and you have never done normal, have we?' I smiled.

'I suppose not,' she replied.

I sighed. 'Rose, I thought you wanted to go? You are the *only* reason I'm going to this thing,' I snapped. I regretted the cross words as soon as they left my mouth. Especially as it wasn't true. As much as I didn't want to go, I had my own reasons. 'I'm sorry,' I told her. Charlotte and Stella were family to Rose. They were more than just godmothers to her. She missed them. At times, they'd been more like mothers. Filling in the gaping parenting holes that me and Taylor had left. I knew how important this week was to her. I reached over and squeezed her arm. 'I know it's been hard for you.' I swallowed as Rose moved her arm and looked away. It wasn't something we'd be talking about. Not today anyway.

CHAPTER THREE

STELLA

Four days before

The old Land Rover bumped along the uneven Cornish roads. I slid around the black plastic seats, every time the car turned one of the tight bends. The airless cab was humid from the midday August heat. Not helped by the fact that I'd had to close all the windows to drown out the sound of the spluttering vintage engine. I would be at Nate's caravan in ten minutes. Then we'd be making the twenty-mile journey to the campsite.

I loved the drive to Nate's. It was hard to find space at this time of year. Roads or beaches or walks that weren't overrun with holidaymakers. The narrow lanes wound high above the valley and were always quiet. Much of the road ran alongside a steep rockface. A moss-covered granite cliff carved out of the hillside. One wrong turn and a car could just tumble into the fast-flowing river below. It kept most drivers away. Even brave locals.

My hair was still damp from the shower I'd had after this morning's run. I lifted the wet blonde waves that finished at the nape of my neck. Tickling my hot skin. Nate had never met any of the group, despite us being together for two years. I had pretended to myself that it was just circumstance that had prevented them meeting. I was the only one who still lived in Cornwall. The rest of them had moved away a long time ago. The meetups had become less and less frequent over the years. As I rumbled along the back lanes, my feelings of dread had forced me to admit that it was anything but circumstance that had kept the group apart.

I turned into the narrow, high-sided entrance that led down to the caravan. The Land Rover lurched wildly as the wheels fell into potholes on the uneven road. Three beige mobile homes were parked at angles in a row. Nate had virtually moved into my cottage now, but on nights that he worked at the farm, he slept in the caravan. It was a place he'd called home since we came back from Europe two years ago.

The door of Nate's caravan was open. At the sound of my car, he strolled down the metal steps. Running a lazy hand through his golden hair. He was wearing shorts. His broad, tanned chest was bare. As he reached the bottom of the stairs, he pulled an old blue T-shirt over his head. It was one he'd had for years. One he used to wear a lot when we were travelling.

I raised my hand in a wave and got out of the car. 'Hi,' he said, walking towards me and pulling me into a tight embrace.

'Hi, yourself.' I laughed as he ran his hands down my back and tugged my hips towards him. He'd been working in the fields all night; I breathed in his sweet earthy scent as I nuzzled my face into his neck.

Nate was nearly twelve years younger than me. He had just turned thirty. It was an age gap I hadn't been comfortable with when we met. It was something I had finally come to terms with a few months ago, when Nate had entered his thirties. My own twenties had seemed like a lifetime ago, years filled with angst and uncertainty. It was another reason I hadn't introduced him to the group.

'Are you ready to go?' I asked, releasing myself from his hug.

'Yep. Let me just grab my kit. Do you have the tent?' I nodded. Nate went back into the caravan and grabbed an old waterproof duffel bag. Everything was simple with Nate. No fuss, no drama. The bag he emerged with couldn't have held more than a couple of T-shirts and jumper. He always travelled light.

When I met Nate, I understood why some people were referred to as 'a breath of fresh air.' The effect he had on me was instant. Like a cool breeze blowing through my tense and muddled mind. I met him during a difficult time in my life. My mum had just died. The pain I'd felt was so sudden and so acute that I thought it might swallow me whole.

After the funeral, I'd packed a bag and flown to Europe. My friends had been shocked. Despite my love of sports and the outdoors, I'd never travelled before. Not even after college when lots of people I knew had gone backpacking. I had no idea what I was doing. Calm, stoic Stella. My predictability and studious nature had got me a law degree. Everyone thought that I was unravelling. The only thing I knew, was that I had to get away from Cornwall. Get away from the tiny wooden cottage by the woods that I'd shared with Mum.

So I left my twelve-hour-a-day job as a solicitor and booked the first flight I found that left the next day. Nate had been working as a surf instructor in Portugal. He'd laughed when I told him I'd grown up in Cornwall and had never surfed. That was how it started, the cliché holiday romance that never ended.

I looked over at Nate's tired, handsome face as I drove out of the farm. He would be a welcome addition to what was bound to be a week of tensions. 'If they're that bad, why are we going?' he'd asked gently. To Nate it was simple. He'd spent his life being a positive person, surrounding himself with positive people. 'It's not like you're family. You can walk away at any time,' he reminded me.

'For a long time, we *were* each other's family,' I'd told him sadly. 'When Annie fell pregnant with Rose, it was me and Charlotte who had held her up. When Mum died, it wasn't my family that I told first... The first number I dialled was Charlotte's,' I'd said defensively. We haven't been together as a group for two years.

We'd seen each other individually and we'd spoken on the phone. The group dynamic had been something that we'd all instinctively avoided. Preferring to bask in the warm memory of what our friendships had once been. Our history was long and our love for one another ran deep, but the cracks had been showing for a while now.

'I understand,' he'd said, pulling me close.

'So many times I've thought about trying to get out of this week...' I told him, biting my bottom lip. The guilt of having said the words out loud. 'But it's Rose's birthday... I can't let her down.' She's had enough of that in her life. If I was honest with myself, it wasn't just about Rose. Two years ago, I'd run halfway around the world to try and find myself again. I'd run for long enough. This week was about closure. It was about shutting a door.

'The only thing I'm really worried about... is what it might do to *us*.' It was a fear that had preoccupied my thoughts these last few days.

'Now *that* is definitely not something you need to worry about.' He'd laughed, tracing the frown lines across my forehead with the side of his thumb. I smiled, but the worry about the week ahead still lingered. A week when everyone's conflicts and everyone's secrets would bubble to the surface once again.

Nate slid his feet out of his flip-flops and placed one tanned foot on the dashboard. 'When are we going to tell them our news?' I could feel his eyes on me.

'Um soon, definitely this week. I just need to find the right time.' I didn't look at Nate when I spoke. I didn't want to see the hurt and confusion. He'd been so patient. 'I've told Rose.'

'Good,' he said with a smile and reached over to place a hand on my thigh. 'It's a happy thing. I'm glad you have someone to share it with.'

Forty minutes later we arrived at the campsite. Ten-foot metal signs sat on either side of the entrance. Protruding from perfectly manicured verges. Tregarrow Farm promised glamping, electric hookups, swimming pool and a licenced restaurant. I took a deep breath as I turned into the site.

The glossy green fields fell away in the middle. Gently sloping down towards each other. A heart-shaped window between the ground and the cornflower-blue sky. You could just make out the coast in the distance. The jagged edges of faraway cliffs above the hazy sea below.

The entrance quickly widened to reveal a small single-storey building with 'reception' in big white letters above the door. A security gate blocked our path. I had no choice but to pull into one of the parking bays outside the front of the shop. We both climbed out of the car, stretching our limbs after the bumpy journey. 'I'll check us in,' I told Nate as I headed for the door. He nodded as he leaned his long back against the passenger door and raised his face towards the hot sun. Every part of me wanted to take Nate's hand and get back in the car. For us to drive back to my little wooden cottage and hide behind the ivy-covered door. To keep everything we have safe from what was coming.

The door pinged loudly as I entered the reception. The entrance was filled with buckets and spades. Inflatable animals hung from the walls and bright seaside postcards were stacked neatly on a white carousel. I was the only person there. I walked to the desk and waited, lifting the end of my T-shirt up to fan my hot face.

'Can I help you?' A middle-aged man appeared from a back

room. He spoke abruptly, like I'd wandered into a prohibited area. I quickly dropped the hem of my T-shirt as he stared disapprovingly at my exposed stomach.

'Um, yes. Stella Winter. I've booked a camping pitch.' Without saying a word, the man leant over a desk chair and started typing keys on the computer. I gently tapped my fingers on the desk to cover the awkward silence. A large bound signing-in book was open on the counter in front of me. I glanced down the column, looking at the long list of guests who had already signed in that day. A few rows from the bottom were 'Jack and Kelly Morris.' The handwriting was Kelly's. Girlish loops danced across the page. Jack and Kelly were already here.

'Two people, seven nights, no electric hookup?' he asked without looking up from the screen.

'Yep, that's the one.' I smiled, trying to soften his demeanour. He lifted his head and fixed me with a hard stare.

'You know that you can't have fires?' he snapped. The man rubbed the back of his neck in irritation. As though his morning had been filled with putting out guest fires.

'Sorry?' I asked. My patience began to fray a little. I could feel beads of sweat prickle at the top of my spine.

'You haven't asked for an electric hookup. So, if you want to cook, it can't be over a fire,' he explained slowly as though he were talking to a child. 'Here is a list of the Tregarrow Farm rules.' He sighed, handing me an A4-printed list. He turned the page over to show me that the list continued on the back. I nodded and went to take the paper from him. He placed the palm of his hand firmly on top of mine. I jumped. 'We've had trouble here with groups in the past,' he warned.

'You'll have no trouble with us,' I said, meeting his glare. I pulled my hand out from underneath his, taking the piece of paper. We held one another's stare for several seconds.

'Tony? I hope you're not scaring this young lady off?' A woman emerged from the back room. Her voice was light and teasing. She put a small hand affectionately on his shoulder. 'I'm Irene and this is my husband, Tony,' she said with a warm smile. They couldn't have been more different, both in character and stature. Irene was tiny. Her small frame disappeared behind her tall, bulky husband. 'Don't mind him, he's just a bit protective of the campsite.' She winked. 'We hope you have a wonderful stay. Let us know if you need anything.' Irene handed me a small plastic card. 'Use this on the scanner by the front security gate and you'll find another one at the entrance to your field.' Irene leant around her husband and looked at the screen. 'You're in Field C.'

'Thank you.' I smiled, taking the card from her. I signed my name in the check-in book under Tony's stony gaze. I lifted my hand in goodbye as I quickly walked to the door. Desperate to leave the airless building.

'All OK?' Nate asked as I walked back to the car. He'd taken his shirt off and had tucked it into the band of his shorts. When Nate was in his early twenties, he'd done some modelling in London. Seeing him standing there, I could see why.

'It's fine, although I'm fairly sure gorgeous men with their tops off is against the rules.' I laughed. I placed my hand on his chest, planting a kiss on his lips. I handed him the long list of rules.

'Wow.' He laughed, glancing down at the sheet of paper.

We got back in the car. The old Land Rover heaved away from the parking bay. As we reached the barrier, I leant out the window and held the plastic card I'd been given against the red light. The metal arm slowly rose in the air, waiting patiently for us to enter. This was it. We were here.

CHAPTER FOUR

ANNIE

Four days before

As soon as we got off the main roads, I pulled over. Pressing the button that folded the roof of the convertible down. 'Please don't, Mum,' Rose begged, but I was too hot to appease her. It wasn't the noise or the wind that bothered her. Rose thought driving with the roof down was brash and ostentatious. In fact, she thought the whole car was pretentious. At least with the roof up, people couldn't see her.

'Rose, it's so hot. It's all country lanes now. It's not like anyone's going to see us.' She nodded, resigned to my single-minded ways.

I breathed in the warm wind that brushed across my face as I drove. I felt my shoulders drop a fraction as some of the tension blew away. The car slowed to a crawl as a brightly coloured pheasant careered across the lane into a neighbouring field. Rose giggled at the awkward bird. I looked over and smiled. It was good to hear her laugh.

'Did you know that Stella's bringing her new boyfriend?' I

asked Rose, trying to change the subject. 'I can't believe how young he is,' I added in a conspiratorial whisper.

'Yes, she told me,' Rose replied. 'He's not exactly new. They've been together for a couple of years now.' She rummaged in her bag, pulling out a pair of headphones.

'When did you speak to Stella?' I asked, trying to keep the annoyance out of my voice.

'A few weeks ago. She phoned to ask how the exams were going. It was one of the weekends you were at the house,' Rose explained. It wasn't an accusation. Rose meant no harm, but I bristled at her words. The suggestion that I hadn't been there. But it wasn't a suggestion, I *hadn't* been there. The business had taken up a lot of my time over the last year. I tried to tell myself that it was all for her. But I knew she relied on Stella a lot these days.

'Why don't you like Stella?' Rose asked gently. She twisted the cable from her headphones around her finger. It wasn't something she had ever asked out loud before.

'What do you mean? Stella is one of my oldest friends... I wouldn't have made her your godmother if I didn't like her...' My denial was over the top. Rose saw straight through it. There *had* been a shift in our friendship over the years. Yet despite our differences, she'd always doted on Rose.

'So why do you always get so defensive whenever I talk about her?' Rose asked. I was about to continue when I saw that Rose was smiling.

'Because... because of how much you like her.' I fired out the words. Neither of us spoke for a moment. Then Rose laughed. The same gentle, wholesome laugh that she had when she was a child. It wasn't a sound I heard much these days. I rolled my eyes at my own petty jealousy and laughed too.

Even with the roof down there was almost no breeze. The Cornish countryside rolled by. Old-fashioned road signs pointing to familiar villages. Lanes I thought I recognised and places I might have been to a long time ago. Like a dream, where everything is recognisable, but nothing quite connects. I'd spent so long trying to get away from this place, it was hard to stop running. I have no idea why Kelly chose for us to camp *here* of all places.

'I tried to convince Kelly to have this week at the Wiltshire house,' I told Rose. She nodded but didn't say anything. 'She *completely* dismissed it. It would have been perfect. We would have had our *own* pool, a chef... and everyone would have had a bed!' I shook my head in wonder at the rejection.

'I think Kelly just wanted to be the one to organise it. She just wants to prove to everyone that she's part of the group. That *she's* Jack's wife now... She's never felt like she fit in...'

'She doesn't,' I replied coldly.

'It must be hard for her... trying to step into Lisa's shoes,' Rose explained patiently. 'You know this is mainly for your benefit? You used to be her boss. She's always found you intimidating.' Rose scrunched up her face like she was delivering bad news.

'Who me?' I laughed, touching my chest with my fingertips in mock outrage. Most people would be horrified at being thought intimidating. I never have. It's what's made me so successful, it's what made me able to do the job that I do. I felt a familiar knot in my stomach as I thought about how much I had to lose.

It had been five years since Kelly had worked for me. She was an inexperienced twenty-two-year-old, desperate to work in public relations. I had risen to the position of senior account manager in the PR firm I'd worked at for ten years. Kelly was obsessed with the famous faces we represented. Her interview for the role as my assistant was terrible. She'd sat open-mouthed as I name-dropped celebrity clients and airily listed the upcoming high-profile events on our roster.

I knew within five minutes of speaking to Kelly that she

wasn't right for the job. I offered it to her anyway. I told myself it was her enthusiasm that had won me over. That her big blue eyes and long blonde hair would bring a bit of glamour to the predominantly male, middle-aged office. In reality, it was because she'd flattered me. She'd been so impressed by me I wanted to have her around. Rose had just turned thirteen. It was painfully obvious that *she* was never going to be impressed by me. Taylor was on tour. Nobody had been impressed by me for a long time. I'm not sure I even realised how much I needed it.

I sometimes wonder if Jack and Lisa would still be together if I hadn't given Kelly the job.

Kelly had only been working for me for a few weeks when I introduced her to Jack. At that time, him and Lisa and the boys were living in a tiny two-bedroom flat. It was just around the corner from my West London office. Me and Jack would often meet for lunch. He was an estate agent. Both our working days were long, and our appointments spread out. We would grab a bite to eat at the tired looking Greek café on the corner. It wasn't the sort of place our colleagues would ever eat lunch. No wine list, no pretentious menu, just great food and good coffee. I realised with a start that neither me nor Jack would ever eat somewhere like that now.

Me and Jack understood each other—back then we did anyway. We both knew what it was to crave more. More from our careers, more money. We were constantly striving for the next goal. Sitting in Apollo's Café, planning our next moves. We used each other as sounding boards for our next venture. We flirted. We always had done, but there was nothing in it. I once asked Jack if Lisa minded our little meetups. 'No,' he'd laughed. 'She's just happy she doesn't have to listen to it.' I liked Lisa a lot. We all did.

One day I was running late, so Jack had popped into the office. I was on the phone. I held a hand up to him, mouthing, 'I won't be long.' Jack took a seat in the small reception area. I watched as Kelly glided across the room towards him. Her red skirt clung to every curve and exposed her long tanned legs. Jack stared, transfixed as she flicked her blonde hair over her shoulder and offered him coffee. They laughed together as I continued my call. Up until then, I'd never known Jack to flirt with other women. Well, no one except me.

By the time I'd hung up the phone and joined them, my body ached with irritation. 'Don't you have work to do?' I asked Kelly bluntly.

'Yes, sorry.' Kelly leapt to her feet and started to make her way back to her desk.

'Have you eaten?' Jack stood up. He fidgeted uncomfortably as he waited for her reply. I'd never seen Jack be anything other than self-assured.

'No,' Kelly replied, looking up at him under long dark lashes.

'Why don't you join us?' he asked. I fixed Jack with a cold hard stare, but he just smiled back. That was how it started. It was how *they* started.

Within a couple of weeks, Jack began lying to Lisa about where he was. He started attending some of the events I'd organised. Something he'd never done in the past. Events that Kelly was at. Jack spoke openly to me about how he felt about her. I think he just assumed that I wouldn't care. That fun-loving, selfish Annie would encourage him to go after what he wanted. He was wrong.

I never told him how appalled I was—it was none of my business. But I did fire Kelly. She shared a photo on her social media from a high-profile event I'd organised. One of our clients was in the background and the image was far from flattering. I told her to clear her desk that day. 'I have no interest in working with a fame junkie.' My voice was low and cold. If it had been anyone else, they would have received a warning. It was the perfect excuse to get rid of her. Kelly cleared her desk. Mascara tears streaming down her face.

I thought that my firing Kelly would bring an end to her affair with Jack. A week later he'd left Lisa and the boys. He moved into Kelly's studio flat. Three years later they were married. I'd never spoken to Jack about what I'd said to her that day. There was no need. He would just shrug and say, 'It's just business, isn't it?' I would nod. But it wouldn't have been true.

Five years later and Kelly had never worked in PR again. She has a part-time job in a clothes shop. I imagine she's never forgiven me, but we're both skilled at keeping up the pretence of friendship. When friends divorce, you have to choose. You can't have them both in your life, it's too hard. I chose Jack. I had to; Jack is family to me. But I hate that I *had* to choose. I can't forgive Kelly for that.

I've been avoiding Jack's calls and emails for weeks now. I know exactly what he wants and it's not something I can give him at the moment.

'Tregarrow Farm.' Rose pointed out the window. 'Mum, we're here!' My stomach lurched as I looked over at her excited face. She looked happier than I'd seen her in a long time. To Rose, Stella and Charlotte are her security. They symbolise everything safe and peaceful in her life. Things that she'd always longed for. Things that I've never quite been able to deliver. Over the last few years, their relationship had become its own entity, something separate from me. Rose didn't have many friends. Even at the boarding school, she seemed to be alone whenever I called her. These days, she spoke to Stella and Charlotte more than I did.

I'm glad that Rose is excited. But I don't think she has any idea how difficult this week's going to be.

CHAPTER FIVE

DCI MELANIE PRICE

The day it happened

I followed an unmarked SOCO van onto the campsite. Two ambulances were parked in front of the reception. The paramedics stood by the backdoors, their heads down and their hands in their pockets. They already knew that their services weren't required. I wondered if the family knew that yet.

After a minute or two of talking to the police officer on the gate, the SOCO van rolled into the first field. I silently held my badge up to the officer and followed the van through. Families watched the macabre procession from their tent village. Their faces solemn and their arms wrapped protectively around their children.

We reached the entrance to Field C. I tapped the steering wheel with my thumb as I waited for the security gate to lift. I opened my window and looked up at a metal pole on one side of the entrance. There was a matching one on the other side. Security cameras. Pointing in different directions, but still fixed on the road. It seemed like an awful lot of security for just a field.

I pulled up in front of a small red brick building. A sign to the right of the entrance indicated that it was the shower block. I nodded my head towards the SOC officers as I climbed out of the car. They were already getting into their suits. Pure white protective clothing and masks that covered their faces. Very soon they'd be moving around a tent that they would erect. Then everyone would know.

It was a sight I'd never get used to. Something I'd seen only rarely in Cornwall in my nineteen years on the force.

'DCI Price?' DI Simon Green stepped out from behind the parked van. We shook hands. It felt too formal considering how long we'd known each other, but that's what these situations called for. There was no other way to do it.

'DI Green,' I replied, sliding the sunglasses on my head down to my face. It had been a while since I'd seen Simon. I didn't want him to see how tired I looked. How much I'd aged in the six months since he last saw me. 'What time did you get here?' I asked.

'About an hour ago. Me and Lyns' live just down the road now.' I nodded. The only acknowledgement that we'd once been friends.

'An accident?' I asked, pulling my notepad from the pocket of my navy blazer. DI Green glanced over my shoulder at the distant crowd of anxious faces.

'I don't think so,' he said quietly with a tight shake of his head. I raised my eyebrows, watching his features curl into a frown. Simon was a good detective. I trusted his instincts. If he said this wasn't an accident, it wasn't an accident.

'Show me,' I told him. DI Green turned without a word, down the wet brick path to the left of the building. A thin layer of water lay on the ground. Left by the rainstorm last night. Small perfectly trimmed shrubs lined either side of the walkway. Square black solar lights sat nestled under the woody trunks beneath. This path would be lit up at night.

'Do we have timings?' I asked, looking up at the side of the shower block for any additional security cameras.

'Some,' he said, pausing to lift the first few pages of his notes. 'Last seen between one a.m. and one thirty a.m. Can't be one hundred per cent on the timings as the group had all been drinking. She was found by a...' Simon checked the name on his notes. '...Tony Western. He's the owner.' Simon pointed his pen towards the campsite. 'He discovered the body at four-ten a.m.'

'Do we know what the owner was doing here at four a.m.?' I asked Simon as he continued down the path.

'He says he likes to get started early.' I nodded, stepping aside to allow the SOCO team by. They already had their hoods up and their masks on. The watching campers would be under no illusions what we were dealing with now. 'It's just around the back of this building.' Simon paused at a spot where the path branched in two. 'This way leads up to where the group were camping.' He pointed to the right, the pen still in his hand. 'They're on Field C, but they have their own little area. It's a sort of a private enclave at the top of the field. They have a path straight down to this block.' Simon turned left, away from the camping area.

Tiredness burnt the back of my eyes. I couldn't have slept for more than three hours last night. I'd been awake since four a.m. My small Victorian flat was above an internet café and sat on a busy road. After the separation, it was all I could afford.

My phone vibrating against the bedside table had woken me from a weak slumber. I checked the time: five twenty-four a.m.

'DCI Price,' I said as I lifted the phone to my ear.

'Mel? Can you hear me.' It was Detective Superintendent Westbury.

'I can, sir... just about,' I'd replied, climbing out of bed.

'We've got a body at a campsite—Tregarrow Farm. It's about an hour away from you. I'd like you to be the Senior Investigation Officer on this.' I searched around for a pen on my messy dressing table. 'Not much info at the moment,' he told me. His words hovered in and out of service. 'SOCO are on route... We'll know more shortly. Are you happy to have DI Green as your number two on this?' he'd asked.

'Yes, of course,' I'd replied. 'Do we have any more on the victim?' I asked, pulling my nightshirt off.

'Not much. Part of a group holidaying from London— couples, kids, the usual... Looks like an accident. Let's catch up later,' he told me before the line went dead.

I continued after Simon. The same neat pathways as before. The campsite was immaculate. Every tree, every path, every fence was perfect. A lot of time and money was spent looking after this place. It was a bit different to the campsites I used to go to when I was a kid. Those were little more than a field and a Portaloo. People just expected more these days.

It was hard to see the body with the number of people crowded into the small space. A strip of thin police tape blocked the path ahead. SOC officers were behind it. Busy collecting evidence. Two uniformed officers who had been preserving the scene stood aside. I didn't recognise either of them. The young men hovered under a rigid plastic roof that protected the dish-washing area from some of the elements. I watched as they fidgeted in their thick black uniforms.

I moved around Simon and stood in front of them, lifting my badge. They stood up tall, muttering 'ma'am' in croaked morning voices.

'Have you spoken to the family yet?' I asked them. They shook their heads.

The taller of the two replied. 'We were waiting for you,' he stammered. I breathed in deeply through my nose.

'Fine,' I replied flatly. 'I need you on the security gate to Field C. No one leaves this area. Not to go to the beach, not to go to the shop. Everyone stays—understood?' I turned to the blonde-haired officer. 'I want you to map out all the tents in this area. Do you have paper?' He opened his mouth to reply. 'Find paper,' I told him. 'Then I want the names of every single person in every single tent by lunchtime. Can you do that?' They nodded briskly and walked away.

'Are you OK?' Simon asked quietly.

'Do you say that to all the investigating officers, DI Green?' I snapped. It was unfair of me. Simon was a good man, a good officer, but I was in no mood to be patronised. Not today. 'What do we know about the victim?' I asked.

'A woman, early forties, lived in London… I need to get confirmation on next of kin. I thought you'd want to talk to them first.' Simon looked down at his notes as he spoke. I gently chewed the inside of my cheek.

'OK.' I cleared my throat and faced the SOCO team. 'Can I come through and have a look?' They looked around at one another. Identical and anonymous, their faces hidden behind protective white masks. The person closest to me nodded. I lifted the tape and crouched underneath it.

The woman lay on her front. Body lying angled across the path. Her feet were bare and the soles muddy. She wore a long white T-shirt. It was soaked through. Almost transparent as it clung to her skin. Her limbs lay at parallel angles. Covered in tiny spots of dirt where the rain had kicked up mud from the path. The T-shirt had ridden up her legs, exposing a small section of black underwear. They looked intact. 'Do we think it's sexual?' I asked Simon.

'Not sure. Possibly. The positioning of the body… the exposed underwear…' he told me. I moved around her torso, carefully checking where I'd stepped in my plastic-covered trainers.

I crouched down by her shoulders, noticing the faint scent of fabric softener on her clothes. Her head was turned to the side. Resting on the step to the dishwashing area. I understand why they thought this might have been an accident. In the dim light of the early morning, it would have looked like she'd tripped and hit her head on the step. The woman's hair would have hidden the blood on the back of her skull.

I leaned in closer to get a better look. The injury was deep and wide. The top quarter of her head was a mess of dried black blood and tangled hair. 'Am I OK to lift her hair?' I asked nobody in particular, holding my pen in a gloved hand above my head.

'Go ahead,' an unknown voice replied.

I hooked my pen under a lock of hair that was draped over her face. I waited as her features slowly came into focus. Her lashes lay heavy on her cheeks. People often say that the dead look like they're sleeping. They don't. There is a visible emptiness to a body. Like a light that's turned off.

I squinted as I took in her face. Pangs of recognition shivered through me. 'DI Green, do we have a name for the victim?' I looked up, hoping that I was mistaken.

Simon tilted his notebook towards me, so I could read the name on the page.

'Shit,' I muttered, rising to my feet.

'What?' Simon asked.

'I know her.' I walked towards the tape, nodding in thanks to the officers.

'You know her? But I thought the whole group were here on holiday...?' He looked confused.

'I don't know her now, but she grew up around here... I went to school with her.'

CHAPTER SIX

CHARLOTTE

Four days before

Our old people carrier bumped along the road into Field C. Theo bounced around in his car seat, waving his soft toy giraffe in the air. The anticipation in the car was palpable.

We had taken my car. It was older than Tristen's coupe, but it was bigger. A proper family car. The side door pockets were filled with litter. The windows were smudged with sticky handprints.

Tristen's car was immaculate. It would give no clues that he had a family. No clues about what sort of person he was. When Tristen lived away, I wondered if other people travelled in his car with him. I wondered if he ever talked about us. He never talked to *us* about the people he worked with. Tristen liked to keep all the parts of his life separate.

When we were together Tristen always drove my car. He drove just like he did when he first passed his test, twenty-five years ago. Seat tilted back, one hand resting on the steering wheel. I never thought to ask if I could drive. I had always just been happy to be a passenger. It didn't matter now anyway. This week could change everything.

I reached behind me and handed Theo his water bottle. He took the bottle without a word. 'Thank you,' me and Tristen spoke in unison as we reminded him of his manners. I smiled at Tristen. He didn't look at me. His eyes remained fixed on the road ahead.

'Are you looking forward to seeing Jack?' I asked brightly.

'It's always good to see Jack… even with the level of shit he brings!' Tristen grinned to himself as he thought about the chaos that was Jack. I looked anxiously at Theo in the mirror. Checking that he hadn't heard the swear word. Tristen noticed and I saw the smile slide from his face.

'It's been ages since you've seen each other…' I tried to work out how long it had been. Trying to keep the conversation going.

'I saw him a few weeks ago…' Tristen stared straight ahead.

'Oh?' I swallowed. 'I didn't know you'd met up. You didn't say.' I tried to keep the hurt from my voice. He shrugged, like it didn't matter. Like there were lots of things that he didn't say.

I was going to ask Tristen not to extend his contract with the army. It was up for renewal in the next three months. I'd been looking for the right time to ask him. I'd been planning on speaking to him about it on the drive down. It was clear that now was not the right moment. I needed to wait. There would be no better time than this week. A week where he's relaxed, where he's with us and his friends. Where he gets to see all the good bits. All the parts he's missing when he's away.

I'd been with Tristen since I was sixteen. My whole adult life. For a long time, I've struggled to know who I am when he's not around. I longed for Tristen to be home so that our family could be complete. But that wasn't the only reason. I needed him. I needed him in a way that I knew he didn't need me. He never had. It made me feel desperate and I hated myself for it.

The Surrey village we'd moved to was beautiful. People

could not have been kinder or more welcoming, but I'd found it hard to make friends. It was an aged community with little by way of entertainment. Sometimes days would pass and the only adult interaction I had was with my elderly neighbours.

'Kelly messaged me yesterday. She said we've got a whole camping area to ourselves.' I tried to sound enthusiastic. 'It's going to be like we've got our own campsite!'

'Great,' replied Tristen without much feeling. I watched his expression for any tiny movement. It was impossible to read his thoughts.

'It's just at the top of the hill, I think.' I directed Tristen through the campsite.

'Wow!' said Theo, his small face pressed against the window. We laughed affectionately.

'It's going to be brilliant!' Tristen told him. His frown had faded away, replaced by a huge grin. It was a grin of relief I realised sadly. Relief that he didn't have to be in the car with me any longer, that the ordeal was over. Relief that I hadn't said something he didn't want to hear.

The site looked full. A sea of bright nylon canopies stretched to the bottom of the gentle slope. A woman crossed the road ahead of us. Carrying a washing-up bowl piled high with dishes. She nodded her head in thanks as we slowed to let her pass. Children ran between pitches. Jumping over guy ropes. Their knees dirty and their hair dishevelled. I used to love camping when I was a child. It was a freedom like no other. I felt a wave of contentment as I realised that these were memories that Theo would have too. As though he'd read my mind, Tristen reached a tanned arm behind his seat and gave Theo's tiny sandalled foot a squeeze.

I saw the area that Kelly had described. It came into view as we rounded the final tarmacked bend. The whole field was enclosed by tall dense bushes. Ten-foot-high laurels lining the perimeter of the site. The only way in by car or foot was through the security barrier. Our section of the site had additional small hedges on either side, shielding us from the other campers. It was a good spot. Kelly had done well.

I saw Jack straight away. Board shorts and an unbuttoned Hawaiian shirt. He had exactly the same confidence, exactly the same swagger that he'd had at eighteen. It emanated from him. Even from across a field you could see it. Jack held a bottle of beer in his hand. I knew without even looking that it would be something expensive, something unusual.

When he saw us, he raised both arms in the air. Tilting his head to the sky in mock euphoria. A cigarette hanging from the corner of his lips. As he lifted his arms, Jack's shirt opened wide, exposing his soft round middle. It wasn't that Jack was a show-off. He was just a man entirely secure with himself. He always had been. It was one of the reasons we loved him.

Tristen beeped the horn of the car in reply. 'Stop!' I giggled, looking self-consciously to the other campers. Tristen's face had broken into a wide smile. He laughed loudly as Jack began to dance. Dance moves we all used to do in the '90s. He was doing it to be ironic. Throwing back to our college days. But in reality, it was who Jack still was. He had been entirely unscathed by adulthood. Unchanged by work, marriage, even children. I envied him.

Tristen and Jack had been best friends since school. They'd been the only ones in the group who had known each other before college.

We parked next to what I assumed was Jack's car. A black Land Rover Discovery. It looked brand new. I wondered how he could afford it. Jack was an estate agent. He was very good at his job, but that car must have been expensive.

'Lottie!' Jack shouted as I climbed out of the car. He was the only person who ever called me that. In fact, he was the only person who had ever shortened my name. I was never a Charlie or a Lotts' as other Charlottes I'd known were called. I had only ever been Charlotte to the rest of them. Plain, sweet Charlotte.

Jack enveloped me in an all-consuming hug. I laughed as my face pressed against his bare chest. He smelt of cigarettes and aftershave. The same aftershave he'd been wearing for years. My stomach lurched with nostalgia. As I pulled away, Kelly walked out of the large tent pitched behind him.

'Charlotte!' I thought she was walking over to hug me. I smiled as I moved towards her. Instead, Kelly put her arms around Jack. She pressed her small body into his back and her fingers crept inside his shirt and settled around his waist.

'How are you?' I asked. My voice sounded unnaturally high.

'Good, babe. Did you find this place OK?' She rested her chin on Jack's shoulder as she spoke. I'd forgotten just how beautiful Kelly was. Her big blue eyes blinked long dark lashes onto her cheeks. Her thick blonde hair tumbled in waves around her shoulders. Kelly didn't wait for me to reply. 'I love this place,' she squealed. 'I'm so happy I found it. You don't even want to know how long it took for me to organise everything...' She kissed Jack on the cheek and released her hands from his waist.

'Thanks for arranging all this, Kelly. It must have been a lot of work,' I told her, forcing my mouth into a smile. 'Do you need any help?' I called over to Tristen as he pulled bags from the boot of the car.

'No, it's fine,' he replied, grinning at Jack as he dropped a big holdall on the ground.

'Be careful with the cooler, the Bolognese is defrosting in there,' I told him. 'Shall we set up in the corner? It's closer to the toilets... in case Theo gets up in the night.' I said, craning my neck to look at how much space there was.

I heard Tristen sigh. 'It's fine, Charlotte. We'll sort it out in a bit.' He sounded weary.

'Of course,' I replied, smiling brightly. I gently chewed my bottom lip. Don't fuss, I reminded myself. Whatever else you do this weekend—don't fuss.

'Big man!' Jack called as Theo came out from behind the car. He walked shyly over to our group and hugged the back of my thigh. 'Lottie, I don't know who this boy is, but that's definitely not Theo. He's way too big to be Theo...' Jack bent down as he spoke. 'How old are you? Twelve? Seventeen?' he asked Theo.

'I'm four!' Theo said loudly as he stepped out from behind my legs. We all laughed. Jack held his arms open and Theo went to him. Jack threw him up in the air and placed him on one of his shoulders. Theo looked delighted. I was so surprised I didn't speak. He never usually went to strangers. Jack wasn't exactly a stranger, but Theo had only met him a handful of times in his short life.

'You're looking good, bud!' Tristen said as he closed the boot of the car. Jack raised his beer bottle towards Tristen. Before he could say anything, Kelly spoke.

'We've only just got back from two weeks in the Maldives,' she said, tossing her hair over her shoulder. Jack looked sharply at Kelly. It was only for a moment, but it was long enough to know that he wasn't happy. He put Theo down gently on the ground.

Kelly ignored his glare. 'We stayed in the same hotel as Tom Cruise, didn't we, babe? I mean, he wasn't there... but it's the one he stayed in a few years ago.' She chattered away happily.

'The Maldives? Jesus, mate, did you win the lottery and not tell us?' Tristen laughed as he piled our camping kit up on the grass. He caught my eye as he spoke. Tristen had seen the car too. He'd thought the same thing.

'Charlotte!' I heard my name called from across the grassy corner. It was Stella. She was carrying a big plastic water container. Next to her was a fair-haired man with a pile of small logs in his arms. We walked quickly to one another and embraced for what felt like minutes. 'It's so good to see you,' she whispered into my hair.

'You too,' I told her as I felt a wave of emotion rise in my throat.

'You look gorgeous, Charlotte,' she told me as she pulled away from my body.

I'd worn a new dress. It was black with tiny white polka dots. When I'd first tried it on a few weeks ago I loved it. It felt classic. Like a summer dress from the 1950s. It somehow felt different this morning. My body felt like it had swelled in the heat. The neckline seemed to have dropped. It clung to every bulge and every bump and seemed to accentuate them. It felt more 'frumpy country fete' than vintage siren. I had never felt less comfortable in an outfit.

'Ah thanks but...' I shook my head as I looked down at the dress in disappointment.

'No, Charlotte, you really do.' Stella took both my hands and held my gaze in sincerity. I felt tears prickle the backs of my eyes. Without saying a word Stella hugged me again. I hadn't realised how much I'd missed her.

'Talking of gorgeous... Nate!' I breathed into her shoulder. We both laughed as we drew apart and I quickly wiped away the tears that were threatening to spill over.

'Nate, this is Charlotte,' Stella said, placing a hand on the small of his back.

'It's really nice to finally meet you, Charlotte.' Nate squeezed my hand. He was the sort of handsome that you usually only see in films. Tanned and muscular, with the bluest eyes I think I've ever seen. He held my gaze and for a moment I couldn't reply.

'It's nice to meet you too.' It came out quickly like one long word. I got the impression Nate had no idea how good looking he was. Or the effect he must have on women. He looked genuinely pleased to see me. I was happy for Stella. She hadn't had anyone special in her life for a long time. Stella deserved something good. *Someone* good.

Waves of conversation ebbed across the group. My ears tuned in to different stories, different voices—laughter. I stood on the peripheral. Pretending to take in the view. Waiting for my hands to stop shaking. Our little camping area was at the top of the field. The site meandered down a gentle slope towards the bottom of the valley. The meadows behind were filled with wheat. Their golden heads of grain stood motionless against the still sky.

I shifted my dress down a little. Trying to move new air to my clammy skin. Trying to pull the cheap fabric away from the sweat that was gathering between my breasts. Stella noticed. 'It's so hot, isn't it?' she said, fanning her thin cotton T-shirt. This heat was making everyone uncomfortable.

The sound of loud music cut through the peaceful campsite. It was Annie and Rose. Gliding along the narrow track. The roof of her shiny blue sports car down and the stereo blaring. This was it. Everyone was here. I should be excited. Grateful that we're all finally together. And yet I couldn't shake this feeling of dread in the pit of my stomach.

CHAPTER SEVEN

ANNIE

Four days before

People stared as I drove through the campsite. Annoyed that my loud music and obnoxious car were stealing their rural peace. I didn't care. I never have worried what other people think of me. But I saw Rose squirm uncomfortably in her seat, so I turned the music down.

As we rounded the final bend, I saw them. Charlotte, Tristen, Jack and Kelly. Stella and her boyfriend were a little back from the main group. They all stood watching as my tiny car bumped onto the grass in front of them. Charlotte waved. Lovely, loyal Charlotte in her best dress. Trying her hardest to please everyone. Rose waved cheerfully back.

I put the car in park and went straight to the boot. I pulled out one of the bottles of Champagne from the ice bag. Droplets of cold water ran down my wrist as I held the bottle above my head. 'Come on!' I screamed into the sky. The group laughed and clapped. We all met between the cars and the tents in a muddle of hugs and kisses. I pulled the cigarette from Jack's mouth and placed it in my own. Inhaling deeply on the dark, acrid smoke. I caught Kelly's eye. She quickly adjusted her face into a smile, but it looked strained.

'You're a sight for sore eyes,' I told Jack with a flirty smile. I grabbed hold of the ends of his shirt and pulled him towards me.

'It's been a minute, hasn't it?' he said, fixing me with a familiar lopsided grin. I wrapped my arms around his middle, pressing my face into his warm chest. He draped his arms over my shoulders and rested his chin on my head. I'd missed this. I'd missed him.

I looked around for Rose. She was hanging back, preferring a more low-key welcome. Stella and Charlotte went to her first. Enveloping her in a maternal embrace. I watched as Stella pulled away, pushing the hair from Rose's young face.

'You look beautiful,' she told her. 'I can't believe you're going to be eighteen this week! Honestly, it seems like just a few months ago that you were Theo's age!' The three of them glowed with affection for one another. I tried to replace the rising tide of jealousy.

Oliver walked out the entrance of Jack and Kelly's tent. Oliver was Jack's fifteen-year-old son from his first marriage to Lisa. By the sound of the welcome he received, this was the first time that the rest of the group had seen him. He looked surly as he scuffed the edge of his trainers on the dry earth. 'Hi, Ollie,' I said cheerfully. 'It's been ages since I've seen you.' Oliver fixed me with a cold glare. 'How's your mum?' I added. Oliver said nothing. He just carried on staring at me. I looked away for a few seconds. I had no interest in trying to carry on the conversation with him. When I turned my head back, he was still there. Still watching me with the same dark expression. It was unnerving.

Oliver had always been a bit of brat. The divorce had been hard on him. But it had been hard on his older brother, Finn, too and he'd turned out just fine. Finn was seventeen now and about to go into his final year at college. He'd decided not to come on this trip, which was a shame. Finn and Rose had always got on. Ollie had always been a bit in his shadow. He'd acted out a few times over the years and I knew there'd been problems at school. I think it was just usual teenage stuff. Drinking and smoking. Jack never went into the details, but I knew him and Lisa were worried. Last year they moved Oliver to a private boarding school. Things must have got pretty bad at home for Lisa to agree to such a drastic move. It must have cost thousands.

We all got to work setting up our camping area. Kelly and Jack had got there early, so they already had their tent set up. It seemed like they'd brought everything. They'd arranged a separate 'kitchen tent' with toaster, stove top, even an electric kettle.

Our yurt had already been erected. Set in the far corner. Charlotte and Tristen's green utility tent was next to us. Stella and Nate were on the other side of them, in their small two-man. A big cream canvas awning was pinned open in welcome. Pastel-coloured bunting hung on either side of the entrance. 'Isn't this nice?' I asked Rose as we ducked our heads to enter. There were twin beds. Low to the ground, swaddled tightly in pale lemon duvets. We slipped our shoes off by the door and tiptoed over soft woven rugs. Fairy lights were draped around the canvas roof. They would look beautiful when it got dark.

Rose climbed onto the bed furthest from the entrance with her old denim backpack. I watched as she crossed her legs, tucking her long cotton skirt under her knees. 'It's lovely, Mum,' she told me as she looked up at the sloped roof. Her face was bathed in the warm, diffused light that shone through the fabric walls. She looked so young. So grateful for this simple space that I'd found her. A surge of regret trembled through my body. A surge so strong it nearly knocked me sideways. Regret that I couldn't go back and do this all again. That I couldn't do it better.

'Shall I leave you to unpack?' I asked. Rose nodded as she

slowly unzipped her bag. There was a small kitchenette area by the entrance. A fridge, a microwave, a little cupboard under the worktop, covered with a bright floral curtain. Maybe I would cook us both something this week, I thought as I searched the cupboard for a wineglass. I thought back to the last time I had cooked for Rose. It was so long ago I had no memory of it. Even eating together was a rare occurrence these days. I turned as I left the yurt. Rose already had a neat pile of books laid out on the bed in front of her. She looked happy.

'Anyone for Champagne?' I called as I popped the cork. Everyone was busy. Banging in tent pegs, blowing up inflatable beds and carrying bags to and from the car.

'Some of us have work to do,' Jack called back, laughing.

'Please yourselves,' I shouted, draining the first two inches of Champagne I'd poured. 'Music! That's what we need!' I placed my glass on the ground and went to the car. After a few minutes I had two speakers set up on the grassy area in front of our tents. I scrolled through my phone until I found what I was looking for. A familiar keyboard rift quivered through the speakers. Jamiroquai. An album we'd listened to on repeat together when we first started college. It was still something I listened to regularly. Every time I heard this tune it took me right back to being sixteen. All the joy and angst and invincibility.

I started dancing. Not in a small, inhibited way that some adults do when they hear a song they like. No, I threw my arms in the air and jumped around. The way I had always danced, the way I *would* always dance. Stella came out of her tent and joined me. We threw our bodies around laughing like we were teenagers again. Like we were back in the Coach & Horses on a Friday night, drinking bottles of Bacardi Breezer. 'Oh my God... do you remember this one?' I squealed as the song changed.

'Charlotte, c'mon!' Stella shouted over.

'Nooo...' Charlotte protested as we dragged her away from the food she was organising in the cool box. We each held one of her hands and tried to force her to dance with us. Jack and Tristen stood by the tents laughing. It felt like no time had passed and, at the same time, like a hundred years had passed. Charlotte shrugged herself out of our grip.

'Hey, don't go,' I laughed, trying to pull her back.

'No, Annie.' Charlotte looked upset. She went back to the cool box. Biting her bottom lip as she tried to organise tonight's dinner. Me and Stella stopped dancing and turned the music down. Tristen watched Charlotte. His features twitched with irritation. It was a look he'd given Charlotte a lot over the last few years.

I thought back to their wedding sixteen years ago. Charlotte had looked so beautiful. It was like she had been waiting her whole life for that day. We all watched Tristen as he waited at the front of the church for his bride to arrive. Jack stood beside him as his best man. A videographer filmed the tense moments before the ceremony. We all saw it. Tristen's expression as he furiously rubbed his forehead. The way his hands clenched and unclenched into fists. It wasn't the normal nerves of a groom. It was regret and the whole room could see it.

Tristen and Charlotte were twenty-five when they got married. They'd been together for nine years. Don't get me wrong, I sympathised with Tristen. I understood that he was in a difficult situation. That he felt like he had no choice. But nobody expected Tristen to stay with her forever. It had been a teenage romance. Nobody expected him to marry her.

Weeks after the wedding Charlotte had complained that the videographer had left out Tristen standing at the altar from their wedding video. Nobody said anything. Not even to each other. But we all knew the reason why. If Charlotte saw his face that day, standing at the front of the church, she would know. She'd know that the only reason he was there, was out of a misplaced sense of loyalty. That he was there out of guilt.

CHAPTER EIGHT

STELLA

Four days before

By the time we'd finished setting up camp, the sun was beginning to go down. The sky was streaked with a peach glow. The kind you only get on summer's evenings. The kind of glow you only get across Cornish skies. The pace of the day had slowed. Families moved gently around the field, basking in the warm light. Even the children had been calmed by the arrival of golden hour.

Nate handed me a mug of tea in an old white enamel cup. He slipped his arms around my waist. I felt his hard body against my back as we watched the sun disappearing behind the horizon.

'I'm sorry,' I whispered, as he nestled his chin into my shoulder.

'For what?' he replied as he gently kissed my neck.

'I'm sure this isn't your idea of a holiday. Camping in a field, just a few miles down the road from our comfy bed... with a group of strangers.' Nate shrugged.

'You know, that bed of yours isn't actually that comfy!' He

laughed. 'When we get married, we should definitely treat ourselves to a new one...'

'I'm going to tell them tomorrow... I promise.' I absently rubbed the finger where my engagement ring usually sat.

'Hey... hey,' Nate said softly. Placing his hands on my tense shoulders. 'I would never force you to do anything. I'm just excited, that's all.' My shoulders dropped a little as he kissed me. A long deep kiss that made me forget where we were for a moment.

'Ahh, get a room, you two!' Annie laughed as she strolled over, a glass of Champagne in her perfectly manicured hand. 'I'm Annie,' she said, stretching out her hand to Nate. 'We didn't get a chance to meet properly earlier.'

'Nate. Good to finally meet you.' He shook her hand warmly.

'You seem familiar...' Annie said, her head tilted quizzically. 'Have you worked in London?'

'Many years ago... a disastrous modelling career when I was nineteen... but I don't think we've met.' He smiled, rubbing his chin awkwardly with the palm of his hand.

'I see why Stella's been hiding you for so long.' Annie gave me one of her slow, lazy winks. 'How old are you, Nate?' she asked, arching one of her dark eyebrows. Her eyes danced with mischief.

'I'm, um... thirty,' he replied, looking at me. Even calm composed Nate could be wrong-footed by Annie.

'Ignore her,' I said. 'She's just jealous.' I laughed, giving Annie a playful nudge.

Annie threw her head back and laughed loudly, nudging me right back. There was so much of her that I had missed and so much of her that I found difficult to be around. She had not changed at all. She was still just as outrageous and untamed and unapologetically Annie as she was when she was eighteen. She still wore her hair in a smooth red bob. Her lipstick was just a more expensive version of the same dark crimson shade she'd always worn. Her clothes were different, but not much. Annie always wore black. When we were at college it was long layered skirts and baggy black T-shirts. It was a sharp contrast to her bold personality. She was the ultimate goth chick. She still dressed in all black. But these days it was more cashmere and Prada.

Tristen had packed an old rusty firepit. We'd set it up a few yards away from the tents. On the grassy area that had become our makeshift front garden. Camping chairs and cushions and blankets were arranged in a circle. A communal space where we all took turns to sit and drink and catch up. Nate had piled a few small logs that he'd found in the corner of the site. I'd reminded him of the no-fire rule.

'It'll be fine. They just don't want us to light fires on the grass—we've got the firepit,' he said

Theo played with Rose on an old fleece blanket. They both laughed as Rose pretended to do the voice of the soft giraffe that Theo carried everywhere. 'Hello there, Theo,' she said in a deep, bumbling tone. 'Do you like tickles?' she asked him as she pressed the giraffe into Theo's neck. He screamed with delight. Rose adored him. She had done ever since he was a baby. Charlotte had lived with Annie and Rose when she was pregnant. They'd all stayed at the Wiltshire house for a few months as Tristen was on a tour of duty. Theo was a few weeks old by the time he finally met him. He never said anything, but I think he found it hard, becoming a father in the way that he did.

I wandered over to Jack and Kelly's tent. Charlotte was in the entranceway, cooking up a cauldron of Bolognese on the camping stove. The air was damp with steam and Charlotte looked flustered. 'Can I help with anything?' I asked her.

'No, I'm fine thanks,' she replied, pushing a strand of limp hair away from her face. 'It won't be long,' she told me, looking up from the pan with a weak smile. Her face looked flushed and anxious. I gave her shoulder a squeeze and left her to it.

Nate and Tristen were kicking a football around with Theo. They all cheered as Theo kicked the ball clumsily between the two sweaters they'd used as goalposts. Even Oliver had wandered over to tentatively join in. It was strange watching Nate and Tristen together. Oddly unnerving. I should be happy. Happy that the part of my life that I'd kept private for so long was merging with the old. But I wasn't. It made me feel uneasy watching my two worlds collide. I looked up at the burnt August sky. Clouds were sliding in from the west. It felt like a storm was coming.

'Dinner's ready,' Charlotte called proudly from the tent. We all made our way over and grabbed a bowl of the steaming stew.

'Thank you,' I told her. 'You're such a good cook.' Nate squeezed Charlotte's shoulder in gratitude as he reached for some cutlery. It was one of the many things I loved about him. The fact that he really saw people. He appreciated them. Charlotte looked relieved that it was over. Relieved that she'd been able to feed ten people.

'Excellent grub, Lottie!' said Jack loudly, helping himself to an extra spoonful.

'How is it?' I saw Charlotte ask Tristen quietly after he took his first mouthful.

'Good,' he replied without looking at her. He left the tent to go and join the others in the outdoor seating area. Charlotte saw me watching and looked away. It was only a small thing, but pain was etched on her brow. This week was more than just a camping trip for Charlotte.

The food was wonderful. The uneasy atmosphere from earlier had settled. The alcohol was in full flow. Everyone had found their role, their place. The laughter had become calmer, more relaxed. So many times I nearly told them about the engagement. When I looked at Nate's kind loving face, I wanted to stand up on my chair and shout it across the field. But I didn't know how they'd take the news—I didn't know how *he'd* take the news.

Up until a month ago he was still calling me occasionally. He was still trying to convince me that it could work. To talk me around. It had been two years. I wish he'd been able to see the finality of it like I had. There was nothing left to make work. I didn't want to announce that me and Nate were getting married, because I didn't want him to think that it was a game. Another hand I was playing. I was done fighting for *us*. There was no *us*. Not any more.

The light was fading fast as we all gathered the dirty dishes into a pile. 'I'll do these,' volunteered Annie as she drained the last of her wine.

'What! Annie, doing dishes? You've got to be kidding me.' Kelly laughed. It was said in jest, but there was something else hiding behind her tone. It had an edge of bitterness. Annie laughed loudly.

'Kelly,' she replied, speaking to her like she was a child. 'I have all *sorts* of talents you don't know about.' She gave her a wink. Kelly looked less sure of herself. Annie was an alpha. Very few people over the years came up against her and came out unscathed. If Kelly's aim was to knock Annie down for the way she'd treated her all those years ago, she'd fail. Kelly was out of her depth.

Annie lifted up a pile of dirty plates and carried them in the direction of the washing-up area. 'I'll give you a hand,' Jack told her, before helping to gather up the crockery. I watched as they walked companionably away from the group. There was a path that ran from our area of the campsite to the toilet and shower block. The dishwashing area was a basic open-air lean-to with a line of sinks. It was around the back of the block.

Nate lit the fire. He crouched in front of the small spark,

blowing on it until the flames crept up the twigs and started crackling at the dry logs. The group began to gather around. Settling themselves on the ground or on one of the camping chairs. Their faces aglow with amber light. Sparks danced into the air as the wood began to catch. I looked up at the black sky as the last of the orange dusk drained away. I bent down towards Nate's ear. 'I'm going to see if Jack and Annie need a hand. I don't think they took a flashlight. They're going to find it hard getting back here with all the dishes.' He looked at me and nodded. We held each other's gaze for a moment. I'm not sure that I had ever been as connected to a person as I was to Nate. It had been almost instant.

I grabbed a flashlight, following the beam in the direction that Jack and Annie had walked. I took small steps along the paved path. Worried I would lose my footing in the blackness. I heard Annie's laugh. The sound was absorbed into the high hedges all around me.

'I'm going to lose it all...' Jack's voice. He sounded upset. There was a desperation that I hadn't heard in him before.

'Does Kelly know?' Annie snapped.

'Of course she doesn't know,' Jack barked. 'Do you think we'd be here if she did?' I froze. Slowly releasing shallow breaths.

'Jack, you can't blame *me* for this. You're the one taking trips to the *fucking* Maldives... driving around in a flashy car,' Annie said accusingly. I knew I shouldn't be listening, but I couldn't join them and I couldn't leave. My feet were fixed to the spot.

'I need it back. All of it. I've only got a few days... then they're taking the lot,' he hissed. Jack sounded really angry now. In all the years I had known him, I had never known him angry, not like this. He had always been the fun one. The life and soul of every party. A lot like Annie really. I thought it was why they had always got on.

'You can't have what I don't have,' Annie replied simply. 'Things aren't great right now...'

'Then sell that massive country house of yours... It's empty most of the time,' Jack replied bitterly.

'No,' Annie said flatly. 'That's my home. That's Rose's home... I just need more time.' I could tell by the way her voice moved that she was still washing the dishes. I could tell by her tone that she didn't care.

'I don't *have* more time,' Jack shouted. There was a loud crash. The sound of plates hitting the ground. I heard Annie gasp in shock. I ran towards the sound. I could feel my heart pounding in my chest.

'*Jack!*' I shouted as I came round the corner. He had hold of Annie by the arms and had pushed her into a corner of the wooden hut. The torchlight reflected on the pieces of white broken plate on the ground.

Annie shoved him hard as he let go of her arms. She leant in close to his face. Speaking so quietly, I almost couldn't hear. 'You wanted to play with the big boys, Jack. Well, this is it. This is the game. You never should have invested more than you can afford to lose.' Annie's voice was spilling over with rage. 'You don't just get to stop, just because you're losing.' She gave him one last shove. Jack stumbled back a little. I watched as he clenched and unclenched his fists. For a moment, I thought he was going to hit her. 'If you *ever* touch me again, I'll tell Kelly everything.'

For a second, nobody moved. Jack turned and walked quickly away. Heading down the path to the main campsite, rather than our little enclave. My trainer crunched on broken crockery. I bent down to pick it up. 'Are you OK?' I asked Annie softly.

'I'm fine,' she said sharply, jutting her chin out in defiance. She bent down to help me pick up the pieces. Even in the dim light of the torch I could see that she was shaking.

CHAPTER NINE

CHARLOTTE

Four days before

The smoke from the fire stung my eyes as it changed direction. I'd stood the electric lamp next to my chair, so I could keep an eye on Theo. He was sitting on a tartan rug with Rose. She was quietly reading him a story by the light of her phone.

Their faces were lit up by the tangerine glimmer of the flames. I sighed. An unfamiliar feeling of contentment whispered through my limbs as I exhaled. My shoulders relaxed a little. Despite my earlier misgivings, I felt contented. It felt good to be here with them all.

'Mummy, I'm tired.' Theo wandered over and tried to climb on my lap. I set my glass of wine down on the floor.

'Shall I put you to bed, darling?' I asked him. Theo shook his head, twisting his knuckle into his eye. 'Do you want to snuggle?' He nodded. 'OK, five minutes and then it's bedtime.' He curled into my lap, burying his face in my shoulder. Rose was watching him fondly. I smiled at her, but she didn't seem to notice. Theo's soft dark hair touched my cheek. I kissed his downy head and reminded myself how lucky I was.

Jack came back empty-handed. There was something different about him. He hadn't come from the direction of the washing up. He seemed to appear from out of nowhere. Striding out of the darkness looking agitated. 'Are you OK?' I asked. For a moment I wasn't sure if he'd heard me.

'Hmm? Yes... I'm fine, sweetheart,' he told me, sitting down on the chair that Kelly had vacated a few moments ago. Nobody else had noticed. They were too engrossed in their own conversations. I watched as he gazed into the middle distance, chewing the corner of his thumbnail.

'Right then, you,' I whispered in Theo's ear. 'It's time for bed.' He attempted a groan, but his heart wasn't in it. He would be asleep in no time. 'Let's say good night to everyone, shall we?' I carried him over to Tristen. He was deep in conversation with Nate about the army. Nate had obviously asked him what it was like. My stomach tensed with disappointment. Listening to him so animated, as he spoke about life in the forces. His life away from us.

'Night night, Daddy,' Theo said quietly as I lowered his head down towards Tristen.

'Night, little man—sweet dreams,' he said, planting a kiss on Theo's head.

'Cute kid,' I heard Nate say as I carried Theo towards the tent.

He was almost asleep by the time I left him. Cocooned in his thick Spider-Man duvet. His giraffe pressed into his face. The tent smelt earthy and comforting. The heat of the day was trapped inside. Me and Tristen had a separate sleeping space from him. We wouldn't wake him when we came to bed later.

'There were a few casualties.' Annie laughed as she returned from washing dishes with Stella. Jack's head snapped around. 'I dropped a couple of plates,' she explained, heading over to the tent to stack the remaining crockery. Stella followed her in silence.

I settled back in my camping chair. Straining my ears for any sound from Theo, tucked up just a few feet away. Oliver had returned with an old acoustic guitar. He positioned himself on the blanket between us. His fingers slid determinedly up and down the neck. It took me a minute to work out what song he was playing. 'Good Riddance' by Green Day. A song we'd all loved in our youth. He looked directly at Rose as he played.

Oliver was good, but it was a little too loud to be relaxing. Everyone had stopped their conversations to listen. He hadn't taken his eyes of Rose. There was something uncomfortable about the intensity of his stare. Rose shifted on the rug, pretending to still be reading. Jack noticed. 'Ollie, that's enough now, bud. Can you put it away please?' Jack asked him, running a hand through his thinning hair.

Oliver stopped playing. He looked at Jack without saying a word. Even by the dim light of the fire I could see the annoyance on his face. Oliver walked slowly back to the tent. His guitar swung limply by his side. There was a collective exhale when he left. A relief from the tension that Oliver seemed to build up around him. I did feel sorry for him. His life hadn't been easy since Jack and Lisa broke up. A new home, a new stepmother—and now he'd been sent to boarding school. Jack should go easy on him. I looked at the faces around me and wondered if everyone was thinking the same thing.

The fire crackled loudly as dry wood caught alight. Small swarms of tiny bugs moved around the group. Their bodies only visible against the bright white of the moon. I closed my eyes. Taking in the smells and the noises. It reminded me of the beach parties we used to have as teenagers. Sitting around a campfire on warm damp sand. I listened to the sound of children's voices, echoing across the campsite as families moved them towards bed. There was something comforting about the sound of other people's holidays. The sound of other people's memories.

'Do you remember Jack's eighteenth birthday party?' Stella laughed as she gazed into the flames. 'We had that huge bonfire on the beach. It was so massive, someone from the village called the firefighters!' It was as though Stella had read my mind.

'I remember... Jack was so drunk he passed out next to the fire... They had no idea he was there when they hosed down the flames. You were soaked, mate.' Tristen was laughing so hard, he struggled to get the last words out. Even Jack in his melancholy mood couldn't help but grin as he pictured the scene.

'Who's up for a drinking game?' Kelly bounced enthusiastically over to the circle, cutting through the nostalgia. Everyone groaned. Kelly slurred her words, like she'd already had a lot to drink. I was still on my first. She must have started early.

'C'mon, guys, it'll be fun,' she pleaded in a girlish voice.

'OK, I'm in,' said Tristen. I watched his enthusiasm in shock. Tristen hated drinking games. He wasn't even really a drinker. I tried to make eye contact with him, but he'd already stood up. 'I'll get more drinks—shots?'

'Ooh yes!' Kelly squealed with pleasure and clapped her hands together.

'Annie, Stella, Jack—you in?' Tristen asked as he walked away from the circle.

'Yes,' they all moaned in unison, before descending into laughter. I tried not to notice that he hadn't said my name. That he hadn't asked if I was playing.

'What was that game called that we used to play at all the beach parties... You know, where you have to drink if you haven't done something, or if you have... I can't remember,' Stella said. She was lying on a blanket in front of the fire, propping the side of her head up on her hand.

'Never have I ever!' shouted Kelly.

'Shhh,' I said automatically, looking over at the tent where Theo was sleeping. Tristen shot me a look. A brief spark of annoyance, before he adjusted his face and put his arm on the back of my chair. My hand automatically went to the scar on my jawline. A twenty-five-year habit.

'You don't have to play if you don't want to,' he whispered. 'Why don't you go to bed? It looks like it's going to be a late one...' He leaned in close, so the rest of the group didn't hear. He thought he was being kind. Giving me an out from a childish drinking game that he knew I didn't want to play. I tried to say something, but no words came out. A huge lump in my throat made it hard to swallow. He would do anything for us, for our family. But the truth was—he didn't want me there. He had more fun without me.

I nodded, willing the tears away. I reached for my wine-glass, which sat almost untouched on the ground.

'So, the rules are, we take turns in making a statement about something. If it's a thing that you've done, then you have to take a drink—a *big* drink! If it's something you haven't done, then you just sit it out—OK?' Kelly explained eagerly.

Tristen returned with a bottle of tequila and a stack of plastic shot glasses. They were piled up his forearm. Everyone shuffled around into sitting position. Placing their bottles of beer and glasses of wine on the ground. He passed around the tiny cups. 'Rose, are you playing?' he asked.

'No thanks,' she replied and started to gather her things up from the blanket. Rose had seen her mother drunk too many times to think that playing would be a good idea. 'Night,' she said quietly to the group and headed towards bed.

'Do you want one?' he asked without holding out a cup to me.

'Yes,' I snapped. Tristen paused for a minute, confused by my tone. He handed me one of the shot glasses. Tonight I would show him. I'd show him that I could be fun and bright and sparkly like the others.

'Night, Rosie!' Annie called out from across the fire. As

Rose walked past my chair, I took her hand and gently squeezed it.

'Sleep tight,' I told her. She tried to return my smile, before heading into the darkness behind.

'Right, I'll go first,' said Tristen, sitting on the ground next to Stella. He filled his cup to the rim and passed the bottle on. When everyone had a drink, he started. 'Never have I ever bunked off school,' he said.

'That's a rubbish one!' Annie scoffed. 'We *all* did that... even Charlotte did,' she laughed, throwing the tequila back in one gulp. Everyone joined in. Giggling as liquor hit their throats. I held the glass to my face. The alcoholic vapour turned my stomach. I drank it down in one and tried to breathe through the burning.

I was always the good girl. Always the one who was scared of upsetting people or getting into trouble. But Annie was right. I did bunk off college with them a few times. We used to go to the beach sometimes on a hot afternoon. We'd swim in the sea and buy chips from the wooden hut by the dunes.

'Charlotte got caught once... Do you remember?' Stella said taking in a sharp hiss of breath as the memory washed over her.

'Oh God... yes!' I hid my giggles behind my hands in embarrassment. 'My English teacher called my mum and told her I'd skipped class. Me and Annie and Stella went back to my house, completely unaware... My mum went mad.' I blushed as I thought of the look on her face.

'Annie managed to talk your mum around,' Stella reminded me. Annie laughed as she did a mock bow, a cigarette smouldering between her fingers.

'Your mum *loved* me!' Annie bragged.

'She did.' I laughed, but that wasn't quite true. My mum had tolerated Annie. She knew exactly what she was like. Fortunately, she knew exactly what *I* was like. That there was nothing that she could say or do that would have stopped me from being friends with her. My mum had watched from the sidelines. Hoping that the friendship would just run its course. Hoping that I would see sense and find a calmer, more suitable friend.

'Your turn, Stella,' Kelly sang from her camping chair.

Stella groaned and sat up, leaning into Nate's outstretched body. She lifted her glass. 'Never have I ever... taken drugs.' She reluctantly drank the shot, shuddering as she swallowed. Jack and Kelly and Annie followed.

'Nate?' Stella turned her head around to face him.

'Nope. Never,' he told her with a grin. 'I've always been a clean-living guy.' He smiled shyly, rubbing the light stubble on his chin. Stella leaned back and kissed his cheek.

Tristen had never taken drugs either. He knew drugs weren't for him even when he was seventeen. He was never swayed.

I hesitated for a moment. Feeling the eyes of the group slowly begin to fall on me. I quickly threw the shot back. The fire in my chest nearly made me gag. 'Charlotte! I never knew you'd taken drugs!' Stella laughed in shock. Her words were thick. Rounded by the alcohol.

'Just once,' I said, staring into the fire. The flames were swimming. The rising heat and tequila had blurred all the faces around me. I wanted to leave but I thought I might be sick if I stood up. I could feel Tristen watching me with concern.

Stella turned to Annie. 'Did you know about this?' she asked her in mock dismay. Astounded by the unlikely reveal. Annie poured herself another drink but didn't reply. A hush fell about the party. Everyone felt the dark shift in mood. Annie glanced up at me. It was only for a moment, but long enough to know that she still remembered.

The only time that I had ever taken drugs was with Annie. The night I nearly died.

CHAPTER TEN

STELLA

Four days before

After a few seconds, the conversation between smaller groups started up again. I knew something had passed between Annie and Charlotte. Maybe something that Annie had said or done to her. Our friendships were littered with times that Annie had hurt one of us. Times she'd let us down. We'd spent a lifetime making excuses for her recklessness.

I tried to catch Charlotte's eye. Offer her a sympathetic smile. But she was staring intently into the fire. 'I'm going to bed,' she said, standing up unsteadily. Tristen came over and supported her arm as she stumbled a little.

'Do you want me to come with you?' he asked her. She shook her head. He released her arm. I watched as she walked back to the tent on precarious legs. I willed Tristen to go with her. Help her to bed, but he didn't. He returned to his seat and poured himself another glass of tequila. I wanted to go with her. But that would look bad. It would look like Tristen didn't care.

'It's my turn,' Kelly said. She lifted a wobbly hand into the air. Tequila sloshed over the top of her glass. It ran down her wrist and landed on her beautiful cream dress. She didn't seem to notice. I didn't want to play anymore. I don't think anybody did.

'Never have I ever... slept with my friend's boyfriend...' Her eyes danced. 'Or girlfriend,' she added with a provocative smile. Nobody drank. We all squirmed in our seats.

'What are you doing, Kel?' Jack asked, taking a long drag on his cigarette. He sounded weary. It was then that we all saw it. The change. An innocent drinking game had turned into an ambush. Jack had obviously told Kelly things that she wasn't supposed to know. She looked over at Annie. I wondered if this is what she had planned all along.

'What?' She laughed, shrugging her shoulders.

'Are you not drinking, Kelly?' Annie asked. She lifted her cigarette to her mouth and slowly inhaled. Her eyes fixed on Kelly. The smile slowly slid from her face. 'Or do friend's husbands not count?' Everybody fell silent.

'If you mean Jack and *Lisa*... I wasn't friends with Lisa when we got together,' she said defensively.

'No, but she was *our* friend,' Annie replied simply, slowly exhaling a long trail of smoke. Oliver stood up from the far side of the circle. I thought he was going to say something, but he just walked back towards the tent. There was a hardness to Oliver's expression. A sort of bitterness that didn't sit right on the face of a child. I think we'd all forgotten that he was there. I thought Jack was going to call after him, but he didn't.

Annie continued. 'I think what the *lovely* Kelly might be referring to, is me sleeping with Danny Sutcliffe... eh, Jack?' Annie was grinning but there was a coldness. She pushed her smooth hair behind her ear and looked up at him. Nobody said anything, too scared break the tension. Annie shrugged and downed her drink in one.

I felt everyone's eyes on me. I tried to soften my expression. I felt my breath begin to quicken as I attempted to hide my shock. Danny Sutcliffe was a name I hadn't heard for years. Jack must have told Kelly what happened. He *must* have known Kelly would use it against Annie. Kelly would do virtually anything to feel superior to her after what she did.

'You forgive me don't you, Stella?' Annie called over to me. I noticed she couldn't quite hold my gaze. It was hard to tell if it was drunkenness or guilt.

'It was a long time ago.' I closed my eyes, pulling warm tequila into my mouth.

I'd watched Danny Sutcliffe for months. I knew every one of his expressions. Every place he hung out. He caught the same bus home as me. I would sit a few rows behind him. Staring at the back of his head as he rested his shoulder against the window. I strained my ears, trying to hear what song he was listening to on his headphones. I was obsessed.

I loved every minute that I spent with my friends, but we were all so different. They didn't study like me or obsess about careers like me. But Danny had wanted to study law too. He was always chasing extra credit. Spending almost as much time in the college library as I did. I had pieced his personality together from a distance. I had decided that we were the same.

It wasn't long before my friends noticed. 'Just speak to him,' Charlotte had pleaded. So one night I did. I'd been working on an assignment in the college library. It was late. The lights had been turned down. There was no one else there. Dark green lamps illuminated the oak tables. I was nearly finished when he walked in.

'Hi,' he whispered as he passed by, not wanting to break the silence. I smiled and nodded. He wore a black hoodie and blue jeans that hung from his hips. 'Is that the research assignment?' he asked, crouching down beside my chair.

'Umm hmm,' I muttered, not trusting myself to speak. 'Do you think we're the only two people who are spending their

Friday night studying?' He laughed. It felt like we were the only two people in the world.

That was how it started. Our Friday nights in the draughty old library. Sharing notes, swapping textbooks. We never kissed, but it felt like it might happen at any moment. Every brush of the hand, every time our shoulders touched. Sometimes we came so close that I thought afterwards that it *had* happened. But he was never my boyfriend.

One Friday he caught up to me in the hall to tell me he wouldn't be in the library that night. He was going to a party. 'I'd rather be studying with you than going to this party.' He laughed. I laughed too. I would rather be in the library with Danny, than literally anywhere else. I thought about going to the party. Annie and Jack were going, even Charlotte was considering it. But I had an exam to prep for.

I didn't see or hear from anyone over the weekend. I tried calling Charlotte, but she didn't pick up. By Monday I knew something was wrong. Charlotte was avoiding eye contact and Annie was nowhere to be seen. Even Jack wasn't himself. 'Charlotte, what's going on?' I asked as we ate our lunch on one of the benches outside. Silence sat heavily between us.

'Annie... had a sort of thing with Danny,' she told me, nibbling the edge of her sandwich without looking up.

'What do you mean... a thing?' I swallowed. I felt my heart pounding in my temples as the colour slowly seeped away from my face.

'She slept with him,' Charlotte told me sadly. I felt like I was going to be sick. Charlotte looked over at me, her face full of pity. I rallied immediately.

'It's OK!' I said, putting my arm around Charlotte. 'It's not like he was my boyfriend.' I gulped down my pain and told her it was fine. It was the only way I could stomach the shame. Hide my embarrassment under a cloak of indifference. How could I have read a situation so wrong.

Worry creased her forehead. She looked like she was about to cry. Charlotte hated conflict.

Later that day I saw Annie. 'Charlotte said she told you about Danny. You two weren't a thing... were you?' she asked, pretending to be confused. Anger clenched hold of my chest. I wanted to hit her. Slap that stupid expression off her face.

'Nope,' I replied, slamming my locker and walking away. She caught up to me.

'Hey... *hey*,' she said and grabbed my arm. 'I never would have done anything if I'd known you two were a thing... he never said anything.'

I knew that if I ended my friendship with Annie, it would be the end of our little group. I didn't want that. I knew she regretted it, even if she didn't say it. Everyone kept Annie at arm's length for a while. Even Jack, who wasn't exactly known for his strong moral fibre. Pretty soon she danced her way back into the fold. Annie was like a cat that way. She always landed on her feet. I never fully trusted her again though. I'm not sure that anybody did.

It made what I did later even worse. I'd felt the pain of betrayal.

It's strange that Jack would have mentioned it to Kelly. I'm surprised he'd even remembered it after all this time. I looked over at her. The serene expression on her face gave nothing away.

'My turn,' said Annie. She stood up and walked slowly over to where Kelly and Jack were sitting. She moved her slight hips between the chairs. Her bum brushed Jack's arm. He stared appreciatively at the back of her body, as she slid seductively through the middle of the circle. I looked at Tristen. He was staring too. Annie had that effect on people.

'No,' we all groaned collectively and began to gather up our things. Annie placed her hands on the back of Jack's chair. Her cropped crimson hair fell over her face as she leaned down close to his. 'Never have I ever... *stolen* anything.' She giggled. Jack looked up, trying to read her expression.

'What the *hell*, Annie?' Jack shook his head, standing up from his chair.

'Stolen anything... What does she mean, Jack?' Kelly asked, talking about Annie like she wasn't there. He let the air escape from his lungs. Rubbing the palm of his hand across his eyes in frustration. Everyone watched from their seats.

'When I was... ahh God...' He sighed. Not wanting to explain. 'When I was seventeen... I stole a car.' Silence fell around the circle.

'*What*?' cried Tristen. 'You stole a *car*! How is it possible that I don't know this?' He laughed, shocked by Jack's admission. He fell silent when he realised no one else was laughing.

'Yeah... I... um... It was in our second year. I was in town one night... It seemed like a good idea. I took it from the car park behind the Grapes Pub.' Jack glanced over at Kelly. It was obvious she didn't know.

'I just... I can't believe you would do something like that.' Kelly shook her head in disbelief. 'What did you do with the car?' She looked like she might cry.

'I left it on the street outside the flat we all shared... I wasn't the smartest thief.' He tried to give Kelly one of his boyish grins. She looked away and the smile quickly slid from his face. 'It was a stupid thing to do. I was impulsive and wild and reckless back then... I didn't want anyone to know about it.' He shot Annie an angry look. 'I definitely didn't want *you* to know about it.' He tilted his head towards Kelly, trying to get her to look him.

'I just don't know why you didn't tell me,' Kelly said sadly. Jack tried to put his arms around her, but she shrugged them off.

We all stood up. Shuffling around awkwardly. Tidying up glasses and collecting the last remnants of litter from around the fire. Pretending we couldn't hear the whispered argument between Kelly and Jack. The night was over.

'Good night,' said Kelly. Trying to walk evenly back to the tent so as not to give away how drunk she was. Trying to hide her humiliation at not knowing Jack's secret.

'Why the hell did you have to say that?' Jack hissed at Annie when she was out of earshot.

'Oh, I'm sorry. I thought we were sharing secrets... It was your wife's idea.' Annie smirked. Jack looked like he wanted to say more but changed his mind. He followed Kelly back to the tent without a word. There was no point in arguing with Annie when she was like this.

The fire flickered angrily as the last of the wood caught. Sending tiny sparks towards the dark sky. 'Good night, everyone,' I whispered loudly as me and Nate headed to bed. Muttered goodbyes drifted out of darkness.

I instantly regretted coming. This was why we rarely met up as a whole group. There were too many secrets. Too much that could and couldn't be said. Everyone had slipped right back into their past selves. That was a person I no longer wanted to be.

CHAPTER ELEVEN

DCI MELANIE PRICE

The day it happened

The pathologist had arrived and was with the body. We waited by the taped-off area for half an hour. Waiting to see if she could give us any early answers before we began interviews. 'Any idea of weapon?' I asked.

'Nothing obvious has been recovered so far.' She pointed to the back of the victim's head. 'It looks like blunt-force trauma. Impossible to say at this stage, what might have been used. I'll know more later.' I nodded.

'OK. Let's go and talk to the friends.' I exhaled deeply through my nose, following the path towards the small enclave.

'We're going to need someone to ID the body,' Simon reminded me. We walked to the camping area in silence.

It was a mess. A rusty firepit sat in the middle of a makeshift seating area. Several inches of black water sat in the bottom of the bowl. Charred embers of wood floated on the surface. Blankets and cushions covered the ground around the old fire. Saturated with rain and covered with muddy footprints. There was litter everywhere. Empty food wrappers, beer bottles, discarded packets of cigarettes. Several camping chairs were positioned around the camp. Their nylon seats sagged under the weight of the puddles that had gathered. One chair lay partially collapsed on the ground, away from the rest of the circle.

The SOC officers would investigate this area. I wanted a record of it before anything was moved. 'Take photos of all of this,' I told Simon quietly, pointing at the firepit and the tents.

A man was crouching on the ground. Gathering shards of broken glass into a bag. He didn't look up as we walked towards him. I counted four tents. Two of them were standard family-sized tents. There was a small two-man tent, simple and low to the ground, and a large yurt, positioned in the corner of the grassy nook.

The tent next to the yurt had been partially taken down. The front awning was collapsed, and the guy ropes released. I pointed to it. Silently asking Simon to capture it on his phone. The boot of an old silver people carrier was open. The back was filled with camping paraphernalia and an overnight bag. It looked as though someone had been packing to leave.

'When were they due to check out?' I asked Simon. He checked his notes.

'Not for another three days,' he said, looking at the full car. I nodded in reply, considering my next move.

A couple stood nervously by a shiny black four-by-four. They watched as I walked towards them. Their eyes wide with shock. The woman was young. Shiny peroxide curls bounced around her shoulders. 'Stop it, Kelly...' the man hissed, his head leaned in close to hers. She flinched like he'd struck her.

'Are you looking for her tent?' the woman—Kelly—asked us as we got closer. Her voice shook. 'It's that one... over there.' She lifted her arm and pointed. I assumed she meant the victim's tent. The man said nothing. My eyes traced his features. Familiar features. It was Jack Morris. We'd been at Porthaven sixth-form college together. We weren't friends; I was in the year below them. But we'd lived in the same town at the same time. In Cornwall that meant something. His hair was thinner and his body was rounder, but there was no doubt it was him. I paused for a moment to see if he would recognise me. He looked away.

We needed to secure the tent. I lifted the canvas entrance and ducked my head as I entered. DI Green was right behind me. Three women were crouched on a bed. Their crying was muffled by the hands over their faces.

A man in the corner cleared his throat. He was sat on the ground, his knees pulled up to his chest. 'Can we help you?' he barked. I saw the flex in his jaw. It was Tristen Stanbrook.

'I'm DCI Melanie Price,' I told the room, holding up my ID. 'I'm very sorry, but I'm going to have to ask you to leave here.' I moved my hand to indicate that I meant the tent. 'This is now a crime scene,' I told them as gently as I could. The women didn't seem to hear me. Tristen's eyes narrowed, like he was trying to piece my words together. Like he was trying to place where he'd seen me.

'Wait... I know you.'

'We went to college together. The year below...' I explained briefly, looking around at their faces. 'I can assure you, this won't affect the investigation.'

Jack walked into the tent. He looked at me in confusion, his face tearstained and his eyes bloodshot. 'Investigation?' One of the women looked up. Her skin was red and mottled and her eyes were wild. I quickly hid my shock. It was Charlotte Bishop. She had hardly changed since college. Her hair was a little lighter, but she'd barely aged at all.

'Was it an accident?' Charlotte asked. Her voice broke with emotion. Another of the women lifted her head from Charlotte's shoulder. Snow white faces looking for answers.

'It's very early in our investigation... We'll have to wait for the results of the autopsy...' I explained. 'But no... we don't think this was an accident. We think that Annie was murdered.'

Nobody said a word. The younger woman tried to stand up from the bed, but her shaking legs barely held her.

'Rose, darling, sit down... please,' Charlotte begged as she tried to support her trembling body.

'We're so sorry, Rose,' the other woman added as she helped Charlotte gently pull her back down to the bed. It was Stella. She glanced up at me. It was only for a moment, but long enough to know that she'd recognised me.

I took a step forward. 'Rose?' I said quietly. The women loosened their grip on her for a moment. 'Annie's your mum?' I made sure to refer to her in the present tense. 'I'm going to need to talk to you...'

'No,' Stella snapped, standing up from the bed and positioning herself in front of Rose. 'It's too soon...' Rose lifted up a slender hand. Like she was answering a question in class. She looked so young. I couldn't believe that she was eighteen. Long dark curls hung around her pale features. Charlotte tried to take hold of her hand.

'No,' she choked, trying to shrug Charlotte away. 'She's my mum... I need to know what happened.' She looked at me desperately. Hoping to find answers in my face.

'Rose... sweetheart, you need to give yourself some time...' Stella wrapped her arm around Rose, hugging her into her body.

'Don't touch me,' she said quietly. Stella looked at Rose in surprise but didn't move.

'Don't *touch* me.' She screamed the words this time. Scrambling away from the bed. She looked wildly from Stella to Charlotte. Then she swung around. Her head moving from Jack to

Tristen. Rose looked terrified. 'Who did this?' she croaked. At first, I thought she was talking to me. But Rose stared at the faces all around her. 'Who *did* this?' she shouted accusingly.

'Rose,' I said gently, approaching her with the palms of my hands up. In the way that a person might approach a wild animal. 'I am so very sorry for your loss. I promise you, we are going to do everything we can to find out who did this.' I kept my eyes on her. Careful not to look at anyone around us. Rose gasped as sobs wracked her body. Tears fell down her face. She sank to her knees. Collapsing onto the salmon pink rug that lined the floor of the yurt.

'What's happening?' a small dark boy of about four or five ran into the tent. His big eyes were round with worry as he took in the scene.

'I'm sorry.' A teenage boy ran into the tent after him. 'I tried to stop him...' The youth ran a hand nervously through his hair. Rubbing the ground with the toe of his white trainers. He looked uncomfortable. It was an uncomfortable situation. But there was something about the awkward way he held himself. Something about the way he avoided my eye.

'Ollie...' said Jack exasperated. 'Where's Kelly gone?' The boy shrugged, but Jack didn't notice as he stormed out of the tent.

Rose shot the teenager a watery smile. 'It's OK,' said Rose, crouching down and holding her arms open to the younger boy. When she knelt on the floor, they were about the same height. He walked over to her and wrapped his little hands around her neck. Rose sobbed into his shoulder. He remained still in her arms. It was becoming clear that something was amiss. It was becoming clear that the only people Rose trusted, were the children.

I stepped out of the yurt with Simon, beckoning for him to walk with me. 'Move them out of there as quickly as you can and secure the tent,' I instructed him. 'Do we have any other relatives who can ID the body?' I asked. 'I don't think we can ask Rose to do it—she's only just turned eighteen.'

Simon nodded. 'There's a mother...' He checked the name on his notes. 'A Cindy Turner. Lives in France. She was informed by local police a short time ago. They've told us there is a passport issue. Expired or too close to expiry—I'm not sure. They're in contact with the embassy to try and fast-track her, but it's going to take a few days,' he told me.

I stared into the middle distance, chewing my lip. 'We don't have that long. OK, I'll talk to them again, see if one of the friends can do it. They've known each other since they were kids.'

'Boss, can I have a word?' One of the officers I'd spoken to by the body approached us.

'Yes of course...' I replied.

'We've been through the security tapes that cover the entrance to Field C. We sped them up. The tapes have been checked from one a.m., the last sighting of the victim, until four-ten a.m., when the body was found,' he explained. 'There's not much.' He glanced at his notes, scratching his cheek. 'A camper van left at around one-forty a.m. We've spoken to the owner. It was a family staying here. They're back home in Devon now. Apparently, their son was ill. It was their last night, so they thought they'd head home, rather than being stuck in traffic with a sick kid. They came here with a group. The other parties have confirmed this.'

'Anyone else?' I asked.

'At two-twenty-four a.m. an elderly female dog walker wandered up to the barrier but didn't go through. The rain was really heavy at this point. Visibility was bad, but you can still clearly see the road. We've tracked her down and she was just letting the dog stretch his legs. Said she was only up for around fifteen minutes and didn't see or hear anything. Finally, we've got the site owner passing through the security entrance at four-zero-six a.m.... the time he told us.'

'Thank you. Can you get full statements from them all? Can you also check the footage on the gate between four a.m. and six a.m. Let's just double check we haven't missed anything. So, the only way in here by foot or by vehicle is via that security gate?' I asked, looking up at the tall dense hedges that surround the park. 'Everyone arriving and leaving is caught on camera?' The officer nodded.

'So the killer is still here. The killer is staying on Field C.'

CHAPTER TWELVE

ANNIE

Three days before

I shielded my face in the crook of my elbow from the bright light. Even the subdued glow of the yurt was too much for me this morning. I thought back to last night. I'm sure there would be an atmosphere this morning. Kelly had brought it on herself. She'd been waiting for a moment like that for years. Revenge for firing her. Reminding the group about how I'd slept with Danny was payback. It had backfired horribly. Everyone already knew.

The thing they hadn't known, that not even Kelly knew, was that Jack once stole a car. I felt a pang of guilt at having exposed him like that. I knew it was something he was ashamed of. I knew it was something he'd trusted me with.

He hadn't left me much choice. He shouldn't have told Kelly that I'd slept with Danny. A memory of her shocked face flickered across my mind. Kelly wouldn't be coming for me again.

'I brought you tea.' Rose pulled back the entrance canvas and stood there for a moment. The sun picked up tiny flyaway strands of hair. They circled her head like a halo.

'Ah, thank you, darling,' I said, propping myself up on my pillows. She passed the steaming tea in a white enamel mug. Rose said nothing as she sat down on my bed. 'Oh, don't be cross with me,' I whined, playfully poking her arm. It felt hard and bony. I looked Rose slowly up and down. Wondering how I hadn't noticed how thin she'd got.

'I'm not cross, Mum... I'm just.' She sighed. 'I don't know why you can't just go easy on people. They're not like you,' she told me. '*Nobody* is like you.'

I laughed. 'Is that a compliment?'

'Not really.' She smiled, but only a little. I wondered how she knew. Rose had gone to bed before the game had started last night. I assumed Stella had told her. I took a long sip of the hot tea. Trying to wash down my irritation.

I got dressed before I left the tent. A black button-down playsuit and gold wedge sandals. It was an outfit I loved. I didn't care how unsuitable it was for walking around a field. It made me feel young. Rose sat cross-legged on her bed. Deep in a hard-back book.

I smoothed my bobbed hair into its sleek curved shape. Painting a full face of make-up on before I joined the others. Charlotte was tidying up. Collecting empty bottles and litter from last night. Crouching on the ground with a black bin liner in her hand.

'Morning, Charlotte,' I said brightly as I put dark shades on.

'Oh, hi, Annie,' she replied, groaning a little as she rose to her feet. 'How did you sleep?' she asked.

'Like someone who had too much tequila!' I laughed. 'You?' Charlotte pushed frizzy hair out of her face. She didn't look like she'd got much sleep.

'Yeah, fine. Lovely. It's so nice to be outside, isn't it?' she replied, but Charlotte looked distracted. Her eyes flickered towards her tent.

'That smells good,' I said. Jack was cooking up bacon on a gas stove.

'There's plenty to go round if you want some,' he told me without looking up. Jack was angry with me. I wasn't sure if it was about the money or that I revealed his secret, but there was an atmosphere. An atmosphere that was very rare between me and Jack. We'd had our ups and downs over the years, but we'd never argued. Not like last night.

'Got any cheap white bread to put it in?' I gave him a knowing smile. Trying to win him over. Trying to remind him of happy times. Bacon sandwiches on cheap slices of bread had always been our thing. A shared love from when we'd lived in a flat together in Porthaven.

'Always,' he replied, holding up a loaf of bread. I could see a smile twitching on his lips. Jack would never be able to stay angry at me. Whatever happened, he would eventually forgive me. He always did.

'Just like old times, eh?' I said moving closer to him. I wrapped my arms around his waist, expecting him to pull me in close like he always did. He didn't. His body felt rigid as he turned over the slices of bacon.

'Do you want some, Charlotte?' he called over to her. I pulled away as he waited for Charlotte to make up her mind. Embarrassed that he'd not returned my hug. Jack's jaw muscles flexed with tension.

Tristen walked out of his tent eating a bowl of cereal. He wore a pair of black pyjama bottoms and his chest was bare. I wolf-whistled. Tristen laughed, a faint blush creeping up his cheeks. I remember when Tristen used to be small and wiry. When we started college at sixteen, he was the smallest out of the group. His hair was coarse and dark. The smattering of freckles across his nose had made him look much younger. It had made it hard for him to get into the local pub we used to drink in.

When he first started going out with Charlotte, she was a good six inches taller than him. A year later he had changed entirely. He towered over her. His back became broad, and his chest muscles pressed against his tight T-shirts. Girls began to notice Tristen. Girls who would never have spoken to Tristen a year ago. He noticed it too, you could tell. But Tristen was with Charlotte. He was someone who didn't like change. Someone who didn't like letting people down.

'Looking good, Tris!' I told him with a flirty wink. 'You're a lucky lady, Charlotte.' I laughed. She smiled and nodded, concentrating on the bin liner in her hand. Tristen said nothing. He carried on scooping cereal into his mouth.

'Is everyone nearly ready?' Kelly ignored me as she walked out of their tent. She was wearing a bright cerise swimsuit with a matching sarong tied around her waist. Jack turned and pulled her towards him. Sliding his arms up her back and looking at her appreciatively. 'Jack!' she squealed in delight, wriggling out of his grip. She'd obviously forgiven him. I wondered if Kelly had seen the awkward exchange between me and Jack. She seemed to be revelling in his attention. Even more than usual. I don't know why it annoyed me so much.

'Where are we going?' I asked, pulling off a small piece of my bacon sandwich without putting it in my mouth.

'To the beach!' Kelly said, tidying away some of the mess Jack had created. 'There's this gorgeous little bay, just fifteen minutes' walk away. You can hire surfboards and kayaks... There's even a little café. It'll be fun.' She flicked her hair over her shoulder. Nobody reminded Kelly that we knew the beach. That it was a beach we used to go to all the time when we were teenagers. She was trying hard to make new memories here. Memories that included her. No one would tell her that every part of this place had ghosts.

'Shall I make sandwiches for everyone?' Charlotte asked, looking around the makeshift kitchen area for ingredients.

'No, let's grab something there,' I suggested.

'I think we should take lunch down there,' Jack said unexpectedly, his eyes shifting around the group.

'Nooo,' Kelly moaned. 'It's supposed to be a holiday. Time off from making sandwiches. There's a lovely little café down on the beach. We can all eat there.' Kelly kissed his cheek as he fried off the last of the bacon.

I watched Jack. His face was creased with worry. Things couldn't be that bad, could they? He couldn't be that desperate that they couldn't afford a few sandwiches? They'd just got back from a holiday in the Maldives... maybe that was the problem.

'Are you going to swim?' I asked Charlotte. She shook her head, stealing a sideways glance at Tristen. 'Shall we just sit on the beach and have a coffee?' I asked her.

'Yes,' she smiled. 'I'd love to.'

We walked down the hill. Leaving the campsite by a small wooden stile in the bottom corner of the first field. The early morning mist had burnt away and the sun beat down on our party as we wound our way along the path. I could feel the heat from the ground through my sandals. My make-up felt thick and tacky against my skin.

The earth had turned to a pale tan dust. It kicked up in small clouds around our ankles as we trudged down the hill.

Nobody spoke much. We followed the hand-carved wooden signs to the beach. The path was narrow, forcing everyone to walk in single file. Laden with bags and towels and sunhats. Grasshoppers crackled noisily in the untamed meadow either side of the trail.

The birds sang high and loud. A throaty celebration of summer. The outdoors wasn't my thing. Nature was never something that made me happy. Not like it made Rose happy. For her it was more of a need. But today was different. Even a city lover like me couldn't help but feel buoyed by the beauty here. Maybe people can change. Maybe I can change.

I smelt the beach before I saw it. A gentle salty breeze that crept around the corner as we approached the dunes. The cove was bigger than I'd remembered it. Jagged orange cliffs surrounded it on all sides. It created a sheltered nook against westerly winds. I was gripped with a sudden moment of nostalgia as I took in the familiar view. Flooded by a jumble of memories.

It was a beach popular with families. Those who didn't want the surfing waves of the north coast. Who wanted still, safe waters where their children could play.

We headed to the café at the top of the beach by the road entrance. Making a base by the small wooden shack that nestled in the dry sand. There were a few people here already. Parents mainly, with small children. The early risers. More would arrive later, but it would never be busy. This had always been a quiet beach.

'Dad, can I hire a kayak?' Oliver asked Jack, pointing to a blackboard sign beside the café.

'No, mate... just swim,' said Jack dismissively, pointing vaguely towards the water.

'But it's not much... just £10 for the hour...' Oliver told him.

'I said *no*,' Jack snapped. Everyone looked up in surprise. 'I've spent enough...'

'Hey... it's my treat,' I said rummaging around for my purse. 'How much do you need, Ollie?' I stood up and walked towards him.

'No, Annie... you don't need to,' Jack said with a sigh.

'I know. I want to.' I smiled. 'Here,' I said quietly, holding out a ten-pound note to Oliver. He leaned in close. I thought he was going to take the money.

'I don't want anything from you,' he breathed. The air left my body. The beginnings of a shocked laughed. I stopped abruptly when I realised he was serious. I looked around to see who had heard. Everyone had gone back to unpacking their bags, changing into their swimming things. Even Jack had lost interest. Only Kelly was watching at us. Her mouth twitched as she tried to conceal a smile. As I turned back to Oliver, he was already several steps away from me. Storming down the beach in a rage.

Everyone went in the water except me and Charlotte and Oliver. We sat at a picnic bench. Nursing cups of burnt coffee in cardboard cups. Two big slices of carrot cake sat untouched on the table between us. 'My treat,' I told Charlotte as we made our choices in the little wooden shop. Oliver sat alone, midway down the beach. Gazing out to sea. Leaning back on hands rolled into fists, digging into the dry sand. He had his back to us, so I couldn't see his face. His body was still rigid with anger.

The hazy sun reflected off the cool waters. Tiny diamonds of light sparkling in the ripples. I tipped my head towards the sun. Allowing myself a rare moment just to be.

'I've missed you,' said Charlotte. 'I've missed *this*.' She stirred her coffee with a small wooden spoon. I reached over and squeezed her hand. We sat like that for a while, looking out to sea.

Stella, Tristen and Nate swam. Heading out to a boatless orange buoy, bobbing in the middle distance. Theo was in the shallows with Rose. His little blue life jacket rucked up around his shoulders, keeping his head above the water. Rose crawled in the sea around him, playing a game. Every so often Theo would scream with joy as she grabbed his foot. Charlotte sat on the edge of her seat, nervously watching them.

'Theo's fine. Rose will take care of him,' I told her. She nodded, forcing herself to look away.

'I'm going to ask Tristen to leave the army,' she told me quietly. I didn't say anything. I avoided her gaze as I picked at the rim of my cardboard coffee cup. 'What?' She sounded defensive.

'Nothing, it's just... do you think that's a good idea?' I asked, screwing up my face in doubt.

Tears sprang into her eyes. 'I need him home, Annie. I'm by myself *all* the time. This isn't...' She waved her hand around as the tears threatened to spill over. 'This isn't a marriage.' Sobs wracked her body as she hid her face in her hands.

'Oh. Charlotte... shh, shh.' I walked around the bench and sat beside her, placing an arm around her shoulder. I lifted a lock of hair that had fallen into her face and tucked it behind her ear. 'Are you sure? It's just... well, be careful what you wish for and all that...'

Charlotte looked up at me with red puffy eyes. 'What do you mean?' she croaked.

I hesitated. 'I mean, having Tris home *all* the time... Is it really what you want?'

'It's what *I* want. I'm not sure if it's what he wants,' she said sadly.

'I'm sure he wants it too,' I said, saying words that neither of us believed.

Jack and Kelly floated in the water, their arms wrapped tightly around each other. They whispered in each other's ears, giggling like newlyweds. Stopping occasionally for prolonged kisses. 'Oh God, get a room,' I said irritably, as Kelly threw back her head and squealed with laughter. It echoed around the rocks. A few people on the beach lifted their heads lazily to watch.

'Why do you dislike her so much?' Charlotte asked, genuinely interested.

'Because she took Jack...' I told her.

'From Lisa?' she asked.

'Yes, from Lisa,' I replied, shifting uncomfortably in my seat. I had no real reason to dislike Kelly and Charlotte knew it.

'I never knew you liked Lisa that much.' Charlotte was right. I didn't like Lisa that much when she was married to Jack.

But I liked the idea of them together. They were a good match. Lisa was calm and cool and funny. She was exactly what Jack needed. Me and him were so similar. It had filled me with hope for the future. That I might one day find exactly what I needed. But then he left her for Kelly.

Charlotte went back to watching Theo. Wiping her tearstained face on the sleeve of her T-shirt. 'She's so good with him,' she whispered.

'Who, Rose?' I asked. She nodded. There was a far-off look on her face. Neither of us spoke for a few minutes.

'Do you ever think... you know?' She asked softly. I lifted my head sharply. 'Do you ever think about how different our lives might have been?' Charlotte still had that distant look. Like she was talking in her sleep.

'No,' I said firmly, standing up from the bench. I turned my back on her. I didn't want to talk about that time. Not today. Not ever.

CHAPTER THIRTEEN

CHARLOTTE

Three days before

It was good to have time alone with Annie. It hadn't happened for a long time. I lifted my fork, pulling away crumbling cake and icing. I took a bite, before returning it to the plate. Annie hadn't touched hers. A wasp crawled lazily across the table. Drunk on sugary leftovers discarded by campers.

Annie was on her phone. Chewing the side of her long nail as she scanned through messages or emails. She looked uncharacteristically anxious. She noticed me watching and closed her phone with a bright smile.

Families began to join other available tables. Piling them high with spare clothes and bags and drinks bottles. The sun blurred against the thin clouds. It reflected off the water, making me shield my eyes with my hand.

I slipped my sandals off under the table. Twisting my toes into the fine white grains. I watched Theo anxiously. Tensing when he disappeared behind a small wave or was blocked from view by Rose. I don't know why I was so worried. He had a life jacket on. He was with Rose.

I wondered if all mothers had a constant knot of worry and fear in their stomach. I worried even when he was by my side. Waiting for something to happen. Waiting for something to take him away from me. In a lot of ways our life suited me perfectly. Most of the time it was just me and Theo. I got to keep him close, to keep him safe.

The tears that had rattled through my body only minutes ago had all gone. I felt a lot better. Like there had finally been a release of the emotions that had built up for so long. I didn't mean to upset Annie by talking about the past. I was so glad she was here. I flashed her a grateful smile.

'Are you still thinking about getting a job?' Annie asked. I hadn't ever talked to Annie about getting a job. It wasn't something I would even consider until Theo started school. To her it was unthinkable. Being at home with a toddler. Not working. Annie had gone back to the office just a few weeks after Rose was born. It was the only way she could cope with motherhood, by pretending that nothing had changed.

'Maybe...' I replied vaguely.

'There was something I wanted to talk to you about,' she told me.

'Anything,' I told her, nodding encouragingly.

'Have you and Tristen ever thought about investing?' she asked, her eyes fixed intently on me.

'Investing?' I laughed awkwardly. 'Investing in what?'

'In me.' She laughed. 'In my PR business. We're about to sign some huge clients next month. It's a good time to get on board. Might be a nice little nest egg for you both... I thought since you'd moved into Tristen's mum's old house... now that you don't have a mortgage to pay.' I was shaking my head before Annie had even finished explaining.

'I don't think we're really the sort of people you're looking for.' I bit my lip. 'Things *are* a bit easier now, but... haven't you got big companies and... I don't know, bankers... people like that who would want to invest?' I was confused. Annie had always kept her work very separate from her friendships.

'Of course! I just thought you might want to... y'know, whilst the going's good.' She gave me one of her cheeky grins, but there was something missing. I watched as she rubbed her forefinger across her forehead. I had known Annie for long enough to know when something was wrong.

'I'm sorry,' I added. 'It's just that... if Tristen *is* going to leave the army, he'll have to find another job. Things are going to be tight for a while...' I explained, wringing my hands together in embarrassment.

'Don't apologise!' Annie held up her hands. 'Just wanted to give you first refusal!'

'I'll speak to Tristen about it,' I told her. She brushed my comment away with her hand. We both turned our heads back to the sea. Each in our own thoughts.

I watched as they all splashed and screamed and swam. Stella and Nate and Tristen had made their way back to where Jack and Kelly were. Everyone was having fun. Everyone except Oliver. He was still sitting alone in the sand. He threw an occasional pebble towards the sea. He wasn't quite close enough for them to reach the shoreline. Even from this far away I could see how annoyed he was. Annie followed my eye line.

'What *is* that kid's problem?' said Annie unkindly. I sighed.

'Still upset that he couldn't get a kayak, I guess.' I shrugged. 'He's been through a lot.' I tried to be fair. Underneath all of the rage, he looked so sad.

'Rose has been through a lot too. You don't see her acting out, throwing tantrums,' Annie said. I didn't say anything. There was no point arguing with her when she'd set her mind on something. 'Doesn't he give you the creeps?' she leaned in and spoke quietly.

'No, Annie... he's just a kid,' I said firmly.

'He doesn't like me. Every time I see him, he just stares.

There's something off about him...' She did a mock shudder. I couldn't tell if she was being serious or just melodramatic. Oliver would never like Annie and I would never tell her why.

Theo trotted out of the water. His little legs kicked soft sand out to the side as he ran up the beach. I unclipped his life jacket and wrapped him in a big towel, rubbing the fabric over his head to dry his hair. The wet tendrils, bounced into dark curls around his face. I held him close. He smelt of salt and fabric softener. The sun glistened on the side of his cheek, illuminating all the little downy hairs. He felt so fragile.

Jack and Kelly waded out of the sea holding hands. 'That was brilliant!' gushed Kelly, squeezing out the ends of her long damp hair.

'I see he's still sulking.' Jack nodded moodily towards Oliver.

'Just ignore him, babe. This is *our* holiday. Don't let him ruin it,' Kelly told him, sliding her slender hands up his bare chest. Jack said nothing. He carried on gazing at his son.

Stella and Tristen and Nate joined us. The men's laughs were short and gasping as they fought for breath after their physical excursion. Stella hid her chest behind her arms as she hugged herself. Her teeth chattered with the cold. Tristen put his arm around her shoulder, pulling her in close.

'How's that?' he asked laughing.

'I need a towel,' she said, pulling away from him.

'Here.' I passed her a towel.

'Thank you,' she said, quickly wrapping the towel around her body.

Theo wriggled by my feet. Pushing piles of soft sand into a small mound in front of him. He stood up. Carrying handfuls of it down to the water's edge. He held out his hands and let the grains of sand flutter into the water. I watched as he crouched down, collecting tiny white pebbles to decorate his sandy dome.

'Don't go any further, Theo—you don't have your life jacket on.' I called over to him.

'He's so gorgeous, Charlotte,' Kelly gushed. We all watched as he carefully laid his stones in a perfect line in the sand.

'Thank you,' I told her, ruffling his damp hair.

'Hopefully we'll have one of our own soon,' Kelly said, looking up at Jack.

'I didn't know you were...' I stuttered, surprised by her openness.

'Oh, no... I'm not.' She laughed, stroking her flat stomach. 'But hopefully soon, hey, Jack?' She looked at him adoringly. Jack pressed his lips together. Like he was holding himself back from saying something. Kelly carried on chatting about babies and pregnancy. Asking me and Annie personal questions about our births. She didn't seem to notice that Jack was standing there in silence.

'Do you want a coffee?' he asked Kelly gruffly as he walked away from the group.

'Yes, please, babe,' she called after him. 'Oat milk if they've got it...' she added. 'Do you think you'll have any more?' Kelly asked, turning to me. I felt Tristen's body stiffen over the other side of the table.

'Erm, it wasn't... I mean... having Theo... it wasn't easy.' I stumbled over my words.

Kelly looked around and realised she had said something wrong; her hand flew to her mouth. 'Oh God, Charlotte, I'm so sorry. I shouldn't have said anything.' Annie raised an eyebrow, but she remained quiet.

'No, it's fine. It's just been a difficult journey,' I told her, as I stroked Theo's soft head.

'There's always adoption,' she told me. Kelly was trying to be helpful. She was trying to be kind, but I just wanted her to stop. I felt trapped. Forced to relive something I didn't want to. The pain never fully leaves you. Not entirely.

'I'm not sure...' I started.

'Adoption is great,' said Tristen. 'It's an amazing thing to do... It's just not for me,' he said without a trace of emotion as he pulled his T-shirt over his head. I was so surprised, my mouth just hung open mid-sentence.

'We *both* decided...' I added, trying to present a united front. I could feel the muscles in my neck begin to tighten.

Tristen stopped getting dressed and looked at me. 'We didn't *both* decide, Charlotte. You'd adopt ten kids if we weren't together.' He was trying to sound teasing. Liking he was gently poking fun at me. But it wasn't funny. Everyone fell silent as Tristen continued pulling his shorts up under his towel. I let his words roll around my head: *If we weren't together.*

I'd always known how Tristen felt about adoption. He'd never made a secret of it. It was a thought that had kept me awake for more nights than I could ever count. Through the miscarriages and failed IVF treatments. The thought that I might never get a chance to be a mother.

Tears stung the backs of my eyes. I forced my breaths down, slow and shallow to keep from crying. I wasn't upset that Tristen didn't want to adopt. I'd accepted that long ago. It wasn't even because he'd told everyone, explained it away like it was nothing. It was because he could no longer see me. We were no longer a 'we'. Connected by an invisible thread of loyalty and trust. Looking over at Tristen, he seemed like a stranger. A man who didn't know me at all.

CHAPTER FOURTEEN

STELLA

Three days before

My teeth chattered as I sat on the bench wrapped in a towel. Head aching from all the conversation. From the effort of it all. I tried to warm myself on the coffee in front of me. Gripping the hot cardboard cup with numb fingers.

Doubts were starting to creep in. Doubts about the wisdom of coming here in the first place. I reminded myself it was for Rose. It was her eighteenth birthday, and this was what she wanted. I reminded myself that us being all together again had been a long time coming. I needed to do this.

I sometimes wondered how much the meetups every few years were out of a genuine desire to be together. Big birthdays, Jack and Kelly's wedding. The odd spa weekend with Charlotte and Annie. Of course we loved each other. Our friendships were the most important of my life. But the years that we'd had that closeness, that depth, had been short. Just the college years really.

Were these trips arranged through a longing to see each other, or just us trying to ignite a spark of who we used to be.

Imitating a carefree version of ourselves for a few days. Jack and Annie have always talked of college as their high point. They have always said it was when they were at their best. They'd assumed we all felt the same.

I would tell them tonight about me and Nate. I was ready. They'll be happy for me. At least most of them will be. It will be a chance to show them how important he is to me. To draw a line under everything that had happened. It still made my heart hammer in my chest as I practised saying the words in my head.

I gazed out at the turquoise water. Oliver was still sitting there by himself. Rose had gone over to check on him. He lifted his head and smiled as she approached. I couldn't hear what was said as she sat down next to him. He seemed happy she was there.

'What's the plan for the rest of the day?' I asked, pulling a T-shirt from my backpack. I was hoping I might be able to slope off for a run. The rear of the campsite was dense with woods. Tall, willowy pine trees. I needed to clear my head. Running through the cool shady forest, soft brown pine needles under-foot, was just what I needed.

'Weellll...' Kelly said, tipping her head to the side. 'There's a BBQ on the campsite this evening! We can drink, sit by the lake... It will be like being abroad,' she said excitedly, looking around at our faces.

'What time is it?' Charlotte asked hesitantly. 'I'm not sure if Theo will be able to stay up that late... after the swimming and...' She gnawed the edge of her thumb.

'He'll be fine,' Tristen said flatly. 'If he gets tired, you can just take him back... or I can,' he said, stuffing his towel into his bag. He didn't look at Charlotte as he spoke. I could feel his impatience. Charlotte flinched like someone had slapped her. He should be gentler with her. We always knew she would be an anxious mother. Tristen more than anyone knew that.

'Shall I walk back up to the shop and grab some drinks for

later? I think there's a store by the site reception,' I said, pulling a brush quickly through my wet hair. 'What does everyone want?'

'Maybe vodka?' Kelly shrugged looking around. 'Wine... a few beers?' she suggested. 'Jack, have you got money on you?' she asked. Jack was staring at his phone.

'Hmmm?' he asked, looking up distracted.

'Money?' she repeated, craning her neck to try and see his screen.

'Oh... um,' Jack muttered, starting to check the pocket of his trousers.

'It's fine,' I said, holding my palm up and gathering my things together.

'Here,' Annie said, holding up a fifty-pound note.

'Jesus, Annie!' I laughed at the extravagant gesture.

'Take it,' she insisted. I sighed and leant over the table, taking the note from her fingers. I saw Jack watching her. A dark cloud crossed his face. I thought back to their argument last night. I'd never seen him behave like that before. Especially not with Annie. Whatever was going on with Jack, it was clear he was in over his head.

'I'll give you a hand,' I heard Nate say as I walked away from the table.

'Honestly, I'm OK,' I told him, turning around and flashing him a smile. Nate would understand. He knew I needed space. I felt bad leaving him here on the beach, sitting amongst a group of virtual strangers, but he'd be fine. He was great in all situations. Nate was someone we all needed this week.

As I turned away, I saw him start a conversation with Annie.

I left the beach. Walking up the sandy path that led back to the campsite. The early afternoon sun was almost unbearable. A burning ball of August heat. I pulled my damp towel out of my backpack. Draping it over my bare shoulders, to keep from getting burnt.

My thighs ached as I climbed the steep slope. I heard foot-steps on the path behind me. Without turning, I moved aside to let them past. Giving myself a moment to rest. A chance to catch my breath. I jumped as a heavy hand suddenly landed on my shoulder. It was Tristen. His face was red with heat and exertion. He must have jogged to catch me up.

'Why are you being like this?' His words tumbled out like he'd been trying to hold on to them for a long time. I could feel my face flush with embarrassment. The familiarity we'd once had was long gone.

'Like what?' I swallowed, trying to shake his hand from my shoulder. Trying to breathe steadily so that I could move forward. Somewhere public. Somewhere that would prevent him from saying all the things he'd wanted to say for so long.

'Like you don't even know me,' he said quietly. I could hear the hurt in his voice. 'I've been nice to Nate. I've welcomed him into the group,' he added, frustrated. I carried on walking. He grabbed my arm, not hard, but hard enough to stop me in my tracks. 'Stella!' he pleaded.

'Why wouldn't you be nice to Nate? He's done nothing wrong,' I reminded him, shrugging my arm free. 'This has to stop, Tris.' I was trying to keep my voice level. Free from emotion. 'You need to think about Charlotte. You need to think about...'

'I do think about Charlotte,' he replied loudly. 'That's all I *ever* do.' His teeth were clenched. He looked like he was fighting back tears. I walked quickly, moving ahead of him, but he caught me up. 'This isn't about Charlotte. It's about us. I don't know where it all went wrong. We just need to go back, retrace our steps...'

'Why now, Tristen? So much time has passed...' I pleaded with him to see reason.

'Because you never gave me the chance to fight for us.' His voice was louder now. 'Your mum died and you just upped and left...'

'I went travelling... I told you... Mum dying changed everything. I couldn't do it anymore. So I...'

'So you *ran*,' he interrupted. 'You ran away for six months and came back with Nate.'

'Tris, we can't go back. We can't change anything that happened,' I said sadly, tilting my head to one side. I felt tears begin to quiver though my body as I looked at his desperate face. 'Charlotte seems unhappy,' I told him. 'You need to focus on her... She's still not...' I struggled to find the word.

'Charlotte is always unhappy,' he snapped, closing his eyes and tipping his head towards the sun. 'We were great together. What happened to us? How did "*us*" get tied up with losing your mum? How did it get tied up with what happened to Charlotte? It turned something great into something awful,' he said softly, reaching for my hand.

'No. What we did *was* awful. I look back now and I don't recognise that person. A person who could do that to her best friend... after everything that happened to her.' Tears spilled over. Pouring down my cheeks.

It was like Tristen hadn't heard me. He stared into the distance. Gazing into the golden wheat fields that crowned the top of the valley. As though he was thinking of something profound to say.

We passed through the stile that led to the campsite in silence. Thanking a family as they waited patiently for us to go through. The shop was in sight now. A large white single-storey building next to the reception.

'I want to be there for Charlotte, I do... It's just.' He put his hands on his hips and looked at the floor, like he was trying to gather all his strength. '...Charlotte wasn't the only victim that night.' He lifted his eyes up to me and we stood there silently

for a moment. The tears stopped. Halted by the hatred that had
begun to gurgle in my chest.

'Charlotte was the *only* victim that night, Tristen,' I said,
struggling to keep the anger from my voice. 'She was the *only*
one who didn't have a choice about what happened to her.' My
face was close to his. 'The rest of us... we made our choices.
Now we have to live with them,' I told him as I turned and
walked away.

A cold gust of air conditioning hit me as I passed through
the automatic doors to the shop. I untucked the back of my T-
shirt from my shorts, letting the cool air fan the beads of sweat
that had gathered in the dip of my spine. I picked up a wire
basket by the entrance. I thought Tristen would follow, but he
wasn't behind me. The small supermarket was bright and
simple. Minimal choice, but everything you might need. My
flip-flops slapped the cool white tiles as I walked along the wide
aisles looking for the alcohol.

'Can I help, madam?' It was the dour man I'd met on reception yesterday.

'Just browsing,' I called back across the empty shop. He
sighed as he lifted a box onto the counter. It came out as more of
a groan. His eyes were on me as I walked along the aisles. I
found the small drinks section and began filling the basket. I
picked up a large bottle of vodka, a brand I'd never heard of. I
pulled two four-packs of cider from the shelves and looked
around for the wine. My eyes flickered under the stark strip
lights. I wondered why they were even on when it was so bright
outside.

I chose three bottles of white wine from the fridge. I had no
idea what I was choosing, just grabbing a selection of
Chardonnay and Pinot. The bottles dribbled with perspiration.
I resisted the urge to hold them against my burning chest.

'Will that be all?' the man said primly as I added the bottles
to my basket. I flashed him an insincere smile and heaved the

basket towards the till. I felt the wire handles bend under the weight of the bottles. I lifted it up onto the counter. The man put his hands on either side of the basket and waited. Like he was deciding whether or not to serve me.

'You're with the group at the top of Field C,' he told me.

'I am,' I replied.

'I don't want any trouble,' he said, looking down at all the bottles.

'As I said before, you won't have any trouble from us... Now if you don't mind,' I said firmly, nodding at my shopping. I grabbed some bags of crisps as he slowly scanned the bottles. The silence broken only by the deep, rapid breaths escaping through his nose and the occasional bleep from the till.

'Do you have bags?' he asked, looking up at me from under his glasses.

'Nope,' I said impatiently, letting my hands fall by my side. Slapping against the skin on my thighs.

He said nothing as he pulled two thin carrier bags out from under the counter and put them next to my things. I held out Annie's fifty-pound note to pay and he reluctantly took it. Holding it up to the light and turning it over for several seconds. I filled my bags and quickly walked towards the entrance.

'Your change, miss,' he said holding out a palm filled with notes and coins. I had to grapple around his hand to collect all of the money. It was a strange encounter. It felt oddly intimate. I knew he was watching me as I walked out the shop.

Tristen was sat on a low wall outside. He silently took one of the bags from me. We walked quietly back to our camping area. The bottles clinked loudly against one another with every step.

'I haven't made choices,' Tristen said quietly. We were nearly back at the tents. 'My *choices* were made up of tiny pieces of guilt and obligation. A life that I managed to scrape together after it happened.' His eyes flashed wildly with anger and regret.

'Don't give me that, Tristen,' I snapped back. 'You have a good life. You have a wife who worships the ground you walk on... a gorgeous son. You're so consumed with what might have been, that you haven't stopped to look at what you actually have,' I told him. 'Even without Charlotte, without what happened to her... without your *"guilt and obligation"*...' My voice was thick with contempt. '...We were *never* going to end up together, Tristen. It's time to let it go. It's time to let *us* go,' I said before walking away on trembling legs.

CHAPTER FIFTEEN

CHARLOTTE

Three days before

The rest of the day had been good. It had been relaxed. Tristen and Jack had taken Theo and Oliver to play pool in the onsite games room. The tension seemed to have lifted between Ollie and his dad. I think he just wanted to spend some time with Jack. It was understandable. I don't think the boys saw him much after the divorce.

It had given me and Annie and Stella a chance to catch up. We sat around on camping chairs, basking in the sweltering afternoon sun. A jug of vodka lemonade and a big bag of salted crisps sat between us.

Kelly dipped in and out of the conversations. Busying herself in the tent for much of the time. She was pretending that everything between her and Annie was fine. Like last night's revelations hadn't upset her. I felt sorry for Kelly.

Rose lay on the warm grass reading her book. The sun beat down on her back. Highlighting the tiny fair strands of hair intertwined between the dark. She looked very content. This was Rose's idea of heaven. Being in the countryside, being alone with her book.

We strolled down to the lakeside barbeque at around 7 p.m. The air was still warm. We'd all dressed lightly. T-shirts and thin fabrics, exposing our sun-prickled skin. The clouds were streaked with burnt orange, staining the mackerel sky. I held Theo's hand tightly. There was a lump of dread in my stomach as we got closer to the water's edge. I could smell the barbeque. The unmistakable aroma of charred sausages and burgers. I felt my stomach growl with hunger. I wore a turquoise wraparound dress, tied tightly at my hip. It was another new one. One I'd bought especially for the holiday. The cheap fabric rubbed uncomfortably against my skin. I'd worn a control bodysuit to help flatten my stomach. To help me feel confident. It was having the opposite effect. I felt old and drab. I'd tried too hard and my desperate efforts were there for everyone to see.

I'd wanted to put on Theo's life jacket before we left. I hated the idea of him playing by the water as it got dark. Even with a group of adults keeping an eye on him. I didn't suggest it. I didn't want it to seem like I was fussing. I just left the life jacket by the entrance of the tent. Hoping that Tristen would see it. Hoping that he would put it on Theo without me having to say anything. He didn't.

As the gravel path turned to sandy earth, I thought about all the places I'd rather be. Curled up in a sleeping bag back at the tent. Curled up next to Theo reading him stories and stroking his soft forehead as he fell asleep. I looked down at him as he bobbed along beside me. He was wearing matching cotton shorts and T-shirt. A blue and white striped set that had been given to him by Annie a few months ago. She wasn't always great with birthdays and anniversaries. Gifts weren't really her thing, but she'd always sent clothes and toys and books to Theo. She'd never forgotten his birthday.

Stella walked ahead with Nate. They looked very content together. It was so good to see her happy. Her mum dying two years ago had turned her whole world on its head.

Stella's mum Connie was amazing. We'd all loved her. The day of Connie's funeral had been a hard day for all of us, but it nearly broke Stella.

Connie had Stella when she was young. I think she was barely twenty when she was born. There was never any mention of her dad and Stella never had any interest in finding out who he was. They lived in a ramshackle cottage by the edge of the woods. The cottage had been Connie's grandad's. It had been a second home for all of us.

Connie was different to our parents. It wasn't just because she was younger. Connie was a free spirit. She wore long flowing dresses and bright headscarves that wrapped around her long tangled hair. She had layers of silver bangles up her wrist, which gently clinked together whenever she raised her hands. I still remember how she smelt—like lavender and patchouli. Connie's warmth was almost visible. You always felt cared for in her presence.

The little cottage in the woods became a haven for us when we were teenagers. Night after night we would light fires out the front of the wooden veranda. Huddled around the flames on an old leather sofa. Wooden armchairs with rickety legs and broken spindles. Connie would bring us blankets and hot cider. We'd sit out there late into the night. She never lectured us on smoking or told us how we should be living our lives. She never wanted us to be anything other than ourselves.

Stella had always pushed herself hard. She had an ingrained ambition that didn't allow her to stop, even for a moment. Connie never tried to change her. She never tried to convince her to go easy on herself or relax. Connie trusted that Stella would find her peace at some point.

It was over two years ago when Stella had called to say that Connie had died. She'd had a massive heart attack. It was unfathomable that she was gone. I could hear Stella's heart break over the phone.

The funeral was held on a cold windy day. We all stood bundled up in black outside the bleak concrete crematorium. We were all thinking the same thing. Connie would have hated this. The buttoned-up formality of it all. We'd wanted to hold Stella up, to support her through the difficult time. She'd held us all at arm's length. Our frequent hugs were met with weak arms and a stiff back. I never saw Stella cry. I think she thought that if she let any emotions escape, she might never be able to close the door again.

The wake was held at the cottage. None of us had been there for a while. Connie was a painter. The walls were covered in her art, thick streaks of bright acrylic on large canvases. I could still feel her energy, I think we all could. Her love of life was embedded in the walls. Stella still lived at home. Even with her enormous salary at the law firm, she'd chosen to live with her mum. None of us knew how she'd be able to carry on living at the cottage. It was like a shrine to Connie's spirit. But she still lived there now.

At the funeral, Stella had walked around with trays of tiny triangular sandwiches. Handing out food to elderly relatives. Topping up glasses with sparkling wine. Me and Annie had tried to help, but she wouldn't let us. Stella was like a robot.

A few months later, Stella went travelling. I don't think that it was just Connie dying that made her go. It was something she'd needed for a long time. It made me so happy to see her like this. Like she'd finally made peace with herself.

The lake looked beautiful. Theo's eyes danced as we walked around the corner. He let go of my hand and skipped the last few metres to the water's edge. I pressed my lips together, to keep from calling out his name. I felt guilty for trying to keep him close. Trying to keep him from the world.

Solar lights were bedded into the ground around the shoreline. They had already turned on, reflecting a warm yellow glow onto the dark water. Families stood around the picnic tables, their hands filled with dinner plates and glasses of wine. Groups of children ran around, chasing each other through the low hedge that bordered the café.

Speakers had been set up outside the wooden hut. The sound of reggae got louder as we weaved our way through the cluttered tables. Festoon lights were draped across the eating area. The faces below bathed in a dusky pink hue. The smell of barbeque food mingled with wafts of perfume and hairspray. Everyone was dressed up for a night out. Like me, everyone was trying their best.

'Do you want a hot dog?' I asked Theo. He nodded enthusiastically. I smoothed his hair across his forehead. The sun had given him a smattering of freckles. I gently tapped the end of his nose and he giggled.

We queued up for food. Engulfed by clouds of sweet-flavoured smoke. We carried plates piled high with burgers and salads and sauces of every colour. We sat down by the lake on the dry sand, balancing our food on our laps. Wedging our drinks glasses into the ground beside us. Tristen was sat about a metre away from me, just the other side of Theo.

'The food looks good,' I told him, pushing a pile of coleslaw across my plate.

'It does,' he replied without looking up.

'Maybe one night this week the three of us could go out for dinner... you know, by ourselves,' I suggested, too scared to look up. Too scared to see his expression.

He paused for a moment. Slowly chewing his food. 'We're supposed to be here all together... Isn't that the point?' he replied. I could tell he was working hard to keep the annoyance out of his voice.

I nodded. Tristen let out a deep sigh. 'I'm sure there'll be a night that we can do that,' he backtracked. But I knew that it wouldn't happen. I knew that the three of us wouldn't be going out to dinner.

Stella cleared her throat and stood up. 'Now that we're all together... I... well, *we*,' she said, looking at Nate, '...have a little announcement.' She was smiling, but I could tell she was nervous. Stella hated to be the centre of attention, she always had. 'Me and Nate are getting married,' she told us, pausing for our reaction. Nate put his arm around her. The other hand was pushed shyly into the pocket of his jeans.

'Congratulations!' we cooed in unison. Me and Jack stood up and went to them.

'Happy for you, Stell,' said Jack, lifting her off her feet as he pulled her into a hug. I could hear the happiness in her voice as she laughed. Tears brimmed in my eyes as I took her hands in mine.

'I couldn't be more excited for you.' My voice was choked with feeling. I watched as she gazed into Nate's eyes. Their love for one another was clear for us all to see. It emanated around the group.

'Oh, Charlotte,' she said in a choked voice when she saw how emotional I was.

'When are you going to do it?' I asked enthusiastically, smoothing down my dress and sitting back down on the sand.

'Erm, well... we're going to do it next month,' she explained. 'Nothing extravagant, really small and *really* relaxed. We're not really "wedding people"...' Stella laughed at her own lack of romance.

'Next month?' Kelly gasped. 'It took us a year and half to plan ours—didn't it, babe?' She looked at Jack, who said nothing. Rose hugged Stella tightly. I could tell by the way they looked at one another that she already knew about Stella's engagement. I'm glad they were so close.

'I've got a whole folder of stuff from ours...' said Kelly. 'We had a wedding planner of course... but I've still got all the catering info and flowers and dress designer stuff. Oooh, we'll have to meet up and go through it.' She clapped her hands together excitedly. Stella nodded. Overwhelmed by the attention.

'Will you get married in Cornwall?' I asked.

'Yeah, we think so...' Stella looked uncertainly at Nate for confirmation. He nodded encouragingly. 'We were thinking maybe a ceremony at the local church, followed by a reception at the cottage...' she explained. 'Do you remember the parties that Mum used to throw? Fires and blankets and random plates of food?' She laughed at the memory. 'I would love to do something like that. It would have made Mum really happy.'

'That sounds wonderful!' said Rose excitedly.

I looked over at Annie, expecting to see her smiling. I'm not sure if she'd congratulated them with the rest of us. She stood there silently, stroking the side of her straight crimson bob.

'Congratulations,' said Tristen, raising his drink in the air. I leaned in close to him. 'It's been a while since we've been to a wedding,' I told him softly. 'Jack and Kelly's wedding a couple of years ago would have been the last one.' He nodded. His eyes fixed on the darkness of the glassy lake.

'I guess I'll have to dig out my suit.' He smiled, forcing his eyes away from the water. 'Hopefully it still fits.' He laughed, patting his stomach. My heart fluttered. Moments like this, moments of closeness were so rare between us. When they happened, my whole body tried to absorb the attention.

I placed my hand on his abdomen and smiled appreciatively. 'Of course it will still fit. You have the body of a twenty-year-old!' I spoke in a low voice. Trying to make my tone flirty and suggestive. My confidence powered by wine. Tristen looked away and the moment was gone.

Theo had finished his food and was playing by the shallows with Rose. She was teaching him how to skim pebbles. His face was scrunched in concentration as he wrapped his tiny fingers around the flat stone. Oliver joined them. Standing with his hands shoved deep in the pockets of his jeans. Rose offered him a piece of wet slate, but he shook his head.

The plates were stacked on the ground beside me. Smeared with sauces and littered with discarded lettuce leaves. It was almost dark. The moon glistened on the black water. All the edges slightly blurred by the glasses of wine I'd drunk.

'I'm tired, Mummy.' Theo dragged his little body up the sandy slope and climbed onto my lap.

'I'll take him to bed,' I told Tristen.

'I can do it,' Rose offered. 'You stay here.'

'No, it's fine... but thank you...' I told her.

'Aww, Charlotte, stay for another drink,' Kelly called loudly over to me.

'Mummy,' Theo whined, rubbing his eyes.

'Just let her take him,' sighed Tristen.

'OK... thank you.' I kissed Theo good night. Clinging to his little hand for too long. I wanted to go with him. I wished I didn't care so much about what people thought of me—about what Tristen thought of me.

'I'll go with you.' Oliver was at Rose's side. His eyes fixed on the ground. He must be so bored here I suddenly realised. It was different for Rose, she was practically an adult. It felt like Oliver was always looking for some place to be.

'I don't... I'm not sure that's a good idea,' Kelly said, nudging Jack and nodding in Oliver's direction. Jack was scrolling on his phone. He glanced up briefly.

'He's fine. Let him go,' he told her, distracted by his screen. I watched Kelly, unsure why she cared. She returned to her drink and the moment passed.

'We'll see you back there,' Rose called out, taking Theo by the hand. He trotted happily beside her. Oliver trailed behind them. Just before they rounded the corner, he turned, staring right at Kelly. Lit up by the silver moon. His dark eyes locked on her. A shadow passed over his face. Something that was very close to hatred.

CHAPTER SIXTEEN

DCI MELANIE PRICE

The day it happened

'We need to notify the owners of the site that nobody is to leave,' I told DI Simon Green.

'Even the families that are due to check out today? I'm not sure we can keep them here...' Simon said uncertainly, scratching his cheek.

'We're going to have to. This is a murder investigation. I can't have people going home... Disappearing across the country when we *know* it was someone here who did it,' I told him firmly.

'Are we absolutely sure that it's someone here?' Simon asked, rubbing his fingers across his chin doubtfully.

'Nobody could have breached the boundary. That hedge is at least ten foot high and impossible to get through.' I pointed at tall green shrubs that bordered the edges of the site. 'Even if they could, there's a fence the other side. It's the same between the fields. The only way in, either by foot or by car is through the barrier... They would have been caught on camera.' Simon looked sceptical. He wanted us to keep our options open.

'If I'm wrong, we'll widen the search later.' I shrugged.

Simon nodded. 'We're going to struggle to keep them here. There's going to be other families arriving...' he reasoned.

'It's unfortunate, but they are going to have to make other arrangements,' I said brusquely, before continuing to check through my notes.

'I'm assuming we're looking at the friend group as the main suspects?' he said in a hushed voice.

'Obviously. So, the sooner we can eliminate the rest of the field, the sooner they can all go home,' I told him. 'Get me timings for the autopsy. We need to know if we got lucky with any forensics. We might be able to get this thing wrapped up quickly,' I added.

'Are we going to keep the group here? The daughter? Can we look into alternative accommodation nearby?' he asked, looking concerned.

I glanced around the field. He was right. This was no place to leave a grieving family. Metres away from the murder scene, under the prying eyes of the other campers. 'OK,' I conceded. 'See what you can find in terms of local hotels and places to stay. I don't fancy our chances though. August in the middle of the summer season? I'll be surprised if you find a single vacancy.' DC Green nodded and walked quickly away.

'Hi, Rose,' I said gently as I went back in the tent. She was still being cocooned in a hug by Stella and Charlotte. Tristen had now left, I assumed that he'd taken his little boy with him. This was not a place for children. I'm sure even in their grief they realised that. I remembered with a jolt that Rose was little more than a child herself.

She tipped her pale tearstained face towards me. 'I'm going to need to talk to you about your mum.' She lifted her chin and nodded. The women moved in closer to her, creating a protective barrier with their bodies.

'Can we go for a walk?' she asked. Her voice sounded small

and distant. I looked behind me and narrowed my eyes. Thinking about the scene beyond this part of the field.

'I'm not sure that's...' I ventured.

'Please,' she said, her voice gathering a little strength. She held eye contact with me. Pleading to get out of the airless tent. I nodded.

'We'll come too,' Stella told her, as the women both got to their feet.

'No,' she told them flatly and followed me outside.

One of the PCs brought us tea. Hot and sweet in beige cardboard cups. Rose cradled it in the palms of her hands. Desperately seeking warmth and comfort. 'Do you want a jumper?' I asked, looking at her thin bare arms. She shook her head. We took the path away from the toilet block, in the direction of the tall trees beyond the site boundary.

'Rose, I can't imagine what you're going through right now. But when someone dies, there are certain procedures we have to follow. Procedures that are going to help us find who did this— but it's going to be difficult for you.' She nodded. It was like someone had reached in and pulled the life out of her.

'What do you need me to do?' she said with all the courage she could muster.

'The first thing we need to do is identify your mum.' I made sure not to call her 'the body.' Rose stopped walking. I saw her dip slightly as her knees shook under the weight of her grief.

'I can do that,' she told me, nodding. Her head continued to move backwards and forwards until I rested my hand on her arm. She looked at me blankly, like she'd forgotten that I was there.

'Usually next of kin would do this,' I agreed. 'But I don't think that's a good idea in this instance.' Rose sipped her tea. It was too hot to drink. It must have scalded her mouth, but she didn't seem to notice.

'Why?' she asked, her voice as thin as paper.

'Because of your age... because she was your mum,' I explained quietly. 'If it's OK with you, I'm going to ask Stella or Tristen to do it. It's going to be a few days before your grandmother is able to travel back here from France.'

'But... I want to...' she stuttered. 'It's the last thing I can do for her.' Big tears rolled slowly down her cheeks. She sucked her bottom lip.

'I know, I know,' I soothed. 'But it's for the best, I promise.' She nodded and continued down the path on unsteady feet.

I watched as Rose dragged herself slowly along the overgrown path. She looked so young, so fragile. Her bony wrists looked like they might break under the strain of clasping the cardboard cup.

'Rose?' I asked levelly, pausing to get her attention. 'What happened last night?' We both sipped on our tea. She lifted her head up slowly. Her eyes took a moment to focus on me.

'Mum had so many secrets. Secrets that even I don't know about. Last night everything seemed to come to a head.' She looked nervously behind her. Like she was checking that no one was listening.

Her body wracked silently in pain. The soft flow of tears finally spilled over. She dropped her cup to the ground. Steaming tea spilled out onto the path as she crouched over, gasping for air. 'I want my dad,' she sobbed. I nodded and put my arm around her, supporting her body as we walked back. Her pain emanated from every part of her body.

Twenty minutes later I was back with DI Green. 'Mel,' he said, tipping his head away from the tent. I followed as he walked the few steps back to the campsite road. I leaned in. 'We've just run a check on the owner—Tony Turnball.'

'Yes?' I waited for him to explain.

'He's had a previous arrest. Six years ago. For voyeurism...' He spoke quietly.

'Voyeurism?' I frowned.

Simon nodded. 'Two women staying at the site contacted the police. They accused Tony of spying on them in the shower block. He said it was a misunderstanding. They didn't want to take it any further, so he was released without charge.' He shrugged.

'Looks like I need to speak to Tony,' I told him, closing my notebook and placing it in my pocket.

Several campers milled around outside. Pretending to be waiting for the shop to open. I'd seen it before. Patient spectators. Waiting for information, for clues. Every crime scene was the same. A dark curiosity would spread from the centre of it like a spider's web.

I kept my head down as I walked into the reception building, closing the door carefully behind me. 'Hello,' I called out.

'Hello, dear.' A woman's voice from a room behind the desk. 'I'm not sure that you're supposed to be here... the police haven't really told us we can open,' she explained gently, stepping out from the room. She had a soft Cornish accent. Her grey hair was gathered into a smart bun. She looked around sixty, but she might have been older.

'DCI Melanie Price,' I told her, lifting up my ID badge.

'Oh, I'm so sorry,' she told me, fingering a crystal that hung on a long gold chain around her neck.

'Are you the owner?' I asked, pulling my notepad from my pocket.

'Yes. Irene Turnball. I own Tregarrow Farm with my husband, Tony,' she explained. 'Such a dreadful business this... I just don't seem to be able to get my head around it,' she added, wringing her hands in front of her. She had a kind face and small piercing blue eyes. She blinked rapidly as she spoke. Just then the door slammed. A man, similar in age to Irene, strode across reception.

'Tony, this is...' Irene started to explain who I was.

'Another one, I assume?' he said, banging his way behind

the desk. His voice was loud and gruff. It ricocheted off the sparse white walls. I didn't react.

'I'm DCI Price. I'm lead investigator,' I said, ignoring his tone.

'Did either of you know Annie Turner or have any contact with her?' I asked. Irene shook her head.

'Yes,' the man snapped. 'I had dealings with the group over the week. Nothing significant, not really. Not until last night.' He avoided my eye. His demeanour stiff and defensive.

'What happened last night?' I asked, pulling my notebook from my pocket.

'The way they behaved at dinner... well, I've been here for over twenty-five years... I've never known anything like it. I was going to tell them to pack their bags and leave this morning,' he said, his face flushed with anger. 'As soon as you've finished up here, I'll be giving them their marching orders. Tregarrow Farm was *not* responsible for what happened to that woman.'

'I'm afraid that won't be possible,' I told him calmly.

'Sorry?' he asked frowning.

'The family and friends will be remaining at the farm until the end of the week, along with the rest of the residents on Field C.'

'Well, that is out of the quest...' He pounded the desk in frustration.

'Sir, we have every reason to believe that the victim was murdered.' For a moment there was silence.

Irene's gasp was audible. The man slumped down on a stool, his face creased in shock. His round belly protruded out in front of him as he sat slumped, deep in thought.

'I need to ask you about your arrest a few years ago. Voyeurism.' I pretended to read it from my notebook, so that I didn't have to look at him. Irene's head shot up. She placed a comforting hand on his shoulder.

Tony's mouth moved up and down for a moment, but no

words came out. 'Mr Turnball, have there ever been any other complaints from guests about you watching them?'

'*No!*' He stood up so quickly from the chair he was perched on. It nearly toppled over. 'It was a misunderstanding. I *told* the police this six years...'

'Mr Turnball, please,' I told him in a calm voice. 'Nobody is suggesting anything else. I'm sure you can understand the need for us looking into every possible avenue when we're conducting a murder investigation.' He felt behind him for his seat. Irene looked like she was going to cry.

'We'll need a list of all employees. You'll also need to go down to the station later today to give a full statement,' I told him. They both nodded silently.

'I'll be in touch,' I said, as I quietly left the shop.

CHAPTER SEVENTEEN

ANNIE

Three days before

I went to buy another round of drinks. I bought a glass of wine for Charlotte, even though she'd asked me not to. She needed to loosen up. I watched as she sipped on her drink, shuffling awkwardly towards Tristen. He stood up to talk to Jack. Charlotte tried to hide the hurt. Pulling her dress over her bare legs. Hugging her cold arms. I wanted to go over to her, to tell her it would all be OK. But I didn't think it *would* be OK. I didn't have it in me to make her feel better about that. Not tonight.

The moon had divided the water with a streak of white light. Every now and then tiny ripples moved out from the centre as fish or flies broke the surface. Moths batted around the small lanterns that circled the edge of the lake. It felt late, much later than it actually was. My limbs felt weak and my mouth felt dry. Alcohol and tiredness had twisted themselves in an uncomfortable knot. I drained the last of my whisky as we all headed back to camp.

I walked alongside Charlotte. Her pace was quick. Eager to get back to Theo. My mind was elsewhere. I scrolled through my phone. Scanning quickly over emails. There was one from the bank. 'Urgent' the subject line read. My stomach dropped. I worked out the date in my head. Payroll for my small team went out two days ago. That was the last of it. The last of my funds. I needed investment this week or it was over. I closed my phone and walked along in silence.

I thought about what Charlotte had said. Asking me why I was going to her. Why I wasn't asking for money from some of the wealthy businesspeople I knew. The truth was, I couldn't. My PR firm was not a sound investment. The minute I opened the books to them they'd run a mile. Not only that, my reputation would be in tatters. Any hint of failure in this industry and everything comes tumbling down.

The only chance I had was my friends. I just needed to keep the business afloat for a little longer, and I could turn it around. I know I could.

The camping area was eerily quiet. Just the distant creak of crickets cut through the darkness. We'd all turned our phone lights on. Beams scattered over the ground and the sides of the tents. I wandered absently next to Charlotte as she went to her tent to check on Theo. I tapped my nails against the entrance as she ducked inside.

'He's not here,' Charlotte's panicked voice sounded from inside her tent.

'Who wants another drink?' called out Jack. He was stood with the others by the firepit.

'He's not *here!*' shouted Charlotte again. There was a sound of scratching canvas and hastily pulled zips as Charlotte battled to get out of the dark tent and on her feet.

'What?' Tristen asked as he moved quickly towards her.

'Shh. It's fine Charlotte... he's with Rose.' I swallowed as I placed my hand on her back. My eyes raked across the dark field for any sign of them.

'Charlotte, it's OK,' Tristen told her, bewildered by her

reaction. 'Rose will have taken him to the toilet or something. I'll go and check.' He jogged off in the direction of the shower block.

I could feel the first rumbles of panic through the group. The realisation that something was happening. Nobody spoke as everyone fanned out and began to search.

'Is she in your tent?' Charlotte asked me abruptly. 'Is Rose in your tent?' she snapped, digging her fingers into my skin as she grabbed my forearms.

'Charlotte... stop. We'll find them. You need to stay calm,' I told her firmly, pulling my arms away. I walked to the yurt, with Charlotte at my heels.

I unhooked the toggles on the thick entrance fabric and pulled one of the flaps aside. I scanned the bed with the light from my phone. Rose's was perfectly made. She hadn't been to bed yet.

'Where *are* they, Annie?!' Charlotte was angry now. Struggling to keep her fears in check. I didn't answer. We walked out of the darkness towards the rest of the group. I moved towards them so that I didn't have to deal with Charlotte alone. I moved towards them because I was starting to feel afraid.

'Theo, *Theo*.' Charlotte was pacing along the path between our camping area and the rest of the field calling his name. Every now and then she stumbled a little. Charlotte was drunk. The wine on top of the vodka we'd drunk earlier was too much for her. Charlotte wasn't a drinker.

'Ollie isn't in our tent...' Jack told us.

'No, Rose isn't in ours either,' I told him. 'Charlotte?' I called over to her in a loud stage whisper. 'Ollie and Rose aren't here either... that's good... it means they're all together.' I spoke in calming tones, like I was talking to a small child.

'That's not *good*,' she shouted. The rage in her eyes was caught in the light from my phone. 'Your kids can take care of themselves... Theo is only four. I *never* should have trusted them...'

'Whoa, whoa... hang on a minute. Maybe you should be looking after your own kid instead of palming him off on ours...' Jack replied angrily.

'Jack, that's enough,' I snapped. I couldn't risk Charlotte getting backed into a corner. I couldn't risk her saying something she'd regret, something we'd all regret.

Tristen was back from the shower block. 'They're not there,' he told us. He was trying to keep his voice level, but I could tell he was beginning to worry. Charlotte heard and started sobbing loudly. My legs had begun to shake. The certainty that I'd felt early was starting to ebb away. A feeling of dread was working its way up my chest. A feeling that something might really be wrong.

'I don't like this...' said Kelly, shaking her head. 'Jack, you need to tell them.' Jack groaned and tipped his head back. Covering his face with the palms of his hands. '*Jack!*' Kelly insisted.

'Tell us what?' I interrupted, striding towards her.

'Mummy!' Theo ran out of the darkness with Rose and Oliver close behind. He ran to Charlotte when he saw her. She knelt down on the grass and cried as she took Theo in her arms. He didn't seem to notice that she was upset. He chatted happily about what he'd seen. The smile fell away from Rose's face when she saw Charlotte on the ground. I stood beside her, putting a protective arm around her shoulder.

'I'm sorry...' she stuttered. 'I didn't mean to worry you...' Her eyes were wide with horror that she might have caused this. 'We took Theo to the bottom field to look for bats...' She looked close to tears herself.

'It was my idea,' Oliver told them, he looked around the faces, as all eyes fell on him. 'The woman at the shop told me that's the best place to see them,' he said defensively.

'It's fine,' Tristen told them, patting the tops of both their backs. 'We just overreacted,' he added.

Rose went to Charlotte, who was still on the ground. Holding Theo's face in her hands as he told her about the bats. 'Charlotte?' She edged slowly towards her. 'I'm so sorry. I didn't mean to scare you,' she told her quietly. Everyone was starting to make their way back to their tents. Other campers who had been drawn closer by the shouting, now moved silently away.

Tristen had taken Theo out of Charlotte's embrace, gently leading him by the hand to bed. He looked embarrassed.

'What were you thinking?' Charlotte said to Rose. She was trying to speak more quietly now, but the words just came out high and strangled. She was still knelt down. Her hands lay limp beside her. 'I thought something had happened,' she added. Tears continued to fall down her face.

'Well, it's all fine now.' I tried to sound pragmatic, but my words came out through gritted teeth. I went to Rose's side and tried to steer her away.

'He's my little boy, Rose... He's only four,' she whined. Charlotte was making no sense, her voice thick with alcohol.

'I didn't... I'm not...' Rose stuttered, turning to face me. Her face full of confusion as to why this had escalated so quickly. I'd had enough now.

'Get up,' I told Charlotte flatly. She stared at me blankly, her face streaked with mascara. 'Get *up*,' I hissed as my anger finally reached the surface. 'Jesus Christ, Charlotte, he's fine. Nothing happened.' I took Rose by the arm and pulled her away in the direction of the yurt.

I turned before I reached the entrance. 'Go to bed,' I told her. I didn't want to hurt Charlotte. She looked broken. But I won't have her treat Rose like that.

CHAPTER EIGHTEEN

STELLA

Three days before

I couldn't stand seeing Charlotte in that state. She looked so exposed, sat there on the floor. The fear of losing Theo, and the alcohol, had sent her over the edge. I didn't want to leave her, but it seemed worse just standing there. Watching her fall apart. Tristen had taken Theo to bed. Annie and Rose were with her. We'd all slunk away back to our tents. I told myself that we were protecting her. But it wasn't that, not really. There was an air of embarrassment. A mortification that even years of friendship couldn't make comfortable. None of us looked at one another as we quietly zipped up the doors to our tents.

I thought about what Kelly had said about Ollie. Why did she look so afraid? What did Jack need to tell us about him? I tried to push it from my mind, but it kept creeping back. There was something not quite right about Oliver. Something unsettling that I couldn't quite put my finger on. I hugged my arms close to my body for warmth.

'Are you OK?' Nate whispered. I nodded, ducking my head under the low ceiling of canvas as I sat on my makeshift bed. 'I know it's been a difficult night, but I'm glad you told everyone.' He gently stroked my cheek. The warmth from his hand spread quickly across my face. I smiled, resting my skin against his hand. He looked so happy.

'I'm glad too,' I told him. 'Was it OK to tell them about our ideas... I know it's not set in stone yet.'

'When you said it out loud tonight... you know, the church and the cottage, the fire and random food... I honestly couldn't imagine a more perfect day.' His voice was low and husky. I leant over and kissed him deeply on the lips.

'What did I do to deserve you?' I asked him with smile.

We sat there for a few minutes in silence. Listening for the sounds around us. An owl screeched nearby. We both laughed a little as we jumped in fear. There was something about tents and the way that they magnify the sound around you. You could almost hear the darkness behind the thin fabric. A moth batted its body against the flysheet, drawn to the glow of Nate's flashlight.

I heard Tristen reading Theo a story. His voice low and calm. He was a good dad. Not always a good husband, but always a good dad. You could never take that away from him.

We could hear Jack and Kelly talking on the other side of us. 'Why do you *never* take my side?' Kelly's voice was loud, as though she was sitting up in bed. I didn't hear Jack's reply, maybe there wasn't one. 'I'm your wife...' she hissed. 'You act like I don't matter whenever you're around them. You let Annie speak to me like *shit*...' She sounded close to tears.

'Babe, I'm too tired for this,' Jack groaned. His voice was muffled, like he was speaking into bedclothes. They both fell silent.

'Do you really want to listen to this?' asked Nate kindly. He lay down on his bed, his T-shirt discarded. The flashlight cast shadows over his bare chest. Highlighting the deep dips of every muscle.

'No,' I replied, tipping my head to the side, smiling at him. I quickly stripped down to my underwear, laying my clothes at the end of the bed. The temperature had dropped and the air had a damp chill to it. I giggled quietly, as I tried to undo my sleeping bag. My teeth chattered as I struggled to open it. Nate leant over and gently pulled the zip down, throwing open the top of the covers. I lay down, reaching for the top half of the nylon bag to pull over myself.

'Don't,' he whispered, moving his hand over to rest on my stomach. Heat moved up my body as I squirmed against the bed. He turned the light off. We were sunk into darkness. His fingers brushed my face as they slid into my hair. I groaned as he pushed his hard body against me. Pressing his lips to mine with such force that I almost cried out.

We kissed slowly. I moved my hand over his broad shoulder. Placing it on his bicep as I pulled his body in deeper. He ran his hand down my torso. Slipping his fingers under the band of my knickers. A bolt of desire spiked through my pelvis. I lifted my hips up to meet him as he slowly slid my lacy thong down my thighs.

I held my breath as he eased inside me. 'Shhh,' he whispered close to my ear. I moaned into the taut skin on his shoulder. Digging my nails into his muscular back, as waves of desire rippled through my core.

Afterwards we lay there. Legs wrapped around each other as he stroked my goose bumps. The silence outside was gaping. A deliberate quiet surrounding the tents either side of us. I wondered how much of that they'd heard. I held my breath as mortification prickled my nerves. Even if I'd known for sure they could hear us. Even if I'd tried to stop, I wouldn't have been able to.

I heard Nate's breathing sink into long, low breaths as he drifted into sleep. His hand went limp on my stomach. I gently slid away. Turning on the flashlight under the blanket, so I didn't disturb him. He lifted his arm sleepily, placing his head in the crook of his elbow.

My eyes traced the contours of his face. It was so different with him. *Everything* was so different. Right from the very start, Nate had made me feel safe. He'd made me feel like I was part of something good. When I went travelling, I'd told myself that what I'd had before was over. But I know that if I hadn't met Nate, I would have gone right back. It was like an addiction.

I wasn't a person who took risks. I had always been cautious and measured. But I'd risked everything to be with Tristen. When you know what you're doing could destroy people, you have to move it outside your body. It's the only way you can carry on. It was like I was looking down on myself. Watching someone else do those things. Watching my own self-destruction. I could split myself in two. One of us good and loyal and incapable of hurting people. The other, bad. A selfish, reckless twin who thought of nobody but herself.

It's only now that I realise that it was all just pretend. You can't split yourself in two. I am all those things.

I pulled on thin cotton shorts and a tank top over my bare breasts. My coldness from earlier had passed. My skin felt damp with sweat. Prickling with oversensitivity. I crawled to the end of my bed and quietly pulled down the zip. The cool breeze hit my face as I emerged, flushed from the humid tent. I reached back and grabbed a cardigan, wrapping the soft wool around my body.

I walked on tiptoes. Pressing my bare feet into the wet grass. The tall hedges rustled in the wind. Their heart-shaped leaves rippled down the border. The campsite was in darkness. Shadowed outlines of the canvas village below, were only just visible. Oliver was sat in the entrance to his tent. He was looking down as his arm jabbed out in sharp, regular movements. 'Are you OK?' I asked, walking towards him. His face was deathly pale. He looked up briefly. Staring up at me

from behind a greasy curtain of hair that had fallen into his
eyes.

He didn't reply. As I got closer, I could see that he had a
knife. He was sharpening a small stick to a point. Roughly
cutting off the end with the blade. I froze as he stared up at me.
It was obvious he'd been crying.

'I'm fine,' he finally replied as he carried on cutting. His
eyes slowly fell on my body, tracing the full length of my frame.
I pulled my cardigan together, crossing my arms in front of my
chest. A small smile spread across his lips.

'Well good night then,' I said uncomfortably as I turned
towards the path. He didn't answer. I rubbed my arms as I
walked away. Trying to push away the rising fear in my stomach. I could still hear the blunt scrapping sound of knife on
wood.

As I left the stark brightness of the toilets, my eyes struggled
to adjust to the dark. The light of the moon was just enough for
me to trace my way back. My feet welcomed the softness of the
wet, muddy ground as I left the hard paving. I rounded the
corner and froze. The crack of a twig breaking underfoot. 'Hello?' I called into the blackness. A pinprick of orange light
glowed from the side of the path. 'Oliver, is that you?' I could
feel my legs begin to shake as I stood fixed to the spot. As I
thought about his knife.

'So, you're getting married?' It was Tristen. He was smoking
a cigarette. His voice sounded low and gruff. I nodded. He
inhaled deeply. His forehead wrinkled in a frown.

Half of Tristen's face was covered by shadows. It made it
hard to read his expression. There seemed nothing left to say, so
I began to walk away. He grabbed my arm. Not in a gentle way
that a friend might do. He grabbed my arm tightly.

Just then there was a noise on the path behind. A scuff of
shoe against stone. We both turned. It was Annie. She just
stood there, staring at us. A look of contempt on her face. I

thought she was going to say something, but she didn't. Annie just walked slowly along the path. Like she didn't know us. Like we didn't exist. It was the same way she had looked at us that night nearly twenty-five years ago.

'It didn't have to be like this...' he said, his voice full of resentment.

'It did, Tristen,' I told him sadly. 'This is the only way it could be. This...' I pointed to the space between us, '...was built on some childhood longing. A pathetic desire to stay young, to stay the people we were back then. If this was *really* meant to be... If it was really something that we couldn't live without, we'd be together. But we're *not*, Tristen.' I could feel my anger peaking. 'Ending it between us two years ago... leaving the country... it was the best thing I ever did.' He took a step back. Shocked that I would dismiss him like this. Dismiss us.

'I've loved you for twenty years... It's always been you, Stella. These two years apart have been the worst of my life. Do you know how many times I almost told Charlotte? How many times I almost left her? You only ended it because you feel guilty... You don't...'

'It's not because I *feel* guilty. It's because we *are* guilty,' I interrupted in an angry whisper. Warning him to keep his voice down. 'We nearly destroyed people's lives. I wake up every single day and celebrate the fact that we didn't.' My face was close to his as I breathlessly let all the rage escape.

'I don't want to be without you. I don't want to watch you marry another man...' he pleaded.

'It's over,' I told him firmly. 'You need to focus on Charlotte and Theo. You need to focus on your future with them.' I walked away on numb feet. A knot of dread in the pit of my stomach. Tears gathered behind my eyes when I thought about how stupid I'd been. How naïve I was to think that this week could bring closure. An end to this awful mess. It would always be there.

CHAPTER NINETEEN

ANNIE

Two days before

Charlotte was nursing a hot mug of tea when I left the tent. I'd left Rose sat on her bed reading. The morning sun was just breaking through the pillowy white clouds. The air smelt sharp and fresh. My nostrils stung as I breathed in its crispness.

Charlotte's skin looked sallow. There was a grey sickly tinge to it. Her eyes were ringed with black circles. Frizzy hair was piled in a heap, high on her head. 'Morning,' I sang brightly as I walked over to the camping chair she was slumped in. 'How are you feeling?' I asked. She shrugged. Her eyes filled with tears.

A wave of irritation washed over me. Irritated by the self-pity.

'Theo was fine,' I told her. 'Nothing happened.' I tried to keep the impatience out of my voice.

'I know...' she choked. 'But...'

'But, nothing,' I told her firmly. I needed Charlotte to know that falling apart wasn't an option. Not this week. I had enough to deal with.

'I'm so sorry,' she said trying to get up off the low camping chair, before sinking back down. Charlotte's eyes flickered anxiously over my face. Looking for signs that she'd annoyed me. 'I know Rose wasn't trying to... I don't know why I said that.' She shook her head and looked away. 'I was really drunk.'

'Stop,' I said as kindly as I could. She nodded like a child. A child who wants to do better. Charlotte looked wild and sleep deprived. There was an unpredictability to her that made me nervous. I hadn't seen her like this for a long time.

Nearly twenty-five years had passed since the night it happened. Charlotte hadn't been OK for a long time afterwards. Even after her parents insisted on having her treated at a psychiatric facility, it took years for her to be stable again. It was understandable. Any one of us would have been the same way if it had happened to us. But Charlotte... Charlotte was fragile *before* it happened. Looking at her now felt like history repeating itself.

'Morning,' Stella walked over to the circle of chairs. She looked svelte in her tight pink running pants and vest. She pulled her arms behind her back, reaching into a stretch. Stella was avoiding eye contact with me. 'How are you?' she asked Charlotte, her brow creased with concern.

'I'm OK, thanks,' she replied with a tight smile. Her eyes darted briefly across to me. Stella nodded, stroking her shoulder affectionately. Charlotte blew steam from the top of her tea like she hadn't noticed.

We'd only been here for two days. Already everyone had slipped back into their old roles. A tried and tested dynamic that we'd played out for years. It wasn't intentional, we just didn't know how else to be with each other.

'Are you going for a run?' I asked Stella, as she bent down to stretch her calf muscles.

'Umm hmm,' she replied, exhaling deeply, without looking up.

'Great! I'll come with you... just give me a minute to get

changed,' I said skipping back towards the tent before she had a chance to protest. Ten minutes later, I jogged out to join her. I was wearing a pair of designer black leggings and a vintage Dior T-shirt and my immaculate white trainers. I hadn't intended to run in any of these clothes, but it was all I had that was even vaguely suitable. The only exercise I did was Pilates.

As I'd got older, the meagre amount of food I allowed myself was no longer meagre enough to stay skinny. Pilates was the exercise I hated the least. The only reason I kept going was because it was a great place to network female executives. The class was at an exclusive members club, two streets away from my apartment. I hated it. I hated the time it took up, I hated the pretentious teacher, but most of all I hated the fact that I'd never missed a class in five years.

'Don't forget, girls' night tonight,' Kelly called after us.

'What?' I turned around. Kelly was dressed in carefully ripped jeans and a tight white T-shirt. Her bouncy curls fell like a blonde waterfall around her shoulders. I took a few steps towards her. On closer inspection, Kelly's flawless skin was caked in make-up. A matt layer, trying to hide the tiredness. The only giveaway was the clogged creases around her eyes. Even Kelly's mask was beginning to slip.

'I've booked a table for us at the bar in town. The taxi's picking us up at seven.' She tilted her head, exposing her long slender neck. Smiling as sincerely as she could.

'Can't we just drink here?' I sighed.

'Nooo,' she whined. 'The place I've booked is lovely—it'll be so nice to have some time with the girlies!' She gave a tinkling laugh and traced a long, manicured nail down her cheek, brushing a stray hair away. I couldn't bear listening to her voice any longer. I nodded, just to get away from the sound.

Kelly just couldn't help herself. Tonight wasn't about spending time with the girls. It was about her showing off a glamorous outfit. It was about her being in control of the evening by booking some expensive wine bar. Tonight was about her proving once and for all that she was part of this group.

This is what the whole trip had been about. Kelly asserting herself as Jack's partner. Chasing away the ghost of his ex-wife, Lisa. The job I fired her from. *His* kids, *his* friends... I get it. It must be hard for her. But this constant one upmanship was wearing thin.

Porthaven was just a short drive away. Our hometown. It would be strange to go back there. Especially in the headspace I was in right now. I caught Stella's eye as we turned to jog away. A moment of solidarity amongst the shards of tension. I knew she felt the same.

We ran steadily towards the tree line. Stella was a runner; she always had been. I knew she was slowing her pace because of me, but I didn't care. This was the only way I could get her on her own.

The woods were dark and cool. A dusty track wound its way through the trees. The ground was a gnarled maze of roots from the old pine trees. Scattered with dead brown needles that cushioned the forest floor underfoot.

I ran just behind Stella's shoulder. The path was too narrow for us to run side by side. Her breathing was smooth and even. The easy pace of an experienced runner. I tried to hide my rapid gasping breaths. My lungs were already burning after just a few minutes.

It was New Year's Eve when I finally knew that Stella and Tristen were having an affair. That their one-night stand two years ago had turned into something more.

We were twenty. Four years before I became a mother. Charlotte and Tristen had been together over three years by then. It had been a difficult three years for all of us. Finishing college. Leaving Cornwall. But for them especially. Charlotte was finally well enough to work after what happened. After her breakdown. She'd got a job as a part-time receptionist. Her and Tristen moved into a small place on the army barracks in Kent where he was based.

We were all staying at Connie and Stella's for the weekend. The place looked magical. Candles were lit on every surface. Homemade paper lanterns were hung from the ceiling in all the colours of winter. A Christmas tree wouldn't fit in the living room, so Connie had put one on the veranda. It was tall and round and draped with tiny lights and carved wooden ornaments.

Wherever we were in the country, whatever we were doing in our lives, going back to Connie and Stella's cottage always felt like going home.

We lit a fire outside. It was like old times. Me and Jack had both brought expensive Champagne with us. Showing off the trappings of our exciting lives in London. We both laughed knowingly at one another as we'd placed them in the fridge. An unspoken acknowledgement that me and Jack were the same. The same vain, brash creatures who had somehow been pulled into the warm embrace of this friendship group. They knew who we were, and they loved us anyway. They were the best thing about us.

The Champagne went unopened. We'd drunk hot cider instead, like we used to. Cuddled up beside the fire draped in jumpers and blankets and knitted hats that Connie had dug out for us. Our faces were frozen in the cold December air, but we didn't care.

'Who wants another drink?' Tristen had asked.

'Yes!' we'd all drunkenly shouted. Raising our empty mugs towards him. He placed his cigarette briefly in the corner of his mouth as he gathered our cups. Hidden in the shadows of the crackling fire. In the darkness between the flames and the woods. Tristen walked behind Stella's chair.

'I'll give you a hand,' she said, standing up. I don't know

why I'd watched them walk back into the house. As they climbed up the wooden veranda steps, I saw their hands touch and their fingers briefly entwine. It was something so small, so insignificant. But it was intimate.

I looked at the faces around me. Everyone was deep in conversation. Nobody had noticed. I stood up from my chair and followed them quietly inside. There was laughter from the kitchen as they poured the drinks. I stood back from the doorframe, watching them unseen. 'Stop!' Stella giggled. Tristen was stood behind her. Pressing his body up against her back as she leant on the counter.

'I don't want to stop...' he muttered suggestively into her neck. I crept away from the door, turning one last time.

'Not now... later,' she whispered breathlessly. I slipped back outside without a sound. No one even noticed I had gone. I could feel my heart pounding in my chest as I took my seat. Like everyone could see what I had just seen. Like it was sketched all over my face.

Tristen and Stella came back with the drinks like nothing had happened. But I knew.

I didn't blame him for trying to find happiness. I just don't know why it had to be Stella.

The love that Charlotte had for Tristen wasn't normal love. It was all consuming, obsessive. It was her reason to carry on after what happened that night. She was so damaged. It made it impossible for him to leave her.

I think Tristen kept telling himself that it was temporary. That he could support her through the aftermath of what happened and then move on with his life. It took two years before Charlotte was anything like recovered. By then, her and Tristen had moved into their own place.

Every time he thought Charlotte was emotionally more stable, something would set her back. It had made it impossible for Tristen to leave. They'd been together since they were sixteen. Their lives were completely intwined with one another. She was like an injured bird. I think at some point, Tristen just resigned himself to the inevitable. That she would never be well enough for him to leave. That his guilt would never let him. So, they got married.

We'd all seen the imbalance in their relationship. How out of control Charlotte's reliance on him was after it happened. I was the only one who had seen it *before* that night. The only one who saw her obsession with Tristen had been there at the start.

We paused by an opening in the path. The sun pierced through gaps in the tall trees. Landing on the dry patch of earth between us. I breathed deeply, bending over to try and catch my breath. There was something comforting about the smell of pine. It reminded me of the woods by Stella's cottage. I wondered if she was thinking the same.

I stared up at glistening leaves and thought about Rose. I thought about how disappointed she would be if she knew what I was doing. How disappointed she would be at who I'd become.

CHAPTER TWENTY

STELLA

Two days before

Annie was gasping for breath just a few minutes into the run. I'd tried to keep my pace slow, go easy on her. But my anxiety had driven me forward. My muscles were fed by fear and apprehension. We stopped at a beautiful clearing in the woods. The dappled light crept through the trees. It was so still. Not even a puff of breeze. It reminded me of home.

'I know it's none of my business... but the fight between you and Jack the other night... Is everything OK now?' I asked. I'd been wanting to speak to Annie about it for two days.

'We're fine.' She spoke the words on an exhale. I nodded. Annie wouldn't be saying any more about it. She straightened her back and met my eye. She looked like she was readying herself. 'Me and Jack will always be fine.' She tried to smile but there was something missing.

'Is everything OK with you?' I asked. Trying to fill the silence. Trying to find out what was going on with her. She shook her head, too out of breath to answer properly. Her pace slowed and I fell back to join her. 'What's wrong?' It wasn't like Annie to present anything except a positive front.

'It's the business...' she panted, slowing a little. I fell into step beside her. '...I'm right on the edge of... of losing everything.' She spoke simply. Staring straight ahead as she spoke.

'Annie... I thought it was all going so well?' I tried to stop, but Annie carried on running. 'But the car... the house? What happened?' I asked, trying to catch up to her. Trying to keep the shock from my voice.

'I overspent,' she said simply. 'I overspent on the Wiltshire house. I overspent on the advertising, on the entertaining. I overspent on all of it. I got the work... big contracts as well,' she said. 'I just need to stay afloat for a bit longer. I need the chance to turn it around.' She glanced briefly over at me.

'Can't you just sell the Wiltshire house? The London flat? That would get you more than enough money,' I told her.

'It's too late. I've defaulted on so many payments that by the time either one of them sells... I will have lost everything. The Wiltshire house was supposed to be for Rose. It's the only place that's ever been home for her. If I lose that, what is the point to any of it...?'

'What do you mean?' I asked, desperately trying to understand.

'All of the sacrifices. All of the nights working. All of the weekends away from Rose. If I lose the business... the house that she loves... there was no *point* to any of it,' she added sadly, slowing to a stop.

'I need investors. I need them quickly,' she told me, her breathing was still short and sharp. 'Stella... I wouldn't ask if this wasn't my last resort.' Her chest rose sharply every few words. 'I'm going to lose it all if I don't do something,' she told me.

'You want *me* to invest?' Things couldn't be bad enough that I was her last resort. 'Annie, I can't... We've got the wedding and...' she stuttered.

'You've got a good job. You're a solicitor... you must have a bit tucked away.' She attempted a cheeky smile, but her heart wasn't in it.

'Yes. A solicitor who went *travelling* for six months not that long ago... How much do you need?' I asked.

'Fifty,' she said, her eyes trying to gauge my reaction.

'Fifty *thousand*?' I gasped. I pushed my fingers into my hair. Cradling my head in shock. 'Annie, I can't... I don't have it.'

'Stella, you're not leaving me with any choice...'

'What do you mean?' I asked cautiously. Her expression gave nothing away.

'I need that money to get back on track. If you don't give it to me...' She shrugged and looked away. 'I'm going to tell Charlotte. I'm going to tell Charlotte about you and Tristen.'

For a moment, neither of us moved. Neither of us spoke. 'What?!' I breathed. I could hardly believe what I was hearing. Annie wrenched her eyes away from me. She stared at a twig on the ground by her foot. Not even Annie had the courage to look me in the eye as she said this.

'I don't have any choice,' Annie reasoned. But her chin jutted out in defiance. A certainty that she was justified in her actions.

'You don't have any choice but to blackmail one of your oldest friends?' The pitch of my voice was climbing, as fear pulled at my vocal cords.

'No, Stella,' she shook her head violently. Her eyes were wild. 'You don't get to take the moral high ground. Not this time,' Annie said bitterly.

'It was complicated,' I pleaded. 'It always has been... You *know* that, Annie.'

'It's not *complicated*, Stella. You slept with your best friend's boyfriend... then you carried on sleeping with him, when he became her husband.'

She knew. Annie knew that it wasn't just one night. She

knew that it had carried on for years. It felt like she'd reached inside me and pulled out everything rotten. Then laid it out for me to look at. I bowed my head. A tear trickled slowly down my cheek. I didn't even attempt to brush it away.

'It's over between us. It has been for two years.' I begged her to believe me.

'It doesn't matter, Stella. That doesn't erase the twenty years you were fucking him...' She spat the words at me.

'Don't pretend you're doing this for Charlotte.' I gulped back emotion. 'We both know this will break her. You could have told her years ago. Why now, Annie?' I asked.

'Because it's all I have. I can't lose everything. I won't... not after all those years of work. Not after everything I've sacrificed to get here,' she said.

'What would Rose say if she knew what you were doing?' I asked desperately. It was my final card. It was all had left. She flinched.

'Fuck you, Stella... You don't get to do that. Not now... What would Rose say if she knew about *you*? About what you've done to Charlotte... Her perfect godmother. Does Nate know? Sweet, kind Nate... does he know what his fiancée was doing with her best friend's husband for twenty years?' She was shouting now. So close to my face that I could feel her words on my skin. I looked behind me in panic. Scared someone might hear us. Scared that it would take away my chance to fix this.

She took a step back. Leaning against a tree before slumping to the floor. All of the rage suddenly gone. 'I'm sorry, Annie. There's nothing I can do,' I told her quietly. My voice was emotionless. Numbed of any feeling. I turned and walked away. Very quickly, my walk broke into a run. I ran away from the direction of camp. Not slowly as I had before. I ran as fast as my legs would carry me. Thinking about Annie, still sat there in the dirt.

The last time me and Tristen had been together was at mum's funeral.

The ceremony at the crematorium had been long and formal. Mum would have hated every moment of it. I'd been so consumed with grief I hadn't known what else to do. I didn't know what other options there were available. What other ways there were to say goodbye. So, I chose the same funeral that everybody else had. I was too scared to do anything different. Too scared to make any sudden movements. The routineness of the funeral was the only thing keeping me upright. I thought that if I followed the same path that everybody else did, I wouldn't get lost. I didn't realise that I already was.

My running had entered a rhythm. The short bursts of breath that fired from my body matched the pulse of my feet on the soft ground. I sped around corners and jumped over the bigger roots. The earth shuddered angrily through my hips each time I landed.

I felt like I was watching someone else that day at the crematorium. Looking on as I shook people's hands and thanked them for coming. Like I'd stepped out of my own body and into an expensive black dress. A dress lined with somebody else's grief. Charlotte and Annie had tried to hold my hand. Hug me and rub my back. They tried to take away some of the pain, share it as their own. I didn't let them. I couldn't. If I'd allowed them to hold me together, I would have broken into a thousand tiny pieces the very next day. The only way I could do it was alone.

Everyone had come back to the cottage afterwards. Somehow it had been even worse than the funeral. Vaguely connected relatives wandered about Mum's things. Sipping freshly poured drinks and telling thirdhand stories about her. I wanted to scream. I wanted to smash the place up, throw everyone out into the rain. Tear Mum's paintings down from the wall. Burn them in a big pile in the garden, so that no one could look at them. I didn't. I just handed out sandwiches, topped up drinks and listened to anecdotes with a faraway smile.

Tristen was sat in Mum's chair. He was wearing a charcoal-grey suit. The jacket was laid over the tatty upholstered arm. I knew he was watching me as I moved around the room. I watched him too. I always watched him. I pretended it was desire. I pretended that it was his taut muscles pressed against his crisp white shirt that drew me to him that day. That day of all days. It was only afterwards that I realised it was something much darker than that. Something much more basic and primal.

We'd slept together many times over the years. Stolen nights away in hotel rooms. Seedy meetups in random military apartments. Sometimes months would go by without us seeing each other. Sometimes only days. Somehow, I knew this was the last time.

When I went to the woodshed to get more bottles of beer, I knew he'd follow. I'd stacked the boxes of lager in the makeshift wooden hut to keep them cold. I took my chance to leave when Charlotte was in the kitchen talking to guests and Annie was on a call.

'How are you?' he asked, leaning against the rickety door-frame. I shrugged, lining up the glass bottles on the ground beside me. He pulled the door closed and slipped the catch over. Neither of us spoke as he moved towards me. Tristen pushed me against the wooden wall. Tiny shards of light entered through the oak slats. Capturing the particles of dust that floated through the air. The kiss hit me like a body blow. It was hard and sudden and exactly what I needed.

My head ground against the splintered wood, as his hands grabbed hold of my thighs. He grabbed the ends of my black dress and pulled it up to my waist. I heard the clatter of his belt unfastening as he buried his face into my neck. Within seconds he was inside me, thrusting me hard into the wall. My toes left the floor as he held me up, suspended on him.

When it was over, I slid down the wall until my feet touched the floor. My dress fell slowly back to my knees. I'd wanted to feel something. I wanted any other emotion than the intense grief that had taken hold of me. For a short moment it had been replaced with longing. A black hedonism. But quickly the pain came back worse than ever. I felt empty and dirty and out of control.

I slunk back into the cottage and carried on pouring drinks. I could still feel him inside me. I hated myself, and for the first time since our affair had started, I hated Tristen. I knew that this was it, that it could never happen again.

It never did. But none of that mattered now. Soon, Charlotte would know everything.

CHAPTER TWENTY-ONE

DCI MELANIE PRICE

The day it happened

I left Irene and Tony and made my way back to the camping area. Simon caught up with me as I ducked under the security barrier to Field C. 'Anything?' he asked.

'I'm not sure,' I replied, tapping the end of my pen on my notebook as I strode along the road. 'They weren't the easiest residents he's ever had. Apparently, he was intending to throw them off the site this morning.' Simon frowned sceptically.

'What, at four a.m.? If there'd been a problem the night before, why didn't he throw them out then?' he asked.

'They were all drunk,' I told him. 'I guess he was waiting for them to sober up, so they could get out of here safely. He seems to run a tight ship,' I added with a wry smile. 'Are you worried about the voyeurism arrest?'

'Maybe. The file's a bit light on facts. But it seems the case was dropped pretty quickly. There's just something I don't like about him,' Simon told me.

'There's something I don't like about a lot of the people involved in this case,' I added, dropping my guard a little. 'Let's speak to his employees and we'll see where we are.' Simon nodded.

We left the tarmacked road and cut across the wet grass. It was already beginning to dry as the sun burnt its way through the cloud cover. Tiny droplets of water glistened on every green blade. The only evidence of last night's rainstorm.

'I thought you were at college with them?' Simon asked after pondering my comment.

'I was,' I replied flatly.

'Didn't you like them?' he asked, lowering his voice as we got closer to the tents.

'No,' I told him. 'Well, I liked some of them,' I said, trying to be fair. 'But no, not really. They just weren't my kind of people,' I added cryptically. We'd reached the yurt. The cream-coloured canvas was now looped with bright yellow police tape. A female officer was guarding the entrance. She stood up straight as we ducked under the cordon, trying to hide her boredom.

The space was hot and airless. It had a musty smell to it. I was sweating into my synthetic blazer. I wanted to take my jacket off. The shirt I'd selected in the dim light this morning wasn't smart enough for that. The officer looked like she was struggling too in her thick uniform. She'd been here for several hours. 'Why don't you go and get yourself a drink?' I told her. She looked a little disappointed. Sent away from the scene when something was finally happening. She gave a brief nod and left.

'Is this the victim's bed?' I asked Simon, not waiting for a reply as I headed over to the mattress on the left. 'OK, let's get some of this stuff bagged up,' I said, putting on plastic evidence gloves. I crouched down by the side of the dishevelled bedclothes. A tangle of sheets and pillows. Faint streaks of fake tan were evident on the white sheets. I thought about Annie's long brown legs. The care she'd taken over her body. Before being dumped behind a toilet block in the pouring rain, like she didn't matter.

'We need to find out what she was wearing last night. I'm assuming the clothes she was found in were items she'd changed into to go to bed?' I worked through my thoughts out loud. Picturing her small wet body. The white T-shirt, made see-through from the rain and clinging to her skin. A charcoal-coloured raincoat was draped over the end of the mattress. I lifted it up by the hem. I could tell just by looking at it that it was wet. 'What time did it start raining last night?' I asked Simon.

'Just after midnight,' he replied. 'I let the dogs out around then. It poured down. The pair of them were soaked when they came back in. I heard it hitting the conservatory roof on and off until... about three a.m. You'd have to check, but I think it was pretty constant.'

'The owner says they were thrown out of the restaurant just before twelve. I'm guessing she wore this raincoat on the way back. It's got to be a good ten-minute walk after a few drinks, don't you think?'

'I guess so,' he replied.

'So, why would she get back here, get ready for bed and then later, go out into a rainstorm?' I pondered.

'To go to the toilet?' Simon suggested.

'In just a T-shirt and underwear? No raincoat, no shoes?' I pointed to a pile of footwear by the end of the bed. Trainers and wedges and a pair of towering heels.

Her clothes were in a messy heap on the floor. They were mostly black. I'd remembered that about her from college. Her love of black clothes and black nails. It had been her thing, even back then. On top of the garments was a gold snake bracelet. The head of the animal protruded ominously in the air. I carefully moved it aside.

On the floor between the two single beds was a neat pile of

items. A novel with a silhouette of a child flying a kite on the cover. Some stationery. A beautiful bound notebook and a packet of brightly coloured pens. Gifts I guessed. Underneath were some birthday cards. All had the number eighteen on the front. I opened the first one. 'Happy birthday, Rosie girl,' it read. 'Lots of love from Dad x.'

At the bottom, was a card four times the size of the rest of them. It was covered in photos. The kind of card that you get made at a printers. You give them a selection of photos and they turn it into a card. Somebody had one made for a work colleague who left last year. A montage of all her best bits.

I looked at the images to see if I recognised anybody. There was a photo of Rose's first day of school. Of her stood in a hessian sack on sports day. One of her sat on her mum's lap, her head thrown back in laughter. There was a picture of Annie when she was a child. I traced the outline of her face. She must have been about four. Stood between a man and a woman who I assumed were Rose's grandparents. Annie once had the same dark curly hair as Rose. Before the crimson dye. Before the smooth bob.

There was a muted photo of Annie and Stella and Charlotte. They were huddled together on a sandy beach. A baby sat on the ground between them. She was dressed in a yellow romper suit and matching hat. A tiny fist held joyfully in the air. It must have been Rose. The women each had a hand on her. Smiling widely into the lens. They all looked so young, especially Annie.

'Boss?' said DI Green awkwardly, clearing his throat. I looked up to see Charlotte, standing over my shoulder, looking at the images in front of me.

'We had that made for Rose's birthday.' She pointed at the card. 'It was Stella's idea.' Charlotte's voice was monotone, almost robotic in its lack of emotion. 'It's her eighteenth. We wanted to remind her how loved she is. We wanted to remind her how many people she has in her life.' Her voice broke as she realised that was more important now than it would ever be.

'I love that photo.' She touched the image of the three of them with Rose. She started chewing her nails. 'I still remember the first day I met Annie,' she said with a faint smile. 'I loved everything about her. I couldn't believe she wanted to be my friend... I don't mean that the way it sounds.' She finally looked at me. 'It's just... Annie could have been friends with anyone she wanted,' she explained. I remembered the effect that Annie had on people.

There was a ball of tissue paper scrunched in her hand. She had a haunted look about her. It was both vulnerable and unnerving. I shuffled the cards into a pile and placed them in an evidence bag. 'Are you taking those with you?' she asked. I nodded.

'We'll make sure they're taken care of. They'll be returned to Rose when we're done,' I told her kindly. Charlotte said nothing.

'How are you?' I asked her.

'I don't know,' she told me, slowly shaking her head. Her eyes focused on my face. A pinprick of light flickered behind her pupils as she tried to place where she'd seen me.

'I remember you.' She held my gaze as the memory returned to her. 'You were nice.' There was a blankness to her tone. It was like she was talking to herself.

'Thanks. I remember you too,' I told her. Charlotte's gaze shifted back to Annie's things on the floor.

'Can I go through her clothes before you...' She bent down on the floor and started to pick up a black dress that had been discarded. I held my hand out to stop her.

'Until we find out exactly what happened to Annie, this is all potential evidence,' I told her. She dropped the dress where she found it and started to back away. 'Was she wearing that last night?' I asked. She shook her head and pointed to a pair of dark, tailored trousers. I could see they were still damp from the rainstorm.

'And the tank top,' she said, indicating a lightweight silk top next to it.

'Was she wearing this jacket when you left the restaurant last night?' She nodded. A shadow spread over her face. Like the memory of last night just came flooding back to her. 'Charlotte? My colleague DI Green here is going to speak to you all.' She nodded mutely. 'He's going to speak to you about identifying Annie's body.'

'What... no, we can't,' she cried, doubling over as if she'd been winded.

I made my voice low and calm. 'We want to make sure that it doesn't fall to Rose,' I explained. Charlotte had her hand over her mouth and was drawing in air through the gaps in her fingers. I took a step towards her and gently pulled her hand away from her face. She sounded like she was about to have a panic attack. I guided her towards Rose's neat bed and sat her down.

'This is going to be an awful time for you all, especially stuck here for the next few days.' Charlotte swallowed back the last of her tears and stood up on shaking legs.

'Can't we leave?' Charlotte was shocked. 'We were going to drive home later today... I've got Theo to think about...' She was horrified at the thought that they might have to stay here.

'I understand. My team are doing everything they can to try and find you all alternative accommodation... but it's high season. That just might not be possible,' I explained gently.

'I'll speak to Tristen,' she said, turning to leave. When she got to the entrance, Charlotte looked back. 'Do you remember Annie from college?' she asked quietly.

'I do,' I replied. She nodded, before pushing her way out of the canvas entrance.

'Right. Let's get them in here to bag this stuff up.' I sighed. 'I want this tent sealed until it's done,' I told Simon.

'Do you think it's one of them?' he whispered. I shrugged.

'I'm not sure,' I replied. 'But what are the chances that this was done by someone random?'

CHAPTER TWENTY-TWO

CHARLOTTE

Two days before

Nausea swirled in my stomach. Sloshing around uncomfortably with feelings of shame. I sat up in my camp bed. I don't know what happened last night. I don't know why I fell apart. I knew Theo was safe.

Tristen had been mortified. I'd tried to hold him when I finally crawled into our tent. Wriggling drunkenly into my sleeping bag with all my clothes and make-up on. His breathing was slow and even. The shadowed line of his shoulder blade etched on his taut back, just visible in the moonlight. I stretched out a shaking hand and traced my finger down the line. He pretended he was asleep, but I knew that he wasn't. I felt every tiny muscle prickle under my touch. Shrinking away in horror.

I shook my head. Tiny involuntary movements as I tried to displace the memory of myself sitting on the ground crying. The sound of my screams was still ringing in my ears.

Last night I'd heard Kelly and Jack arguing as I fell into a drunken sleep. They were too far away for me to hear exactly what they were saying. I heard Oliver's name. Kelly sounded upset.

Stella and Nate were next to us. Whispering words to one another. Every so often the sound of kisses drifted from their tent. The sound of uninhibited sex. Not the perfunctory kind that me and Tristen had over the years.

There are no surprises. Tristen thinks he knows every part of me—from child, to adult, to mother. I think it's one of the things he hates most about me—about us. To him, I'm just an extension of who he is. A broken appendage that he has grown used to. That he works around. He's lived more of his life with me than without.

I thought about all the parts of me he didn't know. All the secrets that would destroy us, destroy everything he thought he knew about me. I closed my eyes, trying to force sleep. I was scared that if it didn't happen quickly, I might tell him. Scream it from my sleeping bag so that everyone would know. A tiny seed of perversion had begun to grow inside of me. It had been growing for a while now. A tiny corner of me that craved chaos. Chaos and revenge.

Sleep had come thick and fast as the Chardonnay numbed my troubled mind. I was just about to fall into the darkness when I'd heard the tent open. A slow ripping sound as Tristen eased the fabric door open. I saw his body disappear into the night, before I fell into a deep sleep.

'Hey, Theo!' I said, I could hear how dry my mouth was. I watched as he played with a pile of toy trucks on the end of his bed. Tristen watched him from his sleeping bag, propping his head up on his arm.

'Mummy, can we go swimming? Uncle Jack said there's a pool here,' he said, lifting a tractor into the air.

'I'll take you, buddy,' said Tristen sitting up.

'No, it's fine. I'll take him. I could do with a swim.' I smiled ruefully, trying to make light of my hangover. He just nodded. I could see the tension in his jaw. Last night's mascara burned my eyes. I longed to lie back down on the bed. 'I was just scared, that's all,' I told him awkwardly. I felt a lump in my throat as I swallowed back my embarrassment.

'I know,' he replied and his face softened a little.

'Look at my turtles!' Theo moved proudly around the group, showing everyone the brightly coloured turtles on his swimming bag.

'Do you mind if I join you?' Rose asked just as we were leaving.

'Of course not!' I told her with a smile. 'You'd love Rose to come swimming with us, wouldn't you, Theo?!'

'Yes!' He threw his arms in the air. Everyone looked on and smiled. Children often have a way of bringing people together.

The pool was outdoors and just a short walk across the campsite. Surrounded by grey concrete slabs and lines of white, plastic sun loungers. A handful of families were already there. They all had young children around Theo's age. The early risers of the campsite. The sun had begun to gather strength. Me and Rose slipped off our clothes, revealing our swimming costumes underneath. I tried not to feel self-conscious as I stood next to her long lithe body.

We sat on the edge of the pool and dangled our legs in the water. It was much colder than I was expecting. We giggled and panted as we lowered our bodies into the shallow end. The sun sparkled on the ripples as they gently lapped against the tiled sides with every movement.

'There is no way this is heated.' Rose laughed. She jumped around, hugging her goose-bumped arms. Theo wore the same blue armbands I'd got for his swimming lessons at our local pool. He'd only gone once. I'd hated it. Watching Theo in the water being cared for by a stranger. Having to speak to the other mums. Making small talk about school catchments and reading levels and play dates. All things I knew nothing about.

I'd secretly hoped that he'd hate it. He didn't. I made up a lie when I phoned the swimming pool. I told them he'd had an allergic reaction to the chlorine. They'd been so nice about it. If Theo had been younger, I would have lied to Tristen too. But he was old enough to be able to tell him the truth. I pushed my wet hair away from my face. I never used to be like this. I never used to lie this much.

Me and Rose took turns catching Theo. He would pull his small body over the edge of the pool and jump right back in. He was beginning to get the hang of swimming. Paddling his arms furiously each time he popped up from under water. His armbands helping him stay afloat.

'I'm sorry,' I told Rose as a wave of water splashed over us. 'I hope I didn't upset you last night.' I touched the top of her arm as we crouched in the cold water.

'You didn't. I understand. I would have been the same,' she told me, looking fondly at Theo.

'I'm sure the wine didn't help.' I smiled, distracted by a new family that had entered the pool.

'Rosie, Rosie,' Theo called. 'Watch this!' Annie, Jack and Stella had always been 'uncle' or 'aunt' to Theo. Rose had always just been Rosie. She caught him in her arms for the hundredth time. 'Mummy!' he called. 'Look... I'm swimming.' We smiled at him indulgently as he pushed his chin above the water and grappled his way to a float that bobbed in the middle of the pool.

I turned to Rose. 'How are you?' It had been a while since I'd seen her. She didn't seem quite herself.

'I'm fine,' she told me, pulling the hairband out of her dark curls. I raised my eyebrows and tilted my head. 'Studying for my exams has just been... It's been a lot. Mum is...' She sighed. 'Mum has been her usual helpful self.' Rose smiled as she rolled her eyes.

'I know that she doesn't always show it, but she does love you,' I explained gently.

'I know,' she replied. 'It's just sometimes... I need her to show it,' she said sadly. I nodded. I love Annie, but I know how she can be.

'Charlotte!' Tristen was crouching by the edge of the pool, beckoning for Theo to come over. 'Why aren't you watching him?' he said. I turned to Theo. He was still playing on the float. Happily kicking water in the air with his feet.

'I... I was,' I stammered. Stung by the injustice of it.

'Time to get out,' he called to Theo, trying to keep his voice light. 'It's my fault. I should have brought him down here myself,' he added coldly, taking Theo's arm and pulling him out of the water.

'He was having a great time... He had his armbands on, Tristen,' I said firmly. 'Of all the things you can criticise me for, how I care for our son is not one of them,' I hissed at him as I climbed out of the pool. Tristen froze. Surprised by my forceful reply.

'I'm sorry,' he said and he looked like he really was. Rose began to swim laps. I tried to catch her eye, to tell her we were leaving, but she was too focused on her strokes. Tristen had both of our towels in his hand. He wrapped Theo tightly up in his, before laying mine over my shoulders. He pretended to tighten it around my body like he'd done for Theo. We both laughed. A moment of lightness. Like old times.

'Do you ever think about Box Heights?' I asked him as we walked back to the campsite. Theo trotted happily ahead, still wearing his swimming shorts. Box Heights was the affectionate nickname we'd given the flat we moved into when we were eighteen. Me, Tristen, Jack and Stella. We moved in together for the last six months of our final year at college. A boxy tan-coloured block of flats on the outskirts of town. Equidistant between the college and the nightclubs. It lacked anything but basic comfort and was devoid of personality—so Annie had called it Box Heights.

'Not really,' he said, stealing a sideways glance at me, wondering where this was going. 'It was a long time ago,' he added.

'They were good times, weren't they?' I asked, pretending to refasten my towel, pretending that I didn't care as much as I did.

'We had some good times there... yeah,' he said carefully.

'I was thinking...' I could hear the slight wobble in my voice. 'Why don't you *not* renew your contract with the army? Stay at home with us.' I twisted my hands in front of me. My voice sounded high and unnatural. I was trying to sound easygoing, flirtatious, but it was coming out all wrong.

'Charlotte, I can't...' A look of panic flooded his face. 'What would I do?' He'd stopped walking now.

'Well, you could find a job closer to home. Be around more for Theo,' I added, sounding more confident than I felt. Tristen rubbed his face with both of his hands, sighing deeply. 'What?' I asked him defensively.

'I just... I don't want to,' he said flatly. I could feel my lips starting to tremble. 'Ahh, I didn't mean it like that...' He saw how much his words had hurt me.

'How *did* you mean it?' I snapped. Angrily wiping away the tears that spilled down my cheeks. Theo turned as he heard my voice rise.

'Mummy?' he asked, a worried look on his face.

'It's OK.' I sniffed loudly, forcing my face into a wide smile. 'Mummy's just being silly.' He nodded and carried on walking. 'Would it really be so bad?' I asked him in a loud whisper.

'No, no... of course not.' He placed his hands on my shoulders. He looked like he was trying to convince himself as much as he was me. 'It's just...' He breathed in as he fought for the right words. 'We've not been happy for a long time, have we?' he said gently.

I felt like I'd been hit by a car. Like someone had pushed all the air from my body. I had an overwhelming urge to shove him. To ram him so hard it took him off his feet. I wanted to yell at him. Shout that *I* was happy, *I* was still in love. But I just stood there numb. Too scared to move in case our marriage ended right there in the middle of the campsite.

'I'm sorry. I shouldn't have suggested it. You're right,' I told him brightly. He searched my face, confused. 'Of course, you should stay in the army, it's your job. We're both very proud of you.' I forced my face into a smile. It made the skin around my cheeks feel tight and twisted.

'Charlotte... that's not really what I meant...' Tristen shook his head slowly. Before he had a chance to say any more, I jogged ahead to catch up with Theo. My heart felt like a lead weight. As I took Theo's hand, I turned briefly to look at Tristen. He was stood, fixed to the spot, looking like his world had just ended.

CHAPTER TWENTY-THREE

ANNIE

Two days before

I tapped my burgundy manicured nail on the edge of my teeth. I was dressed in a short black contour dress and heels. Spiked heels that I know would sink into the grass as soon as I left the yurt. I'd worn my gold snake band. It had been a present from a client a long time ago. It wrapped around my wrist and wound up my forearm. I always felt invincible when I wore it. But not tonight. Nothing would work tonight. Neither the heavy make-up nor the heavy perfume would take away the feeling of self-doubt that was coursing through me.

I hadn't seen Stella since our fight in the woods. I'd been hiding out in the tent for hours. Getting ready, trying not to speak to anyone. It felt like the yurt was getting smaller, like the sides were closing in on me. The taxi would be here soon; then I'd have to face her.

Rose wandered in. 'You look gorgeous, Mum,' she told me. I could tell by her earnest face that she meant it. I kissed her on the cheek as she walked over to her bed.

'Are you coming tonight?' I asked her. She shook her head apologetically.

'I'm going to hang out with Theo and Ollie... and this,' she told me, sitting cross-legged on her bed, waving a book in the air.

'Is Ollie... OK? The other night, when you disappeared with Theo...'

'We *didn't* disappear, Mum...' she interrupted.

'...It seemed like Kelly was going to tell us something...' I tried to remember exactly what she said. 'There's just something not quite right about him. I don't think I've ever met a kid with so much bottled-up anger... Does he ever smile?'

'Mum, he's fine.' She shrugged. 'He's just been through a lot, that's all,' she said kindly.

'You have too,' I reminded her sadly.

'Ahh, but look how well balanced *I* am.' She laughed, cocking her head to the side and fluttering her eyelashes. She had no idea how beautiful she looked. '*And... I* don't have a wicked stepmother like he does.' She laughed.

'Rose Turner! Is that bitchiness... from you?' I said mockingly.

'Kelly's OK,' she told me. 'But... she does have the classic wicked stepmother thing going on! She makes Ollie feel like he's an inconvenience. Like he's not welcome.'

'At least you haven't had to deal with stepparents. Me and your dad have been pretty useless on that front,' I said with a sigh.

'Do you wish things had been different?' she asked, her face full of concern.

'What I wish... is that you were coming tonight,' I pleaded, changing the subject.

'Mum, you know it's not my thing. You'll have a great time... a night on the town, a few drinks...' she replied, picking up her reading glasses and going back to her book.

'Knock knock,' Kelly said as she lifted the canvas entrance.

Me and Rose stole a guilty look at one another, hoping that she hadn't heard us. 'Not long until the taxi—thought we'd have a few cheeky cocktails before we go,' Kelly said in her singsong voice. 'Gorge dress,' she said, pointing in my direction. Long false lashes brushed her cheek as she gave me a slow wink and left.

'Give me strength,' I mouthed silently to Rose. She suppressed a giggle behind her hand.

I left the tent and went to join the others. Kelly had placed candles all around the outside eating area. Cream church candles, all in their own individual jar. They flickered in the fading light, bathing everyone's faces in a peach glow. Kelly knew how to create atmosphere.

I went to stand next to Charlotte. She was twisting the waistband of her dress, trying to pull it down a little. 'I think I might get changed into jeans,' she said worriedly.

'You look great,' I said without looking at her. I was distracted. Wondering where Stella was. Just then the music started. Jack danced out of his tent with a small speaker in each hand. He placed them on the table and pointed his fingers to the sky. It was one of our favourites. It reminded me of being high. Of having sex and having fun. It took me back to a time when I didn't give a shit about a career or how much money I had in the bank. A time when I didn't even care how I was getting home that night.

I caught Jack's eye and he smiled. A smile that told me it was going to be OK between us. He was wearing a pair of white denim shorts and a bright turquoise floral shirt, unbuttoned almost to the bottom. He pulled me into a tight hug. I slipped my hands around his tanned belly and pressed my face into his chest. I looked up at him and laughed as he pumped his fist in the air, cigarette dangling from the side of his mouth.

I took the cigarette and inhaled deeply, tucking myself under the warm nook of his arm. I watched everyone dance

through the smoke that wrapped itself around me. I watched
their faces as they jumped around to the beat. Lit up by the
sunset and the candlelight. We could have all been eighteen
again. I would give anything to go back.

'Babe, put her down... we need to leave,' Kelly laughed at
Jack, but it didn't quite reach her eyes.

The taxi pulled up in front of our camping area. We quickly
downed the last of our drinks. Everyone rushed around trying to
find purses and make-up. The driver sat patiently, listening to
the local radio station.

Charlotte and Stella climbed into the back of the car. I
moved around to the other door. Charlotte apologised and slid
into the middle. A barrier between me and Stella. Kelly sat in
the front of the cramped hatchback. Talking loudly to the driver
as she scrolled through her phone for directions.

'I know the place you mean,' he said in a broad Cornish
accent when she told him the name of the bar. 'It's nice. You
ladies'll like it. Proper fancy it is,' he smiled enthusiastically,
turning the radio down a little. Kelly turned around, beaming at
us like a child.

We were heading into Porthaven. The town where we went
to college. The town where we'd all lived. It had been years
since I'd been back.

The dark lanes slipped by the window. Turning into wider
roads as we got closer to town. Roads I'd once known every
curve and every turn of. Roads I'd learnt to drive on. The streetlights washed over the car, blinking light across my face. I closed
my eyes and let the glow seep through.

We reached the roundabout by the industrial estate. A
place we came a lot for fast food and the cinema. The area
looked tired and uncared for. I remembered it being brand new.
But I guess it was back then. Twenty-five years had passed.

'Me and Tristen were talking about Box Heights earlier,'
Charlotte said, looking over at Stella and then at me. She was

trying to talk lightly, but there was an edge to her. An edge that I'd felt all week. I could hear it catch in her chest when she spoke.

For a moment nobody said anything. 'I wonder if we'll go past it on the way in,' Stella said. But she didn't sound hopeful. She was just filling space. I didn't reply. I could tell Charlotte was trying to lead us both somewhere. It was somewhere that I didn't want to go.

I pressed the button for the electric window, letting the glass slide down a few inches. The warm evening breeze fanned my face. I closed my eyes and breathed it in. The smell of hot dry grass and dew-soaked hedgerows. The smell of summer. I let the sounds of Kelly's voice and the drone of the radio wash over me. Local voices over the microphone, talking about places I knew, places that had been home. It was like being covered in a warm blanket. I rested my head against the glass. I could fall asleep right here. Rocking gently to the rhythm of the engine.

We only moved into Box Heights six months before we left college. I'm not sure why we did it really. All of us could have stayed living at home during that time. We all lived close to campus. We all had great families that let us live our lives. But I think we knew that it was our only chance to do it. We knew that we would all be ricocheting around the country into new lives and new adventures and new friendships. We knew that if we didn't live together then, we never would.

It was supposed to be me, Jack and Tristen who were moving into the three-bedroom flat. Our whole group had been friends for only eighteen months. It felt like a lot longer. It felt like we'd found our people. Stella had decided to stay at the cottage with Connie. Tristen and Charlotte's friendship had developed into a relationship a few months after we'd started college. So, they'd only been together for just over a year. It would have been too soon for them to live together. Nothing had been said. Tristen had just assumed they were both on the same page. They were young. Living together could wait.

A week before we moved in, we'd all been at the bar. Drinking pints of lager at our regular table at the Kings Head. 'How's everyone's packing going?' Charlotte had asked eagerly, looking around at our faces.

'God, awful,' I told her. 'I'm just going to chuck it all in bin liners the day before and sort it out when I get there,' I added.

'We need to think about a toaster, saucepans, that kind of thing. I'm sure my aunt has some stuff we can have...' she chattered happily. Me and Tristen and Jack looked at each other. Not obviously, just slyly out the corners of our eyes, as what Charlotte was saying began to dawn on us. Charlotte thought she was moving into the flat too. I don't know how it happened. How she had misread the situation. Maybe it had been something Tristen had said to her, or maybe she'd just assumed she was invited.

Charlotte had been there when we viewed the flat. Laughed with us at the blandness that was Box Heights, with its plastic pine floors and its stark beige walls. The three of us had chosen a bedroom. I don't remember Charlotte suggesting that she would be sharing Tristen's room with him. In fact, I'd felt sorry for her that day. Sad that she wasn't part of this adventure. I'd even put my arm around her and said, 'Don't worry, you'll be over all the time. It'll be like you're living here.'

It didn't really bother me and Jack. We loved Charlotte, we all did. It was Tristen who it really affected. Sharing a tiny bedroom with his girlfriend. However much he loved her, I knew this wasn't something he wanted. They were only just eighteen.

Tristen never spoke to Charlotte about it. At least, I assumed he didn't, as we all moved in together the following week. He never told her how he really felt. He never told her anything that might upset her. Even then he saw her as fragile. I think we all did.

It's funny how we always thought Charlotte was the weak one in the relationship. Looking back, Charlotte had always managed to get everything she wanted.

CHAPTER TWENTY-FOUR

STELLA

Two days before

We climbed out of the taxi. The bar was down the far end of town. It wasn't an area we used to come as teenagers. We used to hang out in the old part. The pubs there were more lenient with underage drinkers and the beer was cheaper.

The street was getting busy. Groups of young women tottered on high heels under the glare of orange streetlamps. Men in tight shirts and jeans moved like packs between bars. It was Monday night. Most towns would be quiet at this time. But Porthaven was a college town. It was always busy.

Kelly strode confidently up the steps to the entrance. The restaurant was called the Blue Room. The name was written in enormous navy neon lights. The words hung over the glass-fronted eating area. It reminded me of some of the bars in Spain. White stone steps and patio, tall manicured shrubs in pots.

You had to walk through the dining room to get to the bar. It was filled with customers. Almost every table was crowded with people. The noise hit us like a wall as we pushed open the heavy glass doors. There was a long table in the middle that seated about twenty women. Helium balloons were tied to the legs of their table. It looked like it was a birthday party. I had never wanted to be somewhere less than I did the Blue Room.

A waiter showed us to the bar downstairs. It was dark and modern and smelt like sweet vanilla. Most of the tables were empty. Small and low with colourful undersides. Each one was surrounded by upholstered cube stools in dusky pastel shades. The bar was submerged almost entirely in darkness. The only light came from behind the optics, illuminating the bottles of liquor and the smartly dressed barman.

'Here we are,' said Kelly, taking us over to one of the side tables. In the centre was a small plastic card that read 'reserved.' 'What's everyone drinking?' she asked. We all muttered that we didn't know. 'Come *on!*' she persisted. 'This is supposed to be *our* night!' she pleaded, swaying her hips to the low-level bass music. We all followed her obediently to the bar. Kelly rested her elbows on the black polished wood and batted her eyelashes at the barman. 'Two bottles of white wine... a good Chardonnay,' she instructed him, holding up two fingers to indicate what she needed.

The barman pretended not to notice her rudeness. I smiled at him apologetically. He placed four sparkling glasses on the bar and the wine bottles in buckets filled with ice. He told Kelly the price and she quickly held out her card without looking at him. A moment later he returned and leaned in close to Kelly, trying to be discreet. 'I'm afraid your card was rejected,' he told her quietly.

'That's impossible. Try it again,' she barked at him. Kelly didn't care if we heard.

He cleared his throat. 'I've already tried it twice.'

'Try it again,' she said slowly through gritted teeth.

'Kelly, it's fine... I'll pay,' I said pulling my card out of my purse. Charlotte was rummaging in her bag, looking for hers. I looked over at Annie, who was engrossed in her phone, swiping anxiously at the screen like she was searching for something.

'No,' she snapped. 'Run it again.' He nodded and returned to the card machine. 'God!' she said, turning to us and rolling her eyes. He came back shaking his head. Kelly snatched the card out of his hand and began searching for another.

'Please, Kelly, I don't mind,' I told her, handing over my card. The barman looked at me with gratitude. Charlotte clumsily picked up a wine bucket in each hand. Looking nervously from side to side. Charlotte hated this kind of thing.

'I'll bring them over,' the barman told her kindly. She smiled in thanks and clanged the containers back down on the bar, nearly knocking one over.

'Sorry... sorry,' she muttered as her face flushed. She walked away from the bar, shifting the tight waistband of her dress.

We all sat down. Kelly made a big show of pouring the wine. Determined not to let the card incident ruin her carefully planned night. It became very clear, very quickly, that we had nothing to say to one another.

The bar was beginning to fill up. The groups that had been eating upstairs began making their way down to the basement. The overhead lights were turned down even further and the music was turned up. It made it hard to hear each other. Every sentence had to be spoken loudly and with purpose. It made the already stilted chat even more uncomfortable. The silence between us was deafening at times.

'Have I shown you the recent photos of the Wiltshire house?' Annie asked. I wasn't sure if this was another one of her games. Whether she was trying to show me what she had to lose, or just trying to pretend that everything was normal. 'We had the kitchen reconfigured a few months ago—look.' She leaned over the table and showed us images of the beautiful house. 'I'll arrange a weekend for us all there soon,' she added. Her eyes locked momentarily with mine.

'You should have seen this place when she bought it,' Charlotte explained to Kelly, trying to include her. 'It was a complete wreck. Broken windows, peeling wallpaper... There wasn't even any heating. You remember it, don't you, Stella?' I nodded. Trying to show enthusiasm.

We talked about the house for a while. Conversation threatened to dry up. I desperately grappled for a new topic.

'I can't believe how much Oliver has grown since we last saw him.' It was a mistake. I knew it as soon as the words were out of my mouth. I was trying to find a subject that Kelly could talk about. Not something about our shared past and old memories that she knew nothing about.

Kelly nodded slowly, looking around the table as she decided whether to say more.

'I know I shouldn't say this... but Oliver... well it's been difficult these last few months.' Kelly bit her lip. 'Did you know that Oliver's been expelled from his boarding school?' Kelly asked. She already knew that we had no idea. She bent her head conspiratorially towards the table. She knew she shouldn't be saying it, that it was disloyal. I think she was just enjoying the fact that she finally knew something that we didn't. Annie leaned in.

'That kid has always had a problem with me,' Annie said, shaking her head. Charlotte squirmed uncomfortably on her cubed seat. I knew why Oliver didn't like Annie. Me and Charlotte both did.

Jack and Kelly had got married two years ago. It was held at a beautiful country house hotel. Hundreds of people went. It was much bigger and much more elegant than Jack's first wedding, to Lisa. Jack was a show-off. He could be brash and he loved to overindulge in the good things. But the wedding was all Kelly. From the ten-thousand-pound flowers that she told everyone about, to the dress made by a celebrity designer.

Both of Jack's boys were there. Oliver was only thirteen and his older brother, Finn, was about fifteen. It was obvious that they were both struggling. Dressed up in smart grey suits, watching as their dad married his new, much younger wife.

I tried not to judge Jack and Kelly; I wished them both the best as a couple. But I wasn't the only one who wondered where the money to pay for that wedding came from. Jack was an estate agent. He was good at his job, but not *that* good. Kelly had flitted between positions, but nothing had really stuck.

It was a beautiful day. We'd all been drinking Champagne as we waited for the food to be served. I stood with Annie and Charlotte. Huddled on a corner of the terrace that looked out over the perfectly manicured gardens. 'You know, they wouldn't have even got together if it wasn't for me.' Annie giggled, her words thick with Champagne. 'They'd been shagging for weeks before Lisa found out. She phoned me once out of the blue, when we were at an event. Asked if I was with Jack... I made up some lie. I'd just seen him check into a hotel room upstairs with Kelly!' She cackled with drunken laughter. 'I'm like the adulterer's assistant,' she added with a mock bow.

At the same time, me and Charlotte noticed Oliver behind her. He was stood on the terrace steps just below, listening to every word. His mouth was wide open and tears brimmed in his eyes. Before we could say anything, he turned and ran down the steps.

I don't know why Annie said it. She'd always liked Lisa. None of us had approved of his affair with Kelly, but Annie was especially disapproving of it. She may have lied to Lisa, but that would only have been to protect her. Annie had always felt a need to put on this front. Project an image that she was cold and heartless. Annie could be both of those things at times, but it wasn't all she was.

We never told her that Oliver had heard what she said. There didn't seem any point. There was nothing she could do about it. Or rather, there was nothing that she *would* do about it. He was never the same with her after that.

Kelly drained the last of her wine. Grabbing the bottle noisily from the ice bucket. She offered a drink to the rest of the table. Only Annie accepted another full glass.

'Don't tell Jack I said this to you, but Oliver's... become a real problem.' She looked behind her, mouthing the last words silently. 'Since he got kicked out of school, he's been living with us *a lot.*'

'What do you mean?' asked Charlotte, sitting up.

'He's just angry *all* the time,' Kelly explained. 'I don't trust him...'

'Don't trust him with what?' Annie scoffed. But I could tell that it had sparked her interest.

'Just that... you know... if we have a baby... *when* we have a baby...' She held up her hand, showing us she had her fingers crossed. 'It's going to make me nervous having him around a small child.'

'Don't be ridiculous!' said Annie with a laugh, throwing back a big slug of wine.

Kelly looked stung. 'I'm not! You don't even know what he was expelled for,' she replied, sneering at Annie. 'He was actually kicked out for beating up another kid. A *much* younger kid. He put him in the hospital with a broken arm... The police even came to speak to us.'

Even Annie looked shocked. I thought she was going to say something, but she closed her mouth. 'I'm sure that there's... I'm sure that Jack and Lisa have it under control. He's just a kid,' I reminded them, trying to draw a line under the conversation.

Kelly stared silently at the table. I saw her swallow uncomfortably, lifting her drink to her face to hide her remorse. If Jack had wanted us to know about Oliver being expelled, he would have told us. It was a secret Jack hadn't wanted her to share. Jack would not forgive Kelly for betraying him like this. He would not forgive her for betraying his family like this.

CHAPTER TWENTY-FIVE

DCI MELANIE PRICE

The day it happened

I offered to give Simon a lift back to the station in my car. He could leave his car here. We'd be back soon enough. They had set us up an incident room at the station where Simon was based. Mine was an hour's drive away. It made no sense to commute back and forth.

Murders in Cornwall were rare. Random, non-domestic murders were even rarer. 'When are they doing the autopsy?' I asked him, pulling out of the narrow entrance.

'This afternoon, hopefully,' he replied, looking at his watch. 'I'll try and get over there at about two p.m.'

'I want to come too,' I told him. He nodded, eyes fixed on the lane ahead.

It had been six months since me and Simon had last worked together. It had been a truly harrowing case in North Cornwall. A case that had turned out to be what they called a 'family annihilation.' A man named James Keaton had rung police to say he'd come home to find his wife and young daughter dead. There were multiple stab wounds. They were both still in bed.

Forensics believed that they'd been killed whilst they slept. It had been a heart-wrenching case to work on. The whole team had felt it. The whole team knew from day one that James Keaton was responsible.

The investigation had taken it out of all of us. Simon had Lyndsey to go home to. A family to remind him of the goodness there still was in the world. I'd just moved into the flat. For the first time in twenty years, I was alone. Going back to a place that wasn't even close to being home every night.

Simon had tried to support me. Tried to offer friendship in the midst of the separation. But he was Mike's friend really, he always had been. It wouldn't be fair to either of them. When a couple splits up, everyone has to choose a side. I just made choosing a bit easier for him.

Two weeks after the murder, we got a confession. The husband had been having an affair and we had irrefutable forensic evidence. None of us experienced the usual elation we got when closing a case. This one was never going to be a win.

'What were they like at college?' Simon asked, dragging me away from my thoughts. I sighed, pulling forward the memory of their teenage faces. It seemed like a lifetime ago.

'Annie was a force of nature,' I told him. 'You either loved her or you hated her—but you never forgot her. She was loud and confident and obnoxious.' I paused. 'However you felt about Annie, you couldn't help but admire her. She was everything a lot of us wanted to be,' I explained.

'So they were the popular kids?' he said wearily, as though he'd had a lifetime of dealing with popular kids.

'No, not really,' I replied thoughtfully. 'It's as if they only had eyes for each other. This intense friendship that was impenetrable to anyone outside of it.'

'Had they been friends since they were little?' he asked, confused.

'Not as far as I know. I think maybe Tristen and Jack might

have been at school together... It was like they found their
people on the first day of college—and that was it.' I shook my
head in wonder.

'Did you find your people at college?' he asked softly. The
first frisson of familiarity.

'Nope,' I replied simply, closing down any conversation
about my time at college. Neither of us spoke for a couple of
minutes. The narrow lanes and high Cornish hedges had
turned into a wider, busier road. I concentrated on the white
lines that stuttered passed on the concrete ground. 'I think that
was why we all noticed them,' I added, stealing a sideways
glance at him. 'We were all jealous that we didn't have what
they had. Nobody did.'

We'd be at the station in ten minutes. I pulled onto a
familiar roundabout. A busy intersection that joined the
sprawling town to the countryside. There was a drive-through
Starbucks by the far-side exit. A haven for holidaymakers beginning the long journey home. I resisted the urge to turn in and
get a coffee, as tiredness tugged at my eyelids.

'Did Annie leave Cornwall right after college?' Simon
asked.

'I'm not sure. I guess so. I never saw her after their gradua-
tion. I never saw any of them again until this morning.' I turned
on the indicator and took the left exit to Carnley. 'By then, I was
in my last year. I wasn't really the sort to go out clubbing, so
maybe they were still around,' I added.

'A bit of a swot back then, were you?' He laughed. I gave
him a tight smile and changed the subject.

'I was surprised to find out she has a kid,' I told him.

'Why?' he asked.

'I suppose... she just didn't seem the sort.' Simon looked at
me. I wondered if he thought the same about me. That I hadn't
had children with Mike because I wasn't the sort. He might be
right.

Me and Mike had been good friends with Simon and his wife, Lyndsey. We saw each other all the time. Dinners, drinks at the pub after Sunday lunch. Drunken nights in, even a group holiday to Spain a couple of years ago. We all had a good friendship, but Mike and Simon were best friends.

I met Mike during police training nearly twenty years ago. We were so different. None of our friends could have predicted that we would get together. I was quiet and introverted. He was eager and sociable. I'd grown up on a farm. I wore oversized jumpers that hung over my hands. I hid behind my long wavy hair and glasses.

Mike loved to work out. When we did our residential training together, I'm not sure I ever saw him in anything but training clothes. Mike wore suits instead of training gear these days. His hair was now flecked with grey and for the last few years he'd grown a beard. It suited him. I could hardly remember what he looked like without one. It still made me ache when I thought about him.

Talk of babies had been the beginning of the end. I'm not sure why it had caught me so off guard. Why it had been such a shock that Mike had asked about us having children. I was thirty-eight when it came up.

He was relaxed about it at first. Our relationship was wonderful. Why risk what we have? The intensity of Mike's desire to have children crept up on me. I think maybe it crept up on him too. For years, the subject of kids had been on and off the table. Fighting for space between our careers and hobbies and how much we loved our life as a couple. Until one day, it was the only thing on the table. Mike gave me an ultimatum. A hurt, confused ultimatum. One that I didn't take seriously.

I was so angry. I pretended to myself that he was forcing me to have a child. The ultimatum: We have a baby or we split up. That wasn't it. He just wanted to know what our future was going to look like. He just wanted me to talk about it. I didn't want to, so I pushed him away. A stubbornness that I doubled down on when I packed my bags.

He didn't try and stop me. I told myself that it would be temporary, that we'd sort it out. I even told myself that it was what I wanted. But we didn't sort it out. I was still waiting.

Even after I'd rented the flat. Even after he'd updated his social media status to 'single.' I still thought it was him every time the phone rang. Every time there was a knock on the door or a letter. I thought it was him. I was still waiting for him. Waiting for us to find our way back to each other.

'Charlotte and Tristen were a couple at college,' I told him, changing the subject.

'Were they?' he asked, looking mildly surprised.

'Something happened to her...' I tried to retrieve the long-forgotten memory.

'Who, Charlotte?' Simon asked. I nodded. Tapping my thumb on the steering wheel as it started to come back into focus.

'Yeah, I think it must have been a few months before they graduated. I remember there being a lot of rumours about it. I'm not sure if any of them were true. I saw her in town one day. Her face was badly bruised. Cuts all down her neck.' I stroked my own jaw to indicate where it was. 'I heard she was in hospital for a while.'

'Could it have been the boyfriend—Tristen?' Simon asked.

'I knew you'd say that,' I said with a faint smile. A fleeting spark of friendship nestled between us for a moment.

'Maybe the guy beat up his girlfriend, then did the same to her best friend a few years later?' he asked.

'It's a possibility,' I replied.

'If he did it once, there's every chance he did it again.'

· · ·

Carnley police station was an ugly grey building. It was built in the '70s as council offices. It looked like a run-down apartment block. If it wasn't for the sign at the entrance to the car park, nobody would have known what its function was.

I pulled the car into a space over the far side. 'There's only so long we can keep them hauled up at the campsite. Three days at most. After that, they'll all head back home. You know the drill. Chances are another force will step in to take over,' I reminded him.

'Not necessarily,' he told me. 'They didn't the last time,' he said, referring to the murders we worked on a few months ago.

'That was different. That was domestic. You know the press this is going to get in the next few hours. A tourist killed at a sleepy Cornish campsite. Our inexperience in dealing with this sort of thing is going to get brought into question... and they have a point,' I said, getting out of the car. I leant my arms on the edge of the doorframe and talked to Simon over the roof of the car.

'Anyway... we might be running before we can walk. Let's wait for the results of the autopsy. This might all be a tragic accident,' I told him, before heading towards the entrance.

'...But you don't think so?' he called after me.

I turned around. 'No. I don't think so.'

CHAPTER TWENTY-SIX

CHARLOTTE

Two days before

'How young?' I asked Kelly. The bar suddenly felt smaller. Theo is with Oliver. Angry, violent Oliver. I could feel myself start to spiral. She looked at me blankly. I could hear my voice begin to rise. 'How old was the boy he beat up?' I asked. There was a sense of urgency in my voice.

'Oh no... not *that* young.' Kelly was backtracking. Realising that I was nervous about Theo and Oliver being together back at the campsite.

'How young?' I repeated, fixing Kelly in my glare.

'He was... ten,' she said reluctantly.

'*Ten!*' My voice was raised in shock.

'Charlotte, Theo will be fine... Tristen is with him,' Stella said quietly, trying to calm me. I didn't reply. I knew they all thought I was overreacting. Maybe I was, but the fear that was rising up inside me felt very real.

I started tapping out a message to Tristen. *How's everything going?* I typed. *Are you with Theo?* I pressed 'send.' The rest of the table continued their stilted conversation.

'Have you organised any of your wedding yet?' Kelly asked Stella, trying to move the subject away from Oliver.

'No, not really. I've had a quick look at venues. I'm not sure I'm a very bridal person!' Stella said, trying to lighten the mood. I could tell she was watching me.

'It will be the *best* day of your life. Trust me,' Kelly gushed. We all nodded vaguely. Pretending that this was a normal night out. Pretending that we weren't all desperate to leave.

Tristen's face popped up next to my words, telling me he'd received it. I waited. Staring at the bright screen until my eyes blurred. Waiting for the phone to tell me he was typing. There was nothing.

I excused myself from the table. I avoided Stella's eye as she watched with concern. I followed the signs to the toilets. A narrow, carpeted corridor that led away from the bar. The music was a little quieter here and the lights were turned up. I leant against the wall, waiting for my heart rate to slow down.

I tried to call Tristen. Holding my phone to my ear with a shaking hand. 'You've reached Tristen. I'm sorry I can't take your call...' his smooth voice explained down the line. He'd turned his phoned off.

'Shit,' I muttered, leaning back on the bright wallpapered wall. 'Shit,' I said again, throwing my head back in frustration. There was a thud as my skull made contact with the wall. A smartly dressed woman walked past on the way to the toilets. She winced as she watched me hurt myself.

It was a shock to realise that I didn't care any more. I didn't care about the sneers or the looks or the comments. I no longer cared what people thought of me. It should have been a liberating moment. But the realisation terrified me. People's judgement had been the weak glue that held me together. It had stopped me from telling the truth. It had stopped me from screaming out loud how badly I'd been treated. Without it, I'm not sure what I might be capable of.

I returned to the table. Four shot glasses sat in the centre, filled with a clear liquid. I topped up my wine from the cold bottle. 'What did I miss?' I asked, sloshing liquid over the table. I felt them watching me. I knew my eyes were too bright.

'We were talking about awful exes.' Kelly laughed. 'Have you got a psycho ex story?' she asked, leaning in, placing her elbows on the table.

'Nope,' I replied gulping down the wine. 'It's always been Tristen.'

'Of course! I forgot you guys have been together since school,' she said, scrunching up her face. 'It must be so *weird* just being with one person all those years. Don't you get bored?' She laughed.

I watched as she shook out her blonde mane. I imagined grabbing her hair and pulling it. Anger flashed across Annie's face. She wouldn't let Kelly get away with speaking to me like that.

'Are you OK?' Stella whispered, laying her hand gently on my wrist. The sensation of her touch was like water on a fire. The rage drained from my body, leaving me pale and nauseous and full of remorse. I gave her a weak smile and finished my drink.

'So, how's work going, Kelly?' Annie asked. My head snapped up. A tiny smile danced on her lips. We knew what was happening. We knew what she was doing.

'Oh my God, it's amazing!' she gushed, not sensing the trap. Kelly touched the tips of her false eyelashes and added. 'I'm so glad I finally get to work in fashion!'

'I'm not sure I'd call it fashion, Kel.' There was a hard edge to Annie's voice when she shortened Kelly's name. 'It's a shame it didn't work out for you in PR. That was your real dream... wasn't it?' The smile fell from Kelly's face.

'The only reason I'm not still in PR... is because of me and Jack.' Kelly looked hurt. Her bottom lip trembled. She looked like she been wanting to say this for a long time. Annie's face changed. There was a sudden shift in atmosphere. Everyone put their drinks down. We all braced ourselves.

'Is that what you think?' Annie's eyes were cold and hard. Unblinking as she stared at Kelly. Like a predator circling. 'You think I fired you because you were fucking my friend?' She pretended to laugh. It came out hollow and bitter. 'Babe, I fired you because you were shit at your job... I fired you because you were more interested in *being* a celebrity, than representing them. But mostly, it was because I just couldn't *stand* working with you.' Annie smiled and cocked her head to the side. Like she'd just explained something simple to a child.

Kelly froze for a moment. She opened her mouth as if to say something, before closing it again. She stood up with as much pride as she could muster, wriggling the hem of her short dress towards her knees. She walked in the direction of the toilets with her chin in the air.

'Jesus, Annie, was that necessary?' Stella asked. She stood up, following in the direction that Kelly had just gone. Annie looked at me and shrugged. Unable to keep the look of delight from her face.

'Why did you do that?' I asked her stiffly.

'What? I did it for you, Charlotte,' she replied, confused that I hadn't taken her side.

'You didn't do that for me,' I snapped. Annie looked taken aback. I didn't usually speak to her like this. I never spoke to her like this. 'You did it because you hate Kelly. You've always hated her. I can fight my own battles,' I added, looking down at the table.

'Can you?' she asked me disbelievingly. 'Because you've never been able to before,' she said spitefully. Both of us were frozen in her words. Trapped in the truth that had never been voiced before. The anger disappeared from her face and was replaced with remorse. 'Charlotte, I'm sorry... I didn't mean that.'

'Yes, you did,' I told her simply. 'You're right. I've never stood up for myself.'

'That's not true, you...' Annie looked worried now.

'It is,' I said firmly. 'That's not how it's going to be any more.' I could hear my voice echoing in my ears against the loud drumbeat. My words sounded tight and distant. Like someone else was controlling them. I turned to Annie and looked her in the eye. 'Things are going to change.'

Before Annie could reply, Kelly and Stella returned from the toilet. Kelly's eyes looked red and her cheeks were flushed. Stella looked tired. 'Shall we get a taxi?' she asked. I nodded with relief, quickly putting my phone in my bag. Readying myself to leave.

'I'm sorry,' Annie said loudly over the table, wiping her hands on a napkin. Kelly returned her apology with a sweet smile. A smile that didn't quite spread to the rest of her face.

'It's fine,' she said. 'I did love the celebrity thing.' Kelly shrugged. 'Talking of celebrity and ex's... how's Taylor?' The corners of her mouth twitched as she waited for her reaction. Annie didn't flinch. She would have to try harder than that if she wanted a reaction from her.

'Can we go now, please?' I interjected, sitting with my purse in my lap.

Kelly ignored me. 'Do you know he asked me out once,' she said, twisting one of her blonde curls around her finger. She looked like she was suppressing a smile. 'We never did go *out*.'

Stella stood up quickly. I joined her, nearly toppling my empty wineglass over in my hurry. 'Let's go,' she said firmly, starting to walk away from the table. Kelly and Annie didn't move. They locked eyes like two animals trying to decide which one was the prey.

'...But we did sleep together a couple of times... *Obviously* before I met Jack,' Kelly clarified, licking her bottom lip. I held my breath, waiting for the impact. Nobody moved. It felt like the room had fallen silent. 'I knew you wouldn't mind.' She smiled as she searched Annie's face for pain. 'He told me that you two were never a real thing,' she added, waving her hand dismissively.

We all looked at Annie. Her face was still. The only movement was a slight tense in her jaw muscle. Taylor was her one love. He was the only reason she had never found anyone else. It had been an unspoken truth. I wanted to reach out to her, but I knew that would be a mistake.

Annie rose from her chair in one smooth movement. The smile disappeared quickly from Kelly's face. She stumbled to her feet and took a step back in fear. Annie walked slowly around the table, not taking her eyes off her for even a second. Kelly looked desperately at us. Even Stella did nothing. Everything seemed to be happening in slow motion. Like we were watching it under water.

Annie moved into her space until she was just inches away. Kelly looked scared. Her mouth moved up and down as if she was trying to speak. Annie began to laugh. It was slow at first. But the pleasure crept up her cheeks to her eyes. Then she threw back her head and the laugh got louder. Even in the crowed noisy room, people were turning around to stare. Then as quickly as it started, it stopped. She fell dangerously quiet. Kelly flinched as Annie leaned in. Pressing her face against her cheek and whispering something. Something none of us could hear. Annie pulled away and looked at her. Like she was absorbing every moment of Kelly's shock and fear.

'You're a joke,' she told her calmly. 'You're an absolute joke, Kelly.'

CHAPTER TWENTY-SEVEN

ANNIE

Two days before

It took every ounce of my strength not to hit her. My fingers tingled as I dug my nails into the palms of my hands. When I laughed in her face, I wasn't sure I was ever going to be able to stop. It was like someone else had taken control of my body. As I walked towards the heavy glass doors to exit the restaurant, I wasn't sure if my legs would hold me up. They felt numb. As though all the energy had been pulled from my limbs to feed my anger.

The cold night air hit me as I walked out onto the patio. A cool salty breeze that blew in from the sea across the bay. A breeze that I thought would blow away my rage and hurt and humiliation. It didn't. It rushed through my body like iced water, but the anger remained.

Kelly had slept with Taylor. My Taylor. He'd slept with lots of people over the years. Most of them were strangers, some of them were acquaintances. People I knew through the industry. I'd always been able to rationalise that pain. Lock it away in a part of my mind where it couldn't touch me.

Me and Taylor are close. At least we used to be. When Rose was younger and we needed to co-parent. When he toured less. Taylor had known how I felt about Kelly. Taylor would know that my dislike of her was wrapped up in a complicated knot of jealousy and insecurity. The realisation plunged into my body, like being hit by a car. Taylor knew how much it would hurt me and he did it anyway. He knew, and he didn't care.

I'd always told myself that we'd just 'missed' each other. Like sliding doors. Neither of us being in the right place to settle down, to commit. I kidded myself that we were not together only through circumstance—life getting in the way. I thought that I was *his* 'one' too. That someday, he would be ready. Tonight, the truth had come crashing down on me. I finally realised what everybody else already knew. That I'd been waiting for Taylor all these years. Waiting for him to come back to me. Stood alone outside that restaurant, I finally realised that he never would.

I considered getting a taxi back to the campsite by myself. But if I did that, Rose would know. She would know how badly I'd behaved. The only person in the world whose good opinion I still cared about. I hung by the pavement, pretending to check messages on my phone until the other women joined me.

The car was silent on the taxi ride home. A different sort of quiet than the journey there. So heavy you could almost touch it. The only sound was the gentle whirring of the car heater. The warm enveloped me, but the hairs on my arms still stood on end.

The car drove through the centre of town. I pressed my face against the windowpane. Hypnotised by the bright lights from the clubs and streetlights that flashed through the car as we drove by. Every few seconds, Charlotte's profile was lit up by the town. Her scar was still very visible from this angle. An angry red line scratched across her jaw. It had faded since that night. But it still served as a constant reminder of what happened to her.

CHAPTER TWENTY-EIGHT

ANNIE

That night—twenty-five years ago

It's strange the things that I remember from that night. Tiny, inconsequential things. Things that I would have forgotten if the events of the evening were not so pronounced in my memory. The broken clasp on my purse. The way the doorman at the club smelt like sweet vanilla when he lifted his arm to let us in. I still remembered that Charlotte, sweet naïve Charlotte, had decided to take drugs with me that night.

There'd been something different about her. Charlotte had always hated going to clubs. She preferred to be at home or at the cinema. But tonight, she'd asked to come. From the moment I met up with her, she was wired. A sort of electric energy seemed to emanate from her. It was hard to tell if it was good or bad.

She'd walked into the club like she owned it. At first, I'd loved seeing her like that. The music was loud. The sort of loud that pulses through your chest. It had been packed that night. We slid between groups of people, greeting familiar faces as we passed. We ended up on the back staircase that led to the first floor. Hunched together on the widest part of the steps.

We shared a cigarette. Charlotte had always been a nervous smoker. Even at eighteen she still looked behind her, like a teacher was going to come along and tell her off. She didn't look behind her that night. I took a tiny bag of pink pills out of my purse. Pulling one out and placing it on my tongue. I was about to return them to my bag, when Charlotte grabbed my wrist, taking the bag from me. For a moment I thought she was confiscating them. Instead, she took her own pill. Placing it quickly in her mouth before stuffing the rest of the bag in her bra.

We both laughed, but there was something unnatural about the way she looked. I was in no position to judge her on loss of control, but Charlotte looked unhinged. 'Shall we dance?' she'd asked, taking my hand and leading me down the stairs before I had a chance to answer.

I don't remember what songs were playing that night, but we'd danced for about an hour. House music throbbed through our bodies. Other people joined us. We moved around each other in an almost choreographed synchronicity. Charlotte's white T-shirt clung to her curved body. Her hair hung limp, stuck to her face by the sweat that ran off her forehead. I'd played that night over and over in my head. Picturing her expression. I wanted to believe that she was happy, that she was OK. But she looked haunted.

A group of guys I knew started dancing with us. One of them, Damien I think he was called, danced up behind Charlotte. He pushed his pelvis towards her. Rubbing his hips against hers. She didn't react. Just carried on dancing with the same wild expression. A song came on that I loved. I jumped in the air. Throwing my head back in ecstasy as Damien's friend caught me mid-air.

Charlotte tried to get my attention. Beckoning me down from the man's grasp. 'I'm going to go,' she'd shouted in my ear.

'No—stay!' I called back. She shook her head. The man lifted me up again, planting me in the group behind. I just carried on dancing. Occasionally I craned my neck above the crowd to see if Charlotte was still there. I should have asked if she was OK. I should have stopped her from leaving... I should have gone home with her that night.

I'd ended up at a house party. A dirty, scantily furnished flat on the edge of town. I was kissing the man from the club on a grubby beige sofa. My phone rang. I think it might have rung twice before I finally answered it. The loud obnoxious ringtone that we all used to have before cameras and apps and internet were a thing. Charlotte's name flashed up on the analogue screen.

'Where are you?' I said with a laugh, drunkenly moving to a quiet hallway.

'Is this Annie?' A voice I didn't recognise on the end of the line. There was something about her tone that was disconcerting. I could feel my heart beating steadily against my rib cage. I stared at the cracked cream wall beside me. Picking idly at the edges of the paint. I let her words sink in. She sounded like she was far away.

'Annie, I'm Officer Swift,' the woman told me. 'There's been a serious accident...' Time stood still. Everything started to move very slowly. The man I'd been kissing on the sofa appeared from nowhere. He started to stroke my neck. I shrugged him away without turning around.

'Annie, we can't get hold of Charlotte's mother...' I could hear the sound of traffic, like she was standing next to a busy road. '...I'm going to need you to come down to the hospital, right now...' The man rested his head on my shoulder and tried to kiss me.

'Get *off*!' I shouted, pushing him so hard his back slammed against the partition wall. He held his hands up in defeat.

'Annie, are you OK?' the caller asked.

'Yes,' I told her, heading for the front door. People who had been sat in the living room came out to the hallway to see what the noise was. Drunk men and women trying to read a situation that was unreadable. 'I need to go to the hospital... Where is the hospital?' I asked in panic, holding the phone away from my ear. Everyone looked at me blankly.

I hung up the phone and ran out of the flat. I ran down three flights of stairs and out into the cold night before I realised I was barefoot. I didn't care. The soles of my feet slapped on the cold pavement as I ran down the road. The headlights of the oncoming cars blurred my vision. Yellow streaks danced in front of my eyes. I concentrated on the rhythm of my breath.

If I had to tell someone where the party was, or the route I ran, I wouldn't be able to. I knew the hospital was about a mile beyond our flat. I knew I needed to get back there. Not for shoes or a coat, or even to call a taxi. I needed help. The police officer had called *me*. Wild, drunk, irresponsible me. Nobody ever relied on me for anything. If that officer had known a single thing about me, she would have called any other number in that phone first. But she hadn't, she'd called me. I wasn't going to let Charlotte down.

By the time I was one street away from Box Heights I knew I needed to tell Stella and Tristen. I planned out a route in my head. I would go up to the flat to get them... We would go to the hospital... Charlotte would be OK... I ticked them off like a checklist. Repeating the words over and over in my head as the soles of my feet drummed on the hard ground.

When I got back to the flat, I realised I didn't have my keys. Another tenant held the communal door open for me. He didn't even notice my dishevelled appearance, my lack of shoes. Porthaven was a college town. A town of flats filled with teenage students. Nobody kept regular hours here. If you didn't wear shoes on a Friday night—nobody here would notice.

I crept up the stark staircase to our flat on the second floor.

Automatic lights blinked on every time I turned a corner on the stairwell. I looked at my watch. Just after 1 a.m. Stella had agreed to collect us in her car at two. She said she'd still be awake. She was revising for a law exam she had later in the week. Connie had some sort of party, so she couldn't work at home.

I practised how I would tell them as I arrived at our door. Silently saying the words in my head. 'Charlotte's had an accident. Charlotte's hurt. Charlotte might not make it.' Tristen was Charlotte's boyfriend; he should be there at the hospital. He should be the one to call her mum. My thoughts were slow and abstract. Ideas and words dragged themselves slowly together. Bumping against one another in vague solutions.

I lifted the latch of the door to the flat and quietly closed it behind me. There was no sound as I crept quickly along the carpeted hall. The first door I came to was the bedroom Tristen shared with Charlotte. An ugly brown fire door with a small metal plaque attached to the centre, that read 'no smoking'.

'Tris?' I said quietly. Knocking on the door and opening it in one movement. The only illumination in the room, was the arc of light I'd brought in from the hallway. It covered the mess of grey bedclothes. It took a minute for my eyes to adjust to the shadows.

'Tristen,' I said again, more urgently this time. It was then that I saw her face. Pale and shocked. Half hidden by the edge of the sheets. It was Stella. 'Stella... what are you?' I stumbled in my confusion.

'Annie... it's not what it looks like.' Tristen swung his legs out of bed in panic, covering the middle of his bare body with the covers. He held a hand out, trying to explain. The air escaped from my lungs in one breath. I couldn't move. I shook my head. Waiting for them to explain it away. Waiting to wake up from the never-ending nightmare. But there was nothing to say. Silence pounded in my ears as I watched their shame-ridden faces. Tristen and Stella. Charlotte's boyfriend and her best friend. Having sex in her room.

'Annie, please...' Stella was sat up in bed. Tears streamed down her face. I looked at her like she was a stranger. Like I had never met her before in my life.

Then I told them. 'Charlotte's had an accident.'

CHAPTER TWENTY-NINE

STELLA

That night—twenty-five years ago

I threw up on the way to the hospital. I pulled over the car on the short drive there and vomited onto the grass verge. A mixture of shame and regret and fear had turned to bile. None of us knew what we were walking into. None of us knew what had happened to her. All we knew was that it was bad. Really bad.

I still don't know how Tristen's and my attraction to one another had escalated so quickly. How I'd ended up in bed with my best friend's boyfriend.

It was a Friday. Mum was having friends over to the cottage. That usually meant loud drinking and loud conversation. Shouted words across clouds of burning cannabis oil and incense. I'd decided to work at Box Heights that night. Revise for an exam that I had on Monday. I told Annie and Charlotte that I'd pick them up from the club at 2 a.m. when I'd finished. I could drop them home and head back to the cottage.

I always wondered if some part of me had planned it.

Planned to be there alone with him that night. That some part of me knew that it was more than a crush.

Tristen had joined me on the sofa not long after Charlotte had left. She was heading out to meet Annie. I sat cross-legged. A pile of library books stacked high on the coffee table. 'If you want to put the TV on, I can study in Annie's bedroom,' I told him, gathering up my papers.

'No, it's fine,' he told me. There was something different about him that night. Different about us. Like a high-frequency noise that only we could hear. We'd both been aware of it for weeks. An unsaid thing between us. It wasn't how he looked or how he spoke. It wasn't even how he acted. It was just an energy between us. An intense physical attraction that we kept locked in its own room.

'Stella...' He rubbed the back of his neck. 'Me and Charlotte, we're not... we're never going to be right for each other.' He told me what everyone else already knew. Everyone except Charlotte. I'd nodded mutely. 'I'm going to tell her tomorrow. I've been wanting to do it for ages.' He looked over at me.

'OK,' I replied, unsure what else to say.

Tristen leaned over and kissed me gently on the lips. Tiny butterfly kisses that took the edge off. Kisses that didn't count. Not if I didn't kiss him back. My papers fell to the floor with a light clatter as I turned to face him.

'You know we can't...' I pointed to the small space between us.

'I know,' he said smoothly, nodding slowly in agreement. Silence followed. Finally, an acknowledgement that there was something between us. Something that we needed to fight against.

I tucked my knees under my body, until they were pressing into the cheap sofa springs. We were far enough apart that it felt safe. Then he turned to me. Reaching his hands out until they rested on my hips. Fluttering around the top of the low denim waistband. 'Stella...' he whispered. His fingers slipped under the hem of my T-shirt. Just a little, but enough to make contact with my skin. It was like getting hit by an electric current. That's when everything changed.

He grabbed hold of the denim fabric and pulled me towards him. We kissed. Deeper this time, more urgent. I lifted my knee over his leg, until I was straddling his thigh. Shocks fired up my body as I pushed my hips closer to his. My fair hair hung over his face as I kissed him from above. I knew then that there was no turning back. In that moment I didn't care who I hurt or what consequences there would be. In that moment, I would have burnt the building down if it stood between me and him.

He led me to his dark bedroom. Their bedroom. I didn't see Charlotte's clothes or her make-up or her hairbrush. I only saw him. Afterwards, I lay there. Tensing my muscles as waves of guilt and regret washed over me like the tide coming in. I lifted my face from the pillow. 'I'm going to tell Charlotte,' I told Tristen. He nodded silently. 'I can't believe we've done this to her,' I cried, as the full weight of my betrayal came crashing down on me.

That's when we both heard it. The tiny click of the front door latch. I tried to move, but my limbs wouldn't react. Seconds later, Annie was at the door calling Tristen's name. I squeezed my eyes shut like a child. Wishing myself away from his room. Wishing Annie away from the door.

However awful I thought it would be, it was worse. Annie didn't say anything, she didn't need to. Her shock and repulsion was evident. I opened my mouth to say something. But I had no words. There was nothing to say. What me and Tristen did that night was quickly buried by the news that Charlotte was in the hospital. I never spoke to Annie about it. As far as I know, Tristen didn't either.

Charlotte was unconscious when they let us into her room. A cry escaped my chest when I saw her. A deep, unfamiliar guttural noise. I held on to the end of the bed for support. Charlotte was connected to a serious of tubes and machines. Devices monitoring every broken part of her. She still wore the clothes she'd arrived in. The bright white T-shirt she'd left the flat in had been cut, so they could attach wires to her chest. It was drenched in blood. Everything was. It was smeared up her neck where medics had revived her. It covered her face. Two deep cuts, one on her forehead and an even deeper one under her chin that had partially dried.

I moved slowly towards the side of her bed. The palms of her hands were so grazed, it looked like the skin had been peeled off with a knife. I rested my hand on top of hers. Gently stroking her fingers. I looked at Annie. She was staring up at the ceiling tiles, rocking her head back and forth. Like she was trying not to look at Charlotte. Like she was trying to forget.

Tristen sat down on a low chair in the corner of the room. He put his face in his hands. For a long time, the only noise in that room was the sound of Charlotte's heart on the screen. That and the low quiet moan of Tristen sobbing. We stayed like that for what felt like hours. Not looking at each other. Stuck in our own corner of grief. Waiting for someone to save us from the pain. Waiting for someone to save us from ourselves.

An hour later Charlotte's parents arrived. They were talking to a doctor outside. We gathered hopelessly by the door. Charlotte's mum didn't want to come in. I could see her through the small pane of etched glass. Her back was hunched in agony at what she was about to face.

We huddled together on the far side of the room as her parents cried by her bedside. Unsure whether we should stay or leave. Their grief was devastating. It tore through the room like an explosion. 'What happened?' her mum asked us as her dad stood paralysed. None of us answered. 'The doctors don't know; the police can't tell us anything... Tristen, please,' she begged, walking over to him and taking both of his hands in hers.

'I don't... I don't know.' He released one of his hands from her grasp. Lifting his arm and burying his face in the crook of his elbow. 'I wasn't there.' His shoulders shook.

'Oh, Tristen, Tristen... It's not your fault,' she pleaded, trying to pull his arm away and hug him. 'It's not your fault,' she whispered into his hair, stroking his back. The same back I was kissing just hours before. The same back that I'd drawn my fingernails down. I felt like I was going to be sick again.

When their tears had subsided, Charlotte's mum turned to me and Annie. 'Were you with her?' she asked. I shook my head. A small, tight movement. Annie raised her hand a little in the air, like she was answering a question in class.

'I was,' she told her in a small voice.

'Where did she go? What happened?' Annie just stood there. Streaks of mascara trailed under her eyes. Her dark hair was crimped in damp waves. Her sleek bob now gone. '*Annie!*' she shouted. Annie's body visibly jolted as she was shaken out of her trance.

'We went to a club together,' she told them. You could hear how dry her mouth was. 'Charlotte... well she left before me. I think, maybe... it was just after twelve?' Annie rubbed the side of her face helplessly. Her pupils were wide. I wondered how high she was. I wondered if anybody else had noticed.

'So you let her leave by herself?' she asked accusingly. Annie just nodded her head. 'Look at her,' she shouted, pointing at Charlotte. 'She was all by herself... how could you let her just *leave?*' she yelled through gasping, breathless tears. Her husband put his arm around her. I wasn't sure whether he was trying to restrain her or comfort her. Maybe it was both.

'No!' She pushed her husband away. 'This never would

have happened if it hadn't been for her,' she jabbed a finger angrily towards Annie. She moved back to Charlotte's bedside. Bent over as she tried to gain her composure.

'It's not your fault,' said Charlotte's dad quietly to Annie. But he didn't believe it, any more than Annie did.

CHAPTER THIRTY

ANNIE

That night—twenty-five years ago

The little details of that night stand out like brightly lit beacons. Illuminating the memories so that it feels like it happened yesterday.

I looked across the stark hospital room and stroked my arm. My skin still prickled from the last effects of the drugs that coursed around my veins. My eyes ached under the harsh yellow strip lights. I leant against the cold wall. Stuck in a numbed reality. A strange place somewhere between asleep and awake. The door opened and two police officers walked in.

'Annie?' the female officer asked the room. I stood up and took a step forward.

'Annie, we spoke on the phone,' she told me gently. I recognised her voice. She was older than I'd imagined. 'Can we talk to you outside for a moment please?' Her male colleague held the door open, and I walked blankly through it. Into the quiet corridor outside.

I was still barefoot. It hadn't occurred to me to put on shoes when I got back to the flat. The coldness of the polished floor gripped the soles of my feet. It felt like it was grounding me. Pulling my mind away from the horrors in the room behind me. 'Annie? Can you tell us what happened this evening?' I liked the way she said my name. It was strangely comforting. I felt my eyelids droop as I leaned into the sound of her voice. I moved my head slowly from side to side. The movement stretched my neck muscles and it felt good. I saw the officers look at one another. I forced myself to focus. I forced myself to sober up.

'I don't know,' I replied honestly. 'Charlotte left the club at around midnight. She said she was going home... I think.' I wondered why they weren't writing anything down. 'Do you know what happened to her?' I asked. 'She's just so... she looks...' My words trailed off as my voice cracked with emotion. The woman put her hand on my arm.

'We're not sure yet. A member of the public called it in. They found her unconscious in the outside area of the multi-storey car park. Only a few metres away from the busy road. She has several broken bones, significant cuts and broken teeth. We are looking into the possibility that she was hit by a car... or that someone did this to her.' Her words moved slowly around my head. It took a moment for them to connect. My whole body reacted at once. I felt like my legs would fall away from under me.

I'm not sure what I thought had happened to Charlotte. I'm not sure that I'd even allowed myself to consider the possibilities. 'Someone did this to her?' I could feel my heart beating in my neck. I could feel the rage rising up inside me. The woman held up a cautionary hand.

'Now, we don't know that,' she said carefully. 'We won't know anything for sure until Charlotte wakes up.'

'Do you know for sure that she *is* going to wake up?' My words were louder than before, more aggressive. I felt them gather power as the anger pumped through every joint and every muscle. I didn't care how hostile I sounded. The rage was a welcome replacement for the feelings of guilt and fear that rippled just below the surface of my skin.

The door to Charlotte's room opened. Tristen and Stella walked out. 'We're going to get coffee.' Stella told me in a shaky voice. 'Do you want anything?' she asked. Her face was pale and tear streaked.

'No,' I replied coldly. I felt the officer's watching me. Their shoes squeaked on the polished corridor floor as they walked away. My eyes burned into their retreating backs. I wondered how they had the audacity to be alone together. Maybe it was just too hard to be in a room together with Charlotte's parents. Maybe the shame was too much.

'The doctors are doing everything they can,' the officer told me. I didn't say anything. When they realised I wasn't going to be able to help them, they showed me back into the room.

Charlotte's parents stood by her bedside with a doctor. 'I'm going to need you to come with me and fill out some forms,' he told them gravely. They all left the room. Nobody looked at me. It was like I wasn't even there.

I walked over to her bed. Resting my hand on her damaged fingers. 'Fuck, Charlotte. What happened to you?' I whispered, as tears ran down my face onto my neck. It was like a dam breaking. 'I'm sorry,' I croaked. Thinking about the fact that I had let her walk home alone. Thinking about the fact that she'd taken drugs that I'd given her. The memory of the tiny pills crashed into my conscious. What happened to them?

My heart started to race. I looked through the small pane of glass in the door. Checking that no one was coming. Checking that I wouldn't be seen. I told myself I was doing it to protect Charlotte. Keep her from having to answer difficult questions when she wakes up. *If* she wakes up.

My fingers crept under the thin fabric of her ripped T-shirt. Feeling around until I found her bra strap. I stole a quick look behind me. My heart felt like it would crash out of my chest. So loud I was surprised people in the corridor couldn't hear it. There, just under the lacy fabric, where the cup joined the strap was a tiny plastic bag. My shoulders sank with relief. I let all the air escape from my body as I moved away from Charlotte's bed. Scurrying quickly across the room to hide the pills.

I looked at the small transparent bag in the palm of my hand. The resealable opening had been pressed shut. I blinked. Opening my eyes wide to make sure they were working. To make sure what I was seeing was real.

The bag was empty. How many pills had there been? Three, maybe four? I rubbed the palms of my hands together. Sliding the plastic against my skin with frustration. I could feel a scream building up inside me. If I didn't get out of there soon, I'm not sure I could hold it together any more. I flung open the door to the room. I didn't mean to run; I hadn't planned it. I just needed to get out of there.

Once I started, I couldn't stop. I ran down empty white corridors. My bare feet ached as they slapped on the cold tiles. The names of wards and departments that hung from the ceiling blurred as I passed them. I felt like I was suffocating. If I didn't get outside soon, I would stop breathing all together. I pulled at the neckline of my T-shirt. I pulled so hard I heard the fabric tear. It didn't make any difference.

I somehow found the exit. Big sliding doors, just beyond a waiting area. I stumbled out into the cold night. Light rain freckled my face as I walked to the middle of the dark car park. 'Fuuuuck,' I screamed, pressing my fists into my stomach.

I sank to my knees. My bones pressed into the jagged concrete ground. I didn't care. The pain was a welcome distraction. Charlotte had taken the pills. She'd taken all of them. This was my fault. I sat on the damp ground for what felt like hours. Wondering how all of us could have let her down so badly.

The next few days were a haze. Strange, muddled slots of time, pieced together to make a day. We waited for news from the hospital, we waited for Charlotte to wake up. The hours passed very slowly.

Stella had gone back to the cottage. So many times I nearly called her. Nearly picked up the phone to cry with her, tell her that I needed her. But I couldn't. Being angry with Stella and Tristen, *punishing* Stella and Tristen, was the only thing that I could do for Charlotte right now.

Me and Tristen moved around the apartment like ghosts for the rest of the weekend. I picked at food and took long slow showers. Most days were spent in bed, bundled under piles of blankets. Jack would be home on Sunday night. We were bracing for his return almost as much as we were bracing for news of Charlotte. Even though neither of us had spoken, the flat was vibrating with tension.

On Sunday morning there was a knock at my bedroom door. 'Hi,' Tristen muttered as he entered the dimly lit room. His voice was croaky and thick with pain. 'I just want to explain.' He pushed his hands into his hair. He looked desperate. Tired and drawn—just awful. Not as awful as Charlotte though, I thought, hardening my heart to him.

'I love Charlotte. I cannot stand that this has happened to her.' His eyes filled with tears as his voice cracked. 'But what happened to her wasn't my fault. It wasn't my fault, and it wasn't Stella's.' I opened my mouth to say something, but he continued. 'I know what we did was awful. It was unforgivable. But we didn't cause this. Whatever happened to Charlotte, was something separate.' He looked like he was trying to convince himself as much as me. 'Stella is devastated. This wasn't her. This was all me.'

'That's very honourable of you, Tris, but it couldn't have been all you, could it?' I could feel the top of my lip curl with involuntary disgust. 'Was it the first time?' I asked him. The despair and loneliness I'd felt for the last two days begun to bubble to the surface.

'Yes, yes—nothing else has ever happened.' He seemed relieved to tell me something positive. He seemed relieved that I was talking to him. 'I've never done *anything* like this before.' He begged me to believe him. Tristen sat down on the bed and rubbed his eyes with his thumb and forefinger. 'You know, I never meant for all of this,' he waved his hand around. 'I never meant for us to all be living together. For me and Charlotte to be living together. To be honest, before we moved in here, I didn't think we'd be together for much longer. You *know* it was never the plan for Charlotte to live here.' He pleaded for me to understand.

'Why didn't you tell her?' I asked coldly.

'Why didn't you?' he snapped back. 'Sorry,' he added, holding his palms up in peace. 'I just mean neither of us told her for the same reason. We didn't want to hurt her. As soon as she's better I'm going to tell her. I'm going to tell her it's not working between us. I'm going to tell her about me and Stella.'

'Oh God, spare me the self-pity,' I spat, jumping up from the bed. 'You only want to tell her to make yourself feel better. Do you really want to be that guy? The guy who breaks up with his girlfriend after *this* has happened to her? You're going to tell her that she has to find a new place to live? Tell her that her boyfriend and her best friend have betrayed her... after *this*? That's how you're going to manage your guilt, is it? By smashing Charlotte's heart into a thousand pieces.' I pulled breath into my chest as I ran out of air. My body ached with rage.

I stormed out of the room and that was the last time we ever talked about it. I never expected Tristen to stay with Charlotte forever. I never expected him to marry her. I just needed to make sure that Charlotte was better, before her world was turned upside down. But it took so long for Charlotte to get better, that by then, they'd made a life together.

Tristen did love her. I had convinced myself of that. He

wouldn't have married her if he didn't. But they wouldn't be together if Charlotte hadn't been hurt that night.

The fact that Tristen had stayed with Charlotte made it easier for me to forgive them. It was how we ended up saving our friendship. I knew how much their silence had cost them.

We all found ways to manage our guilt. Tristen had married Charlotte. Stella had lost herself in her job. I had made sure that Charlotte's heart wasn't broken. I made sure that she got the life she wanted.

CHAPTER THIRTY-ONE

DCI MELANIE PRICE

The day it happened

Tristen and Jack identified Annie's body that afternoon. They stood outside the police station afterwards, waiting for one of the officers to drive them back to the campsite. 'Thank you for coming in,' I told them formally. Jack was leant against the granite wall smoking a cigarette. Neither of them looked at me.

Jack exhaled loudly and Tristen took the cigarette from him, breathing in the acrid smoke with a frown. Jack turned his head, like he'd only just noticed me. 'You must be pretty pleased with yourself,' he told me with a barely concealed sneer. I looked at Tristen. If he heard Jack's words, he didn't react. He was deep in his own thoughts.

'Sorry?' I asked, folding my arms defensively.

'Getting this gig.' He pointed to the building he was leant against. 'I remember you. The year below us. Always looking down your nose at everyone.' I watched him carefully. 'You were a right swot,' he told me, snorting with disdain.

'Jack, don't do this...' Tristen put a hand on his friend's arm.

'It's fine,' I told them. 'You've had a shock.' I kept my tone even and professional.

'How long are you going to keep us at that place?' Jack asked, looking up from under his dark brows.

'Just two or three days. I know it isn't ideal. We've tried to find alternative accommodation, but it's just not possible at this time of year. My team have screened off the yurt today and are moving your tents to the opposite corner of the top field. We'll send a car for each of you over the next few days, so we can get a formal statement from you all. The sooner we find out the truth, the sooner you can go home,' I told them, before turning and walking back into the building.

At eleven p.m. the incident room was empty apart from myself and DC Green. Simon had insisted on staying with me to find out the results of the autopsy. The lights in the main office had been turned off. Our area was dimly lit by lamps. We sat in the shadows, tapping our pens on the table while we waited. The room smelt freshly painted and the furniture looked brand new. I'm not sure the space had ever been used before. It all felt pretend, like we were playing at being police officers.

Someone had wheeled in an incident board. Annie's name had been written in neat letters on the shiny white surface. The death had not officially been classed as a murder. We had to wait for the results of the postmortem. The investigation had to be ready to begin, but we couldn't waste valuable manpower on a case that might not turn out to be a murder.

The shrill ring of Simon's mobile phone broke the silence. He spoke a few words before hanging up. 'She's ready for us,' he told me. The mortuary was in the next building, a short walk from here. Dr Polly Christchurch was doing the autopsy. An experienced pathologist, but one whose path I'd never crossed.

Seeing Annie's body was no easier the second time. When I saw her on the ground at the campsite, her skin still had some life to it. Now it looked like porcelain. Glowing white under the harsh overhead lights. When you see a body in situ, it feels like a part of them is still there. They usually have clothes and jewellery, maybe a watch or shoes. Something that connects them to who they were. Sometimes, they look like they might just be sleeping. When they get to the mortuary, there are none of those connections.

'Hi, I don't think we've met properly.' Dr Christchurch removed her surgical gloves and extended a hand.

'DCI Mel Price,' I told her as I took her hand in mine. 'It's nice to finally meet you.' I smiled awkwardly.

'Simon. Keeping well?' she asked, returning to her clipboard. 'We don't see as much of each other now that we've got our own fancy canteen.' She laughed. Polly Christchurch had a warm open face. Her hair was cropped and highlighted with ash-blonde streaks that met in a quiff above her forehead. 'I hear congratulations are in order!' She lifted the first page of paper, scanning for the information she needed.

'Thanks,' Simon told her. 'We're trying to get as much sleep as we can before the next one joins us.' He smiled good naturedly. Lyndsey was pregnant again. A wave of sadness washed over me as I thought of everything I'd missed. Everything I was going to miss.

'And how's that working out for you?' Dr Christchurch looked at her watch and laughed again. 'OK, so... Annie Turner. Aged forty-two. I'm not sure where you are with this, so let's go through my preliminary findings,' she told us. 'As you know, toxicology is going to take at least six weeks to come back. I suspect a great deal of significance is going to be placed on those results... especially if this ends in a trial.' Me and Simon looked at each other.

'Whilst I can't tell you right now if any drugs or alcohol were in her system... we do have this.' Dr Christchurch clicked on a small flashlight. She leant over her body, pointing the beam towards Annie's nose. 'Here in the nostril is white residue. Now, I can't say for sure until we test it, but it looks very much like cocaine or amphetamine.'

'Doctor, why is the presence of alcohol or drugs going to be significant in a court case?' I asked.

'Ahh, I'll get to that. So, the cause of death. A subdural haematoma caused by blunt force trauma to the back of the head. An impact that also fractured the skull.'

'Do you have any idea what might have caused it?' I asked.

'It's hard to say.' She shuffled through a pile of crime scene photos, before holding one up. 'There is trace material on the wound. Without testing I can't say with any certainty, but it looks like concrete or stone of some kind.'

'Are you saying this could have been an accident? That the injury could have been caused by her falling onto the path? We know she'd been drinking. Maybe she fell trying to find her way to the toilets... hit the back of her head... somehow got to her feet before her final fall against the kerb.' I played the scene out in my head. Trying to look at all the possible angles.

'No, I don't think so. But I suspect that might be the argument a defence team might make. It's why I think the toxicology results may play a big part. They will try to argue that this is an accidental fall as a result of her being intoxicated.' Dr Christchurch puffed air out of her nostrils and let her shoulders drop.

'But you don't think it is?' I asked. She shook her head.

'Let me explain. First, the traces of blood that were found at the scene. There was the blood that had pooled under her forehead as well as a fine spray patterned across the path. If she'd fallen backwards, hard enough to cause a fracture and a wound of this size, there would have been significant pooling in the first place she fell.

'Do you see this?' She held up a different photo. 'These tiny pinpricks of blood in an arc across the paving.' Her fingers traced the line on the photo as me and Simon squinted at the image. 'I believe that they came from the weapon. The blood pattern is not consistent with where she landed. I think the assailant hit the victim on the back of the head with a hard stone object. The blood spray occurred as they pulled their arm away.' Dr Christchurch lifted her hand in the air to demonstrate.

'Another issue; there are no defensive wounds. When a person falls, there is a moment. A slip of the foot or a trip. A split second when they attempt to save themselves—usually with their hands. There are no cuts or grazes or breaks that I would expect to see on the hands or wrists if this were a result of a fall. Nor is there anything to suggest that the victim fought back,' she told us solemnly.

'In my opinion, this was a single, unexpected blow to the back of the head. A blow so hard and so sudden it caused the victim to fall forward fast enough to not be able to save herself. The injury to the head from hitting the kerb was significant, but it was survivable. The haematoma on the back was, without question, *un*survivable.' The doctor sat down on a low swivel stool.

'Thank you,' I told her. 'That makes my job a lot clearer. Do you have a time of death?' I asked.

'I was waiting for you to get to that. A bit tricky, I'm afraid. You already have a one a.m. to just after four a.m. timeframe. The hours between the last sighting of the victim alive and finding her body. It's been quite hard to narrow it down much. The August temperature dropped considerably last night. Combined with the victim being drenched in rainwater for an undisclosed period of time. Officially, I will be putting in my report that the murder occurred between one-fifteen a.m. and three a.m. Unofficially—and this isn't provable, this is purely based on my instinct, I would say between one-thirty a.m. and two-thirty a.m. is most likely.'

'I really appreciate you taking the time to see us so late,' I said, crossing the room to shake her hand.

'Say hi to Lyndsey,' she called after us. Simon lifted his hand in a wave. I pushed open the swing doors. We walked along the dim corridor, absorbing what we'd been told.

'We'll need to set up a press conference tomorrow. Let them know that this is now a murder investigation.' I rubbed the back of my neck. Fatigue gripped my joints. 'Congratulations!' I told him brightly, looking straight ahead. 'You know, you could have told me,' I said softly.

'I wanted to.' Simon stopped as we reached the exit. 'There didn't seem to be a good time.' I nodded my understanding. 'Lyndsey misses you.'

I pushed opened the security door. 'I miss her too,' I told him, heading out into the dark car park.

CHAPTER THIRTY-TWO

CHARLOTTE

Two days before

The taxi crept through the tent village. The headlights panned over campers as they moved slowly around their pitch, readying themselves for bed. Silhouettes illuminated by torchlights and lanterns. Circles of chairs, filled with blanketed campers. You could just about hear the happy voices as their words were swept away on the night breeze. Congratulating themselves on the great weather and the great campsite and the great company. I watched, unseen from the back of the warm car. Wondering if they knew how lucky they were.

My shoulders sank in relief when I saw Theo with Tristen. There was no sign of Ollie. We all climbed out of the car. Tristen and Nate and Rose sat around a roaring campfire. 'You're back early,' called Nate, walking over to see Stella. It was only just after ten. That's all we'd been able to manage.

He slipped his arm around her waist and offered her a drink from the steaming mug he had in his hand. She sipped it gratefully, licking chocolate off her bottom lip. 'Do you want me to make you some?' he asked quietly. She nodded. They held each other's gaze for a moment. Nate watched her intently, like he knew. Like Stella had told him everything about the night, through just a look.

I had always longed for that kind of connection with someone.

Jack stumbled out of the tent, tripping over one of the guy ropes. His eyes were round and wired. He looked like he'd taken something. 'Heeey,' he shouted drunkenly, staggering towards Kelly with a large tumbler of whisky. He draped his arm clumsily over her shoulder, trapping her hair and pulling her head back a little. She tried to wriggle out of his grasp, but he moved them both towards Annie. Draping his other arm over her shoulder. Annie laughed and leaned into the awkward hug, nuzzling her face into his chest and laughing flirtatiously.

Kelly wasn't smiling. She watched Annie cautiously, like she was scared of what she might do. Scared that she might let Jack know that she'd told everyone about Ollie's violent expulsion from his private school. Scared that she might tell Jack about their altercation tonight. Annie would come off just as bad, but her confidence... her cold boldness put everyone on the back foot. It made her seem unbeatable. Annie wouldn't say anything to Jack—not tonight. That wasn't her style. Annie would wait a while to play her hand. It's what she always did. I think she enjoyed it.

Tristen didn't come over to see me. He didn't even look at me. How had things got so bad, so quickly. He stayed by the fireside, sitting close to Rose. The only thing between them was Theo's small body, crouched on the ground, threading marshmallows onto sticks. 'Hi, baby,' I said, bending down to give him a hug. He was too preoccupied with the sweets to really notice. A familiar stabbing pain of rejection needled at me. A dull ache that I had felt most of my adult life.

I know what people thought. I know what they whispered behind my back. I first noticed it when I got out of hospital.

Then when I got off the psych ward it was even worse. They thought that it was my fault. That I should have picked better. Chosen someone who loved me as much as I loved them. The imbalance between us was obvious. I loved Tristen so much; I thought it would be enough for both of us. I don't think I ever had a choice. I felt like I might have died without him.

'Why's he still up?' I asked Tristen irritably. Annoyed by Theo's lack of interest. He looked up, surprised by my tone. I never spoke to him like that.

'We thought it would be fun to make s'mores and drink hot chocolate, didn't we, buddy?' Tristen replied, talking to Theo rather than me.

'He needs to go to bed,' I told him firmly. 'He'll never get up tomorrow.'

'Let him lie in then. Charlotte, he's on his holiday for Christ's sake,' Tristen said angrily, taking a noisy sip of his drink.

'Nooo,' Theo said, looking up at me. His mouth smeared with chocolate and marshmallow. 'I want to make more smogs,' he whined.

'They're called s'mores,' Rose told him, giggling a little. Tristen joined in, laughing affectionately. Resentment shuddered down my spine. I pressed my lips together to stop myself from saying something. Something I'd regret.

'Hey! What did I tell you lot.' An older-looking man was half running out of the darkness towards our camp. Pointing an angry finger at us and shouting. It was the man I'd seen on reception a few days ago. As he stepped into the light, you could see just how enraged he was. His face was red and sweating. Fine white hairs clung to his wet head. He wore a brown checked shirt. Several buttons were undone, like he'd got dressed in a hurry. He looked crazed.

'No fires... *no* fires!' He waved his hands manically in the air. I led Theo quickly by the hand away from the fire.

'Mummy... you're hurting me,' Theo cried, trying to wriggle out of my grip.

'I'm sorry, darling,' I told him distractedly, watching as the man threw himself around the chairs.

Nate stepped in. 'Whoa, mate, calm down.' He put himself between the man and the fire and spoke in calm even tones.

'*Don't* you tell me to calm down,' he yelled, rubbing his head agitatedly. 'It's always the same with people like you,' he sneered. 'You come here in your fancy cars and your expensive clothes and think the rules don't apply to you.'

'We used a firepit.' Nate pointed towards the base of the flames. 'It won't mark the grass.' He talked to him like he was gently coaxing a child.

'Why don't you just fuck off?' Jack lurched suddenly towards the fire. For a moment I thought he was going to trip right into it. His head swayed precariously as though his neck wasn't strong enough to hold it up.

'Jack... stop, man, what are doing?' Nate turned to him in frustration. Rose got up slowly from her seat and came to stand next to me and Theo.

'That is *it*!' screamed the man, before disappearing back into the darkness.

'Ha,' yelled Jack to no one in particular. He pulled a cigarette from his shirt pocket and tried unsuccessfully to light it. He shuffled his feet like the ground was moving underneath him.

'Shall we pack this stuff up?' Nate suggested. Tristen stood up and started folding up the camping chairs. It was clear that the night was over.

'I'll take Theo to bed,' Rose offered, taking his hand.

'No. I'll take him to bed,' I snapped, walking back towards the tent.

'I was only trying to help,' she said sadly. I didn't reply. I was too embarrassed. Rose was little more than a kid herself.

She was my goddaughter. I was letting my jealousy and bitterness take over every part of me. I turned to apologise when a loud noise crashed through the campsite. The man had come back.

'There!' he shouted triumphantly as he dumped a huge plastic carrier of water over the fire. The metal pit fell to one side and the remaining wet embers tumbled onto the grass. Nate and Tristen leapt away from the spray of water. Silence followed the crash. We all stood there reeling from what had just happened.

The man walked away. The empty plastic water carrier swung happily from his hand. As the smoke began to clear I saw Annie following him. Her folded arms wrapped her long black cardigan around her body.

'Who do you think you are?' she asked. I could see the shadow of some of the other campers in the distance, watching on.

'I'm sorry?' he replied angrily, shocked that he would be confronted so forcefully. She strode confidently up to him, until her face was only inches from his.

'We've paid good money to be here. If we want to light a fire... we will light a fucking fire,' she told him simply, before turning and walking away. The man obviously wasn't used to being challenged. He stood frozen to the spot, his mouth gaping open.

'How *dare* you... I will call the police... This is *unacceptable*,' he stuttered angrily at her retreating back.

'Fine. Do it,' Annie shouted back before going into her yurt. The man slunk back into the shadows from where he came.

'Are you OK?' Tristen asked. I opened my mouth to reply, before I realised he was looking at Rose and Theo. I didn't hear her reply as I went inside our tent.

I helped Theo into his Batman pyjamas. 'Did you have fun tonight?' I asked as he wriggled his legs into his sleeping bag. I stroked his soft dark hair. He nodded with a smile that made his eyes crease. 'I wish I could have been here,' I told him. He shrugged, like it didn't matter to him either way.

'I had Daddy and Rose,' he replied, snuggling into his pillow. I kissed him good night. Crawling to my bed behind the thin partition, before the tears spilled over. What was wrong with me? It wasn't Rose's fault that me and Tristen were having problems. It wasn't her fault that I felt old and unnoticed.

Rose and Annie had bonded with Theo from the day he was born. Tristen was away during my pregnancy. He was there for the missed period and the test and the first few weeks of morning sickness, but by the time I was nine weeks pregnant, he was stationed abroad. I couldn't join him.

I was devastated when he'd left. Knowing what I was about to go through by myself. I went to stay with Annie and Rose at her Wiltshire house for a week. It was before the renovations. Before the swimming pool and the designer curtains and the landscaped gardens. A week had turned into a month and a month turned into six months.

Rose had only just turned fourteen. She was struggling with being a teenager who liked to read and take long walks. A teenager who liked quiet and had a mum like Annie. Her school had agreed to a sabbatical. They knew how dedicated she was to her studies. They also knew how lost she was in the school system. Rose was so like me when I was teenager.

It had worked out perfectly. Rose could stay at the Wiltshire house and study with me there. Annie came and went. Some weekends she would join us, other times she stayed at the London flat. We went for long spring walks. We made the house lovely, a real home. The house only had an Aga to keep us warm. We lit candles and ate pasta and sat in dark panelled rooms every night by the dim lamps we'd scattered around the house. Sometimes we talked. Sometimes we would spend whole evenings in silence. It was a very peaceful time. Probably the most peaceful of my life.

That house made Rose really happy. She was connected to it in a way that I'd not seen someone love a home before. When Annie started renovating it, it was like her soul was being ripped out. I wonder if Annie knew.

I moved from the Wiltshire house into Tristen's mum's old house. I missed it. I missed Rose. But I'd left with a newborn baby. I had Theo. I was finally a mum.

I listened to the hushed conversations outside the tent. When Tristen came to bed a few minutes later, I pretended to be asleep. I was scared to be alone with him. Scared of what he might say to me. I had finally run out of ways to keep him with me.

CHAPTER THIRTY-THREE
STELLA

The day before

I woke with Nate's arms wrapped around me. The rain had come down hard in the night. A loud drumming on the roof of the tent that had made it impossible to sleep. In the early hours of the morning an owl had started screeching. The sound pierced abruptly through the anxious thoughts that swam around my head. It had left me feeling unsettled.

We should have gone home last night. We should have just packed up our things and left. But it's Rose's eighteenth birthday today. My leaving would throw everything up in the air. It would ruin her special day. What reason would I give? That her mum was blackmailing me over my affair with her godmother's husband? No, staying was my only chance of leaving here with my life still intact.

I gently slid out of Nate's grip and climbed out of my sleeping bag. I grabbed a thick jumper from the end of my bed and put it on over my pyjamas. The teeth of the zip grinded noisily as I opened the entrance. I turned to check that I hadn't woken Nate. He was still fast asleep. He looked so peaceful. My mum had an old saying: 'If you want to sleep soundly, take a clear conscience to bed.' Nate always slept soundly.

The air felt damp. I sat on the ground sheet in the covered opening to the tent. Undoing the flaps so I could sit in the dry and watch the campsite wake up. Splashes of raindrops had leaked under the canvas door, pooling around the edge of the entrance.

'Hello, dear. I'm sorry to interrupt.' A whispered voice jumped me out of my thoughts. 'I didn't mean to startle you.' The woman held up her hands in apology. She wore a sky-blue anorak with the hood pulled up. The zip was drawn to her chin. Just her angular milky-coloured face poked out from the fabric. Small piercing blue eyes blinked behind steamed-up spectacles.

'That's OK. I was miles away. Trying to make the most of the quiet.' I smiled. She nodded like she understood.

'This is my favourite time of day,' she told me warmly. There was something very comforting in the way that she spoke. 'I'm Irene. We met when you checked in.'

'Of course,' I replied. Suddenly embarrassed, as I remembered who she was. Remembering what happened last night with the fire. She was married to the man who had angrily put out the flames. The man who had argued with Annie.

'I just wanted to say how sorry I am. My husband has a terrible temper.' She handed me a small basket, packed with food. Eggs and bread and bacon. A glass bottle filled with orange juice.

'You really don't have to...' I shook my head, reluctantly taking the basket.

'No. I insist,' she said firmly. 'Just a few breakfast bits as an apology.' She started to turn as if to leave, before adding, 'You know, he's not a bad man. He has a lot of faults, but he's not a bad man.' She spoke as if I wasn't the first person she'd had to convince. 'We never had children, so this place is his life. He's terrified that something might happen. That he might someday lose it. It's why he's so obsessed with rules.' She shrugged. Not sadly, just a matter of fact.

After she left, the space around me felt very empty. Irene had an energy that filled the air around you with warmth. My mother had the same energy. Familiar feelings of grief washed over me. It was something that hit me regularly. It won't ever go away, but the absence of shock made it easier to deal with.

I watched the dim light brighten over the field. Letting my mind fall back into a pit of memories. I don't know if I was ever in love with Tristen. Intense desire, mixed with a loving friendship is a heady and confusing combination. But I'm not sure if that equates to 'in love.' It wasn't the same as the way I feel about Nate.

CHAPTER THIRTY-FOUR

ANNIE

The day before

'Happy birthday, darling,' I whispered excitedly in the dim hazy light of the yurt. I was sat on Rose's bed, as she slowly twisted her body awake. 'I cannot *believe* my little girl is eighteen today!' I tucked one of her long curls behind her ear.

'Thanks, Mum.' She gave me a sleepy smile as she sat up.

'I've got you a birthday breakfast... it's not much.' I handed her a small white plate with two croissants and a plastic bottle of orange juice. 'It's not exactly the Ritz... but it's all they had in the shop.'

'No, no... this is perfect,' she told me. Rose looked so pleased with my small gesture.

'...And gifts... I have gifts!' I told her happily. Placing a pile of wrapped presents and a handful of cards on the soft bedding. I tucked my bare toes under my legs as I watched Rose carefully tear off the paper. It was a novel. A book she'd mentioned a couple of months ago. I'd checked her shelves before I bought it, just in case she already had it.

'Mum... this is... I can't believe you remembered.' She shook her head in astonishment. Before leaning over and giving me a hug. A hug that lasted longer than any we'd had in a long time. I felt a rush of emotion. It hit with such force I felt dizzy.

I pulled away. 'There are these too... they're only small.' Rose unwrapped two more gifts. A beautifully bound notebook and some pens. She loved stationery. She'd loved it ever since she was big enough to hold a pencil.

'I love them. They're so thoughtful.' Rose looked at me. Her eyes filled with tears.

'Don't! You'll set me off,' I told her, wiping my eyes.

'OK, one last present...' I pulled out a brown envelope from under her bed. I handed it to her. Tapping my foot with excitement.

Rose gently tore apart the paper seal. She pulled out a key and a leaflet. She looked at me confused. 'I got you a car... well, a Mercedes actually... it's a sports car, like mine. It's from your dad too... but it was my idea!' I watched with pleasure as Rose thumbed through the brochure. She didn't need to know that Taylor had paid for all of it.

'I don't know what to say... thank you!' Rose forced the sides of her mouth into a smile and hugged me again.

'I know you haven't started driving lessons yet—but I know you'll pass in no time!' I laughed. Rose nodded, a smile fixed firmly to her face.

'You do like it, don't you? If it's the colour, then we can change it...' I tried to read her expression.

'No, no it's amazing... I'm so grateful,' she gushed hastily.

'OK, great. Well, eat your breakfast. I'm going to have a shower and get dressed.' As I left the yurt, I tuned to look at her. How could she be eighteen? She looked so young, like a child, sat up in bed.

We shouldn't have bought the car. Even Taylor hadn't been sure that it was the right thing to get her. I had insisted. Rose was not a sports car person. She was so touched by the book and the stationery. So happy that I'd chosen presents just for her. That I understood her.

The car had been for me. An over-the-top gesture to make *me* happy. The rest of the day will be all about her. I'll make sure of it.

CHAPTER THIRTY-FIVE

STELLA

That night—twenty-five years ago

Charlotte regained consciousness two days later. As soon as her parents left, me and Annie and Tristen went into her stark room at the hospital. She looked so fragile, so small. 'Hi,' she croaked, offering us a weak smile. I felt my heart break. I actually thought I could feel the moment that it cracked with shame and regret. Sadness for what had happened to her. Sadness for what I had done to her.

'Charlotte, what happened? They won't tell us anything.' Annie sat ashen faced on the bed. Holding her by the hand, pleading for information. Charlotte said nothing for a while. She sipped at the water next to her, silent tears streamed down her face. 'Charlotte, please,' Annie begged.

'I cut across the car park on the way home from the club.' Her voice was flat and emotionless. 'There was nobody around. I was so tired...' We all held our breath. 'When I got halfway across the car park, I heard footsteps behind me. I thought it was a woman... I'm not sure why.' She looked confused. 'I turned around and there was a man just a few feet behind me. He was well dressed, you know?' For the first time, she looked up. 'I just assumed he was going back to his car...'

I watched a tear fall down her face and drop onto the fresh white bed linen. '...And then he hit me. So hard I fell to the ground. I felt my face crack as it hit the concrete.' She touched her cheek with a shaking hand. Her eyes found Tristen's, looking for safety. Looking for him to protect her from the horror she was reliving.

'He punched me and kicked me until I couldn't see any more... that's the last thing I remember.' The room filled with the heaviest of silences.

A few weeks later, Charlotte was admitted to a psychiatric hospital. Stress and exhaustion they said. A gentler way to say that she wasn't coping. A way of saying that she was losing her grip. She stayed there for a long time. When she got out, the stage had been set. Charlotte would be forever fragile, forever damaged. We all tried our best to protect her from the world.

CHAPTER THIRTY-SIX

STELLA

The day before

It was Rose's birthday. Her eighteenth birthday. We'd all promised to go for a walk this afternoon. The weather was awful. The rain was falling in a light mist. A fine spray scattered my face as I pulled on my boots. None of us wanted to go. But Rose didn't ask for much, we would do this for her. We would do it with a smile on our faces and pretend that everything was OK.

It was a ten-minute drive to Greenbank Lake. It was somewhere that we used to come when we were kids. We'd piled into two cars and parked close to the water.

The first time I ever came here was with Tristen. We'd both studied science as one of our subjects at college. We'd been brought here on a field trip when we were seventeen. Measuring water flow and taking the pH levels of the samples we took. Tristen had already been with Charlotte for a while by then. That day was the first time I realised that I liked him. The first time that we'd been alone together outside of the group. It was like meeting him for the first time. He wore a black denim jacket that I'd never seen before. He somehow seemed bigger. His body, his hair. Everything was different. I wondered if he still remembered that day.

I loved this place, even in the rain. We walked in single file along the narrow path from the car park. The sound of wellies in mud was all I could hear with my hood up. Nylon raincoats scratching on the bramble bushes that lined the track. After a few minutes the path opened out onto the lake. A wide stretch of grey water against the dark sky. Raindrops pierced the surface, making tiny ripples. Bringing the fish to the surface.

We trudged through the drizzle. Tall sycamore trees bordered the park. Their leaves like giant hands. Whenever the rain fell more steadily, our path would divert beneath them. We still got wet, but it wasn't as bad. Just the light tap of drops as they ran off the glossy greenery. The sound of birds chirruping as they sheltered in the branches.

I'd never seen the water level as high as it was today. A makeshift sign had been erected. Warning of dangerous currents and unusually large swells in the normally calm lake. Charlotte gripped tightly onto Theo's hand as we followed the path around the water's edge.

We reached a picnic area, settled high above the bank. The rain had stopped temporarily. We all cautiously pulled down the hoods of our coats. Perching on the edge of a picnic bench. The wood now dark and saturated. The view was just beautiful. Even through the grey.

Rose spotted a heron on the far side of the lake. She squealed with pleasure as it took off. Showing us its huge wing-span as it flew over our heads. It was like she couldn't see the black clouds or the mist that was settling. She loved nature and animals. Nothing made her happier. She had always been the same.

I'm glad I stayed. I'm glad we could do this for her.

Charlotte had brought two flasks of coffee. She pulled a

stack of cardboard cups from her backpack. Filling each one halfway with the steaming liquid. It tasted good. Hot and sweet and slightly bitter. I wrapped my cold wet hands around the warm card. Listening to the chatter of conversation. Sharing memories of Rose when she was little.

'Do you remember that cuddly elephant she used to carry around?' Annie asked. 'Jack, you and Lisa bought it for Rose's first birthday.' The air bristled slightly at the mention of Lisa's name. '...Chunky, was that his name?'

'Trunky,' Rose told her. Covering her face in mock embarrassment.

'Yes, Trunky!' Annie laughed. We all smiled fondly as we remembered her small blinking toddler face. Dragging her tattered elephant behind her wherever she went.

'Did you take him everywhere? Like I take Benny everywhere?' Theo asked Rose with interest. Pressing the soft giraffe to his face.

'Yes, I did,' she smiled.

'Where is he now?' Theo frowned.

'Well, when children turn into grownups, they don't need their toys as much... Trunky is very old now—he needs his rest. So, I left him at home.' Rose reached out and stroked Benny's soft body. I felt a lump of emotion rise in my throat. I looked at the other faces around the table and knew they felt it too.

'Ollie, come away from the edge,' Jack called over. Oliver had lagged behind the entire walk. He hadn't said a word to anyone. Not even Rose. Now he was stood on the high bank that cut sharply away to the dangerous current below. He didn't move. His eyes fixed on the swirling waters.

'Oliver, did you hear me? Get back.' He was shouting now. Everyone had fallen quiet. Oliver took a step forward. Only a small one, but it was enough to place his trainer on the very edge. Jack clambered to his feet. Moving carefully along the muddy bank until he was just a couple of metres away from him.

'You and Mum would still be together... if it wasn't for her?' He tilted his head towards the table without turning around. Towards where Kelly was sitting.

'Where's this coming from?' Jack replied, confused. Trying to keep his voice low so that we couldn't hear. 'There are lots of reasons me and your mum split up...' Oliver laughed, but it sounded bitter and angry. 'Oliver, mate, come away from the edge,' Jack pleaded. He sounded worried now. His face anxiously scanned his son's for a sign that he'd heard him.

'You were happy. I know it was a few years ago, but I remember... you two were *really* happy.' He spoke into the air, like he was talking to himself.

'No. We put on a good show for you kids, but we weren't happy. Not really,' Jack tried to explain to Oliver's rigid back. He didn't reply. His upper body leant a fraction towards the edge. Jack leapt forwards, thinking he was going over. He roughly grabbed Oliver's arms from behind and lurched his body clumsily towards the grass.

'Whaaaa,' Oliver called out as he fell backwards. Jack tried to catch him, but he tumbled to the ground. Landing in the deep wet earth. 'What the fuck,' he screamed, slapping the muddy water with the palm of his hand in anger.

'Oliver, I'm sorry...' Jack offered a hand, to help pull him up. Oliver didn't take it. He scrambled to his feet, humiliated. Tristen stood up, realising how angry Oliver was. Realising that something was about to happen.

'Why did you do that?' Oliver's eyes were wild. Tiny specks of saliva sprayed from his mouth as he spat the words close to Jack's face.

'I thought you were going to fall...' Jack pointed helplessly at the edge. Still close enough to be a danger. He looked Oliver up and down. Black mud stained the front and underarm of his sweatshirt. It dripped off his hands that were held out in front of him. His face flushed with embarrassment and rage. 'Let's get you back to the car. Get you cleaned up,' he added, more gently now.

Oliver lowered his hands to his side. Slowly clenching his palms into a fist. Tristen walked quickly towards them, shouting at Oliver. 'That's enough. Go back to the car, Oliver. *Now*,' he told him. Oliver's fist twitched. I thought he was going to punch Jack. We all did. Tristen reached out, and in one smooth movement, hitched his hand under Oliver's armpit and marched him away from the lake. He looked so small alongside Tristen's broad upper body. I saw Oliver's shoulders sink, as all the fight drained out of him.

Tristen and Oliver disappeared towards the car park. Jack just stood there. Sliding his hands slowly down his face in despair. Trying to work out how everything had gone so wrong.

CHAPTER THIRTY-SEVEN

ANNIE

The day before

I leaned my face towards Rose's as we walked through the campsite to get to the restaurant. She smelt of sandalwood soap and grass. Rose was like a perfect rare flower that I'd been given. A flower that had bloomed and flourished, despite the lack of care she'd been given over the years. Her name had been very fitting.

I think she'd had a good time at the lake today. The weather had been miserable. I'm still not sure that the car had been the right choice of gift... but I think she's happy. I found her so difficult to read sometimes. I always had.

The relentless rain had stopped for a while. A layer of water sat on the black concrete road we walked down. The yellow overhead lights shone onto the path. It looked slick and glossy like tar. This was the first time we were eating at the campsite restaurant. It had been Rose's idea to do something low-key. I wanted to spoil her. Show her how much she means to me. But I never seemed to get it right. It was always too much or too little.

Rose linked her arm through mine and pressed her body in

a little closer. Gratitude had always been an alien emotion to me. It wasn't something that I ever felt. But tonight, I felt grateful, despite everything. Grateful for Rose and everything she is. Everything she has brought with her these last eighteen years.

'I'm sure this isn't how you'd pictured spending your eighteenth birthday.'

'It's perfect,' she replied, looking like she really meant it.

'Rosie!' Theo called. His small feet splashed along the wet path behind us.

'You look like a teddy bear!' Rose laughed when he caught up to us. He did look like a bear. His tiny torso was wrapped in a soft brown fleece jacket. His small elfin face poked out from the oversized hood. I felt my neck constrict with emotion. I shook it away. What was wrong with me tonight? Rose's birthday was making me sentimental. It was making me dwell on the past.

Rose picked up Theo and jogged ahead. Theo's laughs rang out in the darkness as she bounced him up and down. I wondered if Rose had ever wished for me and Taylor to be a family. Whether she'd ever dreamt of two parents to live with. Together or apart, me and Taylor could never have offered her any kind of stability. Not in any real sense. We were both too selfish.

I checked my phone again. Three missed calls from a private number. One voicemail. I tucked my phone back hastily in my bag. There was still time. If I could just get some more investment tonight. I just needed to convince Stella or Jack... maybe even Tristen. I can't take out any more loans, but they can. I could still save the business. I could save the house.

The restaurant was big and open. The floors and walls were clad in pale oak. It made it feel like a beach house. The glow of the warm lights made it very inviting. Around half of the tables were full, families mainly. Parents with young children, all scrubbed up for dinner. A corner of the restaurant had been decorated. Balloons had been tied to the backs of the chairs. Gold confetti in the shape of the number eighteen was strewn across the table.

I looked at Charlotte. I knew this was her doing. She gave a tiny shake of her head. To tell me it was nothing. To tell me that she didn't want any credit. Charlotte had set up my daughter's eighteenth birthday party. That's what good mums did. I looked at Theo. He was so lucky to have her.

Rose's eyes lit up when she saw the table. She was someone who *did* feel gratitude, someone who expressed it. She squeezed my hand as we walked to the table. I felt like a fraud, but I said nothing. We all took our seats at the long table. I was sat between Rose and Jack. A weary-looking waiter brought us our menus, setting one down in front of each of us.

I glanced over the menu. The choices were endless. I wondered what bland low-fat meal I would order tonight. I leaned into Rose and whispered excitedly. 'What are you going to have?' I asked her. If I couldn't *be* a good mum, I could act like one. 'It's got to be a nice juicy steak for your birthday, hasn't it?' I smiled, turning the menu over in my hand. Rose stared at me for a moment.

'Mum, I'm a vegetarian.' I saw a lump slide down her throat as she swallowed. Rose had been a vegetarian for nearly ten years.

'God, I'm sorry, darling... they serve big juicy tofu by the looks of things.' I laughed, but Rose's eyes stayed fixed on the menu. 'Tonight's on me,' I called loudly across the table. 'It's not every day that your little girl turns eighteen.' Rose lifted her head, attempting a weak smile.

'...Can we get a round of drinks over here?' Jack called loudly to the nearest waiter, who froze in surprise.

This is what I always did. What I couldn't offer her in terms of interest or affection, I replaced with money. Material things that I thought would fill the void. Rose had no interest in material things.

'We got you a little something... it's from all of us.' Stella reached under the table and handed Rose a huge envelope. That was one of the lovely things about Rose. Even on her birthday she was surprised to receive presents.

She carefully opened the paper sleeve and pulled out an oversized card. Stella had shown it to me earlier. It was something she'd had made a few weeks ago. The cover was printed with photographs. Photographs of Rose's life. Photographs of the people she loves. There were images of her as a toddler, on her first day at school. There was even a rare photograph of me as a child with my mum and dad.

'Everyone contributed pictures...' Stella explained. She watched Rose's face as she stroked the front of the card.

'I love it,' she said, her eyes filled with tears.

'Oh, Rose.' I put my arm around her, giving her an affectionate squeeze. She brushed a tear away and laughed at her own sentimentality. She opened the card and a cheque fell out.

'What... no... this is too much,' Rose stuttered as she looked at the amount she'd been given.

'It's from all of us... We want you to have it.' Stella was firm. 'I know money isn't very personal, but we also know that the only thing you want is books... so we thought we'd let you choose your own!' She laughed. 'I was also wondering if you'd like to go to that literary festival in Sussex you've always talked about? I thought we could make a weekend of it in the summer?'

'That would be... so... that would be wonderful. Thank you all so much.' Rose was a reluctant public speaker. She spoke quietly when she addressed the table. She forced the words out, desperate for them to know how grateful she was.

The chatter across the table continued. It was more relaxed now. The waiter brought over a tray of shot glasses, filled to the brim with a dark liquid. Black sambuca. A tradition from our

teenage years. Everyone politely passed a glass to their neigh-
bour, groaning ever so slightly at the thought of having to do a
shot. Oliver took one of the tiny glasses and placed it in front of
him. Jack noticed. He shook his head from across the table. But
Oliver just lifted the drink and gulped down half of the
contents. He didn't once take his eyes off Jack.

'Nooo,' Stella winced as she smelt the strong alcohol. But
nobody abstained. We would be putting our differences aside
for the night. I tried not to think about how much all this would
cost.

'Three... two... one.' We all threw back our drinks at the
same time. I caught the eye of a couple at the next table. They
were eating with their young children, watching us down our
drinks. The woman fixed her face in a smile when she saw me
looking. But I knew what she was thinking, that we were too
loud, too brash, too irresponsible. She was probably right.

'We need to talk,' Jack leaned in towards me. He smelt of
sambuca and cigarettes.

'Not tonight,' I told him. I placed my napkin on the table
and got up to go to the bathroom. As I walked past the table, I
saw Oliver watching me. Staring at me with anger. He didn't
look away when he saw that I'd noticed. His eyes followed me
across the room.

My heels clipped on the warm wood floor as I headed in the
direction of the toilets. I placed my bag on the edge of the stark
white basin, staring at my reflection in the brightly lit mirror.
The door to the ladies' swung open.

'Jesus, Jack.' I took a step back. I could feel the wine and the
sambuca start to enter my bloodstream. 'I know we need to
talk... but not now, OK?' I pulled some lip gloss from my purse.
I watched Jack behind me as I applied it in the mirror.

'I don't want to talk...' He grinned, holding up a small bag of
white powder. I returned his smile, slowly pressing my glossy
lips together.

'We can't.' I laughed, spinning around to face him.

'Why not?' he asked, tilting his head to the side. Turning on his boyish charm. 'For old times' sake, eh?' he said, pulling a ten-pound note from his back pocket. Holding it up between his middle and index fingers. I paused for a moment, keeping eye contact. Before flirtatiously pulling the note from his hand.

After we'd each snorted the powder, I perched on the edge of the sink. My long bare legs were crossed. Jack leant against the doorframe of one of the cubicles. 'Why were me and you never a thing?' he asked, licking his lips suggestively.

'It's not too late,' I teased. This is what we did. It was what we'd always done. We flirted. We batted eyes at each other. We said inappropriate things and pressed our bodies close when no one was looking. It wasn't that we wanted to be together, or even that we wanted to have sex. Not really.

It was a game. A trick of the light to keep life interesting. To make us feel like we were sixteen again and anything was possible. Twin flames feeding the narcissist in each other. Jack's relationship with Lisa had never bothered me. Lisa was safe and dowdy and everything that I wasn't. I felt superior. I felt that mine and Jack's friendship was superior. That whatever happened, I would still be his number one girl.

It was why I hated Kelly. She had come along and taken him away from *us*. Me *and* Lisa. She was younger and more beautiful. Jack's head had turned in a way that I'd never seen happen with him before. I pretended my dislike was because Jack had been unfaithful. Because Kelly had somehow lured him away from his wife. The truth was that when Jack was with Lisa, it felt like he was still mine.

He took a step towards me. Our eyes danced with the danger of it. When he was just inches away from my face the toilet door burst open. It was Kelly, followed by Stella.

'Jack? What are you...?' Kelly's voice sounded high and

strangled. Stella avoided my eye and headed straight for a cubicle.

'Babe!' Jack said beckoning her into his outstretched arms. Kelly put up a warning hand. Her bottom lip quivered as she eyed my bare thighs. Exposed by my dress that had ridden up my legs. I grabbed hold of the hem and wriggled it down my body as I hopped off the basin.

'Kells.' I stumbled on the polished tiles on my high heels. 'It's not what it looks like...' I caught Jack's eye. That's when it happened. It started off as a small laugh that I hid behind my hand. Seconds later I was doubled over. Taken over by drink and drugs and the ridiculousness of the situation. The anger on Kelly's face or the sobered mortification on Jack's didn't make me stop. 'Sorry,' I mouthed as another wave of laughter rattled out of me.

'Jack!' Kelly snapped, grabbing him by the wrist and pulling him out of the toilet. I turned to face the mirror, dabbing tears from my eyes with the palm of my hand. Stella came out of the cubicle. She stood at the sink next to mine and washed her hands. My face was twisted in a wide grin, still wet from the tears. Stella looked at me like she was seeing me for the first time.

'What happened to you, Annie?' Stella asked sadly.

'Don't be like that!' I scoffed, grappling around in my bag for make-up. Looking for a way to patch up my cracking face.

'It's your daughter's eighteenth birthday. This "I don't give a shit about anyone or anything" just isn't OK any more. Everyone's tired of it, Annie... aren't you?' She dropped the paper towel she'd used to dry her hands in the bin beside me and left the room.

As the door creaked closed, the silence felt deafening. The bright artificial lights burnt the backs of my eyes. I needed water. I needed to sit down or sleep or give myself a rest from my own intrusive thoughts. Stella was right. Everyone was tired.

I was too. But it was too late to change. I wouldn't know how, even if I wanted to.

My phone fell out of my bag as I desperately grabbed at tubes and pots of make-up. It clattered into the basin. Three missed calls and another voicemail. I hit 'play' and put the message on loudspeaker. I gripped the edge of the porcelain until my fingers hurt.

'This is a message for Ms. Annie Turner. My name is Jennifer Hawkins. I'm a senior case handler at Beech Croft Bank. I am calling in relation to your missed mortgage payments over the last few months on your property—West Mill.' I felt the colour drain from my face. 'We have tried unsuccessfully to contact you. The repossession order is now underway. You should have received court documents.' I stabbed at the phone trying to disconnect her voice.

'Ms Turner, I would appreciate it if you could return my call. Unfortunately, this will be happening with or without your involvement.' I rested my elbows on the sink and sunk my head into my hands. It was too late. It didn't matter what I did now. It was too late.

CHAPTER THIRTY-EIGHT

DCI MELANIE PRICE

The day after

Jack's eyes were circled with black rings and red from crying. He looked like he'd slept in his clothes. They were thin and crumpled, as though they hadn't left his body in a few days.

A few minutes ago, Simon had brought a cup of coffee for him to the interview room. He sat across from me at the small plastic-covered table. The sort of table they used to use at primary school. Scratched and chipped with the beginnings of a wobble. I watched as he drank from the steamy cardboard cup. Each sip burnt his mouth, then he'd forget and do it again.

We'd picked him up from the campsite this morning. He'd looked almost relieved when we helped him into the back of the car. A break from their collective grief. An end to the worry of when we'd be coming to get him.

Jack had always been larger than life at college. People used that phrase a lot, but he really was. A caricature of a confident person. A loud unstoppable force. Nothing fazed him. His voice would carry down the halls of the 1950s school building. He had an energy that was infectious. The most outgoing of the tight-knit group. Him and Annie, they were the same.

It's virtually impossible not to be in awe of that as someone younger. Someone outside of their inner circle. Like a celebrity that walked among us. Seeing him now, in front of me, in tatters; it was like watching a faded Hollywood star.

'Interview with Jack Morris commencing at sixteen-zero-three p.m. on the eighteenth of August.' I spoke clearly for the recording. Simon sat very still on the seat next to me. Jack's face twitched as I said the words. 'How was your relationship with Annie?' I asked.

'I loved Annie,' he replied simply. He jutted out his chin, which was covered in several days of dark stubble. 'We all did.'

'Jack, we just want to build up a picture of what happened at the campsite over the last few days. We need to know who did this.' I spoke calmly. He nodded and took another sip of his coffee.

'Did you ever have a sexual relationship with Annie?' I asked. We locked eyes for a moment. His were pale ice-blue. They were hard to look away from. I resisted the urge to shift in my seat. He shook his head. I nodded to the tape recorder.

'No. It wasn't like that. It was intense,' he admitted, wringing his hands together. 'But we never had sex.'

'Did you want to?' I'm not sure why I asked. It wasn't relevant. I felt like I was getting embroiled in these people's lives. He fixed me with a cold stare.

'I'm married.' He spoke with no emotion in his voice.

'Yes... Kelly?' I thumbed through the pile of documents in front of me, pulling out a single sheet of paper. 'You and Kelly have been married for... two years now?' I read from my notes. He nodded reluctantly, wondering where I was going with this. 'Before that you were married to a Lisa Morris? You've got two sons, Finn and Oliver.'

'Is this really necessary?' Jack snapped.

'I'm just checking that we have the correct information. Your youngest son, Oliver, came with you on this trip. Where is he now?'

Jack cleared his throat. 'He's back at the campsite with Kelly.'

I nodded. 'How is your relationship with your son?'

'Will you be checking on my relationship with everybody in my life?' Jack pushed a hand through his thinning hair in frustration.

'Yes,' I replied coldly. 'If we need to.'

'I understand that Oliver has had some trouble at school,' I told him. His head snapped up from the desk. He wasn't expecting this.

'Ollie is a good boy. He's just a kid. He got into a bit of bother at school... it was sorted, it's over.' His eyes darted between me and Simon, scared of what we might be thinking.

'It was only sorted because Oliver was expelled, isn't that right?' I asked. He let out a deep sigh.

'The divorce was hard on Ollie. It was tough on both of them... but Ollie...' He rubbed his hand across his stubble. It made an abrasive sound. '...I don't know. He's fifteen. Do you have kids?' Jack looked at me, his guard finally down. I didn't answer. He carried on. 'Teenagers are hard. When they were babies and toddlers, I spent all this time wishing they were older. Wishing they could just get bigger so it would be easier. Then they got bigger... and it's the hardest bit.' Me and Simon listened silently.

'A couple of months ago, I got a call from Ollie's school. He'd got into a fight. You know, normal kid's stuff. Only, it turns out it wasn't really a fight.' Jack pressed his knuckles into his eye sockets. 'Ollie had beaten this kid up. He was barely ten. A small, skinny little thing.' Now that he'd got talking, his London accent had become stronger. I wondered if he'd spent time there when he was younger, or if it was just something he'd picked up as an adult.

'Ahh, man... you should have seen this kid's face.' Tears welled up in Jack's eyes. 'I don't know how he could have done it. That isn't how he was brought up. Me and Lisa, we might have had our problems, but we love our kids.' I nodded, offering him a weak smile. 'The head teacher said it was the last straw. There'd been other minor issues and they didn't want to work with us to sort them out.' He shrugged his shoulders. 'But there's been nothing like that since. Ollie feels terrible about it. He's not a bad kid.' Jack pointed at the tabletop and started stabbing it with his index finger. 'Ollie had *nothing* to do with what happened to Annie.' His voice was getting louder.

'Jack,' I said calmly. 'Nobody is suggesting that Oliver had anything to do with...'

'Bullshit. That's why I'm here. You lot are desperately trying to pin this on somebody before we all go back to London.'

'I can assure you...' Simon interjected primly. I held my hand up, trying to establish some calm.

I tried a different direction. 'Jack, we understand that you invested a large sum of money into Annie's PR company?'

'I did,' he replied cautiously.

'We also understand that you are facing some financial problems.' Jack snorted.

'That's one way of putting it,' he said drily.

'How would *you* put it?' I was getting tired of playing games. We were quickly running out of time. I was running out of patience.

Jack gnawed at his bottom lip. 'I invested in Annie's company a year or so ago. It all seemed so perfect. Have you seen photos of her country house?' I shook my head. 'Jesus, it's beautiful. Like something out of a movie. It's just paradise, you now? Just staying there, you really feel like you've arrived. I've known Annie my whole adult life, since we were kids. Even I was taken in by that place.' His voice sounded far away as memories came flooding back.

'She used to have celebrities there every weekend. Big A-listers... She had a private chef and staff that helped you with your bags. Me and Kelly were blown away when we saw it. When Annie asked me to invest, I thought she was joking. I'm an estate agent. I'm good at my job, but at the end of the day I'm small fry compared to the people she's in bed with. It seemed like a gift she was handing me. I barely even looked at the paperwork, I was so scared she'd change her mind. I thought it was the beginning of something huge.' Jack squinted slightly. Like he had a nervous tick. I could hear the emotion in his voice. The disappointment that life hadn't turned out the way he'd hoped.

'Is that what's caused your financial problems?' I asked gently.

He shook his head. 'I wish it were as simple as that. I was convinced that I was onto a winner. That if Annie could live the way she was... then I'd soon be living it up too. I borrowed more money. Lots of money against the house. I thought this was a sure thing. I'd never been more certain of anything in my life.'

'Did Kelly know that you'd invested all your money into Annie's firm?'

'No. There was no way I could tell her. Kelly hated Annie...' He paused for a moment as he realised what he'd said. '...It goes back to when they worked together. I was going to tell her as soon as the money started rolling in. I knew she wouldn't have a problem with it then.'

'But the money didn't start rolling in?' I asked. He shook his head.

'Not only that but the repayments on the amount I borrowed is more than I earn.' He looked up at the ceiling and took a deep breath. 'I bought cars and expensive holidays, sent the kids to a fancy private school... we built an extension...' He shook his head in disbelief. 'Kelly just thought I was doing well at work. How the hell am I going to tell her that I've lost it all?' His bottom lip quivered.

'Would it have made a difference if Annie had given you back your investment?' I asked.

'No. It would have given me a bit more time. But it's too late now. I'm in too deep,' he told us sadly.

I took a deep breath and ran the end of my pen down my notes. 'Can you tell us about your last night together?'

'At the restaurant?' he asked, frowning slightly. I nodded. 'It was a mess.' He rubbed the palm of his hand across his forehead. 'Annie was drunk. We all were. It all kicked off and we were thrown out by the owner.' He shrugged as if it was nothing unusual.

'You argued with Annie?' Simon asked.

'Everyone argued with Annie.' He snorted.

I lifted a sheet of paper in front of me. 'The autopsy suggests that Annie took drugs that night. That she might have taken cocaine.' I paused a moment before asking, 'Did you supply the drugs to her, Jack?'

'Shit,' he said and buried his face in his hands. The only sound was his sobs that echoed around the walls of the empty interview room.

'What do you think?' Simon asked when we were out of earshot.

'I think he's going to have a lot of explaining to do,' I said drily. 'But I don't think he did it.'

'He had motive... opportunity?' Simon questioned.

'He did. But he also knows it wasn't Annie's fault he's in the position he's in—not entirely.' We both pushed through the double swing doors that led to the incident room.

'So?' Simon asked as we rounded the corner.

'So, I think we're no closer to finding out who killed Annie than we were at the start of this.'

CHAPTER THIRTY-NINE

CHARLOTTE

The day before

I sat at the back of the long pine table. Tucked into the far corner of the restaurant. I was pinned between Theo and Tristen. Rose and Annie were just across the table from me. The room was dimly lit with a warm orange hue. It hid the animosity that had built up within the group. The gold confetti and brightly coloured balloons masked the darkness that had crept in over the last couple of days. Everyone could feel it. Everyone was just trying to make it nice for Rose.

Theo was bored. He kept gathering small handfuls of the plastic number eighteens and throwing them in the air. Hitting his knife that rested on the table with his adult-sized fork. He'd already had two soft drinks whilst we waited for starters. One of them was a Coke. I was already regretting it. He was only being silly, just playing. But the noise of the metal cutlery clanging together jolted right through me. I could feel the irritation prickling up my neck. 'Stop it,' I snapped quietly, resting my hands abruptly on his to stop the banging. I felt everyone's eyes on me.

We all took a shot of sambuca. Jack had insisted. He'd

become more animated since he found out that Annie was paying for dinner. I pretended to drink it. Sipping the tiniest drop of dark alcohol, before hiding it behind my wineglass.

Annie left the table. Jack followed a couple of minutes later. I looked up to see if Kelly had noticed, but she was deep in conversation. It felt like something was about to happen. A rumbling energy coming from underground, rising to the surface.

Oliver sat a few chairs away. His oily hair hung in his eyes as he looked down at the table. He was holding a steak knife. The tip of the blade was pointed into the white fabric table-cloth. The end of the handle was balanced on the palm of his hand. I glanced down at Theo. He was watching Oliver with interest. Still shocked by his behaviour at the lake earlier today.

Kelly looked over at him. Scanning the table for Jack. 'Don't do that, Oliver,' she told him. Trying to keep her voice light and her smile engaging. 'You'll damage the table.'

'Will I?' he asked. His hand sunk lower. Turning his wrist back and forth, grinding the blade further into the wood.

'You'll have to go back to the tent if you can't behave,' she said, her smile faltering. Craning her neck for any sign of her husband.

'Who's going to make me... you?' He laughed. Oliver lifted his shot glass with his spare hand. Drinking the last of the black liquid in one gulp. He winced as he placed it down on the table. Kelly turned away. Keen to end the scene.

I tuned back to the conversation next to me. 'We should definitely meet up in the autumn for a hike,' Nate suggested to Tristen when he realised they shared a love of the outdoors.

'That'd be great—Charlotte's not really one for climbing.' He laughed. I reached under the table and pulled out two presents wrapped in pink tissue paper. I'd waited all day to give it to Rose when Annie wasn't around. It wasn't that it was a secret. I just knew Rose wouldn't want to share this with her.

I passed the presents over the table. Rose took them quietly, her eyes danced with gratitude. Nobody seemed to notice. They carried on their conversations as she gently slid the paper from the larger of the two presents. She looked at me and smiled, lifting the soft wool to her face. It was a blanket.

When we lived at West Mill together, Rose would always cover herself in a green tartan blanket that she'd found in one of the antique chests. I can still picture her, curled up on the threadbare sofa by the French windows, draped in the musty green checked fabric. It had to be thrown away in the end. It had been destroyed by moths and the wool was so thin in places that it tore. The blanket I'd just given her looked exactly like it. I'd seen it on a stall in the local street market and knew it would be perfect.

Rose opened the smaller of the presents. There was bubble wrap underneath the pink paper. She carefully pulled it away. It was a clay tile with a small handprint in the middle. 'I made it!' Theo called across the table, before hiding his outburst behind his hands. We both laughed affectionately. I felt bad for having been annoyed with him.

'You did *not* make this!' Rose joked.

'I did. I did make it!' he pleaded, his eyes suddenly wide and serious. Worried that Rose might not believe him.

'It's absolutely beautiful,' she told him. 'I will keep it next to my bed and every time you visit you have to put your hand inside the mould to see how much it's grown.' Theo nodded happily.

Rose thanked me. Her eyes telling me what her words couldn't. That it was just what she wanted. That she felt seen. At the end of the day, it's all any of us really want. She gently wrapped the tile back in its protective bubble, sliding it between the layers of woollen blanket. Rose carefully tucked it under her chair, and we shared a look. Rose would not be showing the gifts to Annie. We both knew it. I'm not sure why, we just did.

I looked round at Tristen. Hoping that he'd watched Rose open her presents. That he would see how well I'd done. Even after all this time I still looked for validation from him. I still wanted him to tell me that I'd done good.

Kelly and Jack came back from the toilets. She marched ahead of him, looking like a runway model in her tailored trousers and a jacket with a plunging neckline. They'd obviously had a fight. Kelly turned to Jack and hissed, before taking a seat across the table from him with a practised smile. He muttered something unintelligible under his breath. Jack's pupils were huge and black. He looked unhinged, like he'd taken something. Knowing Jack, he probably had.

The noise around the table increased as the wine flowed. People interrupted each other. Speaking loudly over stories from the past, as we all remembered the old times.

Theo had got bored sitting with the adults. He'd wandered over to the table next to us. The young couple were trying to get their toddler daughter to eat her dinner. She was more interested in the paper and crayons in front of her. I could see how weary they were. Theo wasn't helping. He'd picked up some colouring pencils and had started to draw his own picture. I knew I should go over there, but I just didn't have it in me. I took a long drink of my white wine.

Tristen saw. He moved purposely over to the table and threw a laughing Theo over his shoulder. The family smiled politely. I could tell that we were annoying them. Ruining their already irritating dinner. Tristen sat with Theo on his lap, carrying on his conversation with Nate. Being a dad seemed to come effortlessly to him. I suppose it was easier if you only had to do it for a few weeks of the year.

I sat sipping my wine. I knew I needed to stop. I wasn't really a drinker. The alcohol was going quickly to my head. It was the only thing getting me through tonight. Kelly crouched down behind my chair. She'd been moving around the group, clutching a fizzing gin and tonic in her hand. Her long red painted nails tapped the side of the glass, like she was about to make speech. 'How are you?' she asked patronisingly. A cloud of expensive perfume circled her. She tipped her head to one side, sticking out her bottom lip a little. It was like she was visiting a sick relative.

'I'm fine, thanks,' I replied through gritted teeth.

'Aww, Theo,' she squealed as she spotted him wriggling on Tristen's lap. 'My turn!' she said, placing her drink on the table and lifting Theo into the air. Her slender fingers wrapped around his underarms as she placed him on her hip. Theo looked just as surprised as me. Kelly took the seat next to me. She kept looking at Jack as she bounced Theo awkwardly on her knee. He was paying no attention. 'I can't wait until we have our own,' she spoke loudly to the table as she stroked the back of Theo's dark curly hair. Showing Jack what a good mother she'd make. Showing him how maternal she is.

'Well, if you're as good at being a mother as you are at being a stepmother... that's going to be one *lucky* baby.' Oliver laughed bitterly as he shook his head. Kelly acted like she hadn't heard him.

I pretended that I hadn't noticed that Theo's muddy wet shoe had made a dirty smear down her immaculate white trouser suit. Usually, I would have been horrified. I would have made a big scene of apologising. Trying to help get the stain out. Offering to pay the dry-cleaning bill. I felt immune to it all tonight.

The waiter brought out the main courses just as Annie returned from the toilet. She was unsteady on her heels as she came up behind Rose and wrapped her arms around her neck. I watched as she tipped backwards, only managing to stay upright because she was clinging onto her daughter. Her eyes looked like Jack's. Wide and absent. I wondered what they'd been up to in there. From the look on Kelly's face, she was wondering too.

Steaming plates of food were handed around the table as everyone remembered what they ordered. A seafood spaghetti was placed in front of me. Chilli-covered prawns were piled high on a creamy sauce. It looked incredible, but I'd lost my appetite. Kelly returned to her chair as soon as the food arrived. Theo waved his fork in the air with happiness when his sausage and beans were placed in front of him. I cut up his sausages so slowly that he asked me to stop and did it himself. I felt like I was on a tiny boat, drifting away from everybody. Like their voices were getting quieter. It was a feeling I'd had before. It was a feeling that scared me.

I pushed my spaghetti absently around my plate. Nobody had noticed that I hadn't taken a single bite. The lights seemed to be getting dimmer. I wondered how anyone could see their food properly. The thought made me laugh. I hid it behind my hand, but I know that Tristen was watching me. Tristen had seen this all before.

I watched everybody move as though in slow motion. Rose leaned towards Ollie. She looked like she'd asked him about his food. He smiled and nodded. Annie drunkenly pulled on Rose's arm. Yanking her away from the conversation. She was confused, but waited for her mum to explain. 'Do you know what he did?' she pointed a finger in Ollie's direction. Annie thought that she whispering, but her slurred words were at a volume that everyone could hear. Rose looked panicked. She connected desperately with the eyes around the table, as they tuned in to her words.

'Apparently, he beat up a kid... a reeaally little kid.' Her head slumped onto her propped-up elbow. *'That's* why he got expelled from his fancy school.' Her mouth worked to articulate all the words.

'Mum!' Rose said firmly, looking desperately in the direction of Ollie. His face flushed crimson. He looked over at Jack. His expression gave away how hurt he was.

'What? Mate... I didn't say anything... I promise.' Jack dropped his cutlery and raised the palms of his hands up in innocence. Ollie didn't say a word. He got up from the table and stormed out of the restaurant. 'Did you do this?' Jack yelled across the table at a pale-faced Kelly. She flinched.

'Whoa whoa,' said Nate, jumping to her defence. 'Look, there's no need...'

'Stay out of it, Nate. This has nothing to do with you,' he snapped. Jack turned his attention back to Kelly. 'Did you do this?' he shouted. Kelly gave a very small nod of her head. There was a loud bang as Jack's fist came crashing down on the table. The plates and glasses shuddered under the impact. He looked over at Annie, who was slumped in her seat, unaware of the chaos she'd caused. Before he could launch into an attack on Annie, Rose stood up and took a step forward.

'Instead of starting a fight with everyone at the table. Maybe you should go after him and see if he's OK.' Rose spoke so calmly and so quietly I wasn't sure if Jack heard her. He nodded obediently and walked out of the restaurant to look for his son.

It felt like someone had thrown a bucket of ice-cold water over me. Everything had suddenly come into sharp focus and was moving faster than my eyes could follow. I needed to go home. I couldn't do this any more. Whatever happens, me and Theo are leaving tomorrow. I don't care what she does. I don't care what the consequences are. I don't want to do this any more.

CHAPTER FORTY

STELLA

The day before

Annie was drunk and dishevelled and only just about holding it together. I know she didn't want to tell Charlotte about me and Tristen, but she would if she was desperate enough. Tonight, Annie looked desperate enough.

I was sat between Kelly and Nate. Kelly kept getting up from her chair, chatting her way around the table. Nate was deep in conversation with Tristen. I tried not to feel uncomfortable about my worlds colliding. But sweat tingled across my lower back. I squirmed in my chair as I watched them laugh easily together. I knew this would happen before we came here. I knew it was a risk. It's why I'd left it so long to introduce them. But seeing them here together, turned my stomach.

'How's everything going?' Kelly asked, sliding back into the chair beside me.

'Mmm hmm.' I smiled, picking at the pie I had in front of me. I can't remember what the filling was. I'm sure it was great. Tonight, everything had a sour taste to it.

'Do you think everything's OK with Charlotte and Tristen?'

she said, leaning in close. Feigning concern. Kelly was topless underneath her white jacket. It slid open as she leant over, exposing most of her breast. Kelly didn't seem to mind or notice.

'I think they're fine,' I said coldly, placing some of the bitter sauce on my tongue.

'It's just... they're not really...' Just at that moment, everyone fell silent as Annie started to talk.

'Apparently, he beat up a kid...' She spoke in a loud, whisper which had drawn everyone's attention. I felt my stomach clench as I waited to hear what else she had to say. I turned to Kelly. She had gone a pale shade of grey.

'Did you do this,' Jack shouted suddenly across the table. The restaurant fell silent. I could feel the faces around the room on us. I put my hand on Kelly's arm.

'Whoa whoa,' said Nate, rising protectively from his chair. Before anyone really knew what was happening, Ollie and Jack had left the restaurant. Kelly looked like she was going to cry.

'He's never going to forgive me for this,' she told me in a shaky voice.

'Of course he will,' I said without much confidence.

The gentle hum of the restaurant had returned to a normal level. I could still feel the gaze and judgement of the tables around us. I didn't blame them. I would judge us too.

Tristen got up from the table. I watched as he walked towards the door of the restaurant. He left, pacing in circles on the patio outside. I pretended for a minute that I couldn't see him. Then he waved. Just slightly, but enough that I was worried that he might draw attention to himself. To us. I got up from the table and left the restaurant. If anyone was watching, they would assume we were going to find Jack and Oliver.

We stood beside the big glass entrance doors. Just far enough away that nobody in the restaurant could see us. A clear awning covered the patio. Rain hammered down steadily on the shelter, spilling over the edges. Landing noisily on the stone ground. We had to stand back from the edge to keep from getting splashed.

'What are you doing?' My voice was hoarse with anxiety.

'I need to speak to you.' He raised his hands as if he were about to place them on my waist. Like old times. I flinched ever so slightly.

'There's nothing to say.' I felt like he had his hands around my neck. Gently squeezing the life out of me. I took a step back until I was pressed against the wall. I felt behind me. Fingering the rough brickwork.

Tristen had always been so controlled. It wasn't just because he was in the military. It was something he'd always had. Measured and cautious in everything he did. Tonight, there was an abandon to him. His actions were careless and sloppy and it scared me. 'I love you,' he told me. Loud enough that someone might hear. Jack and Oliver were still outside somewhere. 'I love you' had never been something that we said. Never something we'd admitted to. It was a line. We'd never crossed it.

It felt like we'd reached the top of the tallest mountain and I'd slipped over the edge. Hanging on by the very tips of my fingers.

'You can't say that,' I told him, shocked.

'Why?' he asked. Louder this time. 'It's true.' I wanted to put my hands over his mouth. I wanted to silence him. I wanted him to keep our dirty little secret inside of him, like I had. That's what it was. That's what it felt like. A dirty little secret. Even after all these years. Even though it was over, I didn't want Nate to know. Because once he saw the dirt, he would never be able to unsee it. He would never look at me the same way again.

'Annie knows. Not just about that night twenty-five years ago. She's knows about the affair, Tristen...' I hissed. 'She tried to blackmail me.' It was my last attempt at trying to reason with him. I regretted the words as soon as they were out of my mouth.

'What? How can she...?' He took a step back in shock. 'She *blackmailed* you?' His voice was close to a shout.

'Shhhh,' I pleaded, looking desperately at the restaurant to see if anyone had heard. I'm not sure that I'd ever seen him as angry as this. 'Stop, stop... please stop,' I begged harder than I had ever begged for anything in my life. He must have been able to see the panic on my face. Everything felt so out of control. The most volatile people in the group at this moment, knew the worst thing that I had ever done.

'She can't get away with this,' he said trying to walk away. I put my body in front of his. Trying to block him. Trying to reason with him.

'She can... It's over,' I told him. 'It's over.'

'No.' He brushed past my shoulder, trying to go back into the restaurant. I grabbed his arm in an attempt to stop him. He threw my hand away so violently I lost balance. I stumbled. My back hit the wall. At the moment my body impacted, Nate was there. I hadn't even seen the door open. He was looking at me in shock and confusion. He thought that Tristen pushed me.

'Are you OK?' Nate asked. I nodded, unable to find my voice. 'What the fuck are you doing?' Nate never swore. He rarely even raised his voice. The men stood in front of one another. So close that from the angle I was at, it looked like their noses were almost touching. 'I asked you what you think you're doing?' Nate's voice was terrifyingly quiet and controlled.

'This doesn't concern you,' Tristen told him, looking over at me.

'At lot of things haven't concerned me tonight,' said Nate, rubbing his thumb slowly across his bottom lip. 'Yet here I am.' He shrugged. I saw all the muscles in his upper arm flex with tension through his thin T-shirt.

'Nate, come on,' I pleaded.

'If you *ever* lay a finger on her...' he told Tristen. I slipped my hand around Nate's waist. Trying to pull him away. That's when it happened. Tristen punched Nate in the face. He side-swiped his jaw, almost knocking him off his feet. I heard a high-pitched scream. It took me a moment to realise that the sound had come from my own mouth.

At that moment, a family walked past us, trying to make their way into the building with their young children. The look of horror on their faces seemed to mirror my own. The woman had to jump a little to the side to avoid crashing straight into Nate as he reeled from the impact.

'I'm so sorry...' I said, reaching out a hand in apology. They ignored us. Hurrying inside, holding tightly to their children's hands. As they opened the door, I heard the loud bustle of the restaurant.

Then the singing started.

'Happy birthday to you, happy birthday to you...' I looked through the glass. The waiters had brought out a cake covered in brightly burning candles. They were singing along with the rest of the table. But as the three of us stumbled back into the restaurant, Tristen holding the hand he'd used to punch and Nate covering his jaw, it was clear that nobody was looking at Rose. Nobody was watching the cake as it was gently lowered onto the table in front of her. All eyes were on us.

'Happy birthday, dear Rose...'

I couldn't see the damage on Nate's face. We stood awkwardly behind the waiters, attempting to join in the chorus. I watched as Nate's eyes flit around the table. All of his thoughts slotting slowly together. Adding up what he'd just seen and heard. Adding up what it meant.

Tristen took his seat at the table next to Charlotte just as the singing finished.

'Happy birthday to you.' Everyone held on to the last note for a few seconds. Nobody wanted the song to end. We didn't want to deal with the silence that would follow. Rose blew out her candles and there was a ripple of applause around the table.

I searched desperately for a place to sit. Nate's arm dropped by his side, and I saw his face. A deep purple mark covered the lower half of his jaw. I reached for his hand, but it wasn't there.

'That's it. I want you all out!' A man's voice boomed through the restaurant. The acoustics echoed off the vaulted wooden ceiling. Every person in the room turned to stare. It was the owner of the campsite, Tony. The angry man from the other night who had thrown water onto our fire. He was striding across the dining room with a determined look on his face. Families froze as he passed. Putting down their drinks and cutlery to watch the scene that was unfolding.

'Out!' he shouted again as he reached our table.

'It's you!' Annie laughed, pointing an unsteady finger at the man. 'Don't you ever take a day off?' She snorted, looking around the room for laughs. But nobody was laughing.

'Disgusting behaviour. Shouting and swearing... I've just had a complaint that there were two men *fighting*.' He pointed outside. Everyone looked at me and Nate, who stood lamely behind the chairs. 'You people have no idea how to behave... you should be ashamed of yourselves.'

Everyone stood up silently to leave. There was nothing we could say to defend ourselves. We all shuffled single file out of the restaurant, into the dark rainy night. Not even Annie said a word.

Those of us who'd brought them, threw coats over our shoulders, protecting ourselves from the downpour that was gathering pace. I hid inside my hood. Staring straight ahead at the back of Nate's jacket a few metres ahead of me. We hadn't spoken.

Everyone walked with their family. The only sound was the rain as it bounced off the tarmac road. Most off the lights were out across the campsite. A couple of dim flashlights waved around the shadowed canvas pyramids below us.

'I'm going to brush my teeth,' I told Nate when we got back to the tent. I left before he could reply. I couldn't bear to look at him. I couldn't bear to find out if he knew. If he'd heard my argument with Tristen. If he was going to look at me differently forever.

I walked to the sound of raindrops tapping on my plastic mac. I pulled down my hood when I went inside the cold brick shower block. Standing in front of the mirrors under the white garish light. My hair was flattened by the damp. I drew my fingers down my face. Trying to drag some life into the flesh. I was a deathly shade of pale.

'Are you tired?' I looked up, surprised that I wasn't alone. Charlotte was stood by the door watching me, with a strange sort of smile.

'Yes.' I tried to swallow but I couldn't. 'Are you?' She ignored my question.

'Did you think I didn't know?' she asked, resting her head against the doorframe.

'Know what?' I asked. I could feel bile rising in my stomach.

'About you and Tristen.' Her voice was cold and calm. 'I knew from the very first time you slept together. It was written all over your faces. It was the night I was attacked. That didn't stop you though, did it? Not the coma... or the missing teeth or the broken bones I had. You carried it on for years, didn't you?'

'Charlotte, you have to believe me...'

'I don't have to believe a single word that comes out of your mouth,' she said quietly, before walking back out into the rain.

I burst through the door of the empty toilet stall and threw up.

CHAPTER FORTY-ONE

ANNIE

The day before

The rain was beating down hard on my waterproof jacket. Drops fell from my nose. I licked the water off my lips. Everyone was clamouring to get ready for bed. To climb into their tents and forget about tonight. I didn't want to go inside. I didn't want Rose's birthday celebration to be over. That this was it. All Rose had ever wanted was peace. All I had given her was chaos.

Stella walked in the direction of the toilet and Charlotte followed. I considered going after them. Linking arms with them both as we laughed our way across the campsite. But it didn't feel like something I could do any more. It felt like all the bridges had been broken and burned. It felt like the end. That this trip had drawn a line under all the nostalgia and the memories. That they would all be put where our friendship belonged. In the past.

The coke I'd taken earlier with Jack hadn't worn off yet. My skin tingled. Like I'd been stung by a thousand tiny wasps. I moved my weight from foot to foot, watching as my feet splashed down on the muddy grass. Trying to reconcile my body to my mind. My limbs felt alive, but my head felt foggy and anxious. I looked over at Jack, who was busy helping Kelly secure the entrance to their tent against the rain. He had his head down as he pulled at the entrance ties. There was no indication that Jack was still suffering the effects of the drugs. But he always was better at pretending than me.

There was no sign of Oliver. A fuzzy memory of him storming out of the restaurant fluttered across my muddled mind.

'Mum, it's time for bed,' Rose told me, wrapping her long slender fingers around my arm and guiding me towards the tent. I nodded.

'Good night, everyone,' I called to the dark shapes of people around me. There was a collective muttering of goodbyes. I could feel their resentment. Even after what had happened tonight with Stella and Tristen, it would be me that they'd blame. Me that they'd direct their anger at. Even through the bleak curtain of rain- and my drug-addled state I could feel it.

I didn't used to care what they thought. I didn't used to care what anyone thought. Not giving a shit was my superpower. It's what enabled me to be brave. It's what made me feel like I could do anything. People's judgement was always something that had spurred me on. I'd used it to build ladders. Ladders to climb high above the resentment and rancour. Not tonight. Tonight, it was crushing me.

Me and Rose went into the yurt and let the canvas door fall behind us. The muffled sound of the falling rain was the only thing that felt comforting. My wet dress clung to my legs, sending droplets of water down my thighs.

Rose silently undressed and changed into her pyjamas. The only light in the tent was from her phone. Lying face up on the covers at the end of her bed. I stared at the fabric ceiling, with my hood still up, watching the shadows dance across the milky-coloured roof.

I was too wired to sleep, too tired to undress. The effect of the drugs and the wine were coursing through me, but it felt like it might have just got started. Like there was more to come.

Rose picked up a thick hardback book that she'd been reading all week, using her phone light to scan the pages. My side of the room fell into darkness. 'Did you have a good night?' I asked. Unexpected emotion gathered around my words.

'I did. Thank you,' she said, offering me a smile. Her eyes looked sad. Maybe she was just tired. I would have to tell her about the house. Not tonight, not on her birthday, but I would have to tell her soon. Staying in the house a few days ago was the first time Rose had been there in over a year. I still knew she'd be devastated. That house had always had her heart.

My head ached and my tongue felt thick. I remembered some of the things I'd done tonight. Some of the things I'd said. 'I'm sorry if I embarrassed you.' I slurred the words. An image of Oliver's angry face crept back. I might have had something to do with it. I tried to smile at Rose but the muscles on my face felt numb. I felt like I was sitting in a cold empty bath. Watching the last of the water seep away.

'I had a lovely night. Oliver will be fine. Jack needs to do a better job of looking after him,' she told me. I climbed under the covers in my thin T-shirt. My teeth chattered and my toes felt like ice.

'I'm not sure I ever looked after you. Not properly.' I glanced over at her. The outline of her curls blurred as I tried to focus on her face. 'You've always been pretty great at looking after yourself.'

'You always did the best you could,' she told me kindly. 'We can talk tomorrow—get some sleep.' I huddled into the duvet and the cold damp sheets. Rose put her book down and turned out the light on her phone.

'I love you,' I said into the darkness.

'I love you too,' she replied.

CHAPTER FORTY-TWO

DCI MELANIE PRICE

Two days after

They were eating their breakfast when me and Simon arrived at the campsite the next morning. The salty sea mist hung in the air. Pockets of fog floated weightlessly along the road. Autumn didn't feel far away, just peeking around the corner. The cold breeze and light drizzle seemed to be mocking the group and their attempt at outdoor living.

Stella and Charlotte sat on camping chairs. Huddled protectively around Rose in front of wet black embers. All that remained from a fire that was extinguished days ago. They all clasped mugs of tea. The liquid had been left to go cold and grey, but no one had it in them to relinquish their cup.

They were layered with clothes: joggers and hoodies and boots. Thick socks wedged awkwardly into sandals. None of them looked like they'd slept. Their hair was wild and dishevelled. Their eyes were rimmed with sadness. Rose looked at me desperately. The expression on her face asked a hundred questions at once. I'd seen that look many times before. It was a look

I saw a lot when I worked as a family liaison officer. You were their lifeline, their only hope of getting answers.

I'd worked on cases when there had been no conviction and cases where there was one. It was always the same. The realisation that it didn't change anything. Whilst answers provided an opportunity for some sort of closure, it was also the extinguisher of hope. As long as no one was caught for Annie's murder, Rose would still have a tiny flame of hope burning inside of her. Hope that what she was feeling could somehow be lessened by the arrest of someone. Hope that there was a light at the end of the tunnel. I knew that any arrest would just be a reminder of the foreverness of grief. Especially for Rose. If we made an arrest, it would be one of her friends. Friends who had been like family to her mum. It would be someone whom she'd known her whole life.

Jack and Kelly and Tristen emerged from their tents. 'Good morning,' I said, walking over to the sombre group of women. 'I'm sorry to disturb you so early,' I told them. I really was. Pale faces gazed up at me blankly as I pulled my notebook from my bag. Simon stood beside me, his shoulders hunched. His hands wedged deep in the pockets of his thick overcoat.

'Stella, we're going to need to talk to you. It's nothing to worry about, just routine. Are you OK to come down to the station?' She nodded. Her skin looked washed out, like every bit of emotion had been used up.

'I don't understand why you're doing this,' Rose whispered in a croaky voice. Her heart looked broken.

'We have to speak to everyone. It's the only way to build up a picture...'

'I know, but why her? Why Stella?' Her big eyes brimmed with tears. 'Why not someone else?' she asked. Her gaze flickered over at the small group by the tent: Tristen and Kelly and Jack. It was only for a moment, but long enough for me to see anger flash across her face.

'It's OK,' Stella told her, touching Rose's knee briefly with a trembling hand. 'We will all need to speak to them. They need to know the truth if they're going to catch the person who did this to Annie.' Her voice faltered as she spoke her name. She got up unsteadily from the chair. 'Have you looked into what happened to Charlotte?' she asked me suddenly. Her expression was fixed and determined. Like she'd been building up to saying it out loud. The group collectively froze. The shock at what Stella had said hung thickly in the air.

'I'm sorry, Charlotte. I know we don't talk about it. I know none of us have *ever* talked about it, not properly... but we have to. What happened to Annie is just too... similar.' A tear ran down her face as she finished her emotional plea. Charlotte said nothing. Her mouth opened, but no words came out.

Stella turned to me and took a deep breath. Trying to draw strength into her body as she gathered up the courage to tell me what nobody else had been able to. 'When we were at college, Charlotte was attacked. It happened one night in a car park... A man came at her from behind. She nearly died.' Stella looked at Charlotte. She put her hand to her mouth as her shoulders shook with sobs.

I looked at Simon. This was the first he'd heard of it too. 'Where did this happen?' I asked Charlotte directly. She lifted her gaze from the ground. Her voice was so small, I couldn't make out the words. She looked at Stella for help.

'It happened just down the road from here. It happened in Porthaven... The same injuries as Annie... and they never caught him,' Stella told us. 'It *can't* be a coincidence,' she said, her pitch rising an octave.

'And this was reported to the police at the time?' I asked, scribbling in my book.

'Yes!' There was a desperation to Stella that I hadn't seen before.

'Nobody was ever arrested?' I clarified, watching as the

energy of the group shifted. Some looked relieved that it was finally out in the open—others, like Rose, looked like this was the first time she'd heard of the attack.

'No. The police didn't seem to do anything... Annie even went to the police at one point to complain about the lack of action. What if there's a link? What if it's someone who knew us back then?' Stella looked close to tears.

'A lot of time has passed between the attacks. I understand that you're concerned. But it would be *very* unlikely that it's someone from your past who has targeted both Charlotte and Annie... so many years apart. Unless you feel that there's been a specific threat over this time... a stalker or a...' Rose cut across my words.

'What if it's not someone from their past? What if it's someone in their life *now*? Someone who attacked them both...?' Rose let the sentence hang in the air. Her face fixed on a spot in the middle distance.

'When can we leave?' Tristen called over gruffly. It was abrupt and out of place. Especially as we were discussing a physical attack on his wife. 'We have a child, the weather is bloody awful... quite honestly, we've all had enough.' He walked aggressively towards me, stopping just a couple of feet away. I felt Simon bristle next to me. 'You have no right to keep us here like this.'

'I understand you were booked to stay here until tomorrow?' I asked. I had to concentrate to keep the irritation out of my words.

'Yes, but...' he tried to protest.

'I'm sure one more night won't make any difference. I'm sure you'd rather we got everything we need now, rather than having to get you back again in a few days?' I arched my head to the side in a question. Tristen said nothing. He turned his back on me as he walked away. I noticed that he didn't check if his wife was OK. He didn't even look at her.

'When can we have Annie's things back? You know, the clothes, the things you took yesterday.' Charlotte twisted her index finger into her fist. Rose looked at her confused.

'I'm sorry, but a lot of what we took is currently with the forensics. It will be some time before it's released to the family,' Simon explained.

'OK, are you ready?' I asked Stella. She nodded, giving her boyfriend a kiss on the lips, before following us to the car.

CHAPTER FORTY-THREE

STELLA

Two days after

The interview room was stiflingly hot. The detective dragged an old electric fan across the room. Standing it as close as the taut cable would allow. 'Do I need a solicitor?' I asked. DCI Melanie Price took a seat opposite me.

'That depends,' she replied, holding eye contact with me. 'If you'd feel more comfortable getting legal advice before we start, it's something you should consider. If you have something to tell us that may incriminate you, or someone you know, then it's essential.' She spoke seriously, but she wasn't intimidating. There was something I liked about her, something I trusted. Under different circumstances, I'd want us to be friends.

'I don't have anything to say that would incriminate me,' I told her, pushing my hands nervously into my lap.

'OK then, shall we start?' She introduced DC Green who took a seat next to her and started the recording. 'How was your friendship with Annie?' she asked, taking a sip of her steaming-hot coffee. I thought about her question for a moment. The sound of the fan whirring filled in the space. I could feel the breeze on my legs.

'Annie and Charlotte have been my best friends for twenty-five years. When you've been friends for as long as us, there are always highs and lows...' I shrugged nervously.

'Tell me some of the lows?' said the detective, shifting in her seat.

'Not really lows, just... things weren't the same as when we were kids. That's normal. That would be the same for all childhood friendships. We all grew up.' I added defensively. Melanie Price nodded slowly.

'Were there any *specific* tensions within the group?' she asked. I nodded. 'Tensions within the group, or just Annie in particular?' she added.

'Annie in particular,' I told her reluctantly. 'Her relationship with everyone had become difficult... she could be a difficult person at times,' I said sadly.

'Was there a reason that *your* relationship with her was strained?' I nodded again. Afraid of the inevitable. DCI Price pointed to the recorder.

'Yes.' I knew I had to tell them. I had no choice. I took a deep breath. I just wanted to make sure I told them in the right way. 'Annie knew something about me. She was using the information to blackmail me.' I chewed the inside of my cheek.

'What was it that Annie knew?' she asked quietly.

'She knew that I had an affair with Tristen, Charlotte's husband.' The word still made me shudder. 'I ended it a few years ago... when my mum died. It was before I got together with Nate. We were eighteen when it first happened.' My mouth filled with saliva. I thought I was going to be sick.

DCI Price didn't flinch. She just nodded. 'Thank you for telling us.' She looked at me sympathetically, any judgement tightly under wraps. I think she probably thought I was brave for confessing. There was nothing brave about my honesty. It just didn't matter any more. Me and Tristen... Charlotte. Annie was dead. Nothing else mattered.

'What did she want from you, in return for her silence?' she asked gently.

'Annie wanted money,' I told them. 'Her business was failing. The house was at risk. She wanted me to bail her out.'

'And did you?' she asked.

'No. I didn't have the money she needed. I couldn't even get close to the money she needed.'

'When you didn't give her the money, did she tell anyone?' the detective asked.

'No, I don't think so,' I replied. I didn't tell her about last night. I didn't tell her that Charlotte knew about the affair. That she had maybe known about the affair for many years. I didn't know how she'd found out, but I was sure that it wasn't Annie who had told her.

'You realise that this gives you a motive?' DCI Price told me. I nodded. If I told them that Charlotte knew about the affair before Annie died, then I no longer had a motive to kill her. I wanted to be open with them, but that wasn't something I wanted to share. Not today. Charlotte had her reasons for doing nothing about it all these years. If she wanted to tell them, it was up to her.

'I loved Annie. I loved Annie and I love her daughter. I would never have done anything to hurt either of them. Our friendship was complicated. She was a complicated person. She could be obnoxious and single-minded and insensitive...' I could feel my voice rising with emotion. '...But she could also be kind. I've never known a person more loyal than Annie. Despite the threats and the blackmail, she never would have told Charlotte about me and Tristen.' I took a long gasp of breath into my lungs as I ran out of air. The detectives studied my expression.

I felt tears pushing at the backs of my eyes. 'The truth is, if I'd had the money, I would have given it to her. Not because she blackmailed me, not for her silence. I would have given her the money because I loved her.' A solitary tear rolled slowly down my cheek. 'The saddest part is, that she didn't know that.'

CHAPTER FORTY-FOUR

DCI MELANIE PRICE

Two days after

After the interview with Stella, me and Simon went back to the incident room. Simon tapped away at his keyboard, deep in thought. The room was separated from the main office by a thin Perspex wall. It was still early. I sat listening to the distant sound of phones ringing. Of muffled conversations of officers as they started to arrive for work.

I thought about what Stella had told us. About her and Tristen. How could a marriage be so consumed with secrets and lies. Consumed and yet somehow survive. Held together by tiny fragile strings. Maybe it wasn't a matter of survival. Charlotte and Tristen hadn't worked through anything, they had chosen to simply exist near each other. To move forward at a safe distance from one another. No sudden movements that might alter the straight path they'd cleared for their marriage.

Me and Mike had a great relationship. Our marriage had been full of kindness and respect. But we'd given up at the first hurdle. We'd thrown away so much goodness. The pain I felt when I thought about Mike, when I thought about how far apart we were, it was actually physical.

Ten times a day I thought about picking up the phone. To tell him that I understood. That I knew his ultimatum wasn't about forcing me to have a child. It was about asking me to make a decision, whatever that decision might be. He was asking me to prioritise our relationship. I was just too stubborn to realise it then.

Sometimes you have to lose everything to finally know what matters. Soon I would have to accept that it was over. That one day I would be his ex-wife. One day I would hear that he was with someone else. Soon I would have to accept that he was never going to call.

Simon leant back on his chair. Rubbing his thinning hair with the palm of his hand. 'I've tried to look up the attack on Charlotte Stanbrook, or Bishop, which was her maiden name. There's nothing. No assault, no investigation.' He frowned as he chewed the end of his pen. 'I've requested hospital records, but that's going to take a few days. By all accounts she was in hospital for a while. She nearly died. It makes no sense that there wasn't an investigation.' Simon stood up from his chair. 'I'm going to make a call to Porthaven Central. Maybe someone over there can shed some light on it.' Simon left the room. I went back to my screen.

If Jack didn't kill Annie and Stella didn't kill her, the list of suspects was getting shorter. We only had a few members of the group to interview. We were running out of time. We needed to speak to Charlotte.

I started looking through the notes taken by the first officers on the scene. Nathan King, or Nate—Stella's boyfriend. He was the only person on the trip who had no previous connection to Annie. He'd only been with Stella for a couple of years. This was the first time he'd been introduced to the friendship group.

Nate King used to be a model, I read from the neatly typed

pages next to me. I tapped his name into the search engine: 'Nathan King, model.' The top half of the page was filled with colour and black-and-white images of the man I'd only briefly met. Most were athletic-style shots. Topless and muscley, wearing jeans or crisp white underwear. I checked the credit at the bottom of the photo. Graceland Models. I searched for their website. They had a long list of clients, men and women, none that I'd heard of. I added Annie's name to the search bar: 'Graceland Models Annie Turner.' The first hit was from the website of a PR firm.

'Annie Turner, associate director of West Link PR, lands account with Graceland Models...' the article read. There was a connection between Nate and Annie. There was a chance they'd worked together, or at the very least had met. It was several years ago, but it was a possible lead.

Simon came back into the room, looking confused. 'I've just spoken to someone over at Porthaven. He remembers the case. He wasn't called out, but he was on duty in town that night...' He took a step closer to me and lowered his voice. 'Mel... there was no attack. No assault, no investigation.'

'I don't understand,' I told him. 'Charlotte was in hospital, she nearly died...'

'It wasn't an attack... It was attempted suicide. Charlotte jumped off the top of the car park. They have no idea how she survived. She managed to crawl towards the road and was found soon after. Her parents were aware of the real story apparently. Shortly after, they had her admitted to a psychiatric hospital for a month. How did her friends get it so wrong?' he wondered.

'They didn't,' I told him. 'Charlotte must have lied to them. She told her friends that her injuries were a result of a vicious attack.' I stood up from my desk. 'We just need to find out why.'

CHAPTER FORTY-FIVE

CHARLOTTE

The day it happened

I fidgeted on the hard floor as I tried to fall back to sleep. I'd been drifting in and out for hours. The rain hammered against the taut fabric of the tent. My head was filled with questions. I replayed the night over in my mind. What had happened between Tristen and Nate. What I'd said to Stella. There was no going back now. I didn't know what the future looked like for me and Tristen, but I knew it wouldn't be one that we faced together.

I could feel the ground digging into my hips. The air had escaped from the bed just enough that it no longer held me up. I looked over at Tristen's face. The contour of his features was just visible in the moonlight. I wondered how he could sleep so soundly. How he could rest his mind and his body so easily after everything. I guess that was the problem. I care about us much more than he does.

The sound of a man's voice shouting made me sit bolt upright. I couldn't hear what he was saying, but he sounded panicked. Adrenaline rampaged through my veins. My ears strained to hear the man's words as they were carried away on the wind and the rain outside. The sound of zips tearing open broke through the distant noise. I couldn't work out which direction it was coming from. Maybe Jack or Stella. Still, I didn't move. My legs felt numb as alarm descended on our little camp.

The next shout was louder. 'She's hurt.' I heard the voice yell through the storm. 'Help!' Tristen was up and to the door of the tent in one movement. His reaction was what he trained for in the army. It was who he was. I wriggled out of my sleeping bag and joined him by the entrance.

'What's happening?' I whispered. He was stood so close that if I moved my head two inches to the side, it would be touching his chest. I'm not sure if he heard me, but he didn't answer.

'Hello?' Tristen yelled into the dark rainy night. Out of the shadows stumbled a large man, dressed head to toe in water-proofs. His hood was pulled high over his head, so his face was partially covered. I only realised who it was when he was right in front of me. It was the owner of the campsite. The man who'd thrown us out of the restaurant tonight. I felt a trickle of relief as I realised it wasn't a real emergency. There wasn't someone hurt, this was just another complaint. Another issue this man had with our presence here.

My relief was short lived. 'There's been an accident.' He spoke loudly, his words battling with the hard wind. 'Someone's been hurt.' He was out of breath and panting.

'Who?' Tristen asked, pulling his trainers from the porchway of the tent and slipping his bare feet inside them. The man silently beckoned Tristen to follow him. I lifted the flap of the tent and leaned in. Checking that Theo was tucked up in bed. I knew that he was, I just needed to make sure.

A flashlight momentarily scanned my face. It was Jack and

Kelly, closely followed by Nate. 'What's happened?' Nate asked, throwing a coat over his shoulders.

'I'm not sure,' I replied in a shaky voice. 'Tristen has gone to find out. Is Stella with you?' He nodded.

'Ollie's fast asleep,' Jack said putting a cigarette in his mouth, fumbling around in his pockets for a lighter. 'Has anyone checked on Annie and Rose?' I shook my head. But I'm not sure they saw me in the dim light. My feet felt like ice. I was stood barefoot in the wet grass as the rain lashed against my face. We all waited for Tristen to come back. Replaying the words in our head that we thought we'd heard the man shout. Collectively holding our breath.

Tristen came back. He was alone. Stella's flashlight picked up his face as he marched to Annie's yurt. 'What is it?' Jack yelled nervously. He took a long drag of the cigarette and waited for Tristen to answer. There was no reply. Just the sound of the wind battering against the fabric wall of tents.

Tristen strode over to us. He had one hand on his hip and the other was on his forehead. He was pacing in circles as he struggled to find the words. 'It's Annie,' he said. Tristen was fighting back tears. We all froze. 'She's... she's dead.' The final word was broken by a crack in his voice. He placed the palms of his hands on his knees and bent over. Like he was trying to get more air into his body, like he might faint. When I played this moment over in my mind for years to come, the silence would last forever.

'What do you mean, she's dead?' Jack snapped. He shone the flashlight on our faces, hoping that this was all some horrible joke.

'I mean she's *dead*,' Tristen shouted, dangerously close to Jack's face. I saw a figure moving around the tent behind him. It was Rose, stumbling from the yurt in her pyjamas. She looked so young, so confused. I felt my heart break in two at that very moment.

We all moved slowly towards her. 'What is it? What's happened?' she asked, looking around at the ground to see if she'd missed something. Stella stepped forward.

'Rose?' She put an arm gently around her shoulder as we formed a protective circle around them. 'Something has happened to your mum,' Stella told her. I wanted to turn off the light so I couldn't see the pain on Rose's face.

'What do you mean... what's happened?' Rose sounded annoyed, like someone was playing a trick on her. She slipped out from under Stella's arm and ran back into the yurt calling out for her mum. 'Where is she? Stella, you're scaring me.' Rose's breathing was hard and fast.

'Your mum's dead,' Stella told her. I couldn't see them, but I knew there were tears falling down her face.

'Dead?' Rose said the word as if she'd never heard it before. Rolling it around her mouth. 'How can she be dead?' Her voice was so small we had to lipread her words.

'We're not sure yet,' Tristen said, moving towards her. 'The owner has called the police. They'll be here soon. We'll know more then.' He put his hand on her shoulder and tried to guide her back inside the yurt. I wiped the rain from my eyes with the back of my sleeve so I could see.

'No,' she said, quietly at first. 'No!' she shouted to no one in particular, flailing her arms around until Stella and Tristen were forced to release her.

'Rose, sweetheart... we need to get you back inside,' Jack told her gently. The cigarette still burnt brightly in his hand. I think he'd forgotten it was there.

Rose dropped to her knees. Landing on the wet muddy ground. She opened her mouth and wailed. It was a sound that seemed to reverberate across the valley. It was a sound that I will never, ever forget.

CHAPTER FORTY-SIX

STELLA

The day it happened

The sun had come up over the hill. It seemed to rise suddenly. All at once orange light flooded the campsite like a dam breaking. Everything seemed unnatural. Talking, walking, eating. Nobody knew what to do with themselves. Time passed very slowly.

We'd managed to get Rose back into the yurt. She was calm for now, but there was a vacancy to her. She hadn't spoken to anyone in a while. It was like she was gathering strength for the storm that was coming.

'Are you OK?' Tristen had asked when Nate was out of earshot. I walked away without a word. There was nothing to say. There never would be anything to say—not to Tristen.

There was an ugly purple bruise across Nate's jaw this morning. No one had mentioned it, no one had even looked at it. It seemed inconsequential now. The fight, getting thrown out of the restaurant, none of it was important. I couldn't bear to look at it. That bruise signified all my mistakes. My terrible hurtful choices had now impacted Nate. It had impacted our beautiful relationship and everyone around us. My betrayal had brought a poisonous decay into the lives of everyone around us. Now Annie was dead. It was impossible to see how it couldn't somehow be linked.

I had ruined everything. I would do anything to prove to Nate that I was not that person. Not any more.

There was a collective relief when the police arrived. We found solace in the horror. The white jumpsuits and body bag and yellow police tape. As awful as it was that they were there, it was worse when they weren't. Worse when her body was lying alone behind the toilets. When no one was asking us questions or telling us what would happen next. The police arriving had meant that there was someone in charge of this nightmare. It meant that someone was looking after Annie.

The detective came and spoke to us. Me and Charlotte had been looking after Rose before they took her away. We were both lost for a while. Losing our main focus.

Kelly came back from the toilets. She'd had to walk to the next field. The ones closest to us were closed. They were so near to where Annie was found... I'm sure they would be closed for a long time. 'I've just spoken to a woman at the toilets. She said she overheard the police talking. They're saying she was murdered. They're saying the killer has to have been someone on Field C.' Her eyes were round and troubled.

'Why would some random person want to kill her?' Kelly asked.

'They wouldn't,' snapped Jack. 'They're looking at us.'

CHAPTER FORTY-SEVEN

DCI MELANIE PRICE

Two days after

Rain bounced off the windscreen as I drove home. The wipers struggled to keep up with the river of water that ran down the glass. Dripping noisily from the trees that arched over the lane.

I stared at the dark road ahead. My headlights were only just bright enough to pick up the twists and turns of the high Cornish hedges. I thought about the case. The very different group of individuals that we were looking at for the murder of their friend. I thought about how far we were from a break-through.

We'd tried to get Charlotte in for an interview earlier on today. She'd stalled, told us she was unwell. I'm not sure if it was the truth. She'd looked unwell when I last saw her, but they all had. At this stage, the interview was voluntary, so there was little we could do. We'd arranged to speak to her tomorrow morning. When they left tomorrow afternoon, the investigation would be that much harder. At least until we had some forensic evidence.

I scurried through the rain. Using my coat to cover the pile

of files under my arm. I balanced them on my knee as I scrambled to find my keys. The automatic light clicked on in the
narrow hallway as I pushed open the door. The faded green
carpet was scattered with old takeaway menus that were shoved
through the door on a daily basis. I pushed them aside with my
foot.

I still hated coming home to a dark flat. To an empty flat. I
don't think I'll ever get used to it. The corridor ran alongside the
internet café below me. It was a shared entrance with the flat
above mine. Sometimes when I got home, one of their bikes
would be propped up against the wall. I'd hear the sound of
laughter coming from the door above mine. The smell of their
dinner cooking would waft down the stairs. Not tonight though.
Tonight it was quiet.

I poured myself a glass of red wine. Just to feel a little
warmth, a little comfort. I laid out the papers on the cheap pine
coffee table in the living room. Another strange secondhand
piece of furniture that didn't belong to me. Furniture that made
up part of someone else memories.

I'd left everything except my clothes when I moved out of
the house that me and Mike had shared. I took nothing that
we'd spent years building together. Antiques we'd discovered on
city breaks. The old record collection we were so proud of. The
prints that hung on the walls. Walls that we'd painted in colours
that we'd painstakingly chosen. The truth is, I didn't want to
take anything. If I did that, then we would have needed to
divide everything up. We would have to dismantle the home
and the life and the memories. The only comfort was knowing
that Mike and the house were still there. Just as I left them. This
way I could pretend that it was just temporary.

I'd brought home parts of the police file. The initial statements. The preliminary autopsy, personal items I'd collected
from Annie's things. I dragged a cushion from the sofa and sat
down in front of the table on the hard floor. I took a sip of wine

and set it down next to the papers. The files were still sparse. Over time they would grow in size as interviews and forensics were added. I thumbed idly through the sheets of paper. I wasn't sure what I was looking for. Maybe something we'd missed. Something I could use in the interviews.

I pulled out the pile of cards. Underneath was the oversized card Rose had been given by the group. I laid it on the table and lifted it open. 'Happy 18th birthday, darling Rose! Love from Stella & Nate.' Everyone had written their own message. 'Hope you have a great birthday, Rose! Love from Jack, Kelly & the boys.'

I closed the card and looked at the images on the cover. It was a mosaic of photos. Printed at angles and overlapping. They weren't in any sort of chronological order. They lurched backwards and forwards through Rose and Annie's life. Baby photos, holiday photos, school photos. There was a picture of Annie. She must have been about four. Stood shyly between her parents, Rose's grandparents. Her dark hair and big eyes stared innocently out at me. I brushed my thumb over her face and thought about how fragile life was.

There was a knock at the door downstairs. I didn't move. The neighbours upstairs often had friends over. There was no doorbell for the two individual flats. Visitors just banged on the door and waited. It would take a minute, but they would eventually go down and let them in. The knock sounded again, louder this time. There was no noise from the flat above. No footsteps or doors opening. I threw my cardigan over my thin T-shirt and went downstairs.

The rain was still coming down hard outside. It ricocheted noisily off the pavement. The streetlights skewed the shadows over the man's face. For a long moment, I didn't know who it was. He pulled down his wet hood and my heart missed a beat. It was Mike.

'Hi, Mel,' he said, wiping drops of rain from his forehead.

'Can I come in?' I nodded, not trusting myself to speak. I stood aside and let him in. The front door shut out the sound of the traffic. He seemed so big, stood there in the dimly lit corridor. Everything seemed eerily quiet.

'Do you want to come up?' I asked. Seeing him here, in my flat, it felt like a strange dream. Where everything is disjointed and out of context. He nodded. I felt self-conscious walking up the steep staircase ahead of him. I had never been more aware of the number of steps that led up to my rented flat. Or more aware of the dinginess of the shared entrance.

I showed him silently into the living room and offered to take his wet coat. He looked around the room. Like he was trying to put together all the new pieces of me. Trying to reconcile the old me to these strange new surroundings. He didn't need to. I just existed here. It was only at this moment that I realised it. I hadn't changed at all.

His eyes fell on the glass of wine. 'Do you want some?' I asked, moving towards the kitchen. He shook his head and I stopped moving.

'Simon said you're working on a case together?' He walked over to the tired beige sofa and perched on the edge. He pushed the palms of his hands together anxiously as he waited. Mike had shaved his beard off. He looked younger. It suited him. Seeing him here, in my living room, I'd forgotten just how handsome he was.

'Yes... I heard Lyndsey's pregnant?' I said. Trying to fill the space. Trying to calm my nerves. We locked eyes for a moment. Only Mike would know how much I missed Lyndsey. How hurt I would have been that I was the last to know they were having another child. He opened his mouth to explain, but I interrupted. 'It's fine,' I told him, raising my hand slightly. 'Simon's your best friend... It's... Well, it's complicated,' I reassured him. I wanted Mike's understanding, but I couldn't handle his pity.

'How's the case going?' He glanced down at the papers that were scattered across the coffee table.

'It's a strange one. A group of friends on a camping holiday... one of them was murdered.' Mike raised his eyebrows. Simon obviously hadn't told him all the details. 'I used to go to college with them.'

'What?' he asked, confused. 'Were you friends?'

'No, nothing like that. They were in the year above me... It's all very odd,' I told him, picking up my wine and taking a sip. Mike wanted to tell me something. He was biding his time. It was the reason he was here. I braced myself to hear that he wanted a divorce. That he'd met someone else.

'Mel?' He cleared his throat and rose to his feet. Mike rubbed his chin where his beard used to be. An old habit. 'Mel, I miss you.' He took a step towards me. I replayed his words in my head, to make sure I'd heard them right.

I started to cry. It was as though I was finally giving in to the pain and the loneliness that the last few months had brought. 'Don't cry... Please don't cry.' He came to me, his face filled with anguish.

'I'm fine,' I told him. I tried to turn my back on him, but he grabbed hold of my arms. He pulled me towards him. Kissing me so deeply, I felt all the strength disappear from my body. I sank into the kiss. He tasted just like he always had. A smell so familiar it was almost as though it was part of me.

'Why now?' I asked gently. 'After all this time. Why now?'

'I don't need children,' he told me, pushing away a strand of hair that had fallen into my eyes. 'I don't need anything except you. I'm sorry it took me so long to realise that.'

'I don't know how we got here.' I bit my bottom lip and shook my head sadly. 'It isn't that I don't want children. I just didn't want to...' I tried to explain.

'It doesn't matter,' he said firmly. Mike kissed me again.

Pushing my body against the living room wall. I gasped. I felt every muscle, every movement as he pressed against me.

'Wait...' Something suddenly connected in my head. I pulled away slowly.

'What?' He looked at me concerned.

'No... It's not this... It's just...' I kissed him hard on the mouth to reassure him. I slipped out of his arms and walked over to the coffee table. I lifted up the card, taking a closer look. 'Shit,' I said, covering my mouth with my hand in shock.

'What is it?' Mike's voice was deep and breathless.

'I'm so, so sorry...' I told him, going to where he stood and placing my hand on his soft cheek. 'But I have to go.'

'It's fine,' he said, slipping his arms around me. I wanted to stay here. But I needed to do this. 'Do you want me to drive you?' he asked, looking over at the half-drunk glass of wine. I nodded. I didn't need him to drive me. I'd only had a couple of mouthfuls. But I didn't want to be apart from him. I didn't want to leave him—not like this.

It was still raining when we climbed into his shiny black Lexus. He smiled as he tucked sweet wrappers scattered on the floor into the driver's door. I smiled back. I'd missed his car. I'd missed everything.

We drove in silence along the dark wet roads towards Tregarrow Farm campsite. I found Simon's number on my phone. It took several rings before he picked up. 'Simon?' I said as he answered.

'What's up?' He sounded groggy, like I'd woken him from a deep sleep.

'Simon. I know who killed Annie.'

CHAPTER FORTY-EIGHT

DCI MELANIE PRICE

Two days after

The campsite looked deserted when we pulled into the narrow entrance a while later. A dark car followed us into the parking area. Dimming its headlights as it pulled up behind us. It was Simon. He would wonder why I was with Mike. But he would never ask me about it. Simon knew how private I was.

I reached behind my seat to get the files. 'Thanks for the lift,' I told him, suddenly feeling shy.

'You're welcome.' He smiled at my formality. I could see his eyes laughing in the dim light of the dashboard.

'I'll get a lift to the station with Simon... We, um... We won't be long,' I told him, biting my lip. Hoping this wasn't it.

'You will, but that's OK.' He reached over and kissed me. I nearly pulled away. I knew that Simon would be able to see the outline of us in the car behind. I wanted to tell him to stop, but I couldn't. He breathed in deeply as we separated. 'Let me know when you're done, and I'll come and pick you up. I'll make breakfast.' I nodded, not trusting myself to speak. I gave him one last look, before reluctantly climbing out of the car.

Gusts of wind pummelled my body as I walked over to
Simon's Audi. I turned and watched Mike's taillights leave the
campsite as the rain lashed at my face.

'Hi,' I said to Simon as I got into the passenger seat. 'Sorry
to call you out so late,' I apologised.

'It's fine,' he told me, driving across the dark campsite. 'Do
you want to fill me in?' He didn't mention Mike. He knew I
would tell him when I was ready.

The storm shook the flimsy tents in all directions. The noise
of flapping canvas added to the bleakness of the scene. I walked
slowly towards the campground. My boots sunk into the sodden
earth. Slipping into every step.

Jack sat in his shiny black four-by-four. He was perched on
the edge of the passenger seat with the door open. His legs hung
out of the car. His body was illuminated in the white interior
light. Jack was puffing on a cigarette. Even in this weather,
through the dark and rain, I could tell that he was drunk. Very,
very drunk.

'Where's Charlotte?' I asked. There was no need for formal-
ities, not now. He pointed his finger in the general direction of
the tents. At that moment Charlotte walked out of the tent
closest to us. She had a coat on and a flashlight in her hand. I
felt relieved that no one else was here. This was the best-case
scenario. We would be able to do this quietly, with minimal
fuss.

She knew. She knew before I'd even said a word that we
were here for her. It happens sometimes. People just resigning
themselves to their fate when we arrest them. Other times,
people fight with everything they've got.

'Charlotte Stanbrook. I'm arresting you on suspicion of the
murder of Annie Turner. You do not have to say anything...' As
I read her rights, people moved out of the tents. First Stella,
then Tristen and Kelly, until they were all there. I couldn't see

their faces, but I could feel their shock. They fell silently into the space behind Charlotte. A silhouette audience.

'Charlotte, we'd like you to come with us, please.' I didn't want to handcuff her. Not here. Not in front of everyone. She nodded, her face still lit by the yellow flashlight. Charlotte looked eerily calm. Like she'd been practising her whole life for this moment.

We walked quickly away from the group. 'Are you arresting her?' Rose called loudly, stepping forward from the crowd. The three of us turned. 'Charlotte?' She took another step closer. I couldn't make out her features, but I could hear the hurt in her voice. 'Charlotte... what did you do?' Rose's voice broke as she waited for an answer. I expected Charlotte to explain. To say that it had all been a big mistake. That she hadn't killed her mum. But she didn't. She stared right through Rose as if she weren't there. Then she turned and walked away without a word.

We climbed into the car. I sat in the back with Charlotte. The headlights passed over the pale faces huddled around the tents as we reversed. 'Mummy!' A small figure broke free and ran towards the car. Simon hit the brakes as the child reached the vehicle. Beating his small fists against the bodywork. 'Mummy,' he screamed; you could hear the terror in his voice.

Tristen ran forward and picked Theo up. Throwing his crying, kicking body over his shoulder and away from the car. I turned to Charlotte. Her face was expressionless. 'Can we go now?' she asked in a flat voice. We drove away from the emotionally charged scene. Away from Charlotte's family. I watched her from the corner of my eye as they disappeared from view. She didn't even lift her head. She didn't look at them at all.

As Simon drove steadily through the relentless rain, I thought about the many arrests I'd made over my career. Arrests are never what you expect them to be. They often throw you a curve ball. Suspects are never what you expect them to be either. I glanced over at Charlotte and wondered how she could have done it. How she could have killed her best friend.

CHAPTER FORTY-NINE

CHARLOTTE

Two days after

I sat in the interview room for an hour. Waiting for the duty solicitor to arrive. When he finally did, he said very little. He was a balding man in a brown suit. His tie was covered in faint grease stains. The man sat beside me and wrote notes. I pretended he wasn't there.

The four of us were silent for a while. I'm not sure what they were waiting for. The detectives passed pieces of paper between them. Sheets from a stack of notes that sat on the plastic-covered table. I'm not sure if they were trying to worry me or if they genuinely had information to share. I saw Rose's birthday card under a green folder and my stomach lurched.

'Is this because I lied?' I asked. I was sat on my hands. I could feel myself rocking backwards and forwards but didn't seem to be able to stop. The detective frowned slightly.

'What did you lie about, Charlotte?' she asked. I remember her from college. Melanie Price. She'd worn glasses and had an awkward haircut, like maybe her mum trimmed it. She had a few friends I think, but she was often alone. We were the same me and her. Only I'd accidentally found myself with Tristen and Annie. Stella and Jack. We weren't the popular group. The popular group were the ones who played sports and threw parties. But Annie and Jack were people who mattered. Their opinions mattered. Their presence at college mattered. Before Annie, I was just like Melanie Price.

'Charlotte, what have you lied about?' she repeated the question.

'I lied about being attacked. That night when I was a teenager, in the car park... Stella told you that I was attacked. She seems to think what happened to me and Annie might be linked.' I laughed a little. I couldn't help it. I felt the eyes of my solicitor on me. The detective said nothing. They were all wondering if I was OK. If I was about to snap.

'Why did you lie?' she asked. Her voice was gentle and coaxing. It was oddly relaxing considering the circumstances.

'Because I knew that if I didn't, then he would leave,' I explained simply.

'Tristen?' she asked, knowing the answer. I nodded.

'Have you every loved someone so much that you thought you might die without them?' I didn't expect an answer, but I saw a flash of something in Melanie's eye. 'I would have done anything to keep him back then.'

'And now?' she asked.

'I've run out of ways to hold on to him,' I told her sadly. 'I knew about Tristen and Stella. That week, the week it happened. I'd seen how they looked at each other. They hadn't acted on it, but I'd felt Tristen pull away from me...'

'Was that why you jumped off the car park?' Her voice was low and steady.

'Partly. That... and the drugs Annie gave me,' I said with a smile. My eyes scanned the room. I felt like I'd made a joke, but nobody was laughing. 'I took all of them, the drugs she'd brought. Annie had felt so guilty about it. She thought it was her fault. The pills, letting me walk home by myself. She thought the attack wouldn't have happened if she'd behaved differently.' I don't know if it would have made Annie feel better or worse, that I wasn't attacked. That I'd tried to kill myself. Annie had died without knowing the truth. A trickle of regret wriggled its way down my spine.

'Did you blame her?'

'Did I blame Annie for what happened to me? No. I didn't blame her,' I replied bluntly. 'But I never told her it wasn't her fault.'

'Why did you say that you'd been attacked? Why didn't you just tell Tristen the truth? If you wanted him to feel bad enough to stay with you, surely attempted suicide would have worked too?' Melanie was struggling to understand my motives.

'I'm not sure why I lied. The first time I saw them in my hospital room—Tristen and Stella—I knew it was too late. I knew that they'd slept together. Even through all the pain and the medication I could see it. Their awkward body language and stolen glances. The lie just came out before I could stop it. But actually, being a victim worked quite well for me,' I said casually.

'I kept thinking that they'd find out the truth. The hospital knew that I'd tried to kill myself. The police and my parents knew. I kept waiting for the moment when someone would say something to them. But do you know what I found out? When someone tries to kill themselves—nobody likes to talk about it.' I said the last words in a whisper.

'When they didn't arrest anyone, Stella said she was going to complain to the police. Annie insisted that she do it instead. I knew that she wouldn't. That she'd make up some lie. Annie didn't want any more police involvement than I did. She didn't want any questions to be asked about what I might have taken.' I tapped my thumb very lightly on the table. My solicitor hadn't written anything for a while.

'You must think I'm very strange. Loving someone as much as I love Tristen and standing by whilst he has an affair with my best friend. You just find a way to be OK with it. You'd be surprised the things you find a way to be OK with when you have no choice. You lock it away so that it doesn't hurt you. Or at least, it doesn't hurt as much,' I explained.

'But you stayed friends with Stella?' Melanie asked.

'I did.' The male detective's face was fixed in a sort of grimace. I'm not sure he meant it to be. Not many people would understand. 'I always knew that it was going to be some-body. It was better that it was Stella. Better than some faceless person that I didn't know. Someone that I'd have to stalk through his social media or his messages. Waiting outside their work to find out who they were. I know Stella. I know every-thing about her. I know why Tristen loves her—because I love her too.'

I could see the detectives trying to work out if this was a confession. Trying to work out if I had stalked Stella. Waited outside *her* work. Read her messages or watched her house.

'After you were released from hospital, you went into psychiatric care?' Melanie asked.

'You think I killed Annie because I'm crazy?' I asked her.

'No, Charlotte. We don't think you're crazy,' she told me.

Not long after I was discharged from hospital, my parents had me committed to a psychiatric ward. I was there for a month. I'm not sure my mum and dad really knew what to do with me. I think they were just looking for somewhere safe. Somewhere that they didn't have to feel scared for me all the time. I didn't blame them.

One of the doctors there was called Bryce. We were encour-aged to be on a first-name basis. They said it garnered trust. It didn't really. It was the same kind of awkward as calling your teacher by their first name. I had never spoken more than I did in that month. I had never shared so many secrets or spent more time in the company of people. I never felt more alone than I did in that place.

Bryce had taught me coping mechanisms to get me through difficult times. Scary, anxious times. Times when I didn't trust myself, when I needed distractions. He encouraged me to wear a band on my wrist. To snap the band whenever I needed time to process the feelings rampaging through my mind. The sharp pain of the band hitting my skin would break the destructive cycle. But only for a moment. It was the same self-destructive action. The physical damage to myself replacing the mental damage. The same behaviour in a more palatable costume.

The noisy electric fan drowned out the sound of my heart, pounding in my neck. I clawed at my wrist, looking for the rubber band. Seeking comfort in the pain of the spring back. It wasn't there. It hadn't been there in years. I thought I was better. Cured.

I smiled to myself at the thought that I'd ever considered myself 'better.' The detective saw it. She watched me constrict my face back into neutral. I wonder what allowances they make for being crazy. I wonder if they let you get away with murder.

'They told me I was ill. They said that they could help with it... pills and therapy. But I'd always been that way. Intense. I'd always loved too hard, ever since I was little. But they don't have pills for that. So, I spoke when I was spoken to. Took pills when they were handed to me, and they let me out.' I shrugged as if it had been simple. 'I make people uncomfortable. I make Tristen uncomfortable. It made it much easier when everyone had my attack to blame for the way I am.'

'I wanted to show you this.' The detective pulled Rose's card out from behind the pile of papers. 'Do you know *why* I want to show you this, Charlotte?' I shrugged, but I knew. Melanie placed the oversized greeting card on the centre of the table and waited. My eyes scanned over the photographs on the cover. There was a photo of me and Annie and Stella. We were sat on the beach with Rose between us. She was just a baby. Jack had insisted on taking a photo. We looked so young, so very happy.

I look back at pictures like this, pictures of everyone smiling. Grinning into the camera like we'd just won a competition. I wonder if I was the only one who wasn't really happy. If I was the only one who was pretending. I'd spent my whole life trying to be somebody else. I'd finally achieved it. I *was* somebody else. I just have no idea who that person is.

'I went through these pictures tonight.' My solicitor peered at the card over his glasses. 'I wasn't sure what I was looking for. Probably nothing. Then I came across this photo.' She tapped a picture in the bottom left of the cover. Looking at me for a reaction. I felt my skin go cold.

'I'm not sure how I didn't see it before. The likeness is uncanny. The same dark hair, the same smile... with that little dimple.' I swallowed, waiting for her to say it. 'Theo isn't your son, is he? Theo is Annie's son.'

CHAPTER FIFTY

DCI MELANIE PRICE

Three days after

The colour drained from Charlotte's face. 'Can we take a short break, please?' stuttered the solicitor, suddenly seeing the need for an intervention.

'I don't need a break,' Charlotte told him without looking up.

'Mrs Stanbrook, I really think that you...' he persisted.

'We were pregnant at the same time,' she interrupted. Everyone fell silent. The solicitor returned to his note-taking. Satisfied that he had tried his best. 'It wasn't what she'd expected, but Annie said she would make it work.' She stared at a spot on the table. Looking like this was a story that she'd wanted to tell for a long time.

'I was twelve weeks pregnant and staying at Annie's Wiltshire house. It was before she'd renovated, so it was very rough around the edges. No heating. Peeling wallpaper and rotting wooden floors. But it was beautiful. I woke up one morning and I just knew. Even before the blood, I knew. I just felt empty. Like a tiny piece of my soul had just disappeared. It had happened before—miscarriages. Me and Tristen had tried for so long to get pregnant. We'd done two rounds of failed IVF. We weren't new to the heartbreak. But that time it had felt different. That time, I really thought that we were going to have a baby.

'Have you ever lost a baby?' she looked at me and Simon. Neither of us answered. 'You never stop missing them. You never stop feeling that there is a person who should be here.' Charlotte tugged at a loose thread on the sleeve of her cardigan.

'I didn't want her baby. I wanted *my* baby. I was so consumed with grief. So scared to tell Tristen. Scared that this might be the thing that finally broke us... Annie had made it all sound so normal. As if it was the most natural thing. Almost like fate. I know that part of it was guilt. Guilt about what happened that night. Guilt that she'd carried around for so many years. She just wanted to make me happy. I let her do it.' Charlotte covered her face with her hands and started to sob. Deep, painful sobs. Filled with years of emotion and closely guarded secrets.

I waited for the crying to subside before asking, 'Does Tristen know that Theo isn't his child?' Tears continued to fall down her face unchecked. Charlotte shook her head. She looked like she was crumbling under the strain of it all.

'He was so tiny when he was born,' she told us. 'Tiny feet and hands and these pursed little lips.' She touched her own mouth as she remembered. 'He looked just like her. I couldn't believe no one else could see it. Tristen was posted in Canada. Theo was six weeks old by the time they met. He cried when he held him in his arms for the first time. I should have felt bad. Lying to Tristen about Theo being his son, should have been the worst part. It wasn't. I felt like everything was going to be OK. Like Theo was exactly where he was supposed to be.' I passed Charlotte a tissue and she dabbed at her eyes.

'We are waiting on Theo's birth certificate. It's going to take a day or so. Can you tell us what we can expect to see on there?' I asked her. I tried to keep my voice low and calm. She was right on the edge and I didn't want to scare her.

'We didn't do anything officially. The only option would have been to do a private adoption. That would have raised too many questions. With my mental health history and the fact that I didn't want Tristen to know... I *couldn't* let Tristen know. It would have been too difficult. Her name is on his birth certificate. There is no father listed. Theo's father is not something that was ever discussed. It didn't matter.' Charlotte stared into the middle distance. As though she were back there. Reliving all her decisions over again.

'You must think we're crazy for thinking this would work. Thinking that we could get away with it. But for years it did work. Until this week... nobody knew but us.' She sounded like she was talking in her sleep. 'Annie is my family. I would never have done anything to hurt her.' She lifted her head and looked me directly in the eye. 'If Annie hadn't died, our secret would never have been discovered. There was no way that I benefited from Annie being dead.'

She was right. Charlotte raising Annie's son as her own did not give her a motive to kill her. At that moment there was a knock at the door. A female police officer cautiously entered the room. I paused the tape before she spoke. 'I'm sorry to interrupt, ma'am, but there's a phone call.'

'Can you just take a message?' I asked her irritably. Surprised that she thought it appropriate to interrupt an interview.

'It's Tristen Stanbrook. He's called several times. He says it's urgent...' She looked nervous. Like she wasn't sure if she was doing the right thing.

'Thank you,' I said by way of dismissal. She nodded, closing the door with a look of relief.

'Charlotte, why would your husband be calling the station

urgently at...' I pulled my phone from my back pocket and checked the time. '...nearly one a.m. in the morning?' I hadn't realised it was that late. We needed to bring the interview to a close. We would hold Charlotte overnight and talk to her tomorrow. I unlocked my phone screen and handed the device to Charlotte. She took it, a look of confusion on her face.

'Call him,' I told her, shuffling my papers back into a pile. She carefully dialled the number and held the phone up to her ear. Even over the whirring of the electric fan we could all clearly hear the sound of the dialling tone.

'Hello?' It was Tristen's voice. He sounded panicked.

'What's wrong?' Charlotte asked quickly.

'He's gone...' Tristen's words reverberated through the mouthpiece.

'What do you mean gone... who's gone?' Charlotte's hand flew to her throat.

'Theo... she's taken him. She's taken the car.' He was shouting now.

'Tristen slow down. *Who* has taken Theo?' she asked. Her fingers dug into her neck as she waited for a reply.

'Rose has taken Theo. She's driven off in Jack's car... We're trying to get into Jack's phone to use the tracker, but he's passed out.' There was a rustling sound and muffled voices. 'OK, we're just looking at it now. Kelly said that the car is heading towards the lake we went to on Rose's birthday.'

'Greenbank Lake?' she asked.

'Yes. Why is this happening, Charlotte? Why has she taken him?' She didn't answer him. She let the phone slowly fall away from her face before hanging up.

Charlotte stood up so quickly from her chair, that it slid backwards across the room. Making a shrieking noise as it landed noisily on its back. The solicitor stood up in panic, looking around for an exit.

'We need to find them. We need to go and get Theo.' Charlotte sounded terrified as she pleaded with me to leave. 'Rose can't drive. She doesn't have a licence.'

'You need to calm down...' I stood up calmly, trying not to scare her.

'You don't understand. She's upset. I don't know what she'll do...' She was begging now. Simon stood up and headed for the door.

'We can take my car,' he suggested.

'Charlotte, does Rose know that Theo is Annie's son?' I asked quietly.

She had run to the door and was waiting for Simon to open it. She turned to me, her face ashen. 'Annie isn't Theo's mum... Rose is.'

CHAPTER FIFTY-ONE

CHARLOTTE

Three days after

I had never felt fear like this before. It gripped every part of my body. Even simple things like walking across the car park to the detective's car was difficult. It felt like the connection between my brain and my limbs was broken.

Melanie sat in the back of the car with me, whilst the other detective drove. They had handed me back my phone. I looked up Greenbank Lake on the map. It was about twenty minutes away. The car reversed out of the entrance to the station car park. We left at speed down the narrow lanes. A marked police car was following us. Ready to help when we found them. *If* we found them. The silent flashing of the blue lights reflecting in the rear window of the car made me feel sick.

It didn't feel like the wheels were touching the ground. We glided effortlessly down roads lined with shadowed trees. I clung to edge of the seat to try and ground myself. To try and stop myself from feeling like I was floating away.

The light from the phone shone in my face as I swiped mindlessly through photos of Theo. Melanie reached over and touched my hand. 'We'll find him,' she reassured me. 'Why didn't you tell us... about Rose being Theo's mum?'

'I thought I could protect her. I thought that if I went along with it, you would realise that I didn't kill Annie. That you might take my word for it and not check the birth certificate,' I told her.

'So, it's Rose's name on Theo's birth certificate?' she asked.

I nodded. 'Everything I told you was true. My pregnancy, staying at the Wiltshire house, bringing Theo home from hospital... the only difference is Rose gave birth to him, not Annie,' I told her. 'Rose was fourteen when she got pregnant. Annie wasn't a person who was shocked easily, but... she didn't handle it very well. Rose was at an all-girls boarding school. She was an A-grade student. She met a boy called James, who lived in the next town. I don't think it was a big romance or even a long one. But it was enough to land Rose with a pregnancy at fourteen.

'Rose is so clever. Annie wanted her to have the bright sparkling teenage years that she had. She thought having a baby would ruin Rose's life.' I pulled at a loose thread on my sleeve. Watching as it unravelled.

'Annie asked me to come and stay at the house. Rose was given time off from school. They'd made up some excuse, told the headteacher she was suffering from stress. Annie needed someone to keep an eye on her. She said that they'd make it work. That she would support Rose and her decision to have the baby. But she'd pushed her at the beginning. Pushed her hard to have an abortion.

'Our due dates were only three weeks apart. When I lost the baby... Annie became obsessed with me raising Rose's baby. She saw it as the answer to all our problems. Over time, she just wore us both down.' Melanie watched me carefully. Letting me talk without comment. Without judgement.

'I know that Rose didn't want to give him up. I know what

my taking him did to her. But I convinced myself that it was the right thing to do. I convinced myself that she'd get over it.

'When we left the hospital with Theo, I took him straight back to my house in Surrey. Tristen was still away for another six weeks, so it was just me and Theo. I couldn't carry on staying with Annie and Rose. I couldn't put her through any more heartache.

'We didn't see anybody. We lived in a strange newborn bubble. Every time the phone rang. Every time there was a knock at the door, I thought it was someone coming to take him from me. But no one ever did. Over time it became easier to lie. Most of the time I forgot that I wasn't his real mum. That Tristen wasn't his real dad.' I looked up. Even in the dark I could see that we weren't far away. I placed the palm of my hand on my chest and inhaled deeply.

'Lately Rose has become obsessed with spending time with Theo. Annie had told me that she'd insisted on us coming on this trip. We'd agreed to do it, just to keep her calm. To keep her from doing something stupid—like telling Tristen.'

'Had she threatened to tell Tristen?' asked Melanie.

'No. She hadn't threatened anything, but it was always there, you know? The fear that one day she'd lose it and say something. The phone in my hand rang loudly, lighting up our faces and making me jump.

It was Stella.

CHAPTER FIFTY-TWO

STELLA

Three days after

'Where are you?' I asked Charlotte. My voice sounded breathless.

'We're... we're just a few minutes away,' she told me, her words tight with emotion.

'Don't worry, Charlotte, we're here now. We'll find them,' I said and hung up. I was stood in the Greenbank Lake car park with Nate and Tristen. The only other vehicle, apart from my Land Rover, was Jack's big black car. It had been abandoned in the centre of the gravel area at a haphazard angle. Like Rose had left it in a hurry.

Nate checked the car over. There was no sign that it had been in an accident and no sign of Rose or Theo. He reached into the back seat and pulled something out. Theo's cuddly giraffe. Something he took everywhere. 'I just don't understand. Why would she take him? He's just a little kid,' Tristen cried, pulling the soft toy from Nate's hands.

'Calm down,' Nate was trying to be kind, but it just antagonised him. I shone my flashlight between them. Catching a look of rage pass across Tristen's face.

'Why the fuck are you even here?' Tristen moved aggressively towards Nate.

'This isn't helping,' I snapped, positioning my body between them. 'We need to start looking.'

'Sorry,' Tristen muttered, rubbing his face in frustration. We pointed our flashlights at the ground and followed the path that led to the water. It was only days ago that we were here. That Annie was here, I thought, with a lump in my throat.

The pale moon shone big and bright. Reflecting on the water from the other side of the lake. It had finally stopped raining and the sky was clear. We pointed our flashlights at the track ahead, but they weren't necessary. The moon lit the way. We kept the lights on for comfort. To feel like we were doing something, like we were in control.

Branches scratched at our faces as we scrambled along the path. 'Theo!' Tristen yelled into the shadows. The only sound was his voice echoing back. The sound of the water lapping against the side of the bank.

The path had got a little steeper. A slight incline that lifted the track above the water below. There was now a ten-foot drop to the left of us. The muddy bank created a sharp edge over the dark lake below. The rain had made the water level swell. I pointed my flashlight downwards. Watching the currents swirl dangerously against the side. We were all thinking the same thing. If Theo fell in here, he'd be swept away. He wouldn't stand a chance.

A minute later we saw her. We saw the outline of her. Standing by the high edge, clutching a bundle in her arms. 'Theo!' Tristen called out, as he began to run to them.

'*No!*' Rose screamed. 'Don't come any closer.'

'OK,' I called. 'OK.' We all froze in our places. The bundle in her arms was Theo. He was wrapped in a blanket. Still and silent. She was stood so close to the edge. 'Rose, sweetheart, let me help you,' I pleaded, taking a small step forward. I reached my arm out to her, even though she was still several feet away.

'Stella, don't... please don't,' Rose sobbed. She lurched dangerously close to the edge clutching Theo's body.

'Be careful,' shouted Tristen. He was in agony watching the scene play out. Knowing that there was nothing he could do.

'I just want to get you and Theo back here safely. You want that don't you, Rose? I know you don't want Theo to get hurt,' I told her. Trying my best to buy some time. Trying to talk her down.

That's when we heard footsteps. The hurried scuff of shoes on the path behind us. We swung our flashlights around in unison. Catching the faces of Charlotte and the two detectives running along the track towards us.

'Where is he?' Charlotte screamed. She ran through the middle of us, heading towards Rose.

'Charlotte, *no!*' I shouted, suddenly aware of what she was doing. She stopped when she saw Theo in Rose's arms. When she saw how close to the edge they were.

'Rose... Rose, please. Give him to me... We know how devastated you are about your mum—we all are,' Charlotte called over to her.

'Do you know what it did to me when you took him away from me?' Rose shouted. She was crying hysterically now. I noticed that Theo still wasn't moving. '*Do you?*' she screamed. Tristen took a step forward so he was next to Charlotte.

'What does she mean?' Tristen asked in a low voice. 'Charlotte... what does she mean?' Nobody spoke as the words swam around our heads. As we tried to make sense of them.

'You took him from me. You both did... I didn't stand a chance with you and Mum...' She jabbed a finger angrily in the direction of Charlotte. 'You did this. It's all your fault.' Her words ricocheted out of her between sobs. As she finished, she lurched forward. I thought she managed to catch herself, but she continued to fall. Sliding on the wet earth in front of her. A strangled noise escaped from all of us as Theo tumbled out of her arms. He landed on the ground. Tangled in the thick woollen blanket. I saw him move. Curling his knees into his body as he snuggled into the layers of fabric. He looked like he was still asleep. Rose made no attempt to move him.

'That's *enough*,' bellowed Tristen. His voice was thrown back to him across the water.

'Enough?' Rose shouted back with a bitter laugh. 'You have no idea, do you? No idea what your wife did... what my mum did? He was *mine*. The only thing that I ever had that was just mine... and they took him from me.'

'I don't understand,' Tristen started walking towards her. Like he was wandering through a fog. 'What did they take from you?' By then we'd all realised. Everyone had realised except Tristen. I turned to Charlotte. My jaw hung open, whilst I searched her face for the truth.

'Theo was my baby. He's *my* little boy,' Rose told him. Her words were thick with pain.

'But... I'm his dad,' Tristen said through his tears. He walked towards the small, crumpled boy on the ground. Rose didn't say anything. She didn't say a word when he sat in the mud next to the child who he'd thought was his and bundled him into his arms. Theo stirred. Sensing someone familiar. He reached his tiny hands around Tristen's neck. The outline of Tristen's torso shook with the emotion that had taken over his body. He sat on the ground and rocked Theo backwards and forwards until he fell still again. Nestling his face into his warm neck.

Charlotte cried silently beside me. There was nothing that she could say. No words that could take the pain away from Tristen. The detectives stepped forward. They obviously felt that they'd let us deal with this for long enough.

'Rose, this is DCI Price. I need you to come away from the edge now.' Rose didn't move. 'A lot has happened this evening. I want to make sure that you and everybody else are safe. Let's get you into the warm.'

'You knew my mum, didn't you?' Rose called out to the detective.

'I did,' she replied calmly, edging slowly towards her. Watching her feet as she carefully navigated the slippery ground.

'Was she kind to you?' she asked sadly.

'Was she... kind to me?' Melanie Price asked. 'I didn't know her very well. She was always someone who lit up a room. She was someone who everyone wanted to be.' The detective had her arms out a little for balance. Watching Rose for any sudden movement. 'What happened to your mum was terrible. We are doing everything we can to make sure that the person who did this...'

'Did you know that she lost the house?' Rose called over the top of the detective's head. Talking to me and Charlotte. We both shook our heads. Too scared to say anything. Worried we might make the situation worse. 'The only place that I'd ever felt at home, and she lost it. She lost it because of her vanity and her greed.' She spat out the words like a bitter drink. In all the time I'd known her, I had never seen her like this.

'Rose, what happened that night? The night your mum died?' Melanie asked. There was shift in energy as we stole confused glances from one another.

'She was so drunk that night. I'm pretty sure she'd taken something. Mum woke up about ten minutes after we'd said good night. She told me she was going to be sick.' I held my breath. 'I sat with her at the end of the bed and she told me about losing the house. She said it wasn't her fault. That she'd been banking on other investments... but they'd fallen through.' Her face was scrunched in thought. As though she were reliving the scene minute by minute in her head. Nate stepped into the space behind my body. I felt him gently press against me for comfort.

'It was my home. It was where I was pregnant with Theo. It was the house I should have taken him back to live.' She looked sadly at Tristen as he hugged her son to his chest.

'I told her that now I was eighteen, I wanted a new start. I told her I wanted Theo back. She'd laughed. Told me not to be so ridiculous. Said that giving him up was the best thing that I ever did. That Theo was exactly where he was supposed to be.' Melanie took a step closer. They were only a few feet from one another.

'Mum left the tent. Instead of taking the path to the toilets, she took the one to the washing-up area. She was still drunk. I waited a few minutes, sat there at the end of her bed. I was so angry. Angry that she would say that to me.' Rose wiped the tears from her face with the back of her hand. 'I followed her. I was going to help her. To convince her to come back to the tent. It was raining and she had almost nothing on.'

'I found her staggering around the path in the dark. She laughed when she saw me. As if she knew I'd come to rescue her, like I always did. You could be anything, she told me. A doctor... a lawyer. You can travel around the world. Why would you want to ruin your life with a child? She started to wander away from me, looking for the toilets. It's like I wasn't even there...'

'Rose, I need to take you down to the station. We can talk there, in the warm,' the detective told her gently.

'No,' she shook her head. '"Why would you want to ruin your life with a kid?" she'd said. I couldn't see her very well. Just the outline of her by the washing-up area.

'"Like I ruined yours?" I'd asked her... do you know what she said?' Rose's voice broke. She took a deep breath, trying to compose herself.

'She said "yes." Deep down that's what she believed. That I'd ruined her life. That I'd held her back. She didn't want the same thing for me.' Rose wobbled unsteadily. Taking a small step backwards. A step closer to the drop. Closer to the dark water. Melanie held her hand out, but she didn't take it.

'I felt like my body had been taken over. The rage… it was like I wasn't in control any more,' she told us. We all looked around at each other. Any hope that we had, finally fading away. 'There was a rock on the ground… one of those stones that borders the path. For a moment I thought about hitting myself with it. I just couldn't feel like that any more.

'I hit her. On the back of the head. It was so hard… the noise was sickening. I heard the break. I heard *her* break. That's when she fell forwards. She landed on the edge of the step and I knew it was over. I knew she was gone.' Rose's voice sounded so small and fragile. I wanted to scoop her up and take her away from here. But I couldn't protect her. Not now. None of us could.

Two uniformed officers pushed through the middle of us. They marched along the path towards Rose. Their flashlights picked up the panic on her face. 'No!' yelled Melanie. Rose stumbled backwards in fear. She twisted her body looking for a way out. Her feet slid on the ground, tangling together as she lost her balance. 'No!' shouted the detective as the officers froze.

Rose disappeared. Her slim frame fell from sight as if happening in slow motion. The loud splash made us all run to the edge. Staring into the black water in horror. 'Rose!' Melanie ran along the bank desperately calling her name. '*Rose!*' We frantically raked the water with our lights, but we couldn't see her. Just the rough swirl of the strong currents.

It was then that we heard the second splash of water. We all looked around us. Trying to adjust our eyes to the darkness. To fix on the faces around us. To see who was missing.

'*Mel…*' It was DC Simon Green. He was screaming into the darkness. He was leant over the bank. Searching wildly for any sign of them in the water. *'Melanie!'* His voice boomed across the valley. There was no sound. No screams of help or splashing. No noise of someone fighting for their life. There was no sound at all. Just the ripping waves smashing furiously against the bank.

CHAPTER FIFTY-THREE

CHARLOTTE

Two months after

My black dress felt tight as I entered the cold church. It cut me in half across the middle, making me shift awkwardly. It was a dress I very rarely wore. Smart and formally cut. It was perfect for a funeral.

There was a display in the entrance by the heavy oak doors. Schoolchildren had drawn around their hands and turned them into leaves. They were yellow and brown and red. A celebration of autumn. It made me think of Theo and his tiny hands.

I took my seat on a pew midway down the church. Sitting inches away from the woman next to me as the benches filled up. I looked around the room just as Tristen walked in the building. He was dressed in a black suit and tie. Looking more handsome than I'd ever seen him. My stomach lurched with longing. He sat a few rows back by himself. If he saw me, he didn't look at me.

Theo is back with me—for now. After the camping trip he'd been put into temporary foster care. I felt like my heart had been ripped out. Until the authorities were able to establish the best course of action. That he needs to be with me.

We're living in London, in Annie's flat. I've never really liked London, or any city, but I understood why Annie loved it there. I loved the anonymity of it. The quiet amongst the chaos. We still have a long way to go. But in a lot of ways, we are happier than we've been in a long time.

I drove here by myself. Recently, I've realised how independent I already was. How much I already did for myself before me and Tristen separated. In lots of ways, life is better. Better than it was at the Surrey house. I don't know how long it will last, or what the future holds. But for the first time in my life, I'm not thinking about the future. I'm taking each day as it comes.

CHAPTER FIFTY-FOUR

STELLA

Two months after

We arrived late at the church. Most of the congregation were already seated. A couple of people turned, as me and Jack walked through the stone archway. Our smart shoes tapping on the grey stone floor. Kelly had decided not to come. I didn't blame her. We were all trying to move on with our lives in our own way.

Jack had finally come clean to Kelly about the extent of their debt. He had no choice. Last month, they'd lost the house. His ex-wife, Lisa, was letting them live in her old London flat. It had been her and Jack's first flat as a married couple. She'd got it in the divorce settlement but had recently moved in with her new boyfriend. Jack had basically gone back to where he started. Strangely, it suited him. He looked well. Better than he'd looked for a long time. Kelly had been uncharacteristically stoic about the situation. Sometimes, it's the people who you least expect are the ones who come through for you.

'I had to park the car on the next street,' Nate said, sliding his hand around my waist as we took our seats. Things were good between us. He'd seen all sides of me over the last few months. I was relieved that there were no more secrets. Relieved that he no longer saw me as perfect. I wasn't perfect, but I was trying to be a better person. Nate had nothing to forgive me for. But I did need to forgive myself. Absolve myself of the weight of guilt that I'd carried for so many years.

I looked around for Charlotte. I couldn't see her. We hadn't seen each other since that night. Tristen sat a couple of rows in front of us. I recognised him just from the small part of his head that I glimpsed. I knew every part of him. I felt nothing seeing him here. Nothing other than a sense of loss. Sadness for the past. There had been so much good between us all, so much love. We'd managed to tarnish all of it. Every single happy memory was tainted.

We needed to move forward. We couldn't do that as a group. Not after everything that had happened.

The service was beautiful. So many people had cared about her. Had loved her. They talked about her loyalty, her fairness. Her love of books and the countryside. Nobody spoke about the end. That night by the lake as we all waited for her to climb out of the water. The night that she drowned. A tear slowly rolled down my cheek, as I thought about the pointlessness of it all.

We shuffled back towards the doors in a sombre line. People dabbed at their faces and sniffed loudly. There was a big board by the door. Outlining the order of service. A photo of her smiled back at us. Her hair was a little longer, but she looked just the same.

Underneath it read, 'Melanie Price: 1981–2022'.

The sun was shining when we stepped out into the church-yard. A cold October sun. The kind that reminded you how much you missed summer. We stood around, me and Nate and Jack. Waiting to pass on our condolences. A man stood by the door. A few steps away from the inner circle of immediate family. He was standing next to DC Green. He wore a brown suit and had a thick dark beard. I'd seen photos of him in the paper. He was Melanie's husband, Mike. He looked like his world had ended. I turned away. His grief was too much to bear.

'Hi.' Charlotte was stood at my side.

'Hi,' I replied. We looked at each other for a long moment. Taking each other in. Knowing this was it, the last time we'd see each other.

'I'll go and get the car,' said Nate. Jack leaned over and gently kissed Charlotte on the cheek. He turned and left without a word.

'Rose has changed her plea to guilty. Did you know?' Charlotte asked quietly. I shook my head.

'I haven't spoken to her. Not for a while. How is she?' I asked.

'She's struggling. She doesn't seem to be able to accept what she did. Some days she takes full responsibility and other days... other days she knows that she caused the death of two people. If she hadn't taken Theo to the lake that night... Melanie *drowned* saving Rose,' Charlotte whispered.

Neither of us spoke for a minute. 'I wasn't sure if you'd come,' I told her.

'It felt right to be here,' she replied. I nodded. I knew what she meant.

Tristen walked out of the church. He strolled passed us with his hands in his pockets. He didn't even look up. Neither me nor Charlotte acknowledged that we'd seen him.

'I heard you're living in London with Theo?' Charlotte nodded. There was a glimmer of a smile.

'Me and Tristen aren't together any more. The house in Surrey was his mum's... It made sense.' She looked at the ground as she spoke. 'It's strange, you know? In her flat... most of her things are still there. It feels like we're just visiting. I expect her to walk through the door any moment.' I felt tears spring to my eyes.

'I'm sorry,' I told her. So much had happened. I wasn't sure that I'd ever said the words out loud.

'I know you are.' Charlotte spoke softly, but she seemed stronger somehow. 'Me and Tristen, we were never... It wasn't worth it. None of it was,' she told me.

I squeezed her hand. She squeezed my hand right back as we smiled tearfully at one another. 'There were good times weren't there?' I asked.

'There were *so* many good times,' she laughed, wiping tears from her face. Our fingers touched as we pulled apart from one another. We didn't say goodbye. It didn't feel right. I turned my face into the October sun, and just walked away.

A LETTER FROM AMY

Thank you so much for choosing *The Last Holiday*. I hope you enjoyed reading it as much as I enjoyed writing it.

If you want to keep up to date with all my latest releases, just sign up to the following link.

Your email address will never be shared, and you can unsubscribe at any time.

www.bookouture.com/amy-sheppard

I love hearing what you think of the characters, the plot—and different parts of Cornwall that you think it might be based on! I always appreciate reviews, or you can get in touch with me via my Instagram page.

Amy x

 facebook.com/amysheppardfood
instagram.com/amysheppardfood

ACKNOWLEDGEMENTS

I just wanted to take a moment to say thank you to the people that have made this book possible:

To Paul, Elliot and Sam, you make everything more brilliant —thank you!

Thank you to Mum and Dad for supporting everything I do and for being so lovely whilst you do it.

Thanks to my friends and family for all your support. To Amy Cassidy, I'm so very grateful for you.

Thank you to Clare, my agent. You have been such a great support with all my projects over the years. I wouldn't be doing this without you!

Thanks to my brilliant editor, Lydia. I'm so happy we got to work on another book together! So grateful for your insight and for helping to turn this book into the story I wanted to tell.

I want to thank everyone at Bookouture. You are just amazing. I love working with you!

Finally, I'd like to thank my followers on social media. Your support and your messages over the years have meant the world. I'm so happy to be sharing this story with you.

Amy x